Praise for *A World Without Heroes*

◆

"Brandon Mull is a wizard with words. With Beyonders,
he has conjured one of the most original fantasies I've read in
years—an irresistible mix of adventure, humor, and magic."
—Rick Riordan, author of the Percy Jackson series

★ "Mull moves his story at a brisk pace . . . offering ample
action and feisty dialogue to keep fantasy lovers entertained."
—*Publishers Weekly*, starred review

"Readers will be kept off-guard and on the edge of their seats
from the first page. Perfect for fans of Rick Riordan
and John Flanagan, this is an exhilarating debut in an
exciting new series."
—*Book Page*

"Mull's world-making and character crafting are superb."
—*Bulletin of the Center for Children's Books*

BRANDONMULL.COM

Also by Brandon Mull

Fablehaven
Rise of the Evening Star
Grip of the Shadow Plague
Secrets of the Dragon Sanctuary
Keys to the Demon Prison

BEYONDERS
A WORLD WITHOUT HEROES
✦ BOOK ONE ✦

BRANDON MULL

Aladdin
NEW YORK   LONDON   TORONTO   SYDNEY   NEW DELHI

ALADDIN

An imprint of Simon & Schuster Children's Publishing Division
1230 Avenue of the Americas, New York, NY 10020
First Aladdin paperback edition February 2012
Text copyright © 2011 by Brandon Mull
All rights reserved, including the right of reproduction in whole or in part in any form.
ALADDIN is a trademark of Simon & Schuster, Inc., and related logo is a registered trademark of Simon & Schuster, Inc.
Also available in an Aladdin hardcover edition.
For information about special discounts for bulk purchases, please contact Simon & Schuster Special Sales at 1-866-506-1949 or business@simonandschuster.com.
The Simon & Schuster Speakers Bureau can bring authors to your live event.
For more information or to book an event contact the Simon & Schuster Speakers Bureau at 1-866-248-3049 or visit our website at www.simonspeakers.com.
The text of this book was set in Goudy Old Style.
Manufactured in the United States of America 1112 OFF
2 4 6 8 10 9 7 5 3
The Library of Congress has cataloged the hardcover edition as follows:
Mull, Brandon, 1974—
A world without heroes / Brandon Mull.
p. cm. — (Beyonders)
Summary: Fourteen-year-old Jason Walker is transported to a strange world called Lyrian, where he joins Rachel, who was also drawn there from our world, and a few rebels, to piece together the Word that can destroy the malicious wizard emperor, Maldor.
ISBN 978-1-4169-9792-4 (hardcover)
[1. Space and time—Fiction. 2. Revolutions—Fiction. 3. Wizards—fiction. 4. Magic—Fiction. 5. Heroes—Fiction. 6. Fantasy.] I. Title.
PZ7.M9112Wor 2011
[Fic] —dc22
2010023437
ISBN 978-1-4169-9793-1 (pbk)
ISBN 978-1-4169-9798-6 (eBook)

Once again, for Mary

"A single enduring statement can grant immortality."

—Author Unknown

⟶⟶⊰⊱ PROLOGUE ⊰⊱⟵

Т he prince dangled in the darkness, shoulders aching, ancient manacles digging into his wrists as he tried to sleep. The chains prevented him from lying down. Whether it was truly light or dark he could not say, for his enemies had stolen his sight.

In the distance he heard screaming—the unrestrained wails of a man trying and failing to escape the deepest agony. The unnerving cries echoed from higher corridors, dampened by intervening barriers.

After untold weeks in the dungeons of Felrook the prince could guess what the man might be feeling. Never had the prince imagined anguish so diverse and exquisite as he had experienced here.

He stood up straight, taking some of the pressure off of his wrists. If they kept him chained here much longer, he felt certain his arms would detach. Then again he preferred his current accommodations to the previous room, where the floor bristled with sharp, rusty spikes, and lying or sitting required bloodshed.

The unseen, wretched prisoner continued to scream. The prince sighed softly. Throughout his tortures, no matter what toxins they had forced down his throat, no matter what questions they had asked, he had not yet uttered a single word. Nor had he cried out in pain. He knew that some of the potions devised by Maldor and his minions had power to loosen his tongue and cloud his judgment, so after he was captured, he had firmly vowed to make no sound.

His captors had hounded him expertly. They had tried to bribe him with food and water. They had tried to compel him with pain. Some had come and spoken to him calmly and reasonably. Others had made harsh demands. At times he had faced several inquisitors in a row. Other times hours or days crawled past between interviews. He could not name the array of toxins administered to him, but no matter how they endeavored to blur his mind and weaken his resolve, the prince had focused on one necessity: silence.

Eventually he would speak. He quietly clung to the hope that he would ultimately be brought before the emperor. Then he would utter a single word.

Vaguely, gradually, the prince began to recognize that his mind felt uncommonly clear. A headache persisted, and hunger gnawed at him, but he found himself capable of directing his thoughts deliberately, an ability he had taken for granted before all of his food came laced with mind-altering additives. Aside from holding to his governing rule of keeping silent, his thoughts had meandered hazily over the past weeks, and his identity had felt indistinct.

Without warning, the door to his cell creaked open. He tensed, braced for anything. *Keep silent*, he warned himself. *No matter what they do or say.*

"Well, well," said a warm voice that he had heard before. "You're looking worse every day."

The prince said nothing. He heard other men entering the cell. Three besides the speaker.

The friendly voice hardly paused. "If you're going to host a visitor, we had best get you cleaned up."

Rough hands unlocked the manacles. The prince felt perplexed. He had never been cleaned since arriving at the dungeon. Perhaps this was a ploy. Or perhaps he might finally enter the presence of the emperor!

Large hands gripped his arms. The hands led him forward, then down to his knees. Coarse rags scrubbed his bare flesh. Before long, unseen hands began trimming his whiskers. Minutes later a straight razor scraped across his cheeks.

A man held him on either side, which gave the prince a good sense for how he might attack them. He could use his legs to take out their knees, then get the razor, and add four corpses to his count. Since his capture, he had already slain six guards.

No. Even if he defeated these guards, without his eyesight he would never escape the dungeon. But he might ruin his chance for an audience with Maldor. The prince shuddered faintly. Some of his best men and closest friends had given their lives, and despite their sacrifices he had failed. His only chance for redemption was to come before the emperor.

"You seem especially docile today," the warm voice commented. "Could it be you have finally resolved to become a model prisoner?"

Biting retorts sprang to mind. His consciousness had felt muddy for so long, the prince felt tempted to answer. Surely there could be no harm in responding. No, even if his mind felt clear, even if this particular question were innocent, if he broke his pattern of silence, eventually his captors would coerce him into revealing secrets. He only had one word to share, and it would be in the presence of Maldor.

"Ready for a stroll?" the voice asked.

The men on either side helped the prince rise, then escorted him from the cell. He took shuffling steps. As always he wished for his eyes, but he resolutely reached out with his other senses, noting the direction and temperature of a draft, the acoustics of the corridor, the smells of rot and burning torches.

After some time he heard a door open, and the prince entered a new room. His escorts forced him to his knees—locking him there with shackles on his ankles and wrists—and then placed a heavy iron collar around his neck. Without another word the guards left. Or at least some of them left. One or more could have covertly remained.

Minutes passed. Hours. Finally the cell door opened, and then closed.

"We meet again at last," a familiar voice said.

Chills raced across the prince's shoulders. Maldor had visited Trensicourt years ago, trying to negotiate an alliance. As a boy the prince had studied his every move, this man who his father claimed was so dangerous.

"I promised that one day you would kneel to me," the emperor said, his tone dry.

The prince moved his arms slightly, enough to jangle his chains.

"I would have preferred voluntary reverence," the emperor admitted. "Perhaps in time. I understand you have lost your tongue."

The prince hesitated. He had to be sure. He had learned this word of power at great cost. The emperor could not possibly suspect that he knew every syllable. Otherwise he would never have come here in person. But could the speaker be a trick? An imitator? The prince knew he would only get one chance at this.

"I had no interest in addressing your underlings," the prince said, surprised by how hoarse and weak his voice sounded.

"The heir to Trensicourt speaks?" Maldor exclaimed. "You inhaled a caustic substance. I had begun to suspect you had lost the ability to vocalize. Truly you possess a will of steel. Had I known you merely required my presence, I might have visited you earlier."

If he was an impersonator, he was a very good one.

"What brings you down to the dungeon?"

The emperor paused. "I am here to celebrate the end of my worries."

"You have many kingdoms yet to conquer," the prince protested. "I am one man."

"And a keystone is a single block," the emperor murmured, "yet when it is removed, the structure collapses."

"Others remain," the prince insisted. "Others will rise."

"You speak as though you are already gone," Maldor chuckled. "My friend, I have never meant to kill you. I only needed to prove that you cannot stand against me. The way to confirm this reality was to defeat you. It pains me to see you like this. I would prefer to clothe you in finery and bind up your wounds. You may recall, I have extended my friendship in the past. Not only did you deny me, but you have fought against me, and urged others to do likewise."

"You will never have my loyalty," the prince pledged.

"I wish you would be reasonable," the emperor lamented. "I am fully aware that none of my servants are your equal. You could be my chief lieutenant. I would make you Lord of Trensicourt, and more besides, free to govern as a king in all but name. I could restore your sight, extend your lifespan. You could accomplish much good."

"And all of Lyrian would fall under your dominion," the prince replied. "How do I know this is really you? My eyes are gone."

"Surely you know my voice," the emperor said, amused.

"Years ago you spoke to me in the parlor at Trensicourt. I showed you a toy."

"Has this become a game of riddles?"

"Do you remember the toy?"

"A windup carousel with removable horses. You removed an enameled horse—mostly blue, I believe—and asked me to join you."

The prince nodded in silence. Only the emperor would know that detail. It was too obscure. With hardly a pause he spoke the Word that he had kept secret since his capture. He could taste its power as it escaped his lips, a true Edomic key word.

The prince waited in darkness.

"What a peculiar exclamation," the emperor remarked.

Dismay and confusion left the prince off balance. That word should have been the emperor's undoing! Frantically the prince struggled to recall the Word, but uttering it out loud just once had abolished it from memory.

"You look troubled," Maldor commented knowingly.

"That word should have destroyed you," the prince whispered, the last of his resolve withering, his inner world dimming into a cold place where only the ashes of hope remained.

The emperor laughed. "Come now, my stalwart prince, surely you did not imagine me ignorant of your quest! We are conversing, in truth, but not in person. I am using an intermediary. After all, being a wizard should include a few advantages! My emissary can speak with my inflections, and we can readily communicate from afar. But since he is not me, that perilous word can have no effect on either of us. Now that you are divested of your final weapon, why not reconsider my offer?"

"Never," the prince whispered. All he had left was the fact that he had never let the emperor entice him to switch sides. The prince owed that, at least, to all who had believed in him.

"I am very impressed that you learned the Word," the emperor went on. "You are the first. I have long promised myself that he who learned the Word would be invited to join my inner circle. You have no more options. Do not perish without reason. Further resistance will bring no reward. Work with me, and you can still accomplish much good. Respond with care this time, for you will not receive another opportunity. After all, you just tried to kill me. This introduction to the hospitality of my dungeon has been gentle compared to the horrors that await."

Head bowed, the prince remained silent for a moment. After all the planning, the maneuvering, the bold alliances, the narrow escapes, he had failed! He had said the Word to a decoy! He had even anticipated the possibility, but in the end Maldor had fooled him, had ruined him, as happened inevitably to all of his foes. The prince searched inside for hope or faith and found nothing. Perhaps he should accept the inevitable. He was unsure how much longer he could retain his sanity in this unspeakable place.

The prince raised his head. "I will never serve you. You have defeated me, but you will never own me." He owed these words to those who had died for him. He owed the words to himself. To be destroyed was one thing. At least he had not surrendered.

"Very well. You were my finest adversary, this I acknowledge. But you will break here. You know this. You have my admiration, but not my pity." Footsteps retreated, and a door clanged shut with the finality of a tomb.

❈❈ CHAPTER 1 ❈❈
THE HIPPO

Over the centuries individuals have crossed from our world to Lyrian in a variety of ways. Although some travelers have journeyed between universes deliberately, normally the sudden voyagers are caught by surprise. They become lost in deep caves and emerge into an unfamiliar landscape. They pass through the natural stone arches that occasionally link our realities. They sink into deep wells, enter passageways near mountaintops, or, less often, crawl through petrified logs. But nobody has ever passed from Earth to Lyrian in a less likely way than Jason Walker.

At the age of thirteen Jason resided in the town of Vista, Colorado. Since his father was enjoying a prosperous career in dentistry, and his older brother had just been accepted to dental school, most of his acquaintances expected Jason would one day become a dentist as well. His parents openly encouraged him in that direction. The expectations had rubbed off, and Jason's vague plan for life included earning a baseball scholarship to a university where he could begin his quest for a dental degree.

He could not recall ever deliberately choosing this course— he had no real passion for tooth repair. The routine struck him as dull and monotonous. Scraping teeth. Taking X-rays. Applying fluoride. Deep down Jason craved something else.

Ever since he could remember, Jason had felt drawn to animals. He read books about them, watched nature programs, and begged for pets. After he consulted with his father, this passion inspired his interest in a zoology major on the way to his dental degree. Unlike many prospective zoology students Jason actually worked in a zoo. Understandably, he had never imagined that his volunteer job might lead him to an alternate universe.

During an unseasonably warm week in late February, Jason leaned against the railing outside the fast-pitch batting cage at the local sports park. Tim stood in the cage, knees slightly bent, chipping a lot of foul balls as he struggled to regain his timing. Matt, the best hitter on their club team, had gone first, blasting nearly every pitch to the back of the cage with his fluid swing.

"Don't try to murder the ball," Jason suggested.

"I'd settle for assault and battery," Tim grumbled.

On the next pitch Tim crushed a hard ground ball to the left side of the cage. Jason alternated glances between Tim and a labeled image in his biology textbook. He was memorizing the human skeletal system for a test.

"Get your nose out of that book," Matt murmured to Jason as Tim fouled the next pitch back into the netting.

"I have to head to the zoo after this," Jason apologized. "I won't have much time to study today."

"Trust me," Matt said, nodding toward their left.

Jason turned his head to find a pair of girls coming toward them. They were April and Holly Knudsen, fraternal twins in his grade at Kennedy Middle School. The girls were not much alike in appearance or interests, especially for twins. Prettier and more studious, April was in three of Jason's honors classes, including biology. Louder and sportier, Holly held a softball bat in one hand and a batting helmet in the other.

Only two girls at school made Jason feel queasy and self-conscious: Jen Miller and April Knudsen. They were pretty, and smart, and seemed down-to-earth. Jason harbored secret crushes on both of them.

"Hey, guys," Holly called.

Jason tried to smile. He was suddenly very aware of the textbook in his hands. Would it make him look like a nerd, reading a biology book at the batting cages?

Matt said nothing. He seldom spoke much around girls. Jason tried to make his voice casual. "Hi, Holly. April."

"Getting ready for your last season before high school ball?" Holly wondered.

Tim whacked a hard fly ball.

"Coach Thayer is already scouting Jason," Matt said. "He might end up pitching for varsity as a freshman."

It was true. Jason had hit a growth spurt at the end of sixth grade. His hitting had initially fallen apart as he'd adjusted to his height, while his pitching had started to gain some real speed. He now stood almost six feet tall. His hitting was recuperating, and his fastball was up into the eighties, but his control had suffered.

"Wow, freshmen boys almost never play varsity," Holly admired. "They almost took state last year."

"I'm not sure how much I impressed Thayer," Jason confessed. "My pitches were all over the place."

"Only one guy on next year's high school team throws faster than you," Matt said. "When you throw your best stuff, I can't hit you."

"I tense up lately," Jason admitted with a grimace. Over the past year, during games, he had started to feel very self-conscious, and erratic pitches had been the result. He had blown some games by giving up too many walks, and he'd lost a key game with a wild pitch. He had also hit a few batters, and at the speeds he was throwing, that was a big deal. No opposing batters had been seriously hurt, but they could have been.

At first Jason had assumed the increased speed of his pitches had caused the problem. But then Matt and Tim had begun to notice that he routinely threw better during informal games or practices. It bothered Jason to think that he had lost games because he lacked the guts to throw well under pressure. Maybe the problem came from dwelling on how much others expected from him. Maybe he was expecting too much from himself, fixating on perfection. Or maybe his skills were simply fading.

His friends on the team expected him to overcome his control issues and carry them to glory. But he was not yet the star others expected him to become. He sometimes wished his friends would brag about him a little less.

April pointed at Jason's textbook. "Are you getting ready for the bio test?"

"I'm trying," Jason replied.

"What's the name of your cheekbone?" she quizzed.

He resisted a grin. "The zygomatic arch."

April raised her eyebrows. "Not bad."

Holly rolled her eyes. "You guys are such geeks."

"Geeks rule the world," Jason countered.

Holly grabbed her sister. "We better get over to the softball cage."

Jason wanted to ask them to grab a snack or something. Well, specifically, he wanted to ask April, but asking both of them would be less intimidating. They were two girls; he was with two other guys—it would just be a small group hanging out. There would never be a more perfect moment to casually approach April. Who knew, they might end up with a study date for the biology test.

But he couldn't make his lips move in time. The twins were walking away.

"Hey," Jason called, feeling awkward, squeezing his biology book. "Do you guys want to grab some food when you're done?"

Still moving away, Holly pushed her hair back over her ear as she apologized. "We can't. We have to go to our uncle's birthday party. Maybe some other time."

"Okay, that's cool," Jason said, even though nothing about it was remotely cool.

Behind him Tim exited the batting cage. "You like April?" Tim asked.

Jason winced, stealing a glance over his shoulder. Was he that obvious? "Not so loud. A little, I guess."

"I think Holly seems more fun," Matt mused.

Tim tossed Jason the batting helmet. "You're up. Here's your chance for back-to-back strikeouts."

"You're a riot," Jason said, sliding on the slightly oversized helmet. A red light glowed near the pitching machine. Jason adjusted the strap on his batting glove, grabbed his bat, entered the cage, and took several practice chops, overswinging at first, then settling into his regular stroke.

"You ready?" Matt asked.

"Go for it."

The light turned green. Jason crouched into his batting stance, bouncing a little, anticipating the first pitch, trying to ignore the possibility that April was watching. He tended to swing late on the first ball. It hissed out of the pitching machine and blurred past him. He swung way too late.

"He's a lover, not a hitter," Tim kidded.

Jason focused. The next ball zipped out of the machine. His timing was right, but he swung too low, and the ball skipped up and back off the bat.

On the third pitch he made a solid connection. The ball rocketed to the rear of the cage, a high line drive.

Matt whistled. "Not bad."

Jason glanced back at his friends, grinning. Shifting his gaze, he noticed that April was watching her sister enter the fast-pitch softball cage. When he turned to face forward, a ball was streaking toward him. Jason twisted his head just in time to prevent it from striking his face, but the hard sphere thumped against the side of his helmet, knocking it off his head and sending him sprawling.

Artificial turf prickled against his cheek as Jason tried to fathom what had happened. Suddenly Tim and Matt were at his side, asking if he was all right.

"I'm fine," he muttered, standing up and swaying into Tim, who steadied him.

"You're out of it," Matt warned. "You got tagged hard."

"I'm just a little rattled," Jason protested, shaking Tim off and heading out of the cage. The ground seemed to be teetering, as if he were balancing at the center of a seesaw. "I just need to sit down."

Jason plopped onto the bench outside the cage and put his head in his hands. "I should have warned you," Tim said. "Some of those balls were coming inside for me too. Somebody needs to recalibrate that thing."

"It isn't your fault. I wasn't paying attention. Just bad luck." He put his face in his hands and massaged the sides of his forehead.

"Maybe we should get you to a doctor," Matt suggested.

"No, I'm good. It just shook me up a little. Take some swings; I'll be fine."

"You sure?"

"Yeah. Go avenge me. Knock the covers off some balls."

Jason concentrated on his breathing, trying to ignore the clanging of aluminum bats. He began to feel more centered. He made eye contact with April, who squinted sympathetically. By the time Matt left the cage, Jason could stand without the ground tilting much.

"I want to snag some grub before I hit the zoo," Jason said.

"Sorry, I'm supposed to meet up with my cousins," Matt said. "I'll already be a little late."

Tim checked his wristwatch. "I can't go either. You would have been on your own with the twins. My brother is picking me up in about five minutes. We could give you a lift."

"I have my bike. I'll catch you guys later."

Tim and Matt returned the helmets to the counter, while Jason went to the parking lot and claimed his bicycle from the rack. A string of warmish days had melted the snow, even most of the roadside drifts, leaving the streets unseasonably welcoming to cyclists. Although the sky was currently overcast, the temperature remained much too warm for snow. If anything it might rain.

As Jason pedaled up the hill to Anderson's grocery store, his head began to ache, and he started to feel unbalanced. Rather than push through the discomfort, he opted to walk his bike the rest of the way.

Leaving his bike chained near a soda machine, Jason entered through the automatic door and went to the Chinese food counter off to one side. He ordered the lunch special, and the guy behind the counter spooned orange chicken, beef and broccoli, and chow mein onto a compartmentalized Styrofoam plate. The broccoli was a bright, fluorescent green—a color that would seldom occur in nature. The broccoli always looked that color here, as if it were spray-painted or made of plastic.

After finding a seat at a little table near the deli, Jason started eating. The orange chicken mixed with the chow mein was his favorite, but he only made it through half the food before he began to feel nauseated. He took a long sip of water and rubbed his temples. Then he unwrapped the fortune cookie, cracked it open, and removed the slip of paper. *New experiences await on the horizon.*

They should be a little bolder, he thought, and assert something like, "You are about to suffer from violent food poisoning."

Jason headed outside. As he biked farther up the hill, traversing a few crosswalks, his head felt clearer, although a dull ache persisted, pounding a bit as climbing the slope elevated his heart rate. Before long he reached the Vista Point Zoo parking lot. Although the family-owned institution was no match for the Denver Zoo, Vista Point housed a respectable population, with more than four hundred animals representing almost one hundred and sixty species. Typical for an afternoon in winter, the lot was mostly empty.

At his locker Jason pulled on a set of gray coveralls and replaced his shoes with work boots. He was a few minutes early, so he thumbed through his biology textbook. The words seemed a little fuzzy. Closing his eyes periodically, he recited the names of various bones and processes.

Glancing up, Jason noticed the clock. Time to clean the hippo structure.

When he entered the hippo viewing area, Jason paused to admire a glass case on the wall labeled: MONUMENT TO HUMAN STUPIDITY.

It contained various items workers had fished out of the hippo tank over the years: aluminum cans, glass bottles, coins, cigar stubs, two cigarette lighters, a dental-floss dispenser, a pocket knife, a tangled Slinky, a plastic wristwatch, a disposable razor—even a few rounds of ammunition.

Pacing behind his push broom, Jason watched debris accumulate in front of the dark bristles, wondering how some idiot could top the random dangerous items in the display case. Maybe by chucking in a lawn mower. Or a few bars of uranium.

Jason paused to stare over the railing at the enormous hippo resting motionless below the water on the floor of the tank. Hank was the only hippo in the zoo, an adult male with his fortieth birthday coming up in the summer. Jason shook his head. The majestic hippopotamus—hard at work as usual. They might as well replace it with a statue. No visitor would know the difference.

Faintly, on the edge of perception, Jason heard tinkling music rising from the water. Head slightly cocked, he wandered around the area trying to pinpoint the true origin of the sound. As the volume of the music increased, growing richer and clearer to where he could discern different instruments, he returned to the water and had to admit that the melodic strains seemed to emanate from the submerged hippo.

Had they installed underwater speakers in the tank without his knowledge? Some new technique for soothing the obese mammal? Perhaps it was a pathetic attempt to give the hippo more crowd appeal.

The melody was unfamiliar, supported by harmonies and complemented by interweaving countermelodies. A deep, gentle percussion kept time. Jason leaned over the rail, perplexed by the bizarre phenomenon. He wished another person were present so he could verify that he wasn't having an auditory hallucination.

The hippo stirred, vast mouth momentarily yawning open, and for that instant the music became much louder and more distinct, as if the hippo truly were the source of the elaborate tune. Then the great mouth clamped shut.

The music became muffled again when the mouth closed, but continued to gradually increase in volume. Could the hippo have swallowed a stereo? That was the only plausible explanation, but it seemed just as ludicrous as the idea that the hippo was spontaneously producing the sound.

Maybe there was no music. Maybe he had been thumped on the head more severely than he'd realized. But his mind felt clearer than it had earlier, and the unsteadiness was fading.

Scanning the area, Jason saw no other people around. Would there be time to run and fetch someone else? He thought of the Warner Bros. cartoon about the singing and dancing frog that clammed up whenever witnesses were present.

Leaning his stomach against the top of the railing, Jason teetered far over the metal bar, baffled by the beckoning melody. If he could get an ear closer to the water, he could confirm whether the music was really coming from down there. The hippo remained motionless.

As his ear descended toward the rippling surface, a powerful sensation of vertigo swept over him. Jason overbalanced, lost his grip, and plunged head foremost into the pool above the massive hippo. As if this were the chance for which the lethargic beast had waited its entire captive existence, the hippopotamus surged upward with jaws agape, the music chiming louder than ever.

Before Jason could react, his hands were grasping at a slimy tongue, and his face was sliding against a greasy surface. Sprawled on his belly, he raced along a dark, slippery tunnel. No creature was this big! What was happening? In counterpoint to his distress, melodic music rang clearly as he sloshed along the humid corridor. He tried to brace himself against the rubbery sides to slow his slide but failed, until his arms and head suddenly emerged from an opening in the side of a dying tree, near a river lined with ferny vegetation.

Night had inexplicably fallen. A silver path of moonlight trembled on the water. The music he had heard was coming from a wide raft drifting on the lazy current. He squirmed out of the gap, his coveralls drenched from the plunge into the hippo tank, and turned around to inspect the hollow inside of the tree. The inner walls felt moist and rotten. He could locate no opening save the one through which he had emerged and an aperture directly overhead, at the top of the hollow trunk, through which he could see stars.

This was impossible! Where was the tunnel? How had it led to this tree? Where was the hippo? Where was the zoo? There was no river half this wide in his whole town! Jason blinked, wondering if the blow to his head at the batting cage had knocked him out.

Bracing himself against the interior walls of the trunk, he managed to scramble up until he came out at the top, twelve feet above the ground. Still no sign of a hippopotamus or of the Vista Point Zoo. He did, however, command a clear view of the raft, which had drawn up even with his current location.

Small colored lanterns illuminated the vessel. A narrow man in a pale outfit hammered at a xylophone. A stocky woman blew on a curved flute. Another man alternated between racks of chimes and a tall set of bongos. A flabby woman with at least five chins plucked a strangely shaped stringed instrument. A short figure held an enormous brass horn with tubing that snaked around his broad chest and rested on his shoulders.

The raft swept behind a screen of weeping willows before Jason could apprehend more details, though a few other musicians tinkered with a variety of less discernable instruments. The haunting music permeated the air, floating to him across river and riverbank.

Jason's head swam with questions. How had he gotten here?

Why was it nighttime? How would he get back to the zoo? Falling into the hippo tank was one thing—careless but possible. Passing through the mouth of a hippopotamus into a tunnel slide and coming out of a hollow tree beside a river was tougher to process. Everything he had ever assumed about reality had just been turned inside out. But his surroundings seemed so tangible. There was no denying his senses. He felt the damp, splintery texture of the bark beneath his hands; he smelled the faint odor of decay rising from a standing pool at the river's edge. Oily sap clung to his skin. He sniffed his palm, and the pungent resin reminded him faintly of Fig Newtons and black licorice, but he had never smelled anything quite like it.

Jason sighed. He knew the difference between the vague impressions of a dream and the sharper sensations of wakeful consciousness. He certainly felt awake. Yet he could not help doubting the unreal situation. Perhaps this was simply a vivid dream. After all, a baseball had bashed him in the head. He could still be lying unconscious in the batting cage. Then he shivered. Maybe he had died—there could have been a clot in his brain. Or maybe the hippo really had eaten him. Could he have crossed over to some sort of afterlife?

He scratched his chin. The sensation felt genuine. His wet clothes clung authentically. His head throbbed gently, and he remained mildly dizzy. Would the symptoms of a concussion persist in a dream? In the afterlife? He listened to the music and the gentle lapping sounds of the river. Wherever he was, whatever the explanation, he remained alert, and he was immersed in a vivid, perceivable environment. He surveyed the vicinity—the mossy trees along the river, the shrubs below, the insects buzzing nearby—mildly astonished at how acceptable the impossible became once it had transpired.

Jason promptly discovered that his immediate problem would be getting down. He sat awkwardly on the lip of the tall hollow trunk, trying to position himself so he could descend as he had climbed. He couldn't seem to get it right, and he began to experience light-headedness at the thought of sliding down the interior of the trunk, accumulating splinters, before breaking an ankle at the bottom. Attempting to climb down the exterior of the tree appeared even less inviting. Why was climbing up always so much easier than climbing down?

Finally, after many hesitant twistings and turnings, he lowered himself back into the trunk in a position where he could brace himself. Once he had squirmed down to the bottom, Jason exited the hollow tree, glad for the moonlight, and decided to follow the raft, since it represented the only trace of civilization.

Shortly he came abreast with the music, though foliage along the riverbank hindered his view of the vessel. Jason trotted ahead until he found a gap, and he discovered a little hunched figure squatting on a log.

"Hello," Jason said.

A head whipped around. The face belonged to a kid, maybe ten or eleven. As the boy shifted, Jason realized he had a sizable hump on his back. "Why are you sneaking up on me?" the boy snapped.

"I'm just following the raft," Jason replied defensively.

Looking calmer, the boy scooted over on the log to make room. Jason took a seat.

"What's with the musical raft, anyhow?" Jason asked.

The boy turned a skeptical eye. "You joking? That's the funeral dirge of the Giddy Nine, the best musicians around. Most folks are waiting for them down by the falls. That's the only part they care about. But I like to hear the music. It'll be the last time."

"They're headed for a waterfall?" Now that he listened for it, Jason could hear the distant roar.

The boy nodded gravely. "They're trying to make some kind of statement. They were banned from playing together in public. I don't see how this solves anything." He gave Jason a hard stare. "You must have heard of them. Right?"

"No. I'm a stranger here. Just arrived."

"Where are you from?"

"Vista, Colorado."

"Never heard of it."

Jason hesitated, unsure whether he wanted to hear how the boy answered. "How about America? Or the planet Earth?"

The boy scrunched his face. "Not really."

"Can you tell me where I am?"

"The riverbank, obviously." He returned his gaze to the river with a start. "They've passed us by. We'd better move on or we'll miss the finale."

Jason tromped along behind the boy, who moved surprisingly fast along a good route that skirted several marshy areas and shadowy thickets. The night air seemed to help his head, although a faint pulsing ache persisted.

They climbed a steep rise crowded with vegetation and came out on an overlook high above the river. The falls boomed louder. From the elevated viewpoint Jason peered upriver to see they were now well ahead of the little craft. The music sounded far away. Looking in the other direction, he could see where the river seemed to abruptly end. The falls.

"We'd better keep moving," the young boy urged. "We're ahead of them now, but the river picks up. Soon they'll be traveling much faster than we can."

Jason followed the boy down the rise, back under the gloom of overhanging branches. Soon he could hear the water flowing more swiftly. The roar of the falls grew to a constant thunder, drowning out the distant music. Jason found himself short of breath as he hustled to match the increasing pace of his guide.

They came through a dense stand of trees and beheld a moon-silhouetted multitude congregated beside the top of the waterfall. At the very brink of the falls sat a few tiers of makeshift bleachers crammed with spectators. "Find a good spot," the boy advised before scampering over to the riverbank.

Jason jogged over to the far side of the bleachers, discovering that they came right up to the edge of the dizzying precipice, over which the water tumbled like an endless tsunami. He had been to Niagara Falls once with his family—this looked almost as high with nearly as much water. Cool vapor misted his face.

Jason walked back around the bleachers to the riverbank. People lined the bank upriver from the bleachers for some distance. Some of them looked somber. Others munched on snacks. One group swayed as they tunelessly sang an unintelligible song. Jason moved upriver in search of an open spot. The majority of the people wore simple, homespun clothing, though occasionally he saw a sleek fur coat or embroidered vest. Nobody wore what he considered normal, modern attire.

After jostling forward a little, he found a space that would offer a good view of the craft flowing off the brink, although too far upstream to observe the downward plunge. He stood beside a middle-aged woman wearing a floral bonnet and a dress fashioned from heavy material. She stared anxiously up the river, wringing her hands.

"Can you believe this?" he said.

She turned to him. Her rather wide-set eyes came to his chin. "Can I believe that my brother is about to kill himself to create a ridiculous spectacle?"

Jason's eyebrows shot up. "Your brother is on that raft?"

"He never had any sense. Or any backbone. He obeys whatever Simeon tells him. That madman has convinced the whole group to throw their lives away."

She gazed back at the rushing water. The raft was still not in sight.

"Why are you here watching?" Jason asked.

She shrugged, her cheeks coloring slightly. "To show support. The Giddy Nine believe this sacrifice is important. I suppose that whatever happens, it's better for Darren to leave this world feeling appreciated."

"Is that what brought all of these people?"

She looked down the line toward the improvised bleachers at the brink of the falls. "These are mostly admirers of their music. Nobody gets what this is really about. I imagine many are here simply because it sounds like great fun to watch a raft full of musicians plummet off an enormous waterfall."

Jason inwardly conceded that it would be an impressive sight. But at what cost! The waterfall was much too high for any of the musicians to survive.

"I wish there were something I could do," the woman fretted.

"Why doesn't somebody try to save them?" Jason asked.

"They don't want to be saved. This is a funeral."

Jason looked around. People stared expectantly upriver, some gloomy, some eager.

Should he try to rescue the musicians? It seemed like a tragic waste of lives. If he were out there, no matter what his convictions, he figured he would be changing his mind about going over the falls as soon as he got beyond the point of no return. What sane people would willingly drift off a tremendous waterfall? What sort of useful statement could that possibly make? From what he had been told, it sounded like the others were following the orders of one crazy leader. What if he had brainwashed them, like with a cult? Most of the people on the raft would probably rejoice to be rescued.

"I want to help you," Jason said in a low voice. "Do you know where I could find some rope?"

The woman glanced at him, hope flickering in her gaze. "You want to stop this? The rescue squad has a rope. Don't count on them using it."

"Rescue squad? Where?"

"They're just a precaution. They're not far upriver."

Some in the crowd began to cheer. The raft had come into view. At the very limits of perception Jason heard the music playing.

Leaving behind the group of spectators, Jason took off up the riverbank at a full sprint until he encountered a pair of men. They had a long line secured around the thick trunk of a knobby tree that towered over the rushing water.

"Are you the rescue squad?" Jason asked.

The short man with one arm answered. "Aye."

"Do you intend to rescue them?" The musicians were approaching rapidly on the swift current. Their instruments screeched and hiccupped as the raft pitched on the foamy water.

"Only if they call for assistance," the short man affirmed.

Jason saw that the other end of the slender line was affixed to an arrow held by a slim man leaning on a longbow. The three of them stood approximately fifty yards upriver from the falls. The raft was racing along about twenty yards from the bank.

"Will your arrow reach, carrying that rope?" Jason asked.

"Certainly, long as I aim a little high," the lean man replied.

"You a good shot?"

"None better."

"Maybe you should just save them. I bet they'll end up thanking you."

"Doubtful," the lean man sniffed. "They didn't even want rescuers present. I'll interfere only at their request."

Jason turned to face the imperiled musicians. If he tried to swim the rope out to them, he would be swept away downstream before he got close. The tree did not overhang the river far enough to climb out to them. Time was running short.

"Try to save them," Jason insisted. "This is wrong."

"Not unless—," the short man began.

"I hear them calling for help," Jason lied.

"Go away," demanded the lean man, his wide lips peeling back to reveal yellowed teeth. "The last thing we need is interference from some desperate, aspiring hero. If they really did cry for help, we wouldn't hear it over your racket."

"The sister of one of the musicians sent me," Jason tried.

"I don't care if the king of Meridon sent you," the lean man said. "This is their decision."

The raft would soon draw even with them. There was no time to think. Jason shoved the short man. Caught by surprise, he stumbled back over the steep bank and into the river.

"What's wrong with you?" shouted the lean man, dropping both bow and arrow to dive into the torrent after his fellow rescuer. The one-armed man had already washed some distance downstream and could be seen flailing lopsidedly. Even immediately beside the bank the current ran strong.

Trusting the lean man to rescue his comrade, Jason wasted no time collecting the fallen bow and arrow. He nocked the arrow and pulled it to his cheek, straining against the heavy tension of the string, one eye squinted shut. He hadn't handled a bow since earning an archery badge at a summer camp two years ago.

The raft heaved along, twenty yards out, now exactly perpendicular to his position on the bank. Many of the instruments and musicians appeared lashed in place. He tilted the bow upward, hoping he and the lean man understood "a little high" to mean the same thing.

He released the arrow, and it streaked across the distance to the raft, ending its flight embedded in the shoulder of the man playing the bongos. The percussion stopped as the man sank out of sight. The line on the bank continued to uncoil, paying out as the raft progressed rapidly forward.

Jason gasped. Had that really just happened? Shooting somebody had not been part of the plan. He eyed the uncoiling lifeline. Was it too long? It looked pretty thin. Would it hold?

The line pulled taut with a sudden jerk. The raft lurched in response, sending up a spray of water as it swung toward the riverbank. The crowd cried out in astonishment.

Thirty yards downriver the lean man hauled the short man out of the water. The lean man stood watching the raft arc toward the bank, hands on his hips. Something in one hand glinted in the bright moonlight.

Whether or not the musicians wanted to be saved, the raft was going to collide with the bank. The wounded percussionist must have become firmly entangled with some of the equipment, because the strain on the line was extraordinary. Most of the musicians continued to play. A couple of them seemed to be attempting to free themselves from their lashings.

When the raft crashed against the sheer bank ten yards shy of the falls, buckling somewhat, many of the spectators groaned. But moans turned to exclamations as the impact launched the stocky woman overboard along with her curved flute. The ruckus reached a climax as she washed over the brink and down the thunderous cascade.

Jason's eyes widened in horror, and he felt the bile rise up in his throat, barely able to believe what he had just witnessed. All around him cheering broke out, as the lean man slashed the taut line, and the crippled raft once again surged ahead with the current. Jason thought one person might have jumped from the raft to the bank, but he could not be certain. The uproar from the crowd reached a jubilant crescendo as the raft sailed over the falls directly below the packed bleachers, vanishing with a cymbal crash and a final squeaky note from a woodwind instrument.

Jason stood frozen, feeling like he had been kicked in the stomach. None of those people could have survived!

Knife still in hand, the lean man and his waterlogged colleague were swiftly returning up the riverbank. Jason shook himself out of his paralyzed shock and hurriedly retreated back into the trees away from the river.

CHAPTER 2

THE LOREMASTER

After crashing recklessly through varying densities of foliage for some time, Jason paused, legs tired. In a crouch he listened intently, his head throbbing with every heartbeat. Either he was not being followed, or his pursuers moved like ninjas. To be safe he ran on, until a stitch in his side and an extreme shortness of breath finally forced him to stop. Doubled over with his hands on his knees, Jason still couldn't hear any evidence of pursuit.

He sat on the ground with his back propped against the rough bole of a tree, panting quietly. In what kind of place would anyone applaud as people floated off a deadly waterfall? Had he really just shot a man with an arrow?

Closing his eyes, Jason rested his face in his palms and tried to will himself awake. With his eyes shut he could be anywhere. Unconscious in a hospital bed. Senseless on the artificial turf of the batting cage. Except he still felt the tree at his back, still heard the insects chirping.

The percussionist had been heading toward certain death off a gigantic waterfall. Did it really matter if an arrow lodged in his shoulder a few seconds before the suicidal plunge? Jason gritted his teeth. Through lack of skill he had aimed too low. That didn't make him a criminal, did it? Just a failure as a rescuer. After all, he had been trying to assist people who were already doomed. Right?

The real criminal had been the jerk who cut the line. Jason could hardly believe the man from the rescue squad had felt comfortable cutting loose all of those people. He had basically killed them.

Jason's hands trembled. The night was growing colder, and his damp coveralls magnified the chill. He slapped his cheek. He pinched his arm. The sensations felt genuine.

Tired of sitting and shivering, he got up and continued tramping away from the river. The churning of the falls slowly diminished to a hiss.

The ground sloped generally upward. He kept watch for shelter. In the dimness of the woods, time passed at a crawl. After an hour or two, with his coveralls feeling a trifle less damp and the long walk leaving him exhausted, he settled for squirming beneath a thick bush. It smelled a little like the tree-shaped air freshener in his dad's car. He could no longer hear the falls.

Resting his head on folded arms, Jason clenched his jaw to stop his teeth from chattering. He found that by scooping leaves around himself, curling up, and holding still, he eventually felt a little warmer.

Could he really have crossed over to some other reality? The thought made him shiver. How would he get home? He had seen no evidence of a way back at the tree where he had emerged. No shimmering portal to his home dimension. Where would he begin to look for a way back? What if there was no way back? Had this ever happened to anyone before?

Jason pulled out his cell phone. The glow of the display illuminated the dark bush. Apparently, the phone had survived the wetness of the hippo tank. He was unsurprised to find the phone could not get service. There would be no dialing home. He had one unopened text message. It would be from his mom, probably reprimanding him. He opened the message.

Please answer your phone. Even if you choose to disrespect my opinions, I still love you.

Tears sprang to his eyes. She had it wrong! He just didn't want her trying to control his study schedule.

Earlier today he had let slip that he had a biology test coming up, along with an English project. His mom and dad knew little about his study habits, largely because he routinely brought home really good grades, so they didn't have much to worry about. But every now and then, seemingly at random, his mom decided to play at parenting. She had told him he shouldn't go to the batting cages if he had homework to do. He tried to explain that he had a plan for getting everything done, but she had insisted firmly. So he had just left, biking to the batting cages despite her protests, heedless of the punishments that might follow.

Why was he so stubborn? She had tried to call him, and he hadn't picked up. Would that be how she remembered him? An ungrateful, disobedient jerk? His insides seemed to shrink at the thought. Would this brief message be the last he ever heard from his family?

Jason felt the frustration and fear well up inside him, and his hands involuntarily clenched into fists. He gazed around at the empty forest, wanting to scream, to hit something. How could he really be stuck here, in the middle of this insane place, so far from everyone he knew?

Jason thought about his dog, Shadow, a three-year-old

Labrador. Who would feed him? Walk him? Who would throw around one of the tattered old tennis balls with him? His parents had never wanted a dog. To get him, Jason had promised to take responsibility for all of his needs. Jason had trained him, and had paid for the sofa he chewed up by mowing lawns and washing cars. Jason devoutly cleaned up after Shadow, bathed him, played with him, and roamed the woods with him. He doubted whether his parents knew how much Shadow ate, where he liked to be scratched, or even where to find his leash. If Jason never found his way home, Shadow might suffer more than anyone!

"Hello!" he called out, knowing it was pointless. "I want to go home! Hello! Hello?" He blinked back his tears, trying to get his emotions under control. None of this made any sense, but he had to calm down; he had to figure this out if he ever wanted to see his friends again, his parents, his family.

After taking a deep breath, Jason scrolled through his other messages. There were only five. Four of them were brief, stupid exchanges with Matt. One was from Tim, inviting him to the batting cages. Jason was pretty good about deleting his messages. Now he wished he had more to read. The battery was running low, so he read the message from his mom one last time and then shut off the phone.

Jason closed his eyes. He needed to rest. Hopefully, a new day and a refreshed brain would give him a better perspective.

Back home when he couldn't sleep, he would lie in bed waiting for patterns to appear on the glowing face of his digital clock, including such exciting milestones as 11:11, 11:22, 11:24, 12:12 , 12:21, and his personal favorites, 12:34 and 12:48. Here he listened to night sounds: the sporadic hooting of owls, the occasional fluttering of wings or rustling of leaves, the scraping and squeaking of insects. He shifted around, trying to get comfortable. Just when he was beginning to worry he would never fall asleep . . .

. . . he awoke with sunlight filtering through the trees. He blinked, his head swirling with confusion at his surroundings. Immediately all of the events of the day before rushed back to him, and a heavy weight pressed down on his chest. He had secretly hoped to awaken in a hospital bed back in Vista. Could people fall asleep in a dream, then reawaken with the dream still in progress?

Jason sat up, noticing that his coveralls remained slightly damp. In the light of day he could see that some of the surrounding trees wore a rich purple moss sprinkled with tiny white flowers. A nearby shrub had long, corkscrewing leaves. The clues were subtle, but he was definitely nowhere near Vista, Colorado. An innate sense screamed that he was far from his home, far from his proper place. In fact, judging from the clothes the people at the waterfall had been wearing, he might not even be in his proper time.

Stiff muscles protested as Jason stood. He rubbed at his side where a rock had jabbed him all night. A muscle behind his right shoulder felt particularly sore. He realized it was probably the result of hauling back that bowstring the night before.

Jason sighed. With the surrounding trees obscuring his view, he had little sense of direction. A tiny yellow bird with black markings twittered on a branch. A small fan of feathers frilled the back of its head. More than most people, Jason had always paid particular attention to animals, but this was not a species he recognized.

Hands on his hips, Jason weighed his options. Wherever he was, dying of exposure in the wilderness seemed like a real possibility if he didn't take action. Considering all the people he had seen at the waterfall, he concluded that there must be a town in the vicinity.

With a gnawing hunger growing, he struck off toward the rising sun. He soon came upon a brook narrow enough to jump across. He figured if he wanted, he could follow the brook downstream to the river. The crowd should have dispersed by now.

He crouched beside a place where the water splashed off a little stone shelf. The water looked clean, but he resisted the urge to drink, in case it would make him sick.

He decided to follow the brook. Then if he started dying of thirst, he could always risk waterborne bacteria in order to preserve his life. But he would head upstream first, since the river had been bad luck.

Jason did not travel far before arriving at a pool from which the brook originated. Surveying the area, he was startled to spot a huge building through the trees, constructed entirely of speckled granite. A frieze depicting men at war surrounded the top of the building—foot soldiers armed with spears and shields confronted armored warriors in chariots. Windowless walls of snugly joined blocks hid behind numerous grooved columns. A series of broad stone steps flanked by massive stone figures granted access to a brass door recessed in an arched alcove. The overall effect was that of a fancy museum. Except that the immense structure stood in the middle of a forest without a discernible road or path to grant access.

Relieved to find evidence of civilization, Jason hurried up the stone steps. He hesitated at the door. Maybe it was a huge tomb. The thought froze him momentarily. Did he really want to enter a mausoleum in the middle of nowhere?

He grasped the brass handle and tugged the heavy door, relieved to find it unlocked, because who would leave a tomb unlocked? He pulled it open wide.

An old man wearing a purple hat shaped like a limp mushroom looked up from a great wooden desk as Jason came through the door. A large pair of wire-rimmed spectacles rested on his bony nose, the lenses segmented into bifocals. He tilted his head back and stared at Jason with magnified irises. The skin below his eyes drooped in curved seams.

"Great Mother of Knowledge," the man whispered.

"Hello," Jason said, relieved to have found an actual, nonfurious person.

The man arose and came around the desk. His purple knickers matched his hat and ballooned at the thighs. Bright buckles gleamed on his shoes.

"Welcome, Seeker of Knowledge," he intoned importantly. "Surely you have traveled far and endured much hardship to earn the right to study at the Repository of Learning. Few have the courage to come here, or the skill to find this remarkable edifice."

"I'm from far away, I guess. I'm definitely glad to see you."

The old man rubbed his hands together. "You are the first valiant adventurer in a decade to win through to these hallowed corridors of enlightenment. Truly, you must be an explorer driven by a profound appetite for knowledge. I have been too long without new companionship. Pray, regale me with tales of your journey."

Jason blinked and scratched his cheek awkwardly. "You never get visitors? I just saw a bunch of people at the waterfall not far from here."

The old man scowled thoughtfully. "Locals rarely come as close to the repository as the falls. There must have been some special occasion."

Jason was not eager to recount his accident with the raft. "I guess. You said you wanted my story? Well, I was swallowed by a hippopotamus. Except I didn't go into the hippo. I ended up in a tree. Then I sort of wandered here."

The eyes behind the spectacles narrowed. "You choose to speak in riddles. Very well, you have earned the right to be cryptic. I am the loremaster Bridonus Keplin Dunscrip Garonicum the Ninth. I am custodian of the knowledge hoarded here. How may I be of service?"

Jason regarded the old man thoughtfully. "Nobody has come here in a decade?"

"You are the first in ten years."

"What do you do all day?"

He cocked his head. "I manage the records. I tend the lore. Every volume is catalogued in my mind." He tapped a long finger against his temple.

"So you're a librarian."

His eyes shifted back and forth. "I prefer loremaster."

"Look, my name is Jason, and I stumbled across this place by accident, although it sounds like some people go out of their way to find it. I can see why it takes them a while, since you're located in the middle of nowhere. Can you tell me where I am?"

The loremaster seemed at a loss. "You are in the Repository of Learning," he explained hesitantly.

"No. I mean in general. This world. Does it have a name?"

The loremaster leaned forward, eyebrows twitching upward. "This world?"

"Have you ever heard of Colorado?"

"I have not."

"But you speak English."

"Naturally. Most speak the common tongue."

"Do you know where English comes from?"

"From the Beyond. You ask suspicious questions, traveler."

"Do I?" Jason chuckled. "You would too, in my shoes. As far as I know, you're a hallucination, part of a crazy dream that won't quit."

"I see," the loremaster said. "You are a philosopher."

"No, I came out of my world somehow. I ended up in these woods. I'm from the same place as English."

The loremaster's expression became guarded. "A Beyonder?"

"Maybe, if you say English comes from the Beyond. Do people often visit from my world?"

"Not any longer," the loremaster replied skeptically.

"Do you know how I can get back?"

The loremaster gave Jason a sad smile. "Say no more. Did you journey to this sanctuary simply to mock me? Who put you up to this? My son, perhaps?"

"You think I'm kidding?"

The loremaster placed his fists on his hips. "You would like me to believe that the first Beyonder to visit Lyrian in many decades happened to wander into the Repository of Learning? I may be notoriously gullible, young traveler, but even I have limits."

Jason raised his hands to his forehead. "I don't believe this. You seem like someone who could help me if you believed me."

The loremaster's smile warmed, as if enjoying the absurdity that Jason was remaining in character after having been unmasked. "Enough nonsense. Surely you came here for more than a prank?"

"The name of this world is Lyrian?"

The exasperated loremaster made no response.

"Where is the nearest town?"

The loremaster removed his glasses and rubbed his eyes. "As you well know, there is no settlement in the immediate area. The nearest town is two days east of here."

"Then why were dozens of people watching musicians float off a nearby waterfall?"

"I seldom concern myself with local events beyond these walls."

Jason dug in his pocket and pulled out his keys. A small laser pointer dangled from the key chain. Pressing a button, he shone a red dot onto the wall. "Ever seen a laser pointer?"

"What a curious instrument," the loremaster remarked, genuine interest returning to his voice.

Jason pulled up the blue pant leg of his coveralls. "Look at my boot. Based on what I noticed people wearing at the waterfall, you've never seen shoes like these."

The loremaster leaned down, squinting. "Most uncommon workmanship."

Jason patted his pockets. "I left most of my things in my locker. But I'm guessing my outfit isn't typical either."

"Agreed."

"Well, I've never seen a hat like yours. I'm telling you, it might sound as strange to you as it feels to me, but I'm truly not from around here."

The loremaster clasped his hands together, extending his index fingers and leaning them against his dry lips. "The arrival of a Beyonder would be momentous news. I would be a fool to believe it was possible. An old fool who should know better. Yet you give me pause."

"Good. You say you have books. Are there any books that can tell me where I am?"

"Certainly."

"How about a book that will help me get back to my world?"

The loremaster gave Jason a suspicious glare and lowered his voice. "You should not request imprudent information. Whether you are a prankster or a lunatic, we both know that the emperor forbids open discussion of such topics."

"That's where you're wrong," Jason said, backing toward the exit. "I don't know the rules around here. I'm not trying to offend anyone, but I seem to keep stepping on toes. I don't know about an emperor. If you don't want to help me, I'll take off, no big deal. Sorry I bothered you."

"Wait." The loremaster studied Jason shrewdly. "As I mentioned, visitors have become scarce. Are you really so eager to turn your back on the greatest store of learning in all the land? Suppose I humor your delusion. You claim to know nothing about this world. I know just the volume to provide some background."

"Could it help me get home?"

The loremaster stroked his chin with a liver-spotted hand. "I'm not sure that information could be located in any book. But if you truly are a stranger to Lyrian, this will supply some context. Perhaps the Hand of Providence guided you here. Come."

Jason followed the loremaster out of the entry foyer, past fluted pillars and bearded busts housed in oval niches. They strolled down long passages walled with tall bookshelves. Some held rolled scrolls, others engraved tablets. Jason noticed one shelf laden with books bound in iron. Another shelf showcased miniature books the size of thimbles.

After winding about in the book-lined labyrinth, the loremaster gestured for Jason to take a seat at a wide table of dark cedar. Grunting, the loremaster selected a heavy blue volume almost as tall as his waist, with silver letters embossed across the front in fancy script. He heaved the book onto the table. Not only abnormally tall and wide, the book was several inches thick. Jason read the title.

An Abridged History of Lyrian. The writer was identified as "Author Unknown."

"You're kidding," Jason said, fingering the huge tome.

"This book can provide background regarding our world," the loremaster explained.

"It's enormous. Abridged history? Is that a joke?"

The loremaster shook his head. "Lyrian is an ancient land with a long and complex past. Much of the oldest lore is irrelevant today, but I can guide you to a couple of pertinent passages." He opened the volume and turned past the majority of the pages. The book was in excellent condition—either new or very well preserved.

After leafing through several pages one at a time, the loremaster indicated a florid heading. "You can start here. Each section of the history features a summary at the outset."

"'Decline of the Age of Wizards,'" Jason read. The words were written in large black calligraphy. "You guys have wizards here?"

"Once there were many. Only one remains."

"Wizards who cast spells?" Jason verified incredulously. "Who use magic?"

"Most call it magic. Wizards speak Edomic, the language of creation. Words comprehended by all matter and intellect. You'll see it mentioned in the history. Read the summary."

Jason sighed softly. The handwritten text was fancy but legible.

The three major figures at the end of the Age of Wizards are universally regarded as the only true masters of the high Edomic tongue. While Eldrin and Zokar pursued their ambition to engineer the perfect race, Certius withdrew from the civilized world, content to populate the southern jungles with his creations. Eldrin famously labored in solitude, refusing to share his discoveries. Zokar allied himself with the other notable wizards of the era, taking on Arastus, Orruck, and Maldor as apprentices.

"These guys have weird names," Jason complained.

"Read on," the loremaster prompted. "You needn't absorb every detail."

There can be little doubt that over time Eldrin's mastery of the nuances of Edomic surpassed the abilities of Zokar. Not long after Eldrin created the Amar Kabal, Zokar declared war.

Zokar had spent long years amassing the most fearsome army in the land, and he had forged alliances with the most powerful kingdoms of the age. The races he had engendered served him faithfully in the campaign against Eldrin, as did the torivors. (Despite claims by Zokar to the contrary, there remains much doubt as to whether he actually engendered the torivors. See subsection F, paragraphs 7–33.)

Fearing an alliance between his greatest rivals, Zokar first sent his forces south to eliminate Certius, the lesser threat, and succeeded in the endeavor. The maneuver became known as Zokar's Folly, because an alliance between Certius and Eldrin was highly unlikely, and the operation gave Eldrin time to prepare. In anticipation of the impending battle he created the drinlings.

Prior to the climactic battle, Orruck and Maldor fell out of favor with Zokar, an ironic turn of events considering that it was Arastus who eventually betrayed Zokar in exchange for the right to become Eldrin's first and only apprentice. In the end Zokar was forced to face Eldrin in single combat, and the legendary duel is widely considered the end of the Age of Wizards.

After the victory, with the aid of Arastus, an embittered Eldrin chose to rid the land of all upstart wizards and looted the great stores of learning, effectively ending the study of Edomic. The two wizards passed out of knowledge without ever siring a new race.

"The summary ends here," Jason said, looking up.

"What follows is a much more thorough account of the

condensed events," the loremaster explained. "The serious student can delve into extensive references and commentaries."

"I didn't understand all the words," Jason admitted. "Especially the races. What's a drinling? Or a torivor? What was the Amar Kabal?"

"Unessential details for now," the loremaster assured him. "What did you gather from the account?"

"Sounds like there should be no more wizards. Eldrin and Arastus wiped them out and then took off."

"You understood enough." The loremaster paged farther through the book until he had almost reached the end. "Here is the section describing the current age."

"'Dawn of the Rule of Maldor,'" Jason read aloud.

Lips pursed, the loremaster nodded. "After Eldrin departed from this land, a couple of the races he had engineered established their own kingdoms. Some races mingled with mankind; others remained aloof; others dwindled to extinction. Centuries passed. Nobody expected to see a wizard again. And then Maldor returned."

"One of Zokar's apprentices."

"Everyone, including Eldrin, assumed Zokar had disposed of Maldor. None guessed that he had survived in hiding. Maldor may have been the least powerful of Zokar's apprentices, but he possesses a cunning intellect, and in a wizardless world his abilities were suddenly formidable. Read."

> Maldor exercised extraordinary patience in his bid for power. None knew his identity until after he had established his stronghold at Felrook, fortified by alliances with Caston and Dimdell. In hiding, he successfully rallied many of the scattered and broken races of Zokar, eventually assembling and equipping an impressive force. His greatest advantage undoubtedly came when he gained control of the torivors.

Decades of brilliant political maneuvering followed. Allies became subjects, and enemies were held at bay by a complex system of truces. Maldor proved adept at isolating rival kingdoms, defeating them in battle, and then enlisting their resources in his cause. He managed to forestall unified resistance until such opposition lacked any hope of success. Although scattered free kingdoms remain, Maldor's claim as exalted emperor of Lyrian has effectively gone unchallenged.

"Your emperor is a wizard?" Jason asked.

"The last wizard," the loremaster reported solemnly. "After witnessing the downfall of his master, he has taken no apprentices. The emperor is well aware of the advantage granted by his exclusive knowledge of Edomic, and he has forbidden the study of the language."

"I take it that Maldor isn't a nice ruler."

The loremaster raised his eyebrows. "The emperor is a hard man. Of course, I am in his debt, since he permits me to remain in this post, overseeing this stockpile of learning."

"If he's a wizard, do you think he might know how to send me home?" Jason asked.

"Jason, if you are open to counsel, heed me now. It is unwise to earn attention from Maldor. Most people make a considerable effort to stay far from his thoughts. If you truly are a Beyonder, you might not want to be so liberal with that information. Lie low. Learn slowly and quietly. These days harsh consequences follow those who stand out in a crowd."

Jason nodded pensively. "Who wrote the history I just read?"

The loremaster's eyes shifted from side to side. "Hard to say how these books come into being, author unknown and whatnot. I assume the text was passed down from days of yore."

"The content seemed pretty current. Didn't you say I was the first visitor in ten years?"

The loremaster pressed his lips together. "Maldor has labored for decades to solidify his power. I could have acquired this volume in a variety of ways."

"Maybe. But I bet you wrote the book."

The loremaster reddened and looked away. "Preposterous."

"Don't be shy! I'd be bragging. Look how long it is! And all handwritten!"

The loremaster sighed. "I dislike the idea of associating a written work with a person. Text that has been handed down from unknown origins carries more mystique. It becomes harder to dismiss."

"So you wrote it."

"Yes."

"I liked how even though the summaries were concise, they still told a story. Have you written anything else?"

"Nothing I intend to reveal to you. I wish only to be remembered as Author Unknown."

"Will you ever own up to something you write?"

The loremaster removed his spectacles and rubbed at his eyes. "Perhaps. My father once admonished me to master the laws that govern fine writing until I could weave my words into worlds. If ever I accomplish that feat, I will sign my name to the tale."

Jason surveyed the aisles of books all around him. Books written in another world—many lifetimes worth of stories and insight and philosophy that he would never read. The loremaster replaced his bifocals.

"I'm hungry," Jason said.

"We have nourished the mind," the loremaster said, patting his midsection. "Why not see to the belly?"

* * *

The loremaster served lunch in a room he called the Contemplation Chamber. Giant masks decorated the walls, each a bronze human face, each with one eye squinted shut. Somewhat stained and smudged in places, a detailed mural of thousands of interlocking hands covered the ceiling. Illumination came from a dozen candles in the black iron chandelier and a few oil lamps spaced about the room.

To Jason's surprise, the meal was served by the young boy he had met beside the river the night before. When the boy first entered the room, he locked eyes with Jason and subtly shook his head, a pleading expression flashing across his features. Jason took this to mean that the boy did not want their prior association revealed. The loremaster offhandedly introduced the boy as Hermie.

Jason ate ravenously. A small pile of bitter gray nuts began the meal. The loremaster insisted they were nutritious. Jason washed them down with a cool drink that tasted like diluted berry juice with a hint of honey. The main course was spotted parasol mushrooms, accompanied by a side of dry yellow berries with a flavor like sour candy. The mushrooms were bigger than Jason's hand. They possessed a tender, fleshy consistency and a salty savor not unlike ham. Jason consumed two of the sizable fungi. Dessert consisted of pie stuffed with purple pulp textured like pumpkin innards. Jason was delighted to find the pie sweet and delicious.

"This pie is excellent," Jason said.

"Yes, there is nothing quite like blue root pie."

"I was trying to compare the flavor to something."

"It is unique. How would I describe it? A bit like tasting the opposite of peppered venison in mint sauce."

"I'll take your word for it. Why are all these masks winking?" Jason pointed around the room with his fork.

The loremaster dabbed at his mouth with a frilled purple napkin. "One eye is open to all truth, the other closed to all deception."

"That makes more sense than I expected." Jason reconsidered the bronze faces as symbols of discernment. "Do you mind if I stay the night?"

The loremaster blinked. "I assumed you would stay much longer than a single night."

Jason shook his head. "I have to figure out a way home. My parents must be freaking out. My dog is probably starving. My life is there. Everyone I know, my friends. My school."

"You are a student? What better place for an education than the Repository of Learning?"

"This is a great place, it really is, but I can't stay."

The loremaster nodded regretfully. "I was looking forward to some company."

"You've got Hermie," Jason said.

"A mere lad."

"I'm only thirteen."

"That is the year a boy assumes the mantle of manhood. Hermie is but eleven."

"Maybe you should relocate," Jason suggested. "You'll never have many visitors if you stay hidden away in this forest."

The loremaster shook his head. "Only by my secluded location do I avoid unwanted scrutiny. Those who truly need and appreciate this facility find their way here."

Jason helped Hermie clear the plates and silverware. In the small kitchen the loremaster refused to let Jason help wash.

"Waste no time dallying with trivialities—Hermie will clean the tableware. Explore the library while you can, for tomorrow may be too late. I only ask you not to trespass in the upper level. It is forbidden."

"Forbidden? Why?"

Hermie shot Jason a curious glance.

"I cannot say," the loremaster replied. "But I assure you it is not casually prohibited. My father used to make certain books in our family library forbidden because it was the only way to get me to read them. Boring things, mostly. A clever ruse. That which is not permitted is always most enticing. Do not mistake my intention. I counsel you in all sincerity—resist becoming intrigued. The upper level is completely off-limits for good reason. Understood?"

"Yes," Jason said. Was the loremaster trying to employ the same trick his father had used, immediately after explaining what his father had done? The upper level might be full of boring textbooks and dictionaries and junk. Or it might be unusually cool, housing ancient artifacts or weapons or treasure. More important, the upper level might contain some clue that could help him find his way home. Hadn't the loremaster recently explained that information about the Beyond was forbidden? Where better to look than the forbidden area of a library? The more he thought about it, the more it seemed the loremaster had offered a deliberate hint. He left the loremaster and Hermie behind in the kitchen, determined to sleuth out a staircase.

Jason wandered the maze of books, surprised at how easy it was to become disoriented. Before he encountered any stairs, Jason discovered a large atrium in the middle of the library, visible from all sides behind large panels of glass. He found a sliding door and ventured out into the verdant courtyard.

Overhead, the sun had passed midday. A few puffy clouds stood out against a field of blue. A covered well, complete with winch and bucket, stood in the middle of the atrium beside a stone sundial. Lush fruit trees overshadowed bushes bright with berries. Some of the fruit looked familiar, like colorful variations on plums and apricots, while other fruit appeared completely alien, like the gray furry fruit and the oblong, translucent fruit.

Once the courtyard garden had been properly explored, Jason returned to winding among the bookshelf corridors. Not a wall in the building lacked books. Books even occupied the space above doorways. Occasional hanging lanterns provided most of the light. Time after time Jason encountered dead ends, forcing him to backtrack. Finally, after extensive wandering, he arrived at a helical staircase in a rear corner of the massive building. He dashed up the spiraling steps two at a time and arrived at a large iron door riddled with tiny holes. The perforations were arranged in an orderly grid of columns and rows. Wooden pegs shaped like golf tees protruded from the ten center holes in the uppermost row.

Jason tried the handle. The door was locked. There was no keyhole near the handle. He began counting holes, tallying one hundred in each horizontal row, and about three hundred in each vertical column. A quick computation yielded a total of thirty thousand holes.

He pulled out a peg, hearing a snick as he did so. The peg was slightly longer than his little finger. Inserting the peg into a random hole, he heard it click into place. *Snick-click, snick-click, snick-click*—he tried the peg in various holes. Jason shook his head. It was the most complicated lock he had ever seen. He replaced the peg into its original hole. *Click*. The odds against randomly matching the ten pegs to the right combination of holes were staggering—far beyond something simple like winning the lottery.

Peering closely, Jason detected tiny symbols at the left of each row and at the bottom of each column. Each symbol was unique.

When closer inspection offered no new information, he

retreated down the staircase. With nothing else to do, Jason roamed and browsed. He found books about farming and tool making. Many books were written in foreign languages he did not recognize. One book in English discussed how to construct and fortify a makeshift garrison in hostile territory. Another called *The Epics of Count Galin of Misenmarch* was a hefty book full of long poems. Jason envisioned himself bringing the book home and claiming authorship as a joke. How could it be plagiarism if the material you borrowed came from another world? His English teacher would faint!

Jason was perusing an interesting manuscript called *These Short Lives*, which presented a supposedly factual account of a race of people whose lifespan was only two years, when a big dog with long white fur came into view around a corner. Jason closed the book. The dog just stood there, a juicy pink tongue lolling out. Jason approached cautiously, sinking a hand into the silky fur. "Good boy," he said in a special voice reserved for canines. "You're a good boy. You don't want to maul me, do you?" Petting the animal made him wonder how his own dog was doing back home.

The dog walked away, then stopped to look back. A shiny silver bell dangling from the collar tinkled softly when the dog moved. "You want me to follow?" Jason asked, setting the book down.

The dog led him along a direct route back to the Contemplation Chamber. Dinner awaited on the table. It looked much like lunch, except that these mushrooms were yellow and shaped like stocking caps.

Jason took his seat across from the loremaster and began eating. Hermie was not present.

"That is quite a lock on the door to the upper level," Jason said around a buttery mouthful of mushroom.

The loremaster froze with a bite halfway to his mouth.

"Where would a guy keep a combination to a lock like that?" Jason asked after swallowing.

"You are certainly a forward youth, if nothing else," the loremaster fussed. "The upper level is forbidden. That includes me."

"Did you design the door?"

"No."

"Who did? The Unknown Designer?"

The loremaster shrugged.

"You know the combination, don't you? What kind of librarian would be totally locked out of part of his own building?"

"Would you care to sample a bubblefruit hybrid I produced?"

"I repeat my question."

The loremaster held up one of the oblong, translucent fruits Jason had noticed in the atrium. "The pure bubblefruit is virtually invisible. I mixed this one with a qualine. It tastes rather pleasant."

"I'll stay here beyond tomorrow if you tell me the combination."

The loremaster raised his eyebrows. "If you were to trespass in the upper level, I would have to throw you out. If that is your design, I would prefer you depart at once."

Jason had lost interest in eating. The loremaster took a bite.

"You don't need to give it to me," Jason said with all the nonchalance he could muster. "Just tell me *how* to get the combination. A little clue. I'm only curious about the door. I've never seen a lock like that one."

The loremaster eyed him uncertainly. "A sudden interest in locks, is it? Very well, if you are determined. I have offered ample warning. A book called *The Life I Have Known* may contain a clue."

"How do I find the book?"

"I'll have it delivered to your room."

Jason returned to his food. He bit into the bubblefruit hybrid. The inside was syrupy, but sweet and good. Greenish fluid dribbled down his chin. He finished with a slice of blue root pie.

Afterward, while Hermie cleaned up, the loremaster escorted Jason to a bedroom. The austere chamber contrasted with the lavish architecture prominent elsewhere in the building. A small cot, a stool, a simple table, and a dresser topped with a laving basin were the only furnishings. Bare walls, bare floor, no windows.

Once he was alone, Jason blew out his single fat candle, plunging the room into darkness. Somewhere far off he heard the faint jingle of a bell. Taking a seat on his cot, Jason got out his cell phone, the glow from the screen pushing back the darkness. He reread his messages. The battery was nearly dead.

Jason wished Matt or Tim were with him. They had been his best friends for years. Matt was the most loyal person Jason had ever met, and Tim was hilarious. If they were here, Jason doubted he would feel scared.

But they weren't here. Nobody was here. He wondered if Matt and Tim would blame themselves for his disappearance. They would probably assume the blow from the baseball had given him a brain clot or something. He imagined them searching for his body. He wished he could somehow tell them that he was alive. He wished he could hop on his bike and meet up with them, maybe catch a movie, or throw a ball around, or organize a home-run derby.

Someone knocked softly on his door.

"Come in," Jason said.

Holding a candle, Hermie entered and shut the door. After setting the candle down, he sat on the floor. "Weird light," the boy commented. "Do you dabble in Edomic?"

Jason glanced at his cell phone. "It's from the Beyond. It won't last much longer."

"Thanks for not saying anything about the river. I didn't have permission to be there."

"No problem," Jason said.

"What were you thinking, shooting an arrow at the raft?"

"Going off the waterfall seemed like a bad idea. I wanted to rescue them."

The boy huffed. "Are you trying to be some kind of hero? Is that why you're poking around the upper level?"

"I'm no hero," Jason assured him. "I just want to get home."

"Want to get to Harthenham, I'll bet."

"What's that?"

Hermie folded his arms. "Come on, you're really going to pretend you don't know."

"I really have no clue."

The cell phone died.

"There went your light," Hermie said.

"That was all the juice in the battery. Do you know how to get into the upper level?"

Hermie snorted. "I'm smart enough to stay away. I just help clean up around here and run errands. Here is that book you wanted." He held out a thin book bound in creamy leather entitled *The Life I Have Known and Other Stories*. "You'd have to be a little thick to miss the clue."

Jason accepted the book. "Thanks. Why not save me time and show me the hint?"

He held up both hands. "I'm not a part of this. The dog can help you get around. Anyhow, thanks for not mentioning how we met before. I could get in trouble. I'll keep quiet about you shooting folks with arrows."

"Fair enough."

Hermie picked up his candle and went to the door. "Get some sleep." He slipped out without waiting for a reply.

Jason was left in darkness.

He had hoped Hermie might help him. It would be nice to have a friend. But the boy had only seemed concerned with making sure Jason would keep their previous encounter confidential.

Jason reclined on his cot. This would be his second consecutive night in an alternate reality. Thanks to the loremaster, at least he now had reason to believe others had crossed over from his world to this one. That gave him a little hope that somewhere, somebody might know how he could get back. With luck the answer might be nearby, waiting behind the forbidden door.

Back home his parents would have called the hospitals and notified the police by now. He might even be on the news! They would probably search for him all over the zoo—the last place he'd been seen. He wondered if any evidence would implicate the hippo.

CHAPTER 3

THE WORD

Jason awoke the next morning in darkness. Rolling over, he saw a line of flickering light at the base of the door. He fumbled out of bed, splashed his face with water, ran his fingers through his hair, grabbed the book, and left the room. A guttering lamp in the hallway accounted for the unsteady illumination.

The big white dog lay outside the door. It rose and guided him to breakfast.

"Good day to you," greeted the loremaster.

"Good morning."

"I see Hermie brought you *The Life I Have Known*. Help yourself to some food. I'm off to man the front desk."

"What's the dog called?" Jason asked.

"Feraclestinius Androbrelium Pathershin the Seventh."

"No, I meant his entire name."

"To abbreviate, I call him Feracles. Come by if you need anything."

The loremaster left. Jason drank a hot black beverage, which didn't smell much like coffee. At first the drink was unbearably bitter, but sweetened with plenty of sugar it became palatable.

Messy pieces of dripping fruit and a small bowl of really crunchy nuts completed the meal.

After wiping his hands on a napkin, Jason picked up the book. As with the volume from the day before, it was attributed to Author Unknown. He opened to the table of contents and found the titles of various short stories. Some stood out more than others. Apart from "The Life I Have Known," he noticed "Conversations with an Osprey," "Mysteries of the Deep," and "Last Wishes of a Bumblebee."

Jason thumbed forward to an arbitrary page and read the following:

> "How will you teach your children to fly?" I inquired of the mother. "I do not see how you could ever coax them into the air."
>
> "You do not understand because you are a man. Teaching a bird to fly is similar to teaching a man to swim. Can you swim?"
>
> "Yes."
>
> "Were you frightened when you learned? Frightened you would sink?"
>
> "Naturally."
>
> "So it is with teaching birds to fly. Except we fly better than you swim. The air is our element. We are as clumsy walking on land as you are swimming in water."

Weird stuff. The handwriting looked familiar. He had a guess at who had authored the book. He leafed through the pages, hunting for clues.

Eventually he flipped to the inside of the back cover. On the otherwise blank page a single word had been scrawled: *Moondial*.

Having never heard of a moondial, Jason hoped the term referred to the sundial out by the well.

As Jason closed the book, the white dog stared at him, head tilted, thick fur glossy. Could the dog know the library well enough to guide him to a destination?

"Hey, Feracles," Jason said to the large dog in his special voice. "Will you take me to the atrium?"

The dog immediately padded out of the room. Jason followed skeptically, but sure enough, after zigzagging along a circuitous route, the dog brought him to the glass walls enclosing the garden.

Jason went out through a sliding door. Today was cloudier than the day before, but the sun was currently peeking through.

He crossed to the sundial, studying it closely. The stone pedestal was carved with a frowning sun on one side and a smiling moon on the other. The face of the sundial had ten symbols etched in a semicircular arc, each unique shape composed of fine golden lines. The ten symbols seemed suspicious considering the ten pegs in the grid of holes. None of the designs looked familiar, but he hoped the shapes would correspond with the symbols on the door.

Jason patted his pockets. Beneath his coveralls he wore his jeans and a short-sleeved shirt. He pulled out his wallet and keys. The wallet contained twenty-seven dollars, a student ID, a health insurance card, and an ATM card. The keys were to his house and the padlocks on his lockers at the zoo and at school. He wished his pockets had been stuffed with useful things.

"Think your master would loan me a pen and paper?" Jason asked the dog.

That night Jason did not snuff out his candle when he went to bed. Instead, he opened the journal the loremaster had given him, the new binding creaking. The first page was defaced by scribblings he had made while getting accustomed to the quill. The next two pages showcased the most careful depictions he had been able to manage of the symbols on the sundial face.

Ten symbols would only represent the coordinates along one side of the grid. He had sought more clues at dinner, only to receive further reminders that the upper level was restricted. If the loremaster was playing mind games to pique his curiosity, the old guy was succeeding.

Jason did not think he needed another hint. He had a crazy idea to match a crazy place.

After waiting as long as his patience could endure, he gathered his writing gear and picked up the brass candleholder. Easing the door open, Jason peered out. All other lights had been extinguished. The library looked much more ominous in the wavering luminance of a single unprotected flame.

He crept down a short hall to the first of the shelves. A soft whine behind him nearly startled him into dropping the candle. The white dog nudged its nose against his leg.

"Take me to the atrium, Feracles," Jason whispered. He followed slowly, cupping his hand to protect the feeble flame.

At the atrium he followed the dog outside and then slid the door shut. A hidden moon backlit a large cloud, fringing it with silver. He set his candle down carefully on the lip of the well and turned to inspect the moondial. The gold characters looked silver in the dim moonlight. Squinting closely, he discerned that the symbols were shaped differently from those he had copied during the day.

He impatiently watched the cloud migrate across the sky. One edge of the cloud gradually brightened as the opposite side dimmed. Then the nearly full moon appeared.

Bright silver characters shone in the lunar glow, as finely

traced as their daytime counterparts but completely distinct in form.

Jason began sketching the moonlit symbols, patiently dipping his quill, careful to capture every detail. Since the moonlit markings corresponded with the positions of the daylight symbols, he paired the symbols that occupied the same location as likely coordinates for inserting pegs into the grid of holes. Clouds covered the moon twice as he drew, forcing him to pause for lengthy intervals. At last, with the moon about to vanish behind clouds a third time, he completed the tenth symbol.

Jason went to the atrium door. "Here, Feracles," he called softly. The dog jangled over to him. "Take me to the staircase. Take me to the upper level."

The dog guided him across the garden to a different glass door. Jason slid the door open and followed the dog back into the convoluted passageways. After some time navigating through the gloom, they reached the foot of the stairwell. "Good boy." Jason stooped and rubbed the back of the dog's neck.

When he proceeded up the stairs, Feracles did not follow.

At the top Jason knelt by the door and scanned the symbols along the bottom of the columns of holes. He found one matching a moonlight symbol. Examining the designs beside the rows, he located one matching a symbol copied in the sunlight.

He gathered the ten pegs and began the process of matching each pair of symbols he had copied into his book with the corresponding symbols labeling the columns and rows. After finding each paired column and row, he traced the perpendicular lines of holes to the intersection and inserted a peg. Finding all ten intersections proved to be a tedious task. His eyes began to burn wearily as he triple-checked each coordinate to avoid making an error and having to repeat the entire process.

At last he inserted the final peg. The click was accompanied by a brief metallic tumbling inside the door. He grasped the handle; it turned, and the heavy door swung inward. "I sank your battleship," Jason murmured.

A musty scent wafted from the open portal. Squinting into the darkness with his candle held aloft, he could see shadowy shelves lined with dusty books.

Jason went back down the stairs. "Here, Feracles," he said. "Take me into the upper level."

The dog whined and retreated several steps.

"Come on," he repeated, bending down and patting one knee invitingly.

The dog snorted and shook its coat.

Jason returned to the ominous doorway. Now that the perforated door was open, his conviction wavered. The dog's hesitation was more unsettling than all the warnings the loremaster had expressed. But no matter how creepy it seemed, any chance of finding a way home meant he had to try.

He stepped through the doorway, candlelight pushing back the darkness. His passage stirred up a low fog of dust. The ceiling was lower than below, but otherwise the upper level seemed arranged much like the lower. Except that most of the book spines were obscured beneath cobwebs and grime, making the titles and authors illegible. Maybe the upper level was forbidden because the loremaster was too lazy to clean it. Any respectable librarian would be ashamed.

Jason grabbed a couple of the nearest books and used them as doorstops. He wasn't going to chance the door closing spontaneously.

He wound his way into the book-lined corridors. The long shelves were constructed with undulant curves, giving the dreary passageways a warped, serpentine quality. The farther Jason traveled from the door, the more closely he cupped his hand around the flame. The silence was complete. He stepped softly, breathed quietly. Shadows jittered with the flickering of the tiny flame. The place was creepy, but nothing looked interesting enough to warrant the incredibly complicated lock on the door. He saw no treasure or weapons or intriguing artifacts. The knowledge in the books had to be what made this place off-limits.

His twisting path eventually led to a small reading area with a few tables and chairs. The furniture was sculpted of black stone. Armrests were carved with leering faces, and table legs took the form of fanged serpents. He wiped dusty cobwebs off the spine of a random book. *Subtleties of Manipulation*. The name "Damak" appeared at the base of the spine.

Setting his candle on a nearby table, Jason pulled out the book and opened to the introduction.

> *Manipulation is a quiet tool of majestic power. Artfully manufacturing desires in others to suit one's own needs can be accomplished on an individual basis or on a worldwide scope. Clearly, a study of manipulation requires a profound understanding of the selfish motivators that drive men to action. Different motivators function best depending on the nature of the minds one seeks to dominate. Manifold motivators are available, including fear, the desire for wealth or respect or power, lust, duty, obedience, love, even altruism. Endless combinations may be employed to reduce the staunchest will to a malleable plaything. Learning to discover the appropriate mix of motivators for any given individual or group and mastering how to employ those motivators with a deft touch comprises the essence of manipulative studies.*

> *The master manipulator lies as little as possible. He believes most, if not all, of what he professes. This quality makes him difficult to unmask. Once a subject realizes he is being manipulated, defenses are engaged and future machinations become exponentially more challenging. The most satisfying victories occur over adversaries who do not realize they have been conquered.*

Jason closed the book.

He was beginning to understand why the upper level was restricted. A palpably dark feeling had come over him as soon as he began reading the introduction.

He brushed off a few more spines to reveal other titles. *Religion and Subjugation. Memoirs of a Lost Soul. The Unquenchable Thirst.*

Nothing sounded very wholesome.

He surveyed the multitude of dingy volumes surrounding him. A few sinister books did not confirm that no useful information could be found here. After all, forbidden information was what he needed. Any of the nearby volumes might hold information about hippopotamus portals or contain hints about how he might get home. Didn't a chance like that justify enduring a little creepiness? Probably. But not right now. Such an unsettled feeling had stolen over him that Jason decided to leave the upper level for the moment and return with a brighter light.

Raising his candle in a trembling hand, Jason tried to make his way back to the entrance. Eventually he realized the curving corridors had disoriented him. He should have left a trail of bread crumbs.

He attempted to double back to the reading area, but could not find that, either. Instead he came to a different open area, where the only furnishing was a black pedestal surmounted by a huge book. A plush, dark carpet woven with imagery of cruel thorns covered the floor.

Jason crossed to the book. It had to be important to be situated all alone in such a grand fashion. As he drew nearer, he gasped. Shocked curiosity impelled him forward.

The book appeared to be bound in human skin. Upon close examination Jason observed that the fleshy covering had tiny pores, fine hairs like the ones on his arm, and light blue veins visible beneath the surface.

Aghast, he tentatively touched the surface, withdrawing his finger instantly. It was warm to the touch, with a yielding texture that suggested more thickness than he had expected. It felt alive.

Morbid fascination rooted him to the spot. What sort of book would be bound in living flesh? No writing appeared on the skin to suggest title or author. The publisher must not have owned a tattoo needle.

Rubbing his neck, Jason found the hair there standing upright. He glanced at the dim bookshelves at the edge of his candlelight. Beyond the light the blackness and silence seemed more oppressive than ever.

The surface of the pedestal was slanted, so the book rested propped at an angle. He slid a finger beneath a corner of the cover and flipped it open to a title page written in extravagant calligraphy. The ink was a dark maroon.

The Book of Salzared, *bound in his hide, scribbled in his blood.*

He turned the page.

> *Be cautioned, Reader. Some knowledge can never be unlearned. Such is the secret contained herein. Proceed only in defiance of this gravest warning, for the dire words that follow will set You in opposition to Maldor evermore.*

Jason read the words with mouth agape. What information could be so volatile? How could Maldor possibly know whether he had read this book?

The loremaster had insisted that discussing how to travel to the Beyond was forbidden by Maldor. Jason chewed on his knuckle. What if this book contained the knowledge he needed to return home? This could be it! The next page could hold his passport back to reality.

He turned the page. The writing continued in the same fancy script, almost too ostentatious to read, despite the overlarge characters.

> *I, Salzared, Chief Scribe of Maldor, in a desperate act of betrayal, hereby impart knowledge pertaining to the only vulnerability of my Lord and Master, and do bind these words in my mortal flesh that they might be preserved against those many hands which would otherwise destroy them.*
>
> *Behold, Maldor reigns in fearless might, and rightly so, for none may cause him harm, except by a single Word whose existence is His most closely protected secret.*
>
> *The Word, spoken in His presence, will unmake Him entirely.*
>
> *None, myself included, know all syllables of the Key Word. However, fragments of the Word are known to my fellow conspirators, who stand upon protected ground, awaiting one of sufficient courage to puzzle the syllables together.*
>
> *Speak the Word aloud but once, in the presence of Maldor and at*

no other time, for its utterance will erase all memory of its existence. Writing down the entire Word would provoke a similar consequence.

By reading these words You have nominated Yourself to recover the Key Word, the only hope of deposing my Lord and Tyrant. Move swiftly. The knowledge You now possess marks You for prompt execution.

The first syllable is "a."

Now depart! Let not my sacrifice be in vain. Away!

Salzared

Thumbing through the remainder of the yellowed pages, Jason found them all blank. He closed the tome.

The covering of the book had broken out in gooseflesh. So had Jason.

Could the admonitions he had read be real? Surely the book was of no great importance if it lay up here in this dusty attic. Behind the most intricately locked door he had ever seen. In a library hidden in the middle of a forest. Oh, crud.

Suddenly a flap of skin lifted on the center of the cover, revealing a glaring eye. A human eye.

Jason shrieked, dropping the candle and plunging the room into immediate darkness. Involuntary screams soared from his throat as he cowered on the ground, grasping for the fallen candle. He pressed his hand against scorching wax and cried out even louder.

With deliberate effort Jason clamped his jaw shut, swallowing the remaining screams. He rubbed his burned palm against the sleeve of his coveralls. That eye had looked right at him, slightly bloodshot with a dark iris, pupil adjusting to the candlelight. He shuddered.

Panic threatened to smother him. The oppressive blackness

made him feel alone in the universe except for the texture of the carpet beneath him. Blood pulsed in his throat. What was he going to do now?

Then he heard a faint jingling. It grew rapidly closer.

He groped for his laser pointer key chain. The tiny beam made a little red dot across the room. Until that moment he had not appreciated how inferior a laser pointer was to a candle for purposes of illumination. At least it was something.

The red dot proved sufficient to see Feracles come bounding out of a gap in the bookshelves. Jason pocketed the key chain and clung to the dog as he would to a life preserver. Refusing to hold still, Feracles kept nudging him to stand. Jason rose, maintaining a hand on the dog's furry back, and trotted blindly to keep up as he wound along an unseen route.

Soon he glimpsed light up ahead. They reached the open doorway and passed through to the head of the stairway. The loremaster stood there waiting, a half-shuttered lantern in one hand.

"You could not resist."

"Am I in trouble?"

The loremaster sputtered. "What sort of question is that?"

"I might have made a big mistake."

The old man nodded, eyes narrow. "Have you any idea what the enmity of Maldor means?"

"I'm guessing it's a bad thing?"

The loremaster shook his head sadly. "Perhaps you truly are a Beyonder. May Providence help you. Come."

The loremaster led Jason down the stairs and through the library. Moving at a brisk pace, Jason began to notice how exhausted he felt.

"Most every soul in Lyrian seeks to avoid Maldor's attention. You have just done the opposite."

"I just read—"

The loremaster raised a hand, turning his head away. "Say nothing of what you learned. The burden is yours to bear. Do not inflict the information upon others who willfully chose to stop at the title page."

"Then you know about the book! The one covered in real skin?"

"Of course, my boy." He tapped his temple. "The fact that I have not read that particular tome explains why I am still alive. Were you seen?"

"What do you—"

"You know what I mean."

Jason swallowed dryly. "Yes."

"You must depart at once."

"Actually, that's what the b—"

"Never speak of what you read! You may as well behead me."

"You're going to send me off into the dark?"

"The night is nearly spent. You will find your way. Follow the dawn for a day or two. Seek the Blind King. Perchance he can advise you."

At the front desk the loremaster gave Jason a brown traveling cloak, a blanket roll, and a small sack filled with mushrooms. Hermie awaited beside the main door, regarding Jason with morbid fascination.

"Consume these berries now," the loremaster said, handing him a palmful. "They will help overcome your fatigue. You'll find more in the bag."

"I don't understand what's happening."

"You possess the secret the brave travel here to claim."

"I didn't want it."

The loremaster frowned. "You hinted as though you did, and responded to the clues I offered in return."

Jason felt sick. "It was a mistake! I hoped the book would tell me how to get home. Suddenly I'm public enemy number one. I didn't understand!"

"I regret if that is true. It cannot be undone. You must flee." The loremaster directed Jason to the door. "Take heart. Mighty men have failed to examine the words you read, have quailed at the responsibility and departed as cowards. You leave heroically. Go now. I bid you safe journey." The loremaster hurried him out the door.

"Thank you," Jason said, exiting in a confused stumble.

Feracles barked once as Hermie yanked the door shut.

He was alone.

Gray predawn light glowed at one end of the sky.

Jason took a deep breath, glancing back at the closed door. No doubts lingered that this was real. He was in terrible danger. As a friendless stranger in a foreign land, he had made himself the enemy of a mighty emperor. For the first time Jason fully accepted that he might never get home.

CHAPTER 4

THE BLIND KING

As Jason hiked away from the Repository of Learning, he soon realized that the loremaster was right about at least one thing—those berries had really replenished his energy. He felt like doing karate or acrobatics or a decathlon. All drowsiness gone, he strode toward the rising sun, wrapped against the chill in his cloak, wondering how long it would take to leave the woods behind.

All day he marched, traversing a rolling succession of forested hills, breaking only to snack on mushrooms. There was no denying anymore that somehow he really had been transported into an alternate reality. He could very well live out his life here without discovering a way back. There might not even be a way home. He had to focus on following the one lead the loremaster had offered, and pray the Blind King could help him get home.

Eventually Jason's thirst became irresistible. He stooped beside one of the cleaner-looking streams he had encountered and took a drink, trying to ignore the slimy moss coating the rocks and the bugs gliding across the surface where the water pooled. The cool water tasted good. He figured if he was going to get sick drinking from a stream, he might as well do it in style, so he drank until he was full.

The sun sank behind him, casting a golden glow over the woods. The force of gravity seemed gradually to increase as Jason's berry-induced vigor wore thin. When he crested a final hilltop and found more hills beyond, he spread out his blanket beside a tree and slept instantly.

The following afternoon, with the trees thinning and the hills flattening, Jason found the parallel ruts of a cart track. The weedy track headed generally eastward, so he followed it until it evolved into a narrow lane.

Glancing back at the last of the wooded hills, he froze, certain he had seen a form dive into the shadows a good distance up the slope. He stared at the spot where the half-glimpsed figure seemed to have landed. Leaves whiffled in the breeze. He saw no other movement. Finally he continued along the lane, occasionally stealing quick glances behind, but noticed nothing else out of the ordinary.

After a time a strange cottage came into view, obnoxiously painted in many bright shades, with no length of trim or windowsill matched in color. Sequined curtains shimmered behind octagonal windows. Smoke twisted up from a chimney composed of yellow and blue bricks. A low green fence painted with innumerable flowers enclosed a spacious yard.

"Pssst, hey, you, longshanks, step over here."

The harsh whisper came from a stand of low trees to his left, making Jason jump and turn.

"Be quick about it," the voice urged. Near the base of a tree, obscured by brush, squatted a disheveled man in layers of dark, filth-stained clothing. He wore fingerless gloves of gray yarn.

A shapeless black hat sat on his head like a deflated basketball. His furtive face bristled with whiskers. "Come down here out of sight."

"Are you trying to rob me?"

"I'm harmless. Be quick."

Jason complied, descending the shoulder of the lane to stand above the stranger within the cover of the trees and undergrowth. "What do you want?"

"I know this community," the man said. "You're an outsider. What brings you this way?"

"I'm looking for the Blind King," Jason said.

The man squinted up at him skeptically. "I suggest you move along. There's barely enough pickings around here for one man to quietly skim the cream. Two would starve."

"I'm not here to beg," Jason said.

"Beg?" the man spluttered, obviously offended. "I'm no beggar! I live by my wits! And I don't need interlopers stirring up the henhouse."

"Why are you hiding here?"

"I'm taking measure of the situation," he said. "Franny's been baking. Mind crouching a little? Good lad. Name's Aster." He held out a hand. Jason shook it, certain the courtesy was transmitting fleas.

"I'm Jason. I'm not here to cause trouble for anyone. Once I find the Blind King, I'm sure I'll head elsewhere. I've got plenty of my own problems."

Aster gave a curt nod. "I believe you."

"You're going to steal from that house?"

Aster's face split into a wicked grin. "More than likely. Not enough to do the owner any harm, mind you. Just pinch a pie or two."

"Do you travel much?" Jason asked.

"Don't have much use for it. Travel involves uncertainty. I found myself some well-fed gulls, so I chiefly stay hereabouts. Live off the surplus. Say, you don't happen to have a morsel to spare? Not a handout, mind you. I'll pay you back tenfold in meat pie if you'll wait around for an hour or so. It's just that all this waiting has teased my appetite."

Jason opened his food sack. "I guess I could spare a couple of mushrooms."

The vagrant pulled a disgusted face. "You must be in a worse fix than I am, if you've resorted to dining on fungus. And I honestly have no idea what to make of your outfit. But you strike me as a companionable fellow. Tell you what—sit with me a spell and I'll snatch us a hearty meal. Assuming you'll move along afterward."

The reek of the man alone was sufficient deterrent. "Thank you for your generosity, but I'd better keep moving. I actually meant to knock on the door to that cottage and ask directions."

The vagrant suddenly looked alarmed. "You won't seek to spoil my raid, right, friend? I've been counting on this meal."

Jason wondered if the man could be dangerous. "I'll do my best to repay your friendliness," he replied ambiguously.

"Fair enough," Aster said. "Try not to cause a stir. Give my regards to the Blind King."

Jason returned to the lane, glad for the fresh air, and strolled to a sky-blue gate in the low green fence. "Hello?" he shouted. "Anybody home?"

A moment later the front door opened, and an obese woman with a bright scarf tied round her head leaned out, a cheery smile spreading her cheeks. Her smoothly bloated features gave her face an ageless quality. The smile disappeared when she saw Jason. "What business have you here?"

"I'm just passing through the area," Jason said amiably.

"This town has no use for drifters," the woman warned, scowling. "Keep on walking."

Jason looked around. He saw no town. Her home must be on the outskirts. "I'm wondering if you can direct me to the Blind King?"

Her scowl deepened. "Are you one of his misfits? You ought to know where to find him."

"I've never met him," Jason said. "I need his advice. I'm Jason."

The woman sighed. "I don't mean to be rude, Jason, but these are ugly times. Fair faces and kind words can disguise foul intentions."

"I'm only asking for directions," Jason maintained. "I'm not trying to make waves."

The woman opened the door wider, and an enormous dog padded onto the porch. The beastly canine looked like a bulldog the size of a Saint Bernard. Its hair was short enough to imply it had recently been shaved bald. The animal shook its deeply folded face and emitted a brusque sound between a growl and a cough. Jason would not have been eager to steal anything from a house with such a monstrous guardian. Aster was apparently bolder than Jason had realized.

"Puggles here would prefer if you stopped straining our hospitality," the woman insisted. "I have an alarm beside the door. Don't make me call the militia."

Jason glanced over toward where Aster was hiding. "Listen, lady," Jason confided in a loud whisper. "I don't really need anything from you. I have food in my bag and a destination in mind. But I have important information."

She narrowed her eyes. "What do you mean? Who sent you?"

"Nobody sent me. I just happen to know about a thief who intends to raid your house."

Her expression relaxed, and she chuckled. "You mean Aster?"

"You know him?"

A smile crept onto her face. "That scoundrel takes food from me three times each week, like clockwork. I've known him for years. The loafer refuses to accept charity, but if I let him feel like he's stealing, he'll swipe whatever I leave to cool on the windowsill. He fancies himself a soldier of fortune. I would welcome him to stay in a guest room, but he won't have it. Believe me, I've tried."

"How odd."

"Perhaps. But he keeps his pride, and I perform a service for a friend. He watches out for me. He's run off troublemakers more than once."

"You're a generous person."

Her smile widened, then faltered. "Funny he didn't bother you."

"We spoke," Jason said.

She nodded. "He's an able judge of character. You must have landed on his good side." She looked Jason up and down. "You tried to warn me of trouble. You can't be all bad. You wear strange apparel. Do you come from far away?"

"You have no idea," Jason said. "Look, I don't want to make you uncomfortable, but I could really use directions to the Blind King."

The woman paused, biting her lower lip. "I'm Francine. Franny. I hate to be unwelcoming. It isn't my desire. You can come up to the porch if you like, Jason. I can at least offer you some bread."

"Would you rather I swiped it from your windowsill?"

"Don't try it. Puggles knows Aster. I'd end up finding pieces of you buried around the yard."

Jason held up both hands. "Okay. Maybe the porch would be best." He reached for the gate, and Puggles barked. Jason paused.

"Puggles, heel," Franny ordered, slapping her thigh. She pointed for the dog to go back inside the house, and the bulky canine trundled out of sight.

Jason let himself through the gate. Franny disappeared inside. By the time Jason had mounted the porch steps, she had returned with a loaf of bread wrapped in a coarse bag.

"I have a weakness for the downtrodden," she confessed. "But that doesn't make me gullible. A word from me, and Puggles will tear you apart. If you know boarhounds, you know I'm not exaggerating. And we know Aster is watching as well."

"I hear you," Jason said politely. "About the Blind King . . ."

"It isn't far. Continue down my lane to the crossroads and turn left. You'll pass the Gamester's farm, fork right onto the gravel road, and shortly come into view of the castle."

"So he's a real king with a castle and everything?"

"Not everything," Franny clarified. "He's the unofficial arbiter around here. It would be a stretch to label him a real king. Opinions about him vary. He settles disputes, offers advice. Some do his bidding, but he lacks real authority from the emperor."

"Will it be hard to get into his castle? Do I just knock?"

"Speak with the gatewarden. The king grants audience liberally. You really know so little about him?"

"I only know I need to have a talk with him."

"Your business is your business. By all reports he is a just arbiter. Some who surround him seem odd. You'll have to form your own opinion."

"What do you think of him?" Jason asked.

"He keeps a fairly high profile in a time when it might be more prudent to lay low. You should be on your way."

"Thank you, Franny."

"You seem very open," Franny said sadly. "You should travel

with more care. There are plenty abroad who would take advantage of you."

Jason descended the porch steps and backed toward the gate. "Thanks for the warning, and the bread."

"We never met," Franny said, retreating into her multihued house and closing the door.

Jason waved at the trees where Aster was hiding, then started down the lane. He opened the bag and tore off a chunk of warm bread, which tasted hearty. By contrast it made the bread back home seem ridiculously flimsy. Grateful to have something to eat besides mushrooms, Jason consumed almost half the loaf.

Not long after Franny's home passed out of sight, Jason reached the crossroads. A white stone obelisk marked the intersection. One side of the obelisk was deeply scarred, as if an inscription had been gouged away. Aside from the tall marker and the dirt roads, no evidence of civilization could be seen in any direction.

Jason turned left, passing feral fields of tall grass interrupted by occasional copses of trees. He saw the charred remnants of a house, thorny shrubs growing up among the blackened wood, the scorched chimney still mostly intact.

Presently he came upon tended fields where crops grew in long rows. A fenceless house came into view up ahead: a low, sturdy structure. Out front a burly, shirtless man in overalls sat on a short stool sketching on a large parchment propped on an easel. Another fellow sat nearby on the grass, fiddling with a series of interlocked iron shapes. On a nearby table rested a ceramic dome segmented by lines suggesting it was a complex three-dimensional puzzle. Farther back towered a bronze sculpture comprised of bizarre shapes balanced precariously. Certain portions of the sculpture were on pivots and swiveled lazily in the breeze, squealing faintly.

"Hi, there," Jason said from the lane. "Is one of you the Gamester?"

"I am," said the man in overalls. He stood, a husky man with arms like a linebacker. He seemed a tad wary, but unafraid.

"Did you make that puzzle?" Jason said, jerking his head at the man trying to unlink the shapes.

"I did, along with many others."

"I like that sculpture."

"It can be reassembled in many combinations."

"Do you sell your puzzles?"

He shook his head. "I give them away."

"Do many people come by?"

"Mainly just Jerome here. Most folks would rather not bother. Sometimes a few will come and watch Jerome solve a series of my toughest creations."

Jason gestured at the parchment. "Are you designing a new puzzle?"

The Gamester nodded. "I permit no man to view my designs." He rolled up the parchment, even through Jason could view none of the drawing from where he stood. "What brings you this way, stranger?"

"I need to speak with the Blind King."

"How do you know the Blind King?"

"Isn't he famous?" Jason answered vaguely.

"Locally, yes, to some extent. But you are not from these parts."

Jason was unsure what to say. "It might be best not to ask me too many questions."

"Fair enough," the Gamester replied. "Safe journey."

Jason turned his back on the peculiar pair. The Gamester had not acted very welcoming and had seemed a little too curious. He walked briskly.

After a few miles Jason stopped and stripped off his gray coveralls for the first time, revealing his T-shirt and jeans. A tentative sniff proved that his sweat-marked underarms reeked like unwashed monkeys. It was long past time to wash up and do some laundry. Maybe the castle would have someplace to bathe.

Continuing on with cloak, blanket roll, and coveralls bundled under one arm, he eventually forked right onto a gravel road. Crunching along the gravel sapped more energy than walking on the hard-packed lane. The road wound around a hill, finally bringing him below the shade of broad-leafed trees.

As he rounded the back side of the hill, the castle came into view, constructed atop a shallower hill behind the first. The massive stone complex looked abandoned. Sagging walls topped with crumbling battlements had collapsed entirely in some locations. Only two towers remained standing, one of which was so crooked and damaged it looked ready to topple at a cough from a butterfly. Jumbled heaps of stone and rotted beams marked where other structures had already fallen. The decrepit castle looked like an ideal hideout for thieves or vagabonds. No wonder Aster had told Jason to send the Blind King his regards.

Jason sighed. Had the loremaster misled him? Might he have sent him into a trap? Jason was quickly losing confidence that the Blind King would be able to help him. But with no apparent alternatives, what else could he do?

The gravel path led Jason to a corroded, raised drawbridge with a small door built in its center. A plank led across the shallow, dry moat. Outside the door stood a grave, middle-aged man clad in mismatched armor and clutching a poleax. "Who might you be, sir?" the gatewarden inquired stiffly. Despite the ruins around him he apparently took his job seriously.

"I might be anyone," Jason said. "I'm searching for the Blind King."

"Have you scheduled an audience with His Majesty?"

"No. I've recently arrived from a distant land."

"Do you come on an errand of royal consequence?"

"Of course."

"Your name?"

"Jason."

"Wait here while I inquire within." The man unlocked the door using a key from his belt. Probably not the best defensive strategy to give a lone, exposed guard the key to the door he was protecting. Then again not the best idea to have huge gaps in your walls, either. The gatewarden disappeared through the door.

A few minutes later he returned. "His Majesty bade me to admit you. Take care to show him the respect befitting a sovereign of his magnificence."

The gatewarden escorted Jason across a courtyard where weeds thrived between the cracks of uneven paving stones. They passed close by the precariously teetering tower. The entire complex appeared deserted. Nobody roamed the courtyard, and the windows in the surviving structures looked vacant. Motioning with his poleax, the gatekeeper ushered Jason through a set of double doors into the sturdiest building within the castle compound, which adjoined the only solid tower.

The building housed a great hall. Birds roosted in the rafters, and white streaks of droppings marked the floor and trestle tables. At the far end of the room, upon a moldering dais, a shabby man sat upon a battered throne. A dingy rag bound his eyes, a tarnished crown rested upon his gray hair, and a grimy green robe edged in dirty white fur enshrouded his body. He looked like some old homeless guy playing the part of a wise man in a soup-kitchen Christmas pageant.

Three attendants stood nearby: a mustached man in a stained velvet cap fingering a dented trumpet, an ugly woman with her hair caught up under a faded bonnet, and a humbly clad, young minstrel holding a lute.

"Presenting Lord Jason," called the man in the velvet cap in a proud voice, blasting a flourish on his trumpet for emphasis. The loud notes sounded brassy and annoying, echoing harshly off the bare walls of the cavernous hall.

"One moment," croaked the old king. "First allow my chancellor to complete his report."

"As you will, sire," the minstrel said in a courtly voice, casting a nervous glance at Jason. "As I was recounting, the invading armies have been repelled beyond our frontiers. General Braddock reports staggering enemy casualties. He hesitates at our borders awaiting your command."

"Onward," the king coughed, waving an arm. "Use our initiative to drive them into oblivion before they can reform."

"A dispatch will be sent at once."

"Sooner," the king demanded. "What now?"

"The matter of Lord Jason," said the man in the velvet cap.

"Come forward," rasped the old king, beckoning with one hand.

Jason gaped at the ridiculous scene.

"Go on," urged the gatewarden quietly.

Jason approached the dais. "Greetings, mighty king," he said politely, opting to play along with the charade. It required some effort to restrain his sarcasm.

"Welcome to my realm," the king intoned, spreading an arm outward, sightlessly indicating the damaged walls and dilapidated furnishings. It was embarrassingly clear that the Blind King believed he ruled a grand domain. Jason felt tempted to turn and walk out. There seemed no chance that this pathetic pretender could help him. But it would be rude. And he had no other place to go.

"What brings you before His Majesty?" asked the minstrel, now speaking in a softer, higher-pitched tone.

"I come seeking wisdom," Jason replied, trying to sound formal.

"He comes to the right place," the minstrel declared in a different voice, having changed positions. The others cried out, "Hear, hear," repeating the words in various voices. What an act! Jason threw in a "Hear, hear" of his own.

The king raised his hands for silence. "What wisdom do you seek, young traveler?"

"I'm not entirely sure."

The attendants murmured theatrically.

"What guided you to my kingdom?"

"I was referred here by a loremaster. He lives in a repository—"

"Say no more. I understand." Jason noticed the king's grip momentarily tighten on the arms of the throne.

The attendants mumbled vaguely about the perceptiveness of the king. The woman crept some distance away, coughed loudly, and returned.

"I would converse with Lord Jason at once in the privacy of my chambers," the king proclaimed.

The attendants looked shocked. Apparently this was an infrequent invitation.

"As you command, Your Majesty," the minstrel finally responded in a deep voice.

The woman aided the king to his feet and helped him down the dais steps. "Let young Jason serve as my guide," the king said. The woman stepped away, and the gatewarden hurriedly directed Jason forward. The king placed a hand on his shoulder. Jason followed the gatewarden out one side of the hall.

The gatewarden eyed Jason, making grandiose gestures. Jason took the cue. "You have a spectacular castle," he said.

"Most gracious of you," the king replied in his raspy voice. "We will proceed alone from this point." The gatekeeper bowed and returned to the hall. When they advanced to a curving staircase, the king grasped the banister. "I require no further aid." Jason followed the king up the stone steps, into the more stable of the two towers. The old guy mounted the long flight at an impressive pace. Despite his long gray hair and beard he seemed in healthy condition.

Eventually they spiraled up to the highest room in the tower. The stairs stopped at a heavy door bound in iron. "Here we are," the king said, unlocking the door and leading Jason through the portal.

The room was nicely appointed, with clean furnishings and a canopied bed. The king moved about the room almost as if he could see. With one hand extended probingly, the king found a cushioned chair. "Please be seated."

Jason took a seat across from the king, who sat straight and tall. For the first time Jason noticed the broadness of his shoulders. His bearing somehow seemed more regal than when he had been slumped upon the throne.

"Bridonus sent you," the king stated.

"He did, Your Majesty."

"Then you have seen inside the book bound in living skin?" .

The question surprised Jason. "I have."

The king exhaled. "At long last."

"How do you know about the book?"

"I too have seen within its pages, though few in my kingdom know this fact. You have part of the Word?"

Jason stared at the ragged king. "The first syllable."

"A great burden now rests on your shoulders," the king murmured. "You must think me a fool."

"Excuse me?"

"I have no army. I know I live inside a derelict castle with a handful of well-meaning courtiers. Some of them do not realize I know this, or they pretend not to realize. It gives them great satisfaction to believe they have convinced me that I rule a mighty domain. I do rule here, but my kingdom is the opposite of mighty. For their benefit I put on a stately air, and I play along with the silly intrigues and wars they fabricate."

Recovering from his absurd first impression, Jason was beginning to hope this king might be able to help him after all. "I've come across some weird relationships lately."

"Explain."

"A woman who lets a hobo steal from her because he refuses to accept her charity. A game maker who crafts puzzles for the single person who takes the time to solve them. And now you and your subjects."

The sightless monarch nodded. "People find meaning where they can. These are uncertain times. Part of the reason I play along with our ludicrous pretentions is because it casts us in a ridiculous light. The more absurd we seem, the less we need to fear the emperor." He folded his hands upon his lap. "You have a sharp eye for connections. Where do you hail from?"

"That's hard to explain."

The king stroked his beard. "Are you a Beyonder?"

Jason's heart rate quickened. "Bridonus used that word. I think so."

"How did you come to our world?"

"I know how this sounds." Jason shifted uncomfortably. "I came here through a hippopotamus."

"A water horse? Intriguing. Recount how it transpired."

Jason was thrilled the old guy seemed to believe him. "I worked in a zoo, and one day I heard music coming from the hippo. I got too close trying to listen and fell into the tank. The hippo swallowed me. Except not really. I was suddenly sliding down a tunnel. Then I came out of a tree and couldn't get back."

"What happened next?"

"Well, the music came from a bunch of musicians floating on a raft."

"The Giddy Nine."

"That's right! They were headed for a waterfall. I tried to rescue them, but I messed it up and everyone got angry. Then I found the Repository of Learning, read the book, and Bridonus booted me out and told me to find you."

The Blind King nodded, stroking his beard again, a faint smile bending his lips. "Perhaps those merrymakers were right after all," the king murmured. "They summoned a Beyonder."

"Excuse me?"

"The leader of the Giddy Nine, Simeon, was an adventurous man, more soldier than minstrel. He used their music as a subversive tool, so naturally the performers began to make enemies. He took time off and went to visit a prophetess, one of the few remaining oracles with any real credibility. The act required an arduous journey. Upon his return he consulted with me before implementing her instructions."

"Some oracle told him to float off a waterfall?" Jason asked.

"Essentially. Tell me about your life in the Beyond."

"I'm a student. My dad is a dentist. I live in a nice house. Our world is really different from yours." As Jason spoke, he realized how far away all of that had already begun to feel. He was sitting in an ancient tower—homework and baseball seemed almost surreal.

The Blind King nodded pensively. "Have you ever sacrificed for a cause?"

"Um . . . I've helped with some car washes to raise money for our local soup kitchen. Nothing drastic. I keep trying to understand where I am, and how I can get home. Can you help me?"

"Not many remain who possess the sort of information you seek. Of those who do, few would bother to help you. Maldor discourages the naming of places. He forbids the production of maps. He frowns upon traveling. He teaches the populace to distrust strangers. He wants a fog of ignorance to disconnect our world. None are allowed to discuss the Beyond or the forbidden language. Many have forgotten much, or have never learned it. Others pretend to have forgotten."

"But you're not afraid of the emperor?"

"I am afraid for many reasons. Not so much for myself. I love this land. I do what I can."

"Can you help me understand what I should do to get home? Or maybe where I should start looking? What do you know about the Beyond? I still don't really get where I am."

The king scratched his cheek. "I can't say how to access the Beyond. I'm not sure who might be able to tell you. Others have crossed over from the Beyond, though never frequently, and as of late, traffic between our worlds has come to a standstill.

"I can do my best to orient you. Years ago this particular fiefdom was called Fortaim, and an earl occupied this castle. Fortaim rests upon a peninsula that juts westward from the mainland out into a vast ocean. Following the river westward over the falls, you would have come to the estuary where it empties into the sea. But you went south without a trail until you happened upon the Repository of Learning. From there you came eastward along the peninsula until you arrived at this ruined castle. The river, once called the Telkron, lies a few miles to the north."

Jason was impressed. "Who needs a map with you around?"

The Blind King steepled his fingers. "Once I had eyes, and I used them to travel widely in search of the Word."

"How did you lose them?"

"In a fight with a devious conscriptor. He hurled powdered acid in my face, flaying my skin and stealing my sight. A small inhalation scorched my throat, damaging my voice. The conscriptor captured me. Eventually I came before Maldor. The emperor offered me new eyes. I refused. I would not accept the restoration of my sight at the price of becoming one of his spies. So I was delivered to his tormentors."

Jason swallowed. This old king was something serious.

"Now you must pursue the Word," the king said.

"Honestly, I'd rather find a way home."

"No doubt you would. Should you encounter a way back to the Beyond, I would be the last to blame you for fleeing our world. We teeter on the brink of destruction. But a path back will be difficult to find. Perhaps impossible. In the meanwhile you should seek the Word. Mark my warning—Maldor already pursues you. Seeking the Word is your sole chance for survival. Remain still, or wander aimlessly, and you will be taken."

Jason shifted uncomfortably. He felt no heroic urge to become Blind Lord Jason. "Did you learn much of the Word?"

"I learned some. More than most, I believe. But the syllables I acquired are lost, along with the memories of where I found most of them. Maldor's tormentors used relentless conditioning to abolish many recollections. When it comes to the Word, I remember few specifics. But I retain a few fragmented memories on the subject. I still remember Bridonus, and the book itself."

"So I should leave, then?"

"Rest here for the night. There is somebody you must meet, a fellow traveler. Share a meal with us. I will provide further counsel on the morrow. How does roasted pheasant strike you?"

"I've been living off of mushrooms."

"Go ring the bell twice. It will summon Chandra, my cook."

Jason went to a bell mounted atop a dresser and delivered a pair of sharp blows with the tiny mallet resting beside it.

CHAPTER 5

RACHEL

Jason stood at a narrow window, studying the last embers of the sunset, when a slender man of medium height brought a huge tray to the Blind King's lofty chamber. A shiny scar interrupted his features, starting above his hairline and curving down his cheek almost to his jaw. Offering no introduction, the attendant moved swiftly and silently, rearranging furniture until a seat awaited Jason across from the Blind King, with a small table between them. With quiet efficiency the man shuttled the contents of the tray to the table. Before long the table held three place settings, a bowl of fruit, a charger brimming with mashed vegetables dusted with spices, a carafe of golden fluid, a pitcher of water, and a platter heaped with slices of white meat.

"Thank you, Dorsio," the Blind King said as the attendant picked up the empty tray. "If you would be so kind as to fetch our other guest."

Dorsio snapped his fingers, turned, and exited the room, closing the door silently. From the moment he had entered, the attendant had never looked Jason in the eye.

"Please, have a seat," the Blind King invited.

Jason sat down. "Dorsio seemed really businesslike."

"Forgive his reticence. He cannot speak. In my role as the Blind King I must balance various public and private responsibilities. With my public face as the ridiculous veneer, I privately work to undermine the emperor. Dorsio is part of my private circle. He is quite adept at handling sensitive matters. We have developed a system where he traces messages on my palm, or uses snapping for simple acknowledgments."

"I'm curious about our other guest," Jason confessed.

"Satisfaction will soon replace curiosity," the Blind King said. "Not many of my associates have met her. She arrived here two nights ago. I believe your destinies are linked."

The door opened, and Dorsio escorted a girl into the room. She was almost a head shorter than Jason, and didn't look much older than he was. Her short brown hair had a stylish cut, and she had dark brown eyes and a faint spray of freckles across her nose and cheeks. Her clothes seemed homemade and didn't fit right: The dark yellow shirt sagged in the shoulders, and the coarse brown pants were too loose in the waist, cinched into place with a wide belt. The Blind King rose politely, and Jason awkwardly followed his lead.

Dorsio exited quietly as the girl approached the table.

"Thank you for joining us," the Blind King said with a smile, gesturing toward her seat.

The girl sat down, eyes regarding Jason with interest. "So you're the mysterious visitor."

"You stole my line," Jason said, trying to recover from the shock that the visitor was a cute girl around his age.

"They haven't changed your wardrobe yet," she commented, looking him up and down.

"Those aren't your clothes?" Jason asked.

She smirked, plucking at the yellow top. "Not exactly my style. But my other outfit makes me look too much like a Beyonder."

"You're a Beyonder too?" Jason exclaimed.

The Blind King sat down.

The girl grinned. "They warned me in advance that you're from my world. Totally ruined the surprise."

Jason glanced at the Blind King. Their host waited in silence, a small smile on his lips, listening with his hands folded on the edge of the table. Jason realized he was the only person still standing, and sat down. "How long have you been here?"

"This will be my fifth night," she replied.

"Mine, too!"

"Pardon me," the Blind King interjected. "Would the two of you mind verifying that you both truly come from the Beyond? I do not believe either of you is an imposter, but it never hurts to be certain."

"Ooh," the girl said with delight. "Cross-examination."

"Where are you from?" Jason asked.

"Olympia, Washington," the girl responded. "You?"

"Vista, Colorado."

She nodded vaguely. "What's the capital of Pennsylvania?"

"I don't know. Philadelphia?"

"No. But that's the kind of wrong answer somebody from America would give. Let me guess, you're not a very serious student?"

"Just because I'm not a trivia expert doesn't make me a bad student," Jason complained. "I'm in eighth grade. I take honors classes. What's the actual capital of Pennsylvania?"

"Harrisburg," she replied smugly.

"I'll believe you. Who won the 2004 World Series?"

She shrugged. "The Yankees?"

"The Yankees? And you claim to be an American?" He enjoyed rubbing it in after her attitude about Harrisburg. "It was the Red Sox. The year they broke the curse."

"But the Yankees win the series a lot, right?"

"They've won the most," he conceded.

"Do you play baseball or just watch it?" she asked.

"I pitch for school and on a club team. And I'm a pretty good infielder. What year are you in school?"

"I skipped a grade, so I'm in ninth. But I'm homeschooled. I only go to school to run track."

"How do you skip grades when you're homeschooled? Mom just decides to shorten her teaching career?"

She scowled. "My classes are much harder than anything in public schools."

"If you say so. What track events?"

"Hurdles and pole vault."

"Pole vault?" Jason repeated, impressed. "You must have some guts."

"I like trying new things," she said.

"I'm long past convinced," the Blind King inserted. "Judging from your inflections, I would say you speak English in a similar manner, and based on your intonations, I feel confident that you're both telling the truth. But I already knew that. Consider the exercise a lesson in vigilance. Without extreme caution you will not survive. Shall we eat?"

Jason started transferring meat to his plate. "What's your name?" he asked the girl.

"Rachel," she replied, spooning vegetables onto the Blind King's plate, then helping herself. "You?"

"I'm Jason." Following her example, he shared several cuts of pheasant with the Blind King.

"Don't mind me," the Blind King protested. "My table is set in such a fashion as to enable me to feed myself. Eat your food and get acquainted."

"Can you believe we're actually here?" Rachel asked as Jason made a small pile of mashed vegetables on his plate.

"I've had a hard time getting used to all of this," Jason admitted, trying a bite of pheasant. "Did you get swallowed by a hippo too?"

"Excuse me?"

"Jason came into our world through the jaws of a hippopotamus," the Blind King explained. "The residue of very old magic. There is no rarer or stranger portal connecting our realities."

Rachel pursed her lips. "What, the way I came here was typical?"

The Blind King shook his head. "In these times any visit from a Beyonder is virtually inconceivable."

"You came through a different way?" Jason asked.

"I was hiking with my parents," Rachel said, her eyes losing focus. "We were in Arches National Park, in southern Utah."

"But you're from Washington," Jason said. "Let me guess—the vacation schedule for homeschool is flexible."

"I actually have less vacation time than most kids," Rachel corrected. "Homeschool is portable. My parents are big on first-hand experiences. We do lots of field trips. Museums. Foreign countries. National parks. They're big on nature."

"I've always wanted to travel more. Do you speak other languages and stuff?"

Her eyes lit up. "I love languages. I speak pretty fluent French and Spanish. I'm okay at Italian and Portuguese. And I can sort of get by in Russian, Chinese, and a couple others."

Jason gave a low whistle. "You've been to all those places? Italy and China and everywhere?"

"Yeah."

"Sounds like you guys have some money."

"Dad made a lot as a software designer. He's semiretired. I'm an only child."

"You were telling how you came here," the Blind King prompted.

"Right," Rachel said, raking her fingers through her dark brown hair. "Dad had hired a local guide to take us off the beaten path. He drove us around in a jeep through some amazing country. Have you been to Arches?"

"No. I've been to the Grand Canyon."

"Me too. The Grand Canyon was just a big hole in the ground. Arches and Bryce Canyon seemed much cooler to me. They're full of these awesome spires and bridges made with stones in all these crazy colors."

"You should write a travel guide," Jason said dryly.

"Anyhow, our guide was taking us to some smaller stone arches. The kind you can't find on maps or drive to on a road. He parked beside an arroyo—that's what he called a ravine—and we walked from there. The arroyo branched in a couple places, and while we were stopped for a snack at one point, I saw this beautiful blue and gold butterfly. Each wing was nearly the size of my hand. They almost looked metallic."

"Let me guess the twist ending," Jason said. "The butterfly swallowed you, and you ended up in Lyrian."

"Not quite. The butterfly made me curious. I had never seen anything like it, and I thought maybe I had found a new species. After all, we were in the middle of nowhere."

"I've never heard of a North American butterfly like you're describing," Jason said, proud to sound official with his zoological knowledge.

"We have them here," the Blind King remarked. "Go on."

"I left my parents and the guide and chased after the butterfly. It stayed too far ahead for me to catch up and get a good picture, but I had no trouble following."

"So then what happened?" Jason asked, taking another bite of meat. The pheasant was quite tender, the crisp brown skin on the edges deliciously seasoned.

"I ended up in front of this natural stone bridge, a really impressive one. The butterfly flew forward under the stone arch and disappeared. One second the big, bright butterfly was in plain view—and the next it was gone. I stood there squinting, figuring it must have flown into the shadow of the arch and landed somewhere."

"As I told Rachel," the Blind King commented in his raspy voice, "stone archways have long been a means of conveyance between our worlds. Much more conventional than water horses."

"You followed the butterfly," Jason said.

"The instant I passed below the arch, I was somewhere else," Rachel recounted, her voice quavering at the memory. "The terrain was completely different—a leafy ravine full of gray rocks. I turned around, but the arroyo was gone."

"Did you try to backtrack?" Jason asked.

She shook her head. "Not at first. I saw the butterfly on the ground, not far ahead of me. Its wings quivered weakly. I crouched beside it and watched it die."

"Wow," Jason said. "Then what?"

"I tried to go back," Rachel said. "Whatever mystical doorway I had passed through was either one-way or only open for a second. I called for my parents. I walked up and down the ravine. I threw rocks. Eventually I decided I had better try to find civilization."

"She found the secluded cabin of a friend of mine," the Blind King said.

"It wasn't far from where I came through," Rachel said. "The cabin looked primitive but in good shape. I called and knocked, but nobody answered. The door was unlocked. I found a dead old woman inside. I swear I almost lost it. It was too much."

"Erinda lived in isolation," the Blind King said, taking a sip of the golden beverage from the carafe. He smacked his lips. "Superior honeymelon juice. Be sure to sample some. Where was I? Oh, yes, I had received an urgent message from Erinda the day before, a cryptic missive about doing her part to save Lyrian. Erinda was something of a spellweaver, you see, and she mentioned that she had been in contact with one of the Giddy Nine."

"Was she the oracle?" Jason asked, pouring some of the golden liquid into his glass.

The Blind King snorted. "Hardly. But she evidently played a role in the oracle's designs. Erinda had a fondness for insects. How odd that a Beyonder followed a butterfly through a supernatural portal not far from her cabin on the day she died, all within hours of when young Jason arrived from the Beyond by even less likely means."

"I spent the rest of the day exploring," Rachel continued. "I went back to the ravine hoping I could discover a way back to the arroyo. When I couldn't find a way home, I went back to the cabin and spent the night with the corpse. At least the cabin had provisions."

"Dorsio and Brin the Gamester went and retrieved her," the Blind King said. "The message from Erinda had advised me to send trustworthy men to her cottage."

"The Gamester who lives down the road from here?" Jason asked.

The Blind King nodded. "Another member of my private circle."

"Brin convinced me to come with them," Rachel said. "He seemed to believe I had come from another world. He and Dorsio brought me here."

"And I have been trying to decide what to do with you ever since," the Blind King said. "I am watched too closely for you to remain here for any duration. Given my past, if the emperor believed I was harboring a Beyonder, it would lead to the end of us all. Rachel, I believe your destiny is entwined with Jason's."

"My destiny?" Rachel huffed. "Are you serious? You say it like you mean it."

The Blind King sighed thoughtfully. "There are some oracles who truly possess the gift of foresight. Some pretend, some guess, but a few are legitimate. Indeed some in my family have wielded this true gift of prescience. It seems the last great prophetess in the world helped instigate your arrival here. Where true oracles are involved, yes, I believe in destiny. Or at least potential destiny. The future is never certain."

"I've always thought fortune-tellers were ridiculous," Rachel said candidly. "Then again, after coming here, I'm not sure what to believe anymore. Who knows what might be possible? But enough about me. Jason, tell me about this hippopotamus."

Jason recounted his escapade at the zoo, his arrival at the river, and his failed rescue attempt. Rachel acted incredulous about the hippo, but after Jason pointed out that it was no less plausible than journeying to a new world beneath a stone archway, she listened intently to the rest. The Blind King stopped him before he could relate anything about the Repository of Learning.

"Jason took a detour before joining us here," the Blind King explained. "The details of this detour are perilous to any who learn them. Jason acquired information that directed him toward a quest that could destroy Maldor."

"The emperor?" Rachel verified.

The Blind King nodded. "It must all be part of the oracle's design."

"Wait," Jason said. "Are you telling us that everything we do here is already determined?"

"Certainly not," the Blind King said. "Oracles do not deal in absolutes. They deal in possibilities. The future is always in flux, changing according to the decisions made in the present. Presumably, somewhere in our wide array of possible futures there is a chance that this quest of yours could yield favorable results to those who oppose Maldor. We know nothing more."

"And you think I'm part of this," Rachel said.

"The specifics of the prophecy died with Erinda and the Giddy Nine," the Blind King said. "My best guess is that you two were meant to embark on this quest together. I could be wrong. The choice is yours. The endeavor will be unspeakably dangerous."

"What if I don't want to join him?" Rachel asked.

"I would send you away to a farm owned by distant relatives," the Blind King said. "You would play the role of an orphan brought into the household to help with chores. We would all do our best to hide the fact that you came from the Beyond. Perhaps by lying low and hiding your past, you could eventually build a life here."

"No, thanks," Rachel said. "I want to find a way home!"

The Blind King ran a finger around the rim of a glass. His strong hands looked somewhat younger than the color of his hair and beard would indicate. "If you mean to search for a way home, the endeavor will require much travel. The safest way for you to travel would probably be as a coconspirator in a plot to overthrow Maldor."

"Really?" Rachel asked skeptically.

"Maldor is a complicated ruler. He takes great interest in his enemies, seeking to test them, measure them, and eventually to corrupt or break them. Strange as it may sound, you will meet less resistance on the road if you are part of a known plot against him."

"And Jason's plot is known?" Rachel asked.

"Well known," the Blind King assured her. "Undoubtedly the eye of the emperor is on him. Should you elect to join Jason, the gaze of the emperor will rest upon you as well. As a Beyonder, joining a desperate quest such as this may be your wisest option, as I assume the oracle foresaw."

Rachel rubbed her temples. "I can't believe this! Everything keeps getting worse and worse. I had a good life! It made sense!"

"I can't completely understand how disorienting this must feel," the Blind King consoled.

"I can," Jason said. "It wasn't like I came here looking for a mission. I stumbled across it while hunting for a way home. And I still want to find a way home."

"I would not blame either of you for being reluctant to adopt this quest as your own," the Blind King avowed. "You were both drawn here by forces beyond your understanding."

"For your sake, I'm sorry you're here, Rachel," Jason said. "For mine, I'm sort of glad. It's a relief to talk to somebody who at least knows the Yankees exist."

Biting her lower lip, Rachel pushed some food around her plate. She took a sip of water.

"Take your time, Rachel," the Blind King advised. "For the moment the secret Jason has learned remains his burden alone. Enough of your fate has been involuntary. I will not attempt to force this knowledge upon you. Tomorrow you can depart with Jason, sharing his secret, or you can depart for a quiet life on a farm. With Jason you would be constantly on the run, rushing from one peril to the next. On the farm, if we can manage to transport you there undetected, and if you avoid drawing attention, you would have a reasonable chance of living out your days in peace. You have this night to decide."

"Or there's option three," Rachel said. "Hit the road on my own and take my chances."

"I suppose," the Blind King said. His tone made it clear he thought it would be foolish.

"And I have no choice," Jason grumbled.

"Not much choice," the Blind King agreed. "I suppose you could surrender to the emperor. Otherwise you should pursue the quest. Tonight you will rest under my protection. I will provide you with a room and a bed. On the morrow I will equip you and offer some parting counsel. For the present do your best to relax."

GIFTS

A burst of three brisk thumps rapped against the door. Jason awoke, staring up at the underside of a dark blue canopy emblazoned with a golden sunburst, tucked between soft sheets, head cushioned on a feathery pillow. He occupied the room immediately below the Blind King's personal chamber. Two sets of slatted shutters were latched over tall windows, mostly blocking the predawn grayness. Supercool weapons hung on the walls: several swords, a loaded crossbow, a javelin sharpened to a point at both ends, and a pair of bizarre weapons with short wooden handles from which sprouted many sharp, twisting blades of varying length, intricate as Chinese characters.

Thump, thump, thump.

Jason stretched. Apparently they wanted him to get an early start. Reluctant to leave his comfortable bed, he kicked off his sheets and crossed to the door, the stone floor chilly beneath his bare soles. After removing the bar from its brackets, he slid both bolts and pulled the thick door open. Dorsio stood on the landing, a short sword strapped to his side. He handed a bundle of clothes to Jason and gestured for him to follow.

"Should I put these on first?" Jason asked.

Dorsio gave a nod.

He dressed hurriedly. The shirt, trousers, and loose vest fit better than the clothing Rachel had received. There were no shoes in the bundle. "Do I just wear my same boots?"

Dorsio nodded again.

Jason laced his boots. Remembering his manners, he hastily straightened the covers on the bed. Despite the instructions the Blind King had given to lock his room, the night had passed uneventfully.

Jason climbed the stairs to the king's room, passing the cook as she descended, a gaunt woman wearing a leather choker, clutching a large wooden spoon in one callused hand. He followed Dorsio to the top, where the attendant unlocked the door.

"Enter," the Blind King invited.

Jason complied. Remaining on the stairs, Dorsio closed the door. A tray covered with steaming eggs, dark bread, and fat, crisp bacon sat on a low table. Jason took a seat. At an invitation from the king he piled eggs and bacon onto a slice of bread to make a breakfast sandwich.

"This morning you must depart," the king said. "I will do what I can to help you on your way."

"Where should I go?" Jason asked after spitting a mouthful of bread and egg into his hand because it had burned his tongue. He was glad the king could not see the unappetizing act.

The Blind King scowled pensively. "I have given the matter much consideration, and I've managed to revive a faint memory. I recommend you travel south, well beyond the crossroads, to a place where the road bends east along the top of sea cliffs. At the bend in the road you will leave it, heading farther south until you arrive at a tiny trickle of a stream that seeps away into a crack not far from the brink of the cliffs. Looking down off the precipice near the stream, you will observe a pair of rocks shaped like arrowheads. At low tide jump between those rocks, and swim into the cave at the base of the cliff. A man who dwells inside will give you some of the answers I cannot supply."

"When is low tide?"

"This time of year it should fall around midday."

"How high are these cliffs? Won't I get hurt?"

"The water is deep there. You might drown or be crushed against rocks, but you should survive the fall."

"Comforting." Jason had been blowing on his open sandwich. He took a tentative bite. "Will he give me part of the Word?"

The king crinkled his brow. "He might. I recall that a man in the sea cave assisted me in my quest. I do not remember where I obtained the fragments of the Word I collected, although I know some part came from *The Book of Salzared*. Whether the man in the cave knows part of the Word, or can simply offer some guidance, I am unsure. The memory of his location was all I could salvage."

"How did they erase your memories?"

The Blind King shrugged. "Torture. Toxins. Conditioning. Magic. It is all a miserable blur. I am not quite as old as I appear. I was once a proud, defiant man. The tormentors worked on me until I broke, mind and body. I have attempted to rehabilitate my body, to some success. Healing my mind has proven to be the greater challenge."

With his tongue still feeling scalded, Jason finished his flavorless sandwich. He heard boots stomping up the stairs, followed by a firm rap at the door.

"Who seeks admittance?" the Blind King inquired.

"Brin, bearing urgent tidings."

"Enter."

A key rattled, and the Gamester came through the door, chest heaving, wearing a hooded cloak. "There has been a murder!"

Jason felt uncertain how to react. He wondered if this was more make-believe.

"Go on," the king said.

"Francine, daughter of Gordon, has been taken. There was a slaughter at her home."

"What?" Restrained outrage tightened the king's voice. Jason leaned forward to the edge of his seat, alerted by the king's genuine reaction. Did the Gamester mean Franny?

"Dire news, sire, but accurate."

"Describe the scene." The king had regained his composure.

"When I arrived, the door hung askew on twisted hinges. The parlor was a disaster. Furniture splintered, everything spattered with gore, tattered bits of fabric clinging to the walls and ceiling."

"A mangler," the king stated flatly.

"Assuredly."

"She owned a boarhound."

"I found no traces of the animal in the aftermath."

"Could you identify the victim?"

"Yes." The Gamester produced a bloody rag from inside his cloak, unfolding it to reveal part of a severed hand wearing a gray, fingerless glove.

"Aster!" Jason blurted.

The Gamester nodded at him. "So it would appear. Your Majesty, I found part of a dismembered hand upon a high shelf. I feel certain the hand belonged to the vagrant Aster, and young Jason seems to recognize it as well."

"I spoke with Aster on my way here," Jason recounted, sickened by the news that the vagrant had perished. "He sent his regards."

The king nodded. "Aster was once a very respectable man. He must have tried to intervene when they came for her. Evidently not all heroic inclinations had abandoned him. Jason, I take it you spoke with Francine on your way into town?"

A pang of guilt hit Jason. "I did. I didn't know it could endanger her!"

"This atrocity is meant as a message to you, and also to me. Maldor wants you to know he is watching. And he wants me to know what will happen to any who assist you. Brin, please hasten the preparation of provisions for Lord Jason to take upon his journey. And find out whether Rachel has elected to join him. I lament sending her into danger, but no safe choices remain for her. I still expect her best chance for survival is accompanying Jason, but she must reach that decision on her own. Maintain a guard at the foot of these stairs. Keep a close watch on the road."

"As you wish, sire," the Gamester said, bowing stiffly. He closed the door when he left.

"What will happen to Franny?" Jason asked, embarrassed by the catch in his voice.

"Did you mention the Word to her?" the king asked grimly.

"No, of course not. The loremaster warned me not to talk about it. I only discussed it with you because you brought it up."

"Did you mention anything about the repository? Or your status as a Beyonder?"

"None of that," Jason said. "I just asked the way to your castle."

"Then she will probably live, although she might never return to her home. She will be interrogated and reprimanded."

"I can't believe this," Jason murmured.

The king leaned forward. "Heed my words. I now share a lesson learned through a lifetime of sorrowful experience. Maldor possesses sufficient power that when he wants a person dead, with very few exceptions that individual perishes immediately. Strangely, though, the greater threat an adversary poses, the less vigorously Maldor pursues a hasty demise. He toys with his greatest opponents, baits them, studies them, attempts to shatter their spirits, to drive them to utter ruin rather than merely slay them. For this reason I remain alive. No doubt it amuses him to envision me rotting away in a decaying castle, not dead but defeated. A pathetic monarch astride a throne of make-believe."

"What a psycho," Jason mumbled.

The Blind King raised a finger. "However, Maldor deviates from his sadistically inquisitive pattern when a foe fails to abide by his rules. He abhors the dissemination of sensitive information. He detests the recruitment of neutral parties. It bodes well for you that when Francine is interrogated, she will have no information about the Word or your quest. Had you told her about the Word, I would advise you to hastily gulp down your last meal. Do not take this counsel lightly. If you went around informing every soul you met about *The Book of Salzared*, you and all of the people you had spoken with—and most likely their relatives, friends, and neighbors—would be massacred."

"But you and I have talked a lot about the Word," Jason said.

"You have told me nothing I did not already know. Converse all you want with those of us who share the secret bound in living skin. Once you have been marked as an enemy to Maldor, you are actually safest when consorting with his other enemies."

"Have I brought danger upon you?"

"Undoubtedly. But I would have it no other way. My only remaining purpose of any consequence is advising those who dare to challenge the emperor."

The door opened silently, and Rachel entered, wearing the

same ill-tailored outfit as the day before. Dorsio waited in the doorway behind her.

"Rachel," the Blind King said, tipping his head toward the door. "I take it you mean to join Jason?"

"For his sake," she answered. "It didn't seem like he'd make it far without me."

"Ouch," Jason said. "That's the problem with homeschoolers. They haven't learned to interact with their peers."

"Enough bickering," the Blind King said. "Save your energy for the road. Dorsio, the surrounding countryside remains clear?"

Dorsio snapped his fingers.

"See that we remain undisturbed."

Dorsio snapped again and exited.

"Now that I'm officially coming," Rachel said, "what's the big secret?"

Jason explained about the book and the Word. She listened stoically. The Blind King advised Jason to wait to share the first syllable until he and Rachel were on the road, then repeated his advice about how to avoid provoking Maldor.

"So we're going on a quest to find a magic word?" Rachel asked in the end. She seemed underwhelmed.

"Maldor was apprenticed to an evil wizard called Zokar," the Blind King explained. "As a prerequisite to apprenticeship, dark wizards used to force their novices to allow a destructive spell to be woven into their physical makeup. A key word of Edomic could activate the spell and annihilate them. The practice granted the higher wizard assurance that his pupil would never turn on him."

"And anyone can say the key word?" Jason checked.

"The key words were designed to be the simplest conceivable activation tools," the king said. "This gave the mentoring wizard the assurance that he could overcome his apprentice under almost any circumstances. The main protection to the vulnerable pupil was his trust that his master would keep the key word a secret and never use it unfairly."

"But Zokar shared Maldor's word," Rachel concluded.

"Evidently," the Blind King said. "Zokar must have shared the Word after terminating his relationship with his apprentice. Typically, obscure and slippery words were chosen, to minimize the chances of the destructive spell being triggered accidentally."

Jason grabbed an extra piece of bacon. "*The Book of Salzared* said that I have to memorize the syllables, but to never say the Word or write it down, or it will be erased from my memory."

The Blind King gave a nod. "Edomic words of power can only be retained by the most adept, practiced minds. Part of the magic inherent in these key words causes them to be forgotten upon utterance. Learn the syllables, but only combine them mentally. Do not write or speak them in any combined form, or you risk losing them. You will only get a single chance to utter the Word entire, and that must be in the presence of the emperor."

"You really think this will work?" Rachel asked, taking a piece of bread.

"I have wagered my life, and the lives of many around me, on that certainty," the Blind King affirmed. "Seek the Word diligently. Hope that for a time Maldor will take interest in you and study you rather than speedily crush you. Beware: Even his gentlest tests can be deadly. And be prepared for the moment when Maldor will come for you in earnest. The closer you get to success, the greater peril you will face. The emperor will not let you succeed. Somehow you must triumph in spite of that."

"You didn't," Rachel pointed out.

"Correct," the Blind King said wearily. "We can only hope that you will be clever or skillful or lucky where I was not. The way will be grueling, but with the knowledge you now possess, there is no other option—you must proceed."

Jason nodded, then remembered that the Blind King could not see the affirmation. "We'll do our best."

"Good lad. How adept are you at the art of swordplay?"

"Not at all."

"Have you any weaponry?"

"No."

"Rachel?"

"Uh, I have my camera. And a canteen."

"I have some gifts for you." With a firm shove against the arms of his chair, the Blind King stood and walked over to the headboard of his bed. As he pressed a pair of acorns embossed onto the wood, a panel sprang open, revealing a small compartment. The king removed a couple of articles.

"This poniard is yours now, Jason," the king said, holding out a small dagger. "Its edge is most keen. If you press this blossom on the hilt and slide it forward, the blade becomes a short-range projectile. It is spring-loaded, commissioned from Brin the Gamester. May it serve you well."

The Blind King sheathed the dagger, and Jason placed it in a deep pocket of his trousers. "Thank you."

"I would give you a sword, but openly carrying a weapon you have not mastered is more dangerous than traveling unarmed. Beware men who carry swords. They will know how to use them."

"I'll remember that."

"Rachel?" The king held up a crystal sphere, just smaller than a baseball, with a small stone inside. "This mineral is orantium. It combusts when exposed to air or water. Sealed in the sphere with a pure gas the stone is harmless, but shattering the crystal produces a mighty explosion. An ideal tool for destroying manglers.

Even if a mangler bests you, with this on your person you will not perish alone."

A crease appeared between Rachel's eyebrows. "If it combusts when it's exposed to air, how did anyone get the mineral in the first place?"

The Blind King cleared his throat. "Long ago, at the fringe of recorded history, orantium was mined from the bowels of Mount Allowat, the only place it was ever found. The day came when the miners reached an enormous vein too dangerous to extract, and they abandoned the project. Over time the method of extracting the mineral was lost, as was the location of the mountain. This sphere is a relic from ancient times, one of a dwindling number of orantium explosives."

"What if I crack the sphere by accident?" Rachel asked.

"You would be blasted to pieces. But the crystal casing is quite durable. Fling it with considerable force against a hard surface, or the sphere may not rupture."

The king handed over the globe. "You are very kind," Rachel said.

"As neither of you is a warrior, avoiding confrontations should represent your best hope. Use evasion and persuasion. The knife and orantium are meant as a last resort."

"Live by the sword, die by the sword," Jason said.

"Quite so." The Blind King stroked his beard. "I have an advantage over both of you."

"What?" Rachel asked.

"I know your names. My name is a secret. To all save a few trusted allies I am simply the Blind King. The sharing of my name is no small matter. Many enemies from bygone days would seek their revenge if they knew my location. My beard, my voice, my scars, my premature aging—all of these elements help disguise my true identity. My name is Galloran. The name will open doors. Especially when you claim me as your sponsor. Use my name when you speak to the man in the cave, and with others who share our conspiracy against Maldor. It may bring aid in times of need."

Galloran removed a ring from an inner pocket of his robe and held it out to Jason. "Will this fit?"

Jason slid it on the third finger of his right hand. "Yes."

"It will confirm my sponsorship. My third and final gift. Kneel."

Jason complied. From beneath his shabby robe Galloran drew a magnificent sword, the long blade gleaming like a mirror. He reached forth one hand and laid it on Jason's head to confirm his position, then tapped each shoulder with the blade as he spoke.

"I, Galloran, master of this castle, rightful heir to the throne at Trensicourt, dub thee Lord Jason of Caberton, hereby transmitting all rights and privileges befitting a nobleman of rank and title."

Jason arose, moved by the simple ceremony despite the Blind King's ruined castle, raspy voice, and tarnished crown.

"What about me?" Rachel asked testily.

"You can be my cook," Jason said, unable to resist.

Rachel flushed. "You're going to pay for that one."

Galloran held up a hand. "Tense situations have a way of shortening tempers. Do not misdirect your anxieties. You two only have each other. Your lives depend on getting along."

"Why does he get to be nobility?" Rachel asked with a strained attempt at calmness.

"It is the more believable scenario," Galloran said. "In Lyrian most titles are held by men. If you had land of your own, Rachel, you would certainly not be on the road without an entourage. It would be wisest to travel as Lady Rachel of Caberton, Jason's sister. Since your kinship is pretended, I will not formalize the title.

Do not share your titles liberally. Keep them secret, as with the ring, using them only in times of need, like a hidden poniard. Lord of Caberton is a vacant office which remains my legal right to bequeath. The ring is your evidence. I fear the manor at Caberton is in greater disrepair than this castle, yet the title may serve you if circumstances force you to deal with other nobles."

"Thank you," Jason said.

"My pleasure."

"Sorry if I'm acting ungrateful," Rachel said miserably. "You're right; I am stressed."

"I understand," the Blind King replied.

"Can I be honest with you?" Jason asked.

Galloran folded his hands. "I would not have it otherwise."

"I'm not sure I'm cut out for something like this. I'm a pretty regular guy. All this stuff you've been telling me has almost scared me out of my mind. I don't think I'm what you're looking for. You need a real hero."

Galloran shook his head. "So many misconceptions surround the notion of heroism. Far too many categorize a hero as a champion on the battlefield, a commander of legions, a master of rare talent or ability. Granted, there have been heroes who fit those descriptions. But many men of great evil as well. Heed me. A hero sacrifices for the greater good. A hero is true to his or her conscience. In short, heroism means doing the right thing regardless of the consequences. Although any person could fit that description, very few do. Choose this day to be one of them."

Jason swallowed. "All right."

"I'll try," Rachel whispered.

"Now, *Lord* Jason, *Lady* Rachel, the hour of your departure is at hand."

They descended the stairs together, pausing at Jason's room

so he could collect the remainder of his belongings. He took his wallet and key chain, the cloak and the blanket roll the loremaster had provided, and the small sack of mushrooms and berries. When he grabbed the bundled remains of the bread Franny had supplied, another pang of guilt struck him. He couldn't wrap his mind around the fact that her home had been invaded, Aster had been killed, and she had been abducted, all just for talking to him! How could anyone destroy lives so unfairly? He wanted to hit somebody, but the only real target for his frustrated anger was some faceless emperor in a distant castle.

It was hard to resist blaming himself. Images of Aster and Franny bombarded Jason: recent memories, fresh and vivid. He had brought this disaster to their doorstep. As Jason followed the others down the rest of the stairs, he tried to console himself that there was no way he could have foreseen that his innocent conversation would provoke such extreme retaliation.

Dorsio awaited them at the foot of the stairwell, one hand on the hilt of his short sword, a leather satchel in the other. Dipping his head, he handed the satchel to Jason.

"Additional provisions," said Chandra the cook, approaching to hand Rachel a traveling cloak and a blanket roll of her own. "Safe journey."

Brin the Gamester jogged into view, halting before the king to report. "Sire, a figure on horseback, accompanied by another on foot, has been spied on the access road approaching the gates."

"Unsurprising," the king grunted. "We must make haste. Delay them." Brin trotted away. With the king's hand on his shoulder Dorsio led Jason and Rachel out of the audience hall to a place at the rear of the castle where the wall had tumbled inward in a fan of corroded stone blocks.

"Go swiftly," the king urged. "We will strive to divert any who pursue you. Follow the path. It intersects the road you took out of the hills, Jason, just east of the crossroads. When you reach the road, go west to the crossroads, then south to the sea cave."

"We will," Jason said. "Thank you for everything, Your Majesty."

"Fare thee well, Lord Jason of Caberton. Safe journey, Lady Rachel. Take care of each other. I will do all I can to help from here. May we meet again under friendlier circumstances."

Dorsio clapped Jason on the shoulder and gave an approving nod. He took one of Rachel's hands and gave a squeeze.

"Thank you," Rachel said.

"Hurry," the Blind King urged. "Try not to let others see you on the road. Use your eyes and ears. Keep hidden whenever possible."

Jason tromped out of the gap in the wall with Rachel at his side. He didn't look back. He doubted anyone was watching their departure. And besides, it would do little good to wave to a blind man.

CHAPTER 7

JUGARD

The day was cooler than the previous one. White clouds crowded the sky, billowy masses suspended high above the countryside, casting huge shadows over the landscape. The dirt path, much narrower than the one leading up to the castle gate, wound down through an orchard, then along a fence across pasturelands.

Jason moved at a good pace, impelled by the likelihood that the rider spotted from the castle was after him. Rachel remained beside him, matching his pace, stealing occasional glances back at the ruined castle.

"Do you think any of this is really happening?" she asked.

"It's happening," Jason replied.

Rachel remained quiet for a moment. "Of course you think it's happening," she finally said. "You're just a character in my dream."

"You wish."

"I didn't mean my love interest," she replied defensively. "You'd have better hair. You're the character I dreamed up because the rest of the dream was making me homesick."

"Maybe you're the character I dreamed up to scare myself awake."

"That's not very nice!"

"You made fun of my hair. I like it this way. Short and simple."

"I don't mind short. Mine is short."

"Then what's wrong with mine?" Jason challenged.

"Maybe we should talk about something else."

"Like the guy on a horse coming to kill us?"

"It needs more style," she muttered.

"The horse?"

"Your hair."

"I forgot to bring my gel when I got eaten by a hippo."

"I'm sorry. Your hair is fine. I was trying to be funny."

"I'll give you points for trying." Jason sighed. "This isn't a dream."

"I know," Rachel said heavily. "I just wish it was."

When the path joined the lane, Jason scanned up and down the length of the road. To the east he could see the rooftops and chimney pots of a small town. In the distance to the west he saw the obelisk marking the crossroads. The lane appeared empty.

Jason and Rachel hurried to the obelisk and turned south. He considered how easily a man on horseback could overtake them. Supposedly their pursuer was accompanied by someone on foot. That might slow him. But what if the horseman rode ahead? Taking his poniard from his pocket, Jason fingered the blossom on the handle that could eject the blade. Hopefully, the Blind King would somehow stall their pursuers.

"You got the cool knife and the ring," Rachel grumbled.

"So what? You got a grenade."

"I can only use mine once. And that's if I don't blow myself up first. I can tell women aren't very respected around here."

"I'm not sure anyone gets much respect around here," Jason replied. "So the only stuff you had when you crossed over to this world was your canteen and your camera?"

"Yeah," Rachel said.

"Digital?"

"No, film. We develop our own photographs."

"I should have guessed."

"My parents have a lot of land," Rachel said. "They have some extra houses and workspaces that they lend out to artists and writers and photographers."

"Wow, and I thought I grew up granola in Colorado. Do you guys have campfires and sing together?"

"It isn't that weird," Rachel said. "I do lots of normal stuff too."

"Like attend school at home? Let me guess, were you most likely to succeed? Best dressed? Class clown? All of the above?"

"Very funny."

"I bet you're in a lot of the yearbook pictures."

She shook her head. "I miss out on having an official yearbook. But we take lots of photos."

"Don't you miss having friends?"

"I have friends!"

"Besides your stuffed animals."

Rachel smacked his shoulder. "I have plenty of friends. Public school isn't the only way to meet people. I'm part of a group of homeschooled kids who do stuff together. A few are oddballs, but most of them are cool and interesting. Plus all the visiting artists, and the kids on the track team, and my cousins."

"That doesn't sound too bad," Jason admitted. "If I could still play baseball and do school at home, I might be sold. Especially if it involved lots of fancy vacations disguised as learning." He tried to imagine how that would work. His family had only taken a few vacations together, none very impressive. His brother and sister were quite a bit older, and his mom and dad had always done their fancy trips without kids. His parents had never really shown as much interest in him as they had in his older siblings. He couldn't imagine them taking the time to homeschool him.

Jason glanced back. "I keep expecting to see enemies attacking from behind."

"I know," Rachel said. "Kind of hard on the nerves. Do you get the feeling our lives might never be normal again?"

Jason pressed his lips together. She had just voiced the thought that had been nagging him ever since the Blind King explained their mission. "Yeah."

They picked up the pace, alternating between jogging and walking. Jason was mildly surprised to find that Rachel could match any pace he set. Apparently she hadn't lied about running track.

They ate lunch and dinner walking, feeding on meat and cheese sandwiches created from provisions in the satchel. While scrabbling through the satchel for his dinner, Jason noticed a drawstring bag. Hefting it, he was surprised to find that the small bag felt fairly heavy. Inside he found little pellets of copper and bronze.

"What are these for?" Jason asked. "Slingshot ammunition?"

"Probably money," Rachel suggested.

"Could we be that lucky?" Jason asked.

"The Blind King wants us to succeed."

"Somebody should tell these guys about coins," Jason muttered, putting the little bag away. "It doesn't seem very convenient to have your cash rolling around."

As time wore on, they walked more than they jogged. Jason's

feet felt sore, but Rachel hadn't complained, so he hadn't either. They passed no sign of human life but observed plenty of rodents and birds.

As the sun grew fat and red on the horizon, a moist breeze began to blow in Jason's face. Plodding up a long incline, he debated whether he should fish out his remaining energy berries. Cresting the rise, he finally saw the sea, a blue-gray immensity stretching to the edge of sight, still at least a few miles off down a long slope.

"Low tide won't hit until noon tomorrow," Jason said. "Looks like we'll have more cover up here than we will down there."

"The woods really thin out on the far side of this ridge," Rachel agreed. She crouched and studied the hard-packed dirt lane. "I can see traces of our boots. We should walk down the path a ways, maybe leave it a few times, then double back cross-country. In case they're tracking us."

"You're right," Jason admitted, thinking of Aster's fate. "We should probably take precautions."

Jason followed Rachel farther along the path, stomping his feet. She glanced back at him. "Don't step harder than you were earlier. It might alert them that we're making a false trail."

"Have you done this before?"

"Whenever I escaped from juvie."

Jason chuckled. "Right. You know, we'll have to trade off keeping watch tonight."

She nodded. "Weird that we haven't seen anybody. Nobody using the road, no houses."

"Yeah, it's isolated. I'm going to miss my bed at the castle."

After leaving the path several times, Rachel gingerly followed an improvised route that took them back up the slope into the woods. She selected a spot a good distance from the road, with plenty of trees and bushes to screen their presence. Despite the cover, the location still afforded a view of the lane.

Following a hasty meal, Jason offered to take the first watch. Bundling himself in cloak and blanket, cushioned by flattened weeds, he rested his back against a tree and fought to stay awake. As the light of day faded, the rhythm of Rachel's breathing, the chirping of the insects, and the sensory deprivation of the darkness overcame his fears, and Jason sagged into a deep slumber.

Jason jerked awake. He felt damp. Predawn mist shrouded the landscape, intensifying the morning chill. As he uncurled and stood, his shins felt sore, probably from all the jogging done in boots the day before. The noise of his motion disturbed Rachel. Wiping her bleary eyes, she sat up.

"What time is it?" she asked. "What about my watch? Did you fall asleep?"

"No," Jason lied. "You looked tired. I wanted to let you rest."

"Then why do you have leaf prints and smudges of soil on your cheek?" Rachel asked. "Were you on guard with your face in a leaf pile?"

"I didn't try to fall asleep," Jason apologized. "It got dark and really boring."

"Boring is the goal," Rachel said, pulling her cloak more tightly around her shoulders. "The opposite of boring might be somebody cutting our throats."

Jason winced. Back home several of his classes had bored him. He'd spent tons of late nights trying to find something on television. Much of the time his life had felt planned for him, lacking real purpose, and his boredom had emphasized the problem. But Rachel was right. Boredom was now their friend.

Jason squinted into the mist. "I can't see the lane."

"If somebody is tracking us, the fog should work in our favor," Rachel pointed out.

"I wonder when the mist showed up?" Jason mused.

"Hard to say," Rachel said wryly. "We miss that kind of information when we're both sleeping."

"Don't be that way. At least it worked out. Now we'll be well rested when we throw ourselves off a cliff into the ocean." He stretched his arms wide and groaned. "Want some breakfast? We should probably get going while we have extra cover from the mist."

"Okay. Maybe just a bite before we start."

Jason sorted through their food, selecting some dried meat and tough bread. When he found that the remnants of the mushrooms the loremaster had given him were beginning to smell funny and had fuzzy patches of mold, he threw them out, wondering whether he would regret the loss once their rations ran out.

Munching on bread and meat, Jason and Rachel tramped through dewy undergrowth back to the road, their cloaks wrapped tightly about them. Jason shivered. The damp cold seemed to seep through all layers of clothing.

"Let's check for hoofprints," Rachel suggested.

In the growing light, breathing foggy air, Jason searched inexpertly for fresh signs of a horse. "I don't see anything," he finally announced.

"Then let's be extra ready for our enemies to approach from behind," Rachel replied.

Briskly they followed the lane toward the ocean. After cresting the rise from the day before, the lane wound down to the coast, snaking back and forth to offset the steeper portions of the slope. The farther they descended along the path, the denser the fog became. Jason threw a stone as far as he could and watched it disappear into grayness long before it thudded against the ground, rustling the brush. Before long he could see only a few paces ahead. At any moment he expected a fearsome horseman to lope out of the murk.

As they approached the cliffs, the view of the ocean returned. Low sunlight spread over the water from off to the left, texturing the surface in striking relief by shadowing the troughs between swells.

"Pretty," Rachel commented. "But I miss the cover of the fog."

They reached the point where the road elbowed left, paralleling the cliffs as far as Jason could see. As Galloran had instructed, they abandoned the road, continuing south. They soon reached a gentle trickle of a stream.

The stream flowed toward the cliffs, slurping away into a narrow crack not ten paces from the edge. Unhealthy tufts of scraggly weeds flanked the feeble rivulet.

Jason cautiously approached the rocky brink of the cliff. The view was spectacular. He stood more than seventy feet above the churning surf, at the center of a curving amphitheater of cliffs bordering a wide inlet. At either hand sheer faces of dark stone towered above surging bursts of foamy spray. No reef or shallows slowed the swells as they rose up and flung themselves in frothy explosions against alien formations of rock.

Rachel came up beside him, her stance casual, a hand on one hip. Then she stepped even closer to the edge, leaning forward to gaze straight down. Her proximity to the brink gave Jason chills, but he kept quiet.

"Looks like suicide," Rachel said, drawing back from the edge.

"Maybe it will look better at low tide," Jason hoped.

"There will probably just be more rocks poking up," Rachel said. "You a good swimmer?"

"I'm fine," Jason said. "I'm no Olympian. How about you?"

"I'm pretty good. I've done a fair amount of snorkeling and scuba diving. But no serious cliff diving. This is high."

Turning, Jason stared back at the slope they had descended, realizing that they commanded a clear view of the lane for miles. At least no manglers or other sinister creatures intent on hacking them into confetti should be able to sneak up on them.

"I guess we wait here for midday," Jason said, sitting down and settling back against a little wind-warped tree. Hands in his lap, he gazed at the long slope and its serpentine lane.

"Let me guess; you'll take the first watch? Then we'll wake up at midnight?"

"I'm not sleepy," Jason protested.

"Neither am I," Rachel said, sitting down cross-legged. "So, how do you think we'll get back up?"

"There must be a way. Maybe the person in the cave knows how."

"Are we really going to do this? Jump off a cliff and swim into a sea cave? We'll probably die."

"What else are we going to do?" Jason asked. "If there were any other option I might take it. But it seems clear that if we abandon this quest for the Word, we're doomed. I'd rather risk my life than lose it for sure."

"You believe everything the Blind King told you?" Rachel asked.

"Yeah, I think so. It matched what I read in the book, and what I heard from the loremaster."

"You believe him enough to risk our lives?"

Jason paused. "No. I believe him enough to risk my life. I don't see why both of us should jump."

Rachel scratched her arm. "Why do you get to jump? Because you're the boy?"

"It isn't a prize; it's a punishment."

"It's something important that needs to be done."

"Do you just love to argue? If somebody wanted to jump off a cliff instead of me, I'd be relieved."

"I do want to jump instead of you."

Jason rolled his eyes. "I'm trying to be nice. And fair. I was the one who read the book. This quest is my fault. Besides, I'm bigger than you, which will give me a better chance of surviving the rough surf."

The explanation silenced Rachel for a moment. She picked at the small weeds in front of her. "It's really nice of you to offer," she finally said. "I can tell you don't love heights."

"I don't like edges," Jason corrected. "I'm fine if you give me a guardrail or put me in a plane or send me on a roller coaster. Let's not worry about this for now." He closed his eyes.

"What exactly is a mangler?" Rachel wondered aloud.

He opened his eyes. "We never really had that explained, did we? I guess something nasty that chops people into sushi. I think we'll know it when we see it."

She nodded. "Before we do this, maybe you should tell me the syllable you learned. You know, in case I have to continue alone."

"Are you trying to jinx us? Thanks for the confidence!"

"There's nothing wrong with being prepared for worst-case scenarios."

"You should sell insurance."

She huffed, standing up. "Fine."

"Wow, don't be so touchy."

"You don't have to make fun of everything."

"Maybe we should just enjoy the music of the waves," Jason placated.

She sat back down.

Jason made himself as comfortable as possible against the contorted tree. "The first syllable is 'a.' Just in case."

"Was that so hard?"

Jason grinned, deciding to quit while he was kind of ahead. Rachel certainly wasn't a pushover. She had strong opinions, and little fear of sharing them. A good argument could help pass the time, but Jason found himself wondering whether traveling with Rachel would become annoying. If he were going to meet up with somebody from his world, why couldn't it have been Matt or Tim? They could back him up in a fight, and would be more fun to hang out with. Or if it had to be a girl, why not somebody less obnoxious, like April Knudsen?

The rhythmic crashing of the waves below, like a mighty wind rising and falling with unnatural regularity, lulled him into deep relaxation. Breathing the salt-tinged air, he closed his eyes again.

And woke with a start, Rachel jostling his shoulder. Shadows were small. The sun was high. It was nearly midday. The air was still not warm, though the sun shone brightly.

"Maybe you have narcolepsy," Rachel suggested as he staggered to his feet.

Jason wiped his eyes. "I just love naps."

"Well, warn me before you operate heavy machinery."

Scanning the slope, Jason detected no sign of pursuit. Feeling abashed for having dozed off again, he unlaced his boots and yanked them off.

"What are you doing?" Rachel asked.

"I'm the jumper." Jason proceeded to disrobe until he wore only his boxers—blue with narrow yellow stripes. He reflected that his boxers and boots were now the only clothes in his possession that he had brought from home.

Rachel had turned away. "Not very shy, are you?"

"I'm wearing boxers. They look like swim trunks."

She turned and looked at him. "I can do this."

"You can jump off the next cliff. Don't be stubborn."

"You're the stubborn one," she shot back.

Jason quietly conceded that she had a point. His parents always accused him of being obstinate. At home he often got his way simply by outlasting everyone else.

"We can flip a coin," Rachel said.

"Our coins are pellets."

"No, I have one from our world." She started searching her pockets. "Winner picks who jumps."

"Fine." Shivering, Jason stepped carefully to the edge of the cliff. The sea breeze feathered his cheeks, ruffled his hair. Goose pimples rose all over his body. He folded his arms, rubbing his palms against his sides for warmth.

Far below, the water level had receded. Two rocks shaped like arrowheads stood out clearly now, pointing at each other. To land right between them, he would have to jump outward a good distance.

"Found it," Rachel said behind him. "Heads or tails?"

"Heads." He looked back as she flipped the quarter and caught it.

"Tails," she proclaimed, holding it up with a triumphant grin.

"I lose," Jason said, turning away from her.

"No, wait!"

Swinging his arms forward, he sprang out into empty space, viscera rising within him as his body plummeted downward in a wild acceleration through chill, salty air. The wind of his fall swept over him as the greenish, foamy water came up fast. With his elbow tucked against his chest, he held his nose, straightened his body, and tore through the surface of the water between the two giant arrowheads, his feet barely touching the rocky bottom at the low point of his submergence.

The gentle sting of seawater bothered his vision. He was in a long, narrow pit in the coastal floor, well beneath the churning surface. A couple of nearby sea fans swayed with the current. Vivid anemones clung to the rocks. He swam up out of the trench, angling inward toward the base of the cliff. The closer he got to the surface, the more turbulent the currents became.

His head broke the surface, and he gasped for breath. A half-submerged cave yawned directly before him. A curling swell heaved him in that direction, scraping his shoulder against a rough wall of stone. He stroked madly, bumping a knee against an unyielding face of unseen rock.

The ocean drew him away from the mouth of the cave; then the frothy mass of a breaker heaved him forward out of control. He tucked his head, turning helpless somersaults inside the tumbling rush of water, grimly anticipating the moment his skull would burst against a jagged corner of stone.

When the wave was spent, Jason found himself at the mouth of the cave. He clutched a jutting knob of rock to resist being drawn away as the water withdrew. A fresh influx of roiling spume pushed him beyond the mouth into the cave itself. He could not touch bottom, so he swam fiercely, fading back almost to the mouth before a new breaker shoved him in even deeper.

The cave narrowed. The enclosed space magnified the sounds of the surging sea. He scrabbled for handholds to resist the tide and haul himself farther inward. After he traversed a section so narrow he could almost reach from wall to wall, the cave widened into a spacious grotto. Not much light filtered in from the entrance. In the dimness Jason perceived a still, wiry man seated upon a ledge against the far wall, a good ten feet above the water level.

Finding he could now stand, Jason waded over to the far wall, cautious not to slice his bare soles on the rocky ground. Waist-deep water became ankle-deep. Behind him the ocean roared.

Jason stepped out of the water, too close to the ledge to see the man on top. Regular handholds had been chiseled into the rock. "Hello," Jason called.

No answer. Perhaps the man was asleep. Or dead.

Jason climbed the handholds leading up the sheer face below the ledge. Scents of seawater and stone mingled in his nostrils.

His head cleared the top. The ledge was fairly broad, spanning the entire rear wall of the grotto. The man sat nearby, back to the wall, legs crossed at the ankles, staring at Jason. Tangled gray hair covered his head and face, dangling to his narrow waist. He held a rubbery length of seaweed in his hands.

Jason boosted himself onto the ledge, returning the silent stare.

The man squeezed the seaweed, using both hands to twist it in opposite directions. The action triggered a bioluminescent reaction, bathing the ledge in pale green light.

"Nice cave," Jason said.

The man grunted.

Jason decided to have a staring contest. His eyes began to burn. The man showed no sign of strain. Jason lost.

The man still did not blink. The grave gaze was disconcerting. "I need help finding a word," Jason said.

The man nodded fractionally.

"My name is Jason."

"I am Jugard."

"So you can speak."

The man grunted.

"I was sent by Galloran."

Jugard's bushy eyebrows twitched upward.

"He said you helped him long ago."

A slight nod.

"Will you help me learn the Word to unmake Maldor?"

The man stared. Jason lost the contest a second time.

"You heard me, right?"

The stare persisted. Jugard had obviously heard.

Jason scooted around so his back was against the wall as well. He had asked his question. He would look like a jerk if he kept pushing. Apparently the other man needed time to think about his response. Or perhaps he was crazy. Either way, waiting seemed preferable to coercion. Jason shivered, finally recognizing how cold he was.

Minutes passed. Jason stared at his hands, listened to the echoes of surging waves. He quietly wondered if, somewhere high above, Rachel was worried.

Jason glanced sideways at Jugard. The man had set down his seaweed and was busy untangling his matted beard. Muscles danced in his thin, sinuous arms. Jason returned to contemplating his hands. More time passed. He took the silence as a contest. This time he would not blink. Closing his eyes, he began reviewing the bones of the leg and foot. He had a big anatomy test Friday. No, he had already missed it.

"You are wise for one so young," Jugard said at last. "Most men cannot abide silence. Some fly into a rage. Some become clowns. Some confess all they know. Silence reveals much. I will assist you, Jason, friend of Galloran."

"How can you help me?"

"What do you know?"

"The first syllable. And I know not to say the Word unless I'm with Maldor."

Jugard stopped picking at his beard and started rubbing his ankles. He did not look at Jason. "You are just beginning your search. The Word has six syllables. The fourth is 'en.' I do not know the location of the other syllables, but I know of a man in Trensicourt who might be able to help. If he remains alive, Nicholas should be able to advise you. He once worked closely with Galloran, creating engines of war."

"Okay, 'en.' And Nicholas. Is that all you know?"

"I have dwelled in this cave longer than I can reckon. Most of what I know derives from others who have journeyed here. You are the first in some time. I hope my information remains valid."

Jason nodded. He already had a third of the Word! And he had a new lead to follow. He had worried that the sea cave might represent a dead end. He visualized the portion of the Word he knew.

A ____ ____ EN ____ ____

Jason repeated the name of the contact in Trensicourt.

"That is right," Jugard confirmed.

"Do you know what a Beyonder is?" Jason asked.

"Of course."

"I'm a Beyonder."

The bushy eyebrows twitched again.

"Do you know how I can get home?"

Jugard stared. "I do not. Keep asking your question. There are some who might have answers."

Jason looked around the chamber of stone. He turned to Jugard with a puzzled expression.

"You wish to know how to get back atop the cliffs."

Jason nodded.

"Once, the task was not difficult. Beyond a neighboring chamber, long ago, a colleague of Nicholas helped me construct a means for ascending to a point near the cliff tops. Sometime later, not long after Galloran visited me, the neighboring chamber became inhabited by a titan crab. Since that day five men and one woman have visited me. Two tried to swim out. I know they failed because their corpses washed back into my chamber. The other four attempted to dodge past the crab. I beheld their demise."

"Did any try to kill the crab?"

"Three made an effort to slay the crab once it became clear they would not outrun her. None came close."

Jason silently lamented not bringing the explosive stone. He had nothing to fight with. "What do you suggest?"

Jugard shrugged. "To better understand, you should view Macroid."

"Is that the crab?"

"The name I gave her."

"You can tell it's a she?"

"I know crabs."

They climbed down off the shelf. Jugard, clutching the luminous length of seaweed, led Jason to a long vertical crack in the wall on one side of the chamber. It was just wide enough for a man to walk through without turning sideways. "Why doesn't the crab come through into here?"

Jugard faced Jason, the green seaweed casting strange shadows and highlights across his furry countenance. "She is much too big."

Jason's mouth felt dry.

Jugard handed him the seaweed. "Peer cautiously through the crack before you enter the room. The crab is most likely in the water, but make certain. If she is out of sight, pass through the crack and go two steps beyond. You will notice a small gap on the far side of the room. Beyond that gap lies my ascender. Do not attempt to cross. Macroid will emerge from the water. Be ready. Her speed will astonish you. Retreat when she charges. You should witness her capabilities before you choose your course."

Jason slunk into the crack, shoulders brushing the walls of the narrow way as he crept forward. The cleft ran about six paces before ending abruptly.

Hanging back from the opening, Jason held the seaweed forward, dispelling the darkness in the room beyond. It looked empty. Slowly he eased his head forward, imagining a huge crab waiting at one side of the opening, an enormous claw poised to snap shut on his head as soon as he stuck it out. He peeked quickly and immediately withdrew. Nothing was in sight.

Jason stepped into the chamber. It was maybe twenty yards across. Like the previous chamber, a large portion was submerged in water. On the far side Jason saw the gap Jugard had described. He realized why Jugard had warned him not to make a break for it. With no giant crab in sight it appeared temptingly close. The intervening floor was smooth and largely free of obstacles. It was tempting even with the warning. Maybe the crab was asleep.

At his second step into the chamber the crab erupted out of the salty pool in a single tremendous leap. A geyser of brackish water splashed against the ceiling, spraying the entire length and breadth of the room. In his shock Jason dropped the seaweed, taking an involuntary step backward as he wiped brine from his face.

He gaped in awe at the titan crab. The massive creature was the size of a car, not including a huge pair of claws bigger than public mailboxes. The shiny black armor of its carapace gleamed wetly, reflecting the green luminance of the seaweed. The creature stood at the edge of the water, great claws upraised, snipping open and closed with a harsh shearing sound.

Without warning the crab scuttled toward Jason in a horrifying burst of speed. He lunged back into the crack as the nimble creature sprang, hurtling through the air, black claws flashing. Jason fled through the cleft back to Jugard, pursued by the grating scrape of shell against stone and the shearing snip of eager claws.

Jugard caught hold of Jason's shoulders, steadying him as he tried to stop hyperventilating. "Now you comprehend your peril," Jugard said. "Come."

Without the seaweed the chamber was once again lit only by daylight filtering in from outside. Jason followed Jugard back up to the ledge, where the wiry man squeezed a fresh length of seaweed. This one had a more bluish tint.

"Is there a way to kill the crab?"

"Probably not even with an army. Those claws are razor keen. I watched an excellent sword shatter against the shell."

"I can't imagine surviving a swim out of here."

"You would have to swim a great distance. Those who have tried did not get far."

Jason considered the turbulent coastal waters. He had only survived because the waves had pushed him into the cave. Swimming against them would be suicide. Could he at least shout the syllable up to Rachel? He doubted she could hear him over the roar of the ocean. It might be worth a try. Then she could continue the quest on her own. It wouldn't be fair to leave her stranded and exposed with the horseman after her.

"How do you survive in here?" Jason wondered.

"The sea provides. Fish, shellfish, urchins, kelp. They can all be eaten uncooked. And a trickle of fresh water runs into that basin over there." Jason walked over to where Jugard indicated.

At one end of the shelf, water tinkled into a natural basin, slowly overflowing off the shelf into the sea. The fresh trickle had to be a byproduct of the little stream atop the cliff. Unfortunately, the water emerged from a split in the rock the width of his finger—there would be no climbing up that way.

"What should I do?"

"I have no right to say. You are welcome to remain here as long as you choose. The variety is limited, but food and water exist in abundance."

"None of the others stayed."

Jugard shrugged his bony shoulders. "I presented them with similar cautions. They were heroes on important quests. They believed that where others had failed, they would succeed."

Jason returned to the wiry, grizzled man and sat beside him, back against the wall. He rubbed his cheeks, looking for stubble. He hardly had any facial hair. He wondered how long it would take for him and Jugard to look alike.

CHAPTER 8

MACROID

"Someone else is approaching," Jugard said, disturbing Jason's reverie. "Were you with anyone?"

"Yeah," Jason said, standing up. He could see a figure swimming out of the narrow passage into the grotto. "Rachel! Do you need help?"

"I'm okay," she gasped. "Something's coming."

"What?"

"I'm not sure. A mangler, maybe." She reached the shallows and waded hurriedly toward the ledge, her homespun shirt clinging wetly.

"A mangler couldn't follow you in here," Jugard said. "It would sink like a stone."

Coughing, Rachel climbed the handholds to the ledge. She had removed her vest and shoes. Her shirt and pants dripped copiously.

"I'm Rachel," she told Jugard.

"Jugard," the shaggy man responded.

"What happened?" Jason asked.

"I freaked out," she apologized, trying to wring out her shirt.

"Not too long after you jumped, something came tearing down the slope. It ignored the road, racing straight at me. It wasn't a horseman. It kept low enough that all I could really see was the motion."

"What did you do?" Jason asked.

"I thought about using the orantium. But I didn't really know what was coming. I knew it was fast and could keep low. I started to worry I might make a bad throw and miss it. Once it got past the bend in the lane and kept heading straight for me, I panicked."

"Did you bring the orantium?" Jason asked hopefully.

Rachel shook her head. "I was worried it might detonate when I hit the water. So I stashed it, took off my vest, and jumped. I didn't have time to think it through."

"Rough swim?" Jason asked.

She laughed shakily. "It almost killed me." She slapped his chest with the back of her hand. "By the way, I didn't appreciate you cheating after the coin toss. We need to be able to trust each other."

"I had your best interest in mind."

"Whatever followed you is still coming," Jugard announced.

"How do you know?" Jason asked.

"I know the natural sounds of this place," Jugard assured him. "I can hear something snorting and gasping, something bestial."

"I don't see anything yet," Jason said.

"You will," Jugard replied.

Gurgling growls and churning splashes heralded the creature's arrival to the grotto. Jason, Rachel, and Jugard clustered at the front of the ledge to observe as the animal entered the cavern, struggling toward the shallows from the deeper water across the chamber. The beast seemed inept at swimming, its sizable head bobbing in and out of sight. Jugard twisted a short piece of seaweed and tossed it into the water to better illuminate the approaching creature.

"Boarhound," Jugard murmured, astonished.

Rachel backed away from the edge as the oversized bulldog reached the shallows and charged, baying wildly, to the base of the ledge, ten feet below Jason and Jugard. The animal began hopping ferociously, coming within a foot or two of the ledge despite its bulky body and stubby legs. Foam lathered its wide jaws.

"Boarhounds are not typically fond of water," Jugard said. "Do you know this animal?"

"Puggles," Jason said. "I think I saw this boarhound at a woman's house a couple of days ago. I heard she was attacked and captured yesterday."

The dog continued bounding at them tenaciously despite repeated failure. Jugard stared intently. "This animal has been conscripted."

Jason turned to Jugard. "What does that mean?"

Jugard pinched some of his whiskers and started twirling them. "Conscriptors have been known to turn animals to their own uses."

"What are conscriptors?" Rachel asked.

Jugard gave her a bemused look. "You must be a Beyonder as well. Conscriptors recruit for Maldor. They are among his most elite soldiers, trained to raise armies from conquered towns or kingdoms. Some specialize in recruiting animals. This dog knew your scent. A conscriptor has transformed it into an assassin, warping it until its only purpose became to track you down and slay you."

"I jumped off a cliff to escape a dog?" Rachel asked bitterly.

"Take another look at the dog," Jugard invited. "If it had your scent, you made the right choice."

"We have a conscriptor trailing us?" Jason asked.

Jugard shrugged his bony shoulders. "Possibly not. That may be why he sent the animal. Out in the open this crazed boarhound could have finished both of you."

Jason stared down at the snarling canine, impressed by the rippling muscles under the short-haired pelt. The black gaping mouth held vicious teeth.

"What do we do now?" Rachel asked.

For the first time Jugard smiled. "The Hand of Providence accompanies you. This potential threat may represent your salvation."

"How?" Jason asked.

"Bait."

"What do you mean?" Rachel asked.

"Macroid is attracted to fresh blood like nothing else. Twice I have cut myself accidentally. Both times the crab rushed to the cleft, reaching madly, beating and snipping at the very stone of the cave. The futility of her efforts did not daunt her. She did not desist for hours after the wound was dressed."

Jason shuddered.

"Noting the thirst for blood, I tried cutting myself once immediately after a man dashed for the ascender. The crab hesitated, but went for the man. Had I been within her reach, however, I have no doubt the crab would have attacked me first."

"Macroid is a crab?" Rachel asked.

Jason described the colossal crab in the neighboring cavern, explaining how it currently impeded their way to the top of the cliff. Rachel turned to Jugard. "So you think if we wound the dog, and it chases us into Macroid's cavern, the crab will attack the dog, leaving us time to escape."

"That is your best chance. It will require perfect timing. No blood must be drawn until after you are in Macroid's chamber.

Otherwise she will block the cleft, and you will find yourselves trapped between crab and boarhound."

Jason ran a nervous hand through his damp hair. He looked down at the ferocious dog, saddened by the thought of the crab destroying it. "If Puggles follows too far behind, the crab will mutilate us before the dog enters the room."

Jugard rubbed his palms together. "She may mutilate you regardless. But good timing should improve your chances."

"How do we get the timing right?" Rachel wondered.

Jugard turned his back on them, hands on his hips. He grabbed a wooden spear with a sharp stone tip from against the wall. "I will wound the boarhound once you are through the cleft, then turn it loose."

"How can we restrain the dog?" Jason asked.

First propping the spear against the wall, Jugard gathered up a coiled rope of amber seaweed. He fashioned a knotted loop at one end. "Here is my leash." After examining the length, he secured the other end around a stone protuberance.

They peered over the ledge. Puggles continued to rage up at them, twisting and leaping and scraping its claws against the stone below the shelf. Jugard dangled the loop, slipped it around the dog's thick neck on the first try, and jerked it snug. The dog continued bounding at them, heedless of the rubbery noose.

"I left enough slack for the dog to get close to the cleft. You two will go to the end of the ledge, over by the cleft, and drop down. I will come up behind the dog, slash its hindquarters, and sever the restraining line. The animal should pay me no mind. As the conscriptor desired, it will be fixated on you two. Let me figure out the timing. At my signal your duty is to run as fast as you are able. Don't hesitate. Macroid may be sufficiently quick to get all of you."

Jason could feel his heart hammering.

Jugard squeezed a strand of blue-glowing seaweed and fastened it around Jason's wrist. "You remember what I told you concerning the Word."

Jason recited all Jugard had told him. Rachel listened with wide eyes.

"Very well," Jugard said. "Ready?"

"Now?" Rachel asked.

"Is the crab underwater again?" Jason asked.

Jugard nodded. "Macroid is too bulky to stay out of the water long. I would stake your life on it."

Jason managed a feeble smile.

"Take heart," Jugard said. "You have a real chance. Get into position."

Jason and Rachel walked along the length of the ledge until they reached the wall with the crack in it. Puggles moved with them along the base of the shelf until restrained by the seaweed leash. Jugard skillfully descended the ledge behind the dog, spear in one hand, stone knife in the other. The dog didn't even glance at him.

The cleft in the wall was about fifteen feet beyond the base of the ledge. Jason turned around, dangled from the shelf, then dropped to the cavern floor. The boarhound snarled in ferocious frustration, testing the elastic limits of the seaweed rope. The effort only tightened the noose, strangling the dog's growls.

Jason could not help feeling like this was happening too quickly. He wished he had more time to get used to the plan. After all, the crab was huge, and it had killed before! Rachel dangled from the ledge, and Jason placed his hands on her slender waist, helping her land lightly. The enraged boarhound retreated a few paces, then rushed forward, stretching the restraint enough to get frighteningly close as Jason and Rachel edged toward the crack. When the dog lost momentum, the seaweed recoiled, dragging the boarhound end over end like a spasmodic fish on a line.

Jason stood at the cleft, trying to prepare his mind. "Wait," Jugard called. "The boarhound is strangling."

Sure enough, the beefy dog had not regained its feet. It thrashed on its back, emitting choked snorts.

"I will sever the rope at the neck, slashing the dog with the same motion. When I spring forward, you run."

"Ladies first," Jason murmured, relieved that his voice didn't betray how tense he felt.

Face rigid with worry, Rachel entered the cleft.

Jugard discarded his spear and moved in close, stone knife poised. He jumped forward, bringing the weapon down in a savage arc. Jason did not see the blow strike. He propelled himself through the cleft in five long strides, and bolted into the chamber of the titan crab, only a pace behind Rachel. The bit of seaweed he had dropped earlier still glowed green on the ground, mingling its light with the blue luminance of his seaweed bracelet.

Water sprayed in his face. Macroid had been surging up from the water before they had even entered the chamber. Jugard must have drawn blood. As Jason sprinted forward, intent on the gap across the room, the titan crab, after the briefest pause, darted toward him, a massive blur glimpsed in his peripheral vision.

There was nothing Jason could do except run, even though the crab would be on him before he was halfway across the room. Where was the dog? What if it was too asphyxiated to get up and chase them? What if it was attacking the convenient target of Jugard?

Rachel was fast. Running full speed, fueled by desperation, Jason could barely keep pace with her. When the crab sprang, he would try to dodge, maybe buy Rachel some time.

Deep baying rang harshly behind him. The black crab skidded to a stop. Jason hazarded a glance back. The boarhound was racing into the chamber, gaining ground even as the crab pounced at the bleeding canine, slicing Puggles in half with a lethally timed snip.

Jason stumbled, taking several awkward steps forward before Rachel slowed enough to grab his arm and keep him upright. To fall was to die. The gap loomed before them, slightly wider than the previous cleft. Jason could hear the crab scuttling after them, closing fast. The scuttling stopped. The crab must be airborne! They were almost there.

A tremendous force slammed into his back, pitching Jason forward through the gap. Whether the impact came from outstretched claw or armored body he could not distinguish, but it struck him with the blunt power of a battering ram. He bounced and rolled forward out of control, bare skin colliding with stone. Beside him Rachel tumbled as well. As she lost the momentum of her fall, she scrambled onward. Shouting in pain and fear, Jason rolled deeper into the recess, ignoring the scrapes and bruises on his elbows and knees.

The shearing snip of razor claws rang desperately behind him. Looking back, he saw a black claw reaching into the gap, scissoring open and closed well out of reach. Jason panted, watching in mesmerized horror as the crab returned to the gory remains of the boarhound and began dissecting the corpse in a frenzy.

"Oh my gosh!" Rachel exclaimed, voice trembling. "We almost died. I can't believe we made it!"

"That was close," Jason grunted.

"You alive?" The hoarse shout came from across the cavern.

"We made it!" Jason cried out, still trying to fully accept that they were out of danger.

"First since Galloran! Good luck to you. Safe journey."

"Thank you!" Rachel called.

Jason crawled deeper into the cleft, emerging into a small room with no visible exit and no water. Sunlight filtered in through a tall shaft in the ceiling. He slumped onto his back and closed his eyes, hesitant to examine his injuries. Shock had dulled the pain, but even so he could feel his skin burning where it had torn, throbbing where it had bruised.

"Are you all right?" Rachel asked, crouching beside him.

"Just banged up," Jason replied. "How about you?"

"I made a luckier landing," Rachel said. "Having clothes on must have helped. These pants may not be the most stylish, but they're made of tough material."

Suppressing a groan, Jason sat up and began checking his wounds by the light on his wrist. No elbow or knee had escaped abrasions and bruises. One thigh had the largest scrape, beneath where his boxers had torn—a blotchy discolored wound streaked with thin lines of blood and sensitive to the touch. His palms were raw. Thankfully, nothing felt broken. Just sore.

"The scrape on your thigh looks nasty," Rachel commented.

"Could have been worse," Jason said, finally beginning to relax. "I could have lost a limb. Or my head."

"I've never seen anything like that crab," Rachel said. "I thought we were goners. Did you see what it did to that dog? I mean, that was a big, strong dog."

Jason winced. He didn't expect to get the image of the dog's violent death out of his head anytime soon.

"It was probably a good thing," Rachel consoled. "The conscriptor had turned it into a monster."

Jason shook his head. "Nothing deserves to die like that."

"It was disgusting."

"Thanks, by the way," Jason said, "for helping me keep my balance."

Rachel smiled. "I heard you stumble. You might not have fallen. I hope I didn't slow you down."

"I probably would have fallen," Jason admitted. "You pretty much saved my life."

"What are friends for?"

Jason stood up. "We should keep moving." He could hear the crab snipping frantically at the narrow gap again, probably drawn by his open wounds. The passageway curved, so Jason could not see Macroid from his current position. He wondered if the dog had already been devoured; then he tried to shut down his imagination.

Jason and Rachel examined the room. Off in one corner a wooden platform attached to a chain dangled perhaps a foot off the ground. An iron lever projected from the wall beside it. Jason crossed to the platform and looked up. Most of the rocky ceiling was dark, but daylight spilled in through a single tall shaft. The chain from the platform stretched up the center of the shaft, which had to be nearly as high as the cliff. Sunlight came in through an opening in the side near the top. In the lofty sunlight he saw where the barbed chain disappeared into the rocky ceiling.

"A primitive elevator?" Rachel asked, gazing up as well.

"Looks like it," Jason said. "Should we see if it still works?"

"Give me a second," Rachel said, lacing her hands behind her head and blowing out air. "I've never almost died before. Not really."

Jason noticed that her eyes looked a little misty. "Are you okay?"

"Yeah. No. I don't know. I mean, a giant man-eating crab? Seriously? What have we gotten ourselves into?"

"A big mess," Jason agreed. "At least we survived. And we already have a third of the Word."

She took a shuddering breath. "Way to find the bright side."

Jason fingered the iron lever. "Think the lever will make the elevator rise?"

"I sure hope so," Rachel said. "If we have to climb a barbed chain, I might walk back to Galloran and ask to be put on his secret farm."

"Hop on," Jason suggested. "I'll lean over and pull the lever."

"I'll throw the lever," Rachel corrected. "I should do something."

Jason almost argued, but stopped himself. "Fine. Then we'll be even."

"No. I still jump off the next cliff."

"I'm hoping we're finished with cliffs."

"You know what I mean. I'll take the next big risk."

"I really was trying to be nice."

She studied him skeptically. "I think it also had a lot to do with getting your own way. If we want to succeed, we need to be able to trust each other. I can be stubborn too. But we need to be teammates."

"You're right that I like getting my way," Jason admitted. "But sometimes stubbornness can be a good thing. Like when Coach Bennion tried to quit."

"Who? What?"

"I was in seventh grade, playing baseball with a club team. Coach Bennion was an assistant. He really helped me with my swing. Anyhow, our real coach was very strict. One day he had to go out of town, so Coach Bennion was running practice. Bennion was more laid back, and a bunch of the guys started goofing off, since Bennion wasn't much of an enforcer."

"Were you one of those guys?" Rachel asked.

"We were all guilty. Bennion tried to put his foot down, but we smelled weakness, and some of the guys talked back to him. I'd never seen Bennion mad, but his face went red, and he told us he was done; we could coach ourselves. I felt horrible. I followed him off the field, apologizing and telling him we'd do whatever he wanted to make it up to him. He told me to run a hundred laps. He wasn't being serious. He was just trying to get rid of me. He got in his car and left."

"And you ran a hundred laps?" Rachel asked.

"Most of the other players went home. A few ran part of the way. But I ran a hundred laps. I mean, I walked part of it. When my mom came to pick me up, I explained what had happened, and she let me keep going. It took until after midnight. Somehow Coach Bennion heard. And he decided not to quit."

"That's pretty cool," Rachel said.

"Being stubborn can be good!"

"Not if it makes you a bully. I'll never be able to trust you during a coin toss."

"True, I may do something terrible like risk my life instead of yours."

"You had good intentions," Rachel acknowledged. "It was even sweet. But with the kind of danger we're in, trust matters a lot."

Jason folded his arms. "Okay. I'll make you a deal. Next time instead of taking matters into my own hands, I'll argue until you give up."

"That would be better. But don't count on me always giving up."

Jason stepped onto the platform. Splintered and rotting, less than three feet square, the planks thankfully felt solid. Rachel climbed on as well, gripping the heavy chain below where the barbed wire links started as the platform gently swayed.

"Should we do this?" Jason asked.

"I'm ready," Rachel confirmed, leaning over and placing a hand on the lever.

"We don't know how this will work," Jason warned. "Might be a rough ride."

"I'll hold on tight. You do the same." She pulled the lever and quickly gripped the chain with both hands. A tumbling sound rattled inside the walls of the cavern, and the platform started rising.

The chain and platform hauled Jason and Rachel upward, accelerating alarmingly, clattering ever louder as the speed of the ascent increased. Jason squeezed the chain. Pulleys shrieked. The chain vibrated. Near the top the speed decreased. For a moment the chain slackened in his hands as inertia continued to carry them upward. After they reached the weightless apex of their climb, gravity took over, and they fell until the chain jerked tight again with bone-wrenching abruptness, nearly breaking Jason's desperate hold.

Jason and Rachel stood face to face, separated only by the chain. Her eyes were shut. The platform pendulumed calmly in a weird silence broken only by the dreamy sounds of the surf. Glancing down, Jason beheld the dizzying drop to the stone floor below.

Rachel opened her eyes. "Are we alive?"

"For now."

"That went faster than I expected."

Jason heard a clicking sound. He noticed a simple iron dial on the wall, like the hand of a clock. It had pointed upward at first, but it was turning downward as the clicking continued.

"I think we have a time limit," Jason said, jutting his chin at the dial.

A large, irregular opening in the wall of the shaft beside them overlooked the ocean. The afternoon sun shone down on the ranks of approaching swells.

"Should we pump?" Rachel asked.

Jason nodded.

Synchronizing their efforts, Jason and Rachel began to lean backward and forward, swinging the platform in the direction of the opening. The clicking continued as the dial passed the three o'clock position. Before long Jason kicked out a leg and hooked his foot against the side of the opening. Rachel hopped off the platform to the narrow shelf. Bracing herself against the side of the opening, she steadied Jason as he released the chain and stepped onto the shelf beside her.

They stood high on the cliff face. A small flock of gray gulls hung motionless, gliding into the breeze. A few worn handholds led up to the top.

When the dial reached six o'clock, another tumbling sound came from within the walls of the rocky shaft, and the platform rapidly descended. Once the platform had reached the bottom, the dial reset, pointing upward. Staring at the barbed links of the chain, Jason was glad he didn't have to descend this way. He looked up the final portion of the cliff face. "I guess we climb."

"It isn't far," Rachel encouraged. "It looks easy."

"After you."

Rachel reached for the first handhold and started up the remainder of the rocky face. After taking a few seconds to steady himself, Jason followed, the sea breeze tickling his naked back. Teeth chattering, he tried not to think about the drop behind him, or to heed the churning surf far below. By focusing on finding secure places to put his hands and feet, he was soon pulling himself over the lip of the cliff.

Standing, Jason scanned the area. The trickling stream lay at least fifty yards off to one side. Rachel was jogging toward where they had left their gear. Nobody else was in sight. His clothes lay scattered around the bush where he had stashed them. Jason ran to catch up to Rachel.

Crouching near the bush, she held up the crystal globe with the orantium inside. "Safe and sound."

"Looks like Puggles chewed on my clothes."

"He was probably excited to get a full dose of your scent. At least he left our gear alone."

Jason collected his clothes, fingering spots where they had been torn or punctured by boarhound teeth. It felt good to put on clothes and wrap up in his cloak. His boxers only retained a trace of dampness.

"Are you cold?" Jason asked.

She had bundled up in her cloak. "Not with my cloak on. My clothes are still damp, so I was feeling that wind."

Jason surveyed the area. "I don't see anybody else."

"We should take advantage of the daylight while it lasts," Rachel said. "Get away from here, find a place to camp."

"We should have asked for directions to Trensicourt," Jason said.

"We'll keep following the road," Rachel replied. "It has to lead somewhere. Eventually we'll find someone who can tell us."

They walked back to the road, and began hiking eastward along the cliffs. Gazing back, Jason felt immense relief to have the ordeal of the sea cave behind him.

"Can you believe we survived?" Jason asked after they had been walking for some time.

"I know . . . Once the boarhound showed up, everything happened so fast," Rachel responded. "Now all I can think about is how close we came to ending up just like Puggles."

Afternoon dwindled to twilight, and twilight deepened toward night. They found shelter in a recessed thicket. After a hasty meal Rachel insisted on taking the first watch.

"I won't fall asleep," Jason promised. "I had a big nap, and you didn't."

Rachel eyed him warily. "Are you sure? If we both fall asleep, we might wake up dead."

"We probably wouldn't wake up. We'd just be dead."

"No, I think you'd wake up just long enough to feel incredible pain and realize the shame of your failure."

Jason chuckled darkly. He raised his right hand. "I'll stay awake. I promise." His mind flashed back to the image of Macroid tearing apart the boarhound, and he gave his head a shake. He couldn't let himself think about what either creature would have done to him and Rachel if given the chance. "I've been scared straight," he reassured her.

"Let's decide on a punishment if either of us dozes. You know, extra motivation."

"Besides a possible death penalty?" Jason paused, then smiled. "How about whoever messes up has to smell the other person's socks?"

Rachel raised her eyebrows and cocked her head. "Not bad. I would have a much smellier punishment than you, but I'm not going to mess up. Okay, here it is—whoever naps while on watch has to smell the other person's sock *and* stick it in their mouth."

"You're disgusting!"

"The punishment needs to be brutal, or it will be worthless. Remember, our lives are at stake."

Jason sighed. "Fine. I'm not going to mess up either. If you want to eat my socks, that's your business."

"Is it official? Deal?"

"Deal."

CHAPTER 9

TARK

Three days later, in the early afternoon, Jason and Rachel reached the area where the peninsula joined the mainland. The cliffs had leveled to a beach of silvery sand that mirrored the sky when moistened by waves. An oval, narrow-mouthed bay reached inland from where the peninsula and the mainland met. Beyond the mouth of the inlet desolate beaches stretched southward to the horizon.

Ever since the sea cave, Jason had remained wide awake during his watches, and he had failed to catch Rachel napping. They had felt tense on the road, since many expanses had offered little cover. Nevertheless the days had passed calmly, with no frenzied dogs, horrible manglers, or even fellow travelers passing them on the road. Their food supply had steadily dwindled however, leaving them with only enough for another day or two.

As the road meandered toward the rear of the bay, a fishing village came into view, huddled near the water. A sizable wharf with many docks projecting into the inlet stood devoid of any vessel bigger than a rowboat. A few small crafts floated in the calm harbor, rocking as fishermen slung nets. Two men sat at the end of a worn dock, holding long fishing poles and talking.

The houses in town were boxy structures painted in fading colors. Most of them looked to have been constructed from driftwood and flotsam. On many sagging porches, crates and casks served as tables and stools. Plain canvas curtains hung in malformed windows. Seashells or wildflowers in colored bottles invariably decorated the sills. Atop one house a figurehead of a plump mermaid, paint peeling, leaned out over the yard. A lazy mood pervaded the town. Few people walked the street—those who did seemed to wander.

One structure in town stood out from the rest—a wide, round building with a shallowly sloped conical roof. It drew attention because it ponderously rotated like an overgrown carousel. The bizarre rotunda sat high on a slope, the farthest structure from the water.

Jason glanced at Rachel. "Our first town," he said quietly.

"It's almost weird to see people."

"Nobody stares," Jason said, "but everybody glances."

"They seem wary," Rachel said. "Should we check out the spinning building?" Jason nodded.

Through streets powdered with orange dust they walked up to the odd edifice. A freestanding sign posted out front dubbed the building THE TAVERN-GO-ROUND. Up close the walls whirled by fast enough that Jason wondered how anyone came or went. Since laying his eyes on the peculiar structure, he had not yet noticed it stop. A platform with a few steps led up to the moving wall. The door came by. A square-faced man leaning out called, "You want in?"

"Yes!" Jason shouted, mounting the platform.

The man and the door spun out of sight. When he came around again, wind ruffling his hair, the man held a meaty arm outstretched. Jason caught hold, and the man swung him through the portal.

"The lady also, I expect?" the man asked.

"Yes, please."

Inside, Jason found a single large common room, with a circular bar curved around the center. Tables and chairs were fixed to the floor. Rafters strewn with glowing kelp added a turquoise radiance to the sunlight flashing through the moving windows.

Only a few patrons sat at tables, a few more at the bar. Two of the men seated at tables were dressed as soldiers. A pair of barmaids navigated the room with trays, leaning expertly to keep balanced. Here by the door the outward pull was difficult to resist.

Rachel came through the door, supported by the square-faced man. "Look at this place," she murmured.

"I'm surprised there isn't more puke on the floor," Jason mumbled back. He strode to the bar, noticing how the pull lessened the closer he came to the center of the room. Rachel joined him at the bar, where the sensation was minimal.

"What can I do for you? I'm Kerny." The bartender, a lanky man with a huge overbite and hair visible in his ears, introduced himself.

"Why is this place spinning?" Jason asked.

Kerny blinked. "An underground river turns a wheel far below us."

"Does it ever stop?" Rachel asked.

"Only if the river does. The speed varies with the season. We're going round pretty good right now. Takes some folks a little time to get accustomed, like earning your sea legs. The Tavern-Go-Round put us on the map. Back when maps were legal."

Kerny turned to a man squatting on a nearby stool. The man mumbled something, pulled a copper pellet from his pocket, and handed it to Kerny. Jason began rummaging through his satchel.

"What food do you serve?" Jason asked, after Kerny had placed a bowl of stew before the man.

"All kinds of seafood. Best we serve is puckerlies. We keep them alive in a tank. You ever had puckerlies?"

"No," Jason said.

"Nothing beats a platter of puckerlies served live."

"How much?"

"Three and a half drooma. But worth it."

"Did that guy just pay a drooma for that stew?" Rachel verified.

"Yeah. It's really hearty."

Jason and Rachel glanced at each other indecisively. At least Jason now knew that the copper balls were each a drooma. The bronze ones would hopefully be worth more.

"Can't we get parasites from raw seafood?" Rachel asked the bartender.

"Not every puckerly is fit to serve," Kerny said. "We're selective. We don't get complaints."

"Haven't you had raw fish?" Jason asked Rachel. "You seem like the type who would eat sushi."

She narrowed her eyes. "Of course I've had sushi. How it's prepared matters a lot."

"How's this," Kerny offered, clapping his hands down on the bar. "I'll let you each sample a puckerly. If you like them, order the platter. Agreed?"

"Sure." Jason said.

Kerny returned quickly. In each hand he held a black thimble-shaped shell roughly the size of a plum. Jason accepted one and peered at the squirming, multicolored tissue inside. Rachel was right that raw seafood could be dangerous. He remembered his biology teacher expounding on the perils of consuming raw fish. Jason glanced at Rachel. "Ladies first."

She gave him a snotty grin. "You're such a gentleman when it's convenient. I vote you be the guinea pig."

Jason was acutely aware that Kerny was waiting and listening. Now was not the time to argue. Mutely dreading the unseen parasites about to turn his body into their vacation resort, Jason raised the shell to his lips.

"Squirt a little pulpa oil in there to loosen it up," Kerny interrupted. "Otherwise you'll have to suck like a tube-billed mud strainer." The bartender held out a glass vial with a tiny mouth and inky blue liquid inside.

Jason tipped the vial above the puckerly, wrinkling his nose as the colorful flesh writhed at the contact from the dark drops. Tossing his head back, he dumped the contents of the shell into his mouth, disturbed that it kept squirming.

The texture was like raw egg yolk, the flavor slightly salty, richer than any seafood he had ever tasted. He chewed briefly, then swallowed, the slimy mass coating his throat on the way down.

"What do you think?" Kerny asked.

"Really good," Jason said, surprised.

"Honestly?" Rachel asked.

"Try it," Jason challenged.

Rachel dripped some oil into her shell, then downed the contents. Her expression brightened. "We'll take a platter."

Just then a man jostled into Jason from behind. Turning, he saw a short, stocky fellow who had been seated at a table near the door. The man had thick black hair and dense stubble on his face. The sleeves of his shirt were rolled back over hairy forearms bulging with muscle.

"I'll have the chowder," he growled in a deep voice.

"Not until you bring in some money or wash some dishes," Kerny responded, overly articulating his words. The bartender glanced apologetically at Jason.

"I'm not good enough to wash dishes," the man blubbered in

despair. "I'm not good enough for chowder. Sorry to bother." He wheeled around and plopped down at a nearby table, laying his face on folded arms.

"What's his problem?" Rachel asked softly.

Kerny shook his head. "He's depressed and dizzy. Nobody should sit near the outer wall when we're spinning this briskly. I extended him some credit, but there are limits to what a person can do. I pity him for his mishap, but I can't let him bankrupt me."

"What mishap?" Jason wondered.

"Where have you been? He's the sole survivor of the Giddy Nine. Poor sap."

Jason whirled. So somebody did jump from the raft! His rescue attempt had not been a total failure. He felt a rush of relief knowing he'd saved at least one person's life.

"Will you take your food at the bar or at a table?" Kerny asked.

Jason turned back. "At a table. And I'll buy that man some chowder."

"Suit yourself. What will you and the young lady drink?"

"Water," Jason said.

The bartender shrugged and moved away.

"Notice he didn't ask me what I wanted," Rachel whispered.

"Now is not the time to discuss women's rights," Jason whispered back. "Did you want chowder too?"

"Water is fine. But I wanted to be asked."

Jason sat down beside the man he had rescued. Rachel sat across from them. "I'm Jason," he said. "This is Rachel."

"Tark," the man replied in his gravelly voice, not looking up.

"I ordered you some chowder."

Tark raised his head, smiling. He leaned back as he looked at Jason, as if trying to bring him into focus. "That was right gentlemanly of you."

"No problem. I heard about your friends."

"They were the lucky ones," Tark moaned, clutching his hair.

"But didn't they die?" Rachel asked.

"Like I was supposed to."

Jason tried to cover his surprise and confusion. The one person he'd saved was devastated at having survived? He cleared his throat. "So, uh, what instrument did you play?"

Tark eyed him. "You aren't from hereabout."

"We come from far off."

"I play the sousalax."

"What is that?" Rachel asked.

Tark huffed. "Merely the largest of all lung-driven instruments. Only six or seven men along the coast have the capacity to sound it properly. Away north they use the instrument to summon walruses and sea elephants."

"That sounds handy," Jason said, sharing a small smile with Rachel.

Tark nodded obliviously. "I was supposed to play to the end. The sousalax lays the foundation for the other instruments. You know? And it was more than that. Listen, this stays between us. Simeon, our leader, had been absent a long while. He had a habit of going on excursions. One day Simeon shows up claiming a prophetess told him if we floated down the river to the waterfall playing music, we would summon a hero to help depose Maldor. He had an exact date and time in mind. At first we thought he was having fun with us, but he just kept staring, grim as a widow on her anniversary. We discussed the idea a long while, and eventually came to a unanimous accord. I mean, what do we need today more than a real hero? Not these fakers looking for a free ride to Harthenham—I mean the kind of heroes we sing about, the kind who actually stand for something. Simeon convinced us to play right up to the end and summon a hero by our sacrifice." Tears brimmed in his eyes. "But I reneged."

A barmaid approached and laid down a platter of puckerlies beside two tall glasses of water and a wooden bowl of chunky chowder. "Don't let him get started," she warned Jason. "You'll be trapped here all night with him repeating the same sorry story."

"I'll keep that in mind," Jason said. He turned back to Tark. "Go on."

Tark raised the bowl to his lips, took a long sip, wiped his mouth, and sighed contentedly. Jason dripped some pulpa oil onto a puckerly and swallowed it. Rachel grabbed a puckerly as well.

"It was all the fault of that sadist who fired the rescue arrow," Tark resumed, gazing at his chowder. Jason stiffened, biting his lip. "We were all resolved to our course of action until a chance for escape thrust itself upon us. With the arrival of that line to shore our determination slackened.

"The arrow took Stilus through the shoulder. Funny thing, he had been the one most opposed to the idea of our sacrifice. It took a good deal of cajoling to convince him. Old Stilus was superstitious, you see. I'd wager he took the arrow for a sign he'd been right all along. No sooner had he fallen than he began wrapping the line in a figure eight around one of the cleats. Stilus never did have much luck. I suppose he thought he was doing the right thing, trying to save us.

"When the boat started swinging in to shore, a bunch of us assumed we would be saved whether we liked it or not. A few kept playing, but most of us, myself included, began stripping away our bindings. We had lashed ourselves in place, you see, so we could keep playing through the rough water. By the time we collided with the bank, even the few folks still playing were having second thoughts. Our chance to survive was so near. I jumped to shore the same instant the line was severed, and found myself alone, the sole defector, watching my comrades float away."

Tark sniffed and ran the back of his hand across his nostrils. "By that time everyone thought they would be saved. I saw it in their eyes. Because of that hope of survival they experienced true terror as they reembarked toward the falls. Most couldn't play their instruments, either out of fear or because they had unlashed themselves and toppled over."

His voice became painfully intense. "What should have been a proud occasion of willful self-sacrifice degenerated into a pathetic farce where a raft full of cowering musicians plunged frantically to their deaths. Gelpha got off a blast on the clarinet. And some brave soul crashed the cymbals."

Jason felt a growing sense of horror, each word of Tark's like a punch to his gut. He'd only tried to help, and he'd caused so much suffering. How could he ever make up for it?

Tears leaked down Tark's face. He took a hasty sip of chowder.

"That was my responsibility. I was to crash the cymbals at the end of the finale. Not only did I fail, but some poor terrified soul covered my mistake."

He sobbed, banging a fist against the table. Then he wiped his nose against his shoulder. It took a moment before he went on.

"Afterward people acted like they were glad to see me, happy I had cheated death. But it was an act. Soon I understood the incident had branded me a coward and a mutineer. So I left. There was no place for the Giddy One among those people. I considered returning to the mines. I was an able miner once. But I felt too low even for that. You see, no hero appeared after my friends plunged off the falls. The prophecy went unfulfilled. And for the rest of my days I'll be burdened with the knowledge that it was my fault. Nobody will ever know whether the prophecy could have come true, because I abandoned the sacrifice. The Giddy Nine were supposed to go over those falls. Instead, eight frightened musicians plunged to their deaths, leaving one wretched craven behind."

"You shouldn't be so hard on yourself," Rachel consoled.

"Right," Tark huffed in disgust. "I should congratulate myself for betraying my friends and protecting the emperor. Suicide has tempted me. But I resolved that since I was not man enough to lose my life among friends, I don't deserve to be coward enough to take my life on my own. So now I am a wanderer. A vagabond whose sousalax rests upon the ocean floor, probably inhabited by a giant transient crab."

"That's—it's awful," Jason said. He opened his mouth to form some further expression of sympathy, but he couldn't speak through the knot in his stomach. Could he possibly be the hero these musicians had summoned? Galloran had made it sound like anyone, even some kid from the suburbs, could become a hero. Hearing in detail the sacrifice these nine people had made just to bring a hero to Lyrian was overwhelming. It filled Jason with a sudden, intense desire to actually be the hero they needed. But was he capable of that?

"I wish I could find the lowlife who shot that arrow," Tark grated, fists clenched. "He's the one who ruined our sacrifice. Without his interference I would have remained true to our cause. Paying him back is my sole remaining purpose."

Rachel and Jason exchanged an uncomfortable glance.

"What does he look like?" Jason asked.

Tark eyed him. "By the description I got, he looks a bit like you. Tall. Sandy hair."

Tark snorted, finished his chowder, and wiped his mouth on his sleeve. "Until the day I die I'll be watching for him."

"Maybe you shouldn't target the poor guy who shot the arrow," Rachel blurted out.

"Why not?" Tark barked.

"He was probably just trying to help," Rachel said weakly.

Jason bowed his head. "I think we all know who the real villain is," he muttered.

Tark eyed Jason narrowly. "Maldor," he mouthed, considering the idea.

"If you want to lose your life doing something useful, go after him," Jason said, keeping his voice low. "That would be the best way to honor the sacrifice your friends made. Who knows? Maybe you are the hero they were trying to summon."

Tark sat up straighter, eyes clearing. "I think you're onto something. What could be more fitting?" He pulled a heavy, saw-toothed knife from his waistband and stuck it fiercely into the tabletop.

Jason stared at the imposing blade in silence.

Tark stood up, stroking his chin. "Mark my words: I may not have died, but my life ended on those falls, so I have nothing to fear. Like a ghost I will stalk Maldor and his minions." He furtively glanced to see if anyone had overheard him. "Keep this conversation between the three of us. We never met. Good luck to you, friend Jason." He slapped Jason on the shoulder. "You have revived me."

Tark sheathed his knife and marched to the door. He tumbled out with help from the square-faced man.

Jason and Rachel each picked up another puckerly. As Jason sipped the squirming flesh, he thought about the heavy knife. Up until a minute ago it had been destined to slit his throat. He hoped Tark's resolve held. Although he was haunted by Tark's story of those final moments at the waterfall, he wasn't ready to die to make amends.

Jason finished his share of the puckerlies, and Rachel did likewise. They grew on him more with each he ate. After his last swallow he leaned back, satisfied, relishing the filmy residue lining his mouth. A truly delightful aftertaste.

The barmaid came back.

"What do I owe?" Jason inquired.

"Four drooma."

Jason pulled a bronze pellet from his pouch. "What's this worth?"

"Five," she said, as if she suspected he was teasing her.

"Here you go. Keep the change."

She stared at him.

"What?" Jason asked.

A smile spread across her face. "Thank you very much." She sounded so sincere, Jason decided that people in Hippoland must be lousy tippers. Immediately she went over to Kerny, talking excitedly and glancing toward Jason.

"Hey, big spender," Rachel hissed. "You still with me?"

"I was just tipping. Twenty percent is pretty standard where we're from."

"For the record you tipped twenty-five," Rachel said. "It doesn't matter. We should probably get going."

Jason turned to face the door. "Did we just send Tark to his death?" he murmured.

"Later," Rachel whispered.

"We probably did," Jason said. "He seemed like he was in the mood to do something stupid. I guess it beats getting that huge knife through our backs some dark night."

Rachel stood up.

Kerny hurried over, as if worried they would leave without talking to him. "How were they?"

"Delicious," Rachel said. "You know your seafood."

Kerny gave Jason an awkward glance, as if surprised Rachel had spoken first.

"She gets excited about her food," Jason quipped, earning a grin from Kerny. Rachel's lips compressed into a thin line. "And she was right. Puckerlies were a great suggestion—I have a new favorite meal. By the way, do you know where Trensicourt is located?"

Kerny steepled his eyebrows, forehead wrinkling. "Away inland a good ways."

"Do you know specifically?" Jason asked.

"Can't say I do. I've heard of the place, naturally. Never made it out that way."

"Do you know anyone who could tell us how to get there?"

Kerny scratched his head. "I doubt anyone in town could tell you. You know how travel has dwindled. Not too wise these days, what with folks disappearing and such. No offense. I'm sure you know your business. Say, do you need a place for the night?"

"Maybe," Jason said, glancing at Rachel, who gave an infinitesimal shrug.

"My mother runs a small inn," Kerny said. "Only rooms for hire in town. Good price, nine drooma, and lodging comes with breakfast."

Rachel offered Jason no clues to her opinion. He supposed it would be nice to have a bed. The last few nights had been chilly, waking up in fog. "I'll take you up on that. But we'll need two rooms."

Kerny raised his eyebrows.

"She's my sister," Jason explained.

Understanding dawned on the bartender's face. "Two rooms, you say? Might elevate the price to twelve."

"That should work," Jason agreed.

"Gerta," Kerny called, removing his apron. The young woman who had served them hustled over. "Watch the bar. I want to escort these good people personally."

CHAPTER 10

NED

The square-faced man helped them out the door. They landed rolling on a long mattress stuffed with straw. Kerny used his momentum to somersault expertly to his feet, then gave Jason and Rachel a hand up.

They walked together down the dusty road into town.

Kerny waved at a couple of people they passed. A tall man with curly orange hair and more freckles than skin came up to them, wearing what looked like a long sack with holes cut for his head and arms, the rough material dangling almost to his knees. His elbows were the widest part of his thin, speckled arms. He wore a black leather glove on one hand and no shoes. Even without shoes he stood a few inches taller than Jason. The stranger walked uncomfortably close to them.

Kerny steered Jason and Rachel away from the man. "That one's not well," he muttered.

"Who are your friends?" the stranger asked, following them, sniffing.

"They're none of your business, Ned."

"Sure of that, barkeep?" Licking his chapped lips, the tall man came up right beside Jason, matching him stride for stride.

Kerny wormed between Ned and Jason. "Shove off, Ned."

Ned puckered his lips. "Not yet. Share the secret first. Who are the outsiders?"

"My guests," Kerny growled. "Dignified visitors."

"Don't look dignified," Ned remarked. "They look barely grown. They been sleeping outside."

"Enough!" Kerny exclaimed, making Rachel flinch. "Shove off!"

Ned stopped trailing them, and Kerny led Jason and Rachel to one of the largest houses in town, right on the water. The residence stood up in the air on tall pilings. They climbed a coarse rope ladder up to the porch. A short woman with her gray hair knotted in a bun came to the door.

"I brought you customers," Kerny said hurriedly. "This is Jason and his sister, Rachel. They're staying the night. Twelve drooma for two rooms."

The old woman's eyes widened briefly. She regained her composure quickly, smiling kindly, but not before Jason recognized they were paying more than usual for the rooms. Jason considered haggling, then reconsidered, since he had already informally agreed to the price. Kerny left, and the old woman escorted them to a pair of small, neighboring rooms. In Jason's room a wide canvas hammock stretched from wall to wall. A trunk with a big lock sat in one corner. Nets hung over the window instead of curtains, partially impeding the view of the harbor.

The old woman gave Jason the key to the trunk and told him he could stow his belongings there. Then she took Rachel next door. After the old woman finished, Jason entered Rachel's room. She sat on her hammock, legs dangling, rocking gently.

"Do you think our hostess left us with the only keys to our trunks?" Rachel asked.

Jason frowned. "Good point."

"Let's never leave our belongings unattended."

"Really? I was thinking we might hit the local cineplex, see what's playing."

Rachel folded her arms. "I know it isn't your fault, but I didn't like how I was treated in the tavern. People acted like I didn't exist."

"You did a good job rolling with it," Jason said. "We have to blend in."

"I know," Rachel said. "But it makes it hard for me to help. I knew Kerny wanted to overcharge us. Didn't you notice how the waitress went straight to him after you tipped her, and how extra friendly he became?"

"Sort of," Jason said vaguely, embarrassed at having missed the signals. "I just thought it might be nice to have a roof over our heads. Who knows when we'll get another chance to sleep indoors?"

Rachel scowled thoughtfully. "We were probably safer alone in the woods. Everyone seems too interested in us. Have you noticed the eyes on us since we walked into town?"

"Yes."

"That weirdo Ned was the only person with the guts to say what everyone else was thinking. People don't travel around here. We've drawn a lot of attention."

Jason scratched his forehead. "Should we leave?"

"I don't think so," Rachel said. "If we take off before tomorrow, it will just make us look more suspicious. But we should be on guard."

"I hear you," Jason said. "We'll lay low, stay in our rooms. Do you think they have HBO?"

"Only in the fitness center," Rachel replied.

"I'm a little tired," Jason said. "Might be a decent time to sneak a nap."

"I think I have you figured out," Rachel said. "When in doubt, sleep."

"No fair," Jason complained. "Aren't you tired too? We've been hiking for days and staying up half the night on watch."

"I've been too keyed up to sleep well since I got here," Rachel said. "It might feel good to rest behind locked doors."

"Okay, I'll be in my room."

"Just a second. Quick question. Do you think you're the hero the Giddy Nine were trying to summon?"

Jason paused, pondering the story Tark had shared. It had been the music of the Giddy Nine that had caused him to topple into the hippo tank. Could he possibly be the hero they were hoping to call? After all, he had already begun a quest to destroy Maldor.

"If I was the hero they were looking for, those musicians were crazier than anyone ever realized."

"It is quite a coincidence," Rachel said softly. "Galloran seemed to think we were the people the oracle wanted."

Jason shrugged. "Just in case, I'll try not to die."

"Probably smart."

On returning to his room, Jason locked the flimsy door and tried out the hammock. Lying back comfortably, swaying gently, he closed his eyes. How could he be the hero they wanted? What had he ever done? Pitch a few shutouts? Get good grades? What about Rachel? The lady working with the Giddy Nine had apparently called her to Lyrian as well.

Could the fate of an entire world really depend on them? Did either of them stand a chance of succeeding? Galloran seemed to have faith in them. Could they possibly live up to his expectations?

The hammock was seductively comfortable. Content to rest for the moment, Jason let his worries melt away.

Somebody was knocking on the door. Jason realized he had dozed. He hadn't slept long. It was still bright outside. Did Rachel need him? Or did his hostess have a question? The soft knock was repeated. He tipped clumsily out of the hammock and opened the door.

It was Ned. "Hi, blue eyes," the tall man said, stepping into the cramped room.

Jason backed into his room as Ned pressed forward presumptuously, eyes roving, one of them twitching a bit. "What do you want?" Jason asked.

"You're a man on the move. Or maybe on the run?" Ned smiled. His gums looked pulled back too high. A few teeth were missing. "You ever swallowed a swallow? Ever badgered a badger? Ever outfoxed a fox?"

Jason found he had backed into his hammock. "What are you talking about? This is my room. I'm a friend, Ned."

Ned eyed him knowingly. "They are all looking for you. I found you, though. Tell me true—you seen the book?"

"What book?"

"The one that saw you."

Jason swallowed. "What do you mean?"

"Keep playing the fool, and I lose the glove." Ned held up a gloved hand, and put his other hand in position to remove it. "Last chance: Tell me true."

This was insane. "Yes, I have seen the book." Jason had no idea what danger there was in Ned removing his glove, but he did not wish to find out.

Ned showed his smile. It reminded Jason of a picture his dad had shown him to scare him into brushing his teeth. "I once defied

Maldor. Bad choice. Worst choice. The more you defy him, the more you deify him. He is the puppet master. He holds all the strings."

Jason was speechless. His hand strayed beneath his cloak.

"Want to see my string?" Ned asked, tugging at his glove.

Jason pulled out his knife. The sheath was still on it. Quick as a mousetrap Ned chopped Jason's wrist with one hand and stole the knife with the other. Jason pressed back against the hammock, rubbing his wrist. Ned calmly inspected the sheath. "Where'd you get this?"

"None of your business." Jason prepared himself, muscles tense, ready to spring. The guy was tall and quick, but skinny. If he could just get a hold of him, he would slam him around the room a bit.

"Violence will not serve you. Answer me. Answer right, and the glove stays on."

"Forget it."

"You stole it."

"No."

Ned yanked the sheath off.

"Found it."

"No."

"Your silence is not loyalty. Don't protect information I already know. Tell me who gave it to you." Ned pointed the dagger at Jason, thumb covering the trigger that could eject the blade.

Jason did not want to get Galloran in trouble. "I won't tell you."

Ned licked his lips. One eyelid fluttered. "As a lad I served one man I would never betray. His mark lies upon the sheath."

This surprised Jason. He wavered. "Galloran gave me the knife."

The dagger dropped to the plank floor. Ned's lips trembled. "He lives?"

Jason nodded.

Ned plunged his fingers into his orange curls. Emotions warred on his freckled face. "I pity you. Poor dupe. Poor gull. Listen. Ned never saw you. Leave in the night. A road departs town to the northeast. The Overland Loop. Or a trail leads southeast."

"What's under your glove?"

Ned grimaced. "My string. I will come in the night." He cackled. "I'll scout for you." He rushed out of the room.

Jason collected his knife and sheathed it, returning the weapon to his pocket. As he locked his door, he heard a soft knock.

"Jason?" Rachel asked from the far side.

Jason opened the door. "Did you hear my visitor?"

"Thin walls," she said, entering. "I missed a few words, but I got the gist."

"He knows who I am," Jason said. "He knows about our quest."

"Should we leave?" she asked.

Jason thought for a moment. "We should stay. If Ned knows who we are, others will figure it out too. We may need somebody who knows the area. He said he would scout around and come for us after dark."

"He seems nuts. I'm not sure we can trust him."

"I'm not sure about anything," Jason admitted. "But I think he's sincere. If we've drawn unwanted attention, slipping out of town after dark probably makes the most sense."

"Unless people come for us before then," Rachel pointed out.

"You have your explosive crystal ball?" Jason asked.

"Yes."

"Keep it handy."

She nodded. "I'm going to find Kerny's mother. Maybe she can go buy us some provisions."

"Not a bad idea," Jason said. "We're running low. And we might want to think twice before hanging around another town."

"I'll need to give her money," Rachel prompted.

Jason got out the little bag with the pellets. "How much?"

"Fifteen should buy a lot. I got the feeling those puckerlies were pricey."

Jason handed over three bronze pellets. "She may keep the money and betray us."

"It beats openly roaming the town, trying to buy provisions ourselves," Rachel said. "I'll pay attention. If she stays away too long, we can make a run for it."

"Tell her to keep a drooma for her trouble," Jason said.

"I was thinking two."

"Whatever."

"Can I borrow the satchel?"

"Sure."

"You should probably keep the door locked."

"I will."

After Rachel left, Jason practiced drawing his knife. Pulling it out still in the sheath had failed to intimidate Ned. He rehearsed until he could slip a hand into his cloak and swiftly produce a naked blade.

It was well into the afternoon. If they were going to sneak away in the night, Jason realized he should probably sleep. It took some time to calm his mind, but eventually he dozed.

All was dark when Jason woke. He could barely make out the shape of the trunk on the floor. He had no idea how late it was, but the night was quiet. He wondered if Rachel was all right. If there had been commotion, he supposed he would have awakened.

Jason got out of his hammock and stood at the window. He

saw no stars. Where was Ned? Should they wait for him? What if he failed to come?

After gathering his belongings from the trunk, Jason tiptoed to the door. A tap on the window startled him. Whirling, he saw Ned's face beyond the warped glass, upside down. Jason undid the latch, and Ned swung nimbly from the roof through the open window.

"Come with me," Ned whispered.

"What?"

"Listen."

Jason held still and focused on his hearing. After a tense moment a faint creak reached his ears. "That? What is it?"

Ned's breath was in his ear. "Somebody failing to move silently."

Panic jolted through Jason. "What about Rachel?"

"Already on the roof," Ned whispered. "Follow quietly."

Without awaiting a reply, Ned smoothly boosted himself onto the windowsill and disappeared onto the roof. Momentarily stunned, Jason again heard the creak of stealthy footsteps in the hall, this time just outside his door. The handle turned gently. It was locked.

Jason ducked under his hammock and climbed stealthily onto the windowsill, glancing at the fifteen-foot drop to the dim ground. Why did the little inn have to be on stilts? Standing awkwardly, Jason reached up for the eaves above his window. Ned caught hold of him and helped pull him onto the roof, where Rachel sat waiting, as promised.

Following Ned's example, they lay flat, listening. A gentle scrape of metal against metal suggested someone picking a lock. Jason heard a door creak open, followed by hurried footsteps.

"He's not here," a man exclaimed in a loud whisper.

"Maybe he escaped this way," a different voice said, right below Jason, at the open window.

"And flew out to sea," the first man spat sarcastically. "Come along."

They clomped out of the room, and Jason heard the door to Rachel's room crash open. Footsteps shuffled noisily, all pretense at stealth gone.

"Nothing," a voice said.

"What did you expect?" the other voice chided.

Heavy feet clomped hurriedly away.

Ned held a finger to his lips. The three of them waited in silence. Finally, Ned spoke. "You have a friend."

"What do you mean?" Jason asked.

"A riderless horse wandered into town this evening. I went up the Overland Loop, found a conscriptor facedown on the road-side. Stab wounds in the back. Dead mangler not far off. Such a thing has not been seen in some time. I dragged the corpses deep into the woods. You have a friend out there. Strange folk in town tonight. Leave by the main road. That way may be clear a while. You never knew me."

Ned crept across the roof in a crouch. Nothing creaked. He dropped out of sight.

"How late is it?" Jason asked.

"Maybe an hour past nightfall," Rachel answered. "When Ned showed up at my window, he almost gave me a heart attack."

"We should take his advice and get out of town," Jason whispered. "That was way too close. Do you have the new provisions?"

"In the satchel," Rachel said. "I'm ready."

"I think Ned dropped onto the porch. That's probably the only decent way down."

Jason and Rachel slunk along the roof to the front of the house, cringing as shingles creaked. By the time they got there, Ned was no longer in view—not on the porch, not down on the street. Jason saw no sign of anyone else, either.

"It looks clear," Rachel whispered. "We should move."

Jason slid into position to drop from the roof to the porch. Suddenly several of the wooden shingles overhanging the eaves of the house snapped, and he crashed to the porch on his back.

Lying stunned on the splintery planks, Jason tried to breathe. His lungs refused to function. All he could think was that his back was broken. He rolled onto his side. A feeble croak escaped his lips, then abruptly he was breathing again. Never had the wind been so brutally knocked out of him.

He sat up, holding still and listening to ascertain if his clumsiness had attracted attention. Both the house and street remained quiet.

Rachel dropped down lightly beside him. "Good thing I'm carrying the explosives," she whispered.

Jason drew a shuddering breath. "No kidding. Let's get off this porch before somebody comes."

They hurried down the rope ladder. The night was overcast. They moved quickly along dark streets, light bleeding through a few shuttered windows. Jason stayed a step ahead of Rachel, one hand inside his cloak, fingering his knife. The moving windows of the Tavern-Go-Round flashed from the slope above the town.

Jason thought he knew the road Ned had meant. The road he and Rachel had followed into town left the village angling toward the northeast.

As he passed quiet houses, Jason heard the lapping of the water in the harbor and the distant crash of breakers. A goat bleated from a pen beside a shadowy house with a big anchor half-buried in the front yard. Jason jumped, drawing his knife.

When they reached the main road, Jason set a brisk pace, taking long, quick strides. Rachel stayed silently at his side. For a good while they mounted a steep incline. The night was so dark they proceeded by feel and by faith that there would be no obstacle in the road. Like a dead mangler. Or a live one.

When dawn began to turn the sky gray, they took a break, ravenously devouring some of their newly acquired bread, sausages, and cheese. Jason eyed the energy berries the loremaster had given him. They showed no sign of spoiling, so he decided to conserve them.

As daylight brightened the overcast sky, Jason and Rachel resolved to walk the day away before sleeping. Around noon they ate again. While they were eating, a wagon appeared up ahead on the road. Jason and Rachel rushed for cover, ducking out of sight in the trees, remaining hidden until well after the wagon had rattled past.

A couple of hours after lunch they walked through a small village of tall, steep-roofed buildings constructed of stone and mortar, all crowded close together. A few were shops; most were residences. All of the buildings looked old. People watched them as they passed, their suspicious glares burning into Jason.

He noticed a group of young kids laughing as they played a game that involved throwing rings around a pair of stakes in the ground. A few of the kids chased one another. One spun in place until she got dizzy and fell down.

Jason frowned. This world was no place for children. What sort of future would these little ones have?

"Maybe we should have gone around the town," Rachel muttered, "made our way through the woods."

"Too late now," Jason answered.

By the time the sun was setting, both Jason and Rachel were trudging along wearily. They roamed a good distance off the road and swallowed a few bites of food. Jason threw himself down in his blanket between the sprawling roots of a thick tree with smooth brown bark and fuzzy green leaves shaped like pieces of a jigsaw puzzle.

"I'll take first watch," Rachel yawned.

"I can," Jason offered, half asleep.

"I've got it. You rest. I'll wake you soon."

CHAPTER 11

FERRIN

The following morning Jason awoke to something tickling his face. He brushed his cheek and sat up quickly. A shiny red centipede longer than his middle finger lay upside down on the ground beside him. The creature wriggled over and disappeared under a root.

Jason shivered. How long had that thing been crawling on him? One of the little drawbacks to sleeping out in the open.

Sitting up, he looked over at Rachel, sound asleep, wrapped in her cloak and blanket. Had she ever awakened him for his watch? He didn't think so. Could she have fallen asleep on guard? She looked pretty and vulnerable, lying there serenely. He felt a sudden desire to protect her.

Famished, Jason started rummaging for food. Although he tried to be quiet, the noise disturbed Rachel, and she sat up, gasping and blinking. After looking around for a moment, she turned to Jason. "I'm so sorry! I don't remember falling asleep!"

"We survived," Jason replied.

Rachel squeezed fistfuls of her blanket, her jaw tight. "Take off your socks," she said bravely.

"It might be hard to get them off. They feel pretty stiff."

"Ha-ha."

"Seriously, I might need your help. Some of my blisters popped yesterday. The socks feel plastered to my soles."

"I feel bad enough. You don't need to rub it in."

Jason had to admit she looked miserable. "Tell you what. We were exhausted. And I got a warning the first time I fell asleep on watch. You deserve one also."

Rachel scowled. "I don't deserve a break. I could have gotten us killed."

"Next time you blow it, you will smell and taste my socks. Same goes for me. No mercy from now on. Have some breakfast. We should get back on the road."

As they proceeded, the forest dwindled to meadowland, still interspersed with groves of trees, but primarily featuring broad expanses of brush and wild grass. From the position of the climbing sun Jason could tell that the road was generally bending northward.

Around midmorning Jason and Rachel came to a crossroads. This was no footpath branching off the main thoroughfare—it was the junction of two major roadways. A tall post with a crossbeam lashed near the top marked the intersection. A bag hung from the crossbeam, well out of reach.

Jason paused, hands on his hips. The roads joined at right angles, and all looked to be in good repair. "Which way?"

"West would take us back toward the Blind King," Rachel said. "And we came from the south. So north or east."

"Ned called this road the Overland Loop. That might mean if we continue north, it will circle back to where we started following it."

"Hello?" called a weak male voice, startling both of them.

Jason turned in a circle. Nobody was in sight, and there did not appear to be any cover for a good distance. "Who said that?" he asked sharply.

"Praise the fates," the voice cried, gaining strength. "Help me. I'm up here."

Rachel shared a befuddled glance with Jason. "Could that have come from the sack?" she asked.

"Sounded like it." Jason stared up at the bag dangling from the crossbeam. The sack looked barely large enough to hold a bowling ball. Jason raised his voice. "Who are you?"

"I'm Ferrin," the voice responded, muffled by the bag. "I'm a displacer. A gang of ruffians robbed me and left me here to die. Please get me down."

"How do you fit in the bag?" Rachel asked, baffled.

"Like I said, I'm a displacer. I understand you may not be terribly fond of our kind, but please don't leave me here to rot."

"We come from far away," Jason said. "We don't know what displacers are."

"It's unkind to tease the helpless."

"We're serious," Rachel assured him.

"They chopped off my head and buried my body. Things like that don't kill displacers. Parts severed from my body remain linked by cross-dimensional connections."

Jason gazed at the sack in disbelief. "So just your head is in there?"

"Yes, and I'll be just fine once you reattach me to my body."

"Where is your body?" Rachel asked.

"Hard to say. I can feel that I was buried. I could tell they didn't take me far. Look around."

Jason and Rachel searched the surrounding area. Off at a diagonal between the northbound and eastbound roads Rachel noticed a rectangular patch of churned-up earth. "I think I see where they buried you."

"Good. Go exhume me, and I'll help you get my head down."

"You still have control over your body?" Rachel exclaimed.

"My body doesn't feel disconnected," Ferrin explained patiently. "Blood from the heart in my body under the ground is still flowing into my head up here. The air I breathe in this sack is still filling my lungs. All my nerves remain in contact with my brain. That is what makes me a displacer."

"And you can reattach your head?" Jason asked.

"Nothing could be simpler. Coming apart doesn't serve much purpose unless you can put yourself back together. But I need you to dig me up first."

"Should we do this?" Jason whispered to Rachel.

"We can't just let him die," she replied softly.

"What if he's lying? What if he's a criminal?"

"Then he's probably on our side."

Jason and Rachel shed their cloaks. Crouching in the freshly turned soil, Jason began scooping away loose dirt with his hands, getting gritty bits of earth under his fingernails. Rachel set to work alongside him. The hole had been recently filled, so the dirt moved easily. Before long they reached the body, maybe three feet under, lying supine. They worked to clear the soil from atop the length of the body, mounding it off to either side. Soon the body sat up and started helping.

Jason and Rachel stepped away from the hole as the headless body clambered out like some monstrosity from a horror movie. Hearing about a headless body from a voice in a sack was one thing—watching a headless body rise from a shallow grave was another.

"I can't see a thing through this sack," Ferrin declared. "Could one of you lead my body over here?"

Rachel shook her head and gestured for Jason to do it. He approached the body, which stood motionless beside the hole, one hand outstretched. It wore a gray shirt, canvas pants, and rope-soled shoes, all caked with earth. As Jason drew near, he stared down at the headless neck, observing a perfect cross-section of muscle, skin, fat, blood vessels, bone, the spinal cord, the esophagus—everything. Strangely, no soil clung to the exposed tissue. Measuring himself against the body, Jason found that the neck came up to the top of his chest.

Jason took the hand of the body and led it over to the gibbet below the bag. "Pleasure to meet you," the muffled voice said, while the body shook his hand gratefully. "Can you see how they fastened me up here?"

Rachel approached cautiously, keeping her distance, an expression of morbid fascination on her face.

"A cord holding the bag shut is looped over a hook," Jason said.

"Can you reach it?" Ferrin asked.

"Not even close."

"Could you reach if I put you on my shoulders?"

"I think so, but I don't want to scramble your insides. What if I hurt your spinal cord or something?"

"Don't worry. The displacement field that keeps me connected protects the exposed portions of my anatomy."

The body crouched down.

"I'm not sure I could balance on you without a head there. Plus I'm taller than you. Why don't you climb on my shoulders? You should be able to unhook the bag by touch just fine."

"Fair enough."

Jason knelt down, and the body, feeling its way, sat on his

shoulders. Rachel came forward and helped Jason stagger to his feet. He moved under the bag.

"I have it," Ferrin announced.

Jason knelt again, and the body dismounted. The body opened the mouth of the bag, removed the head by the hair, and held it so that it could see Jason and Rachel.

"Many thanks," the head said. "You saved my life."

"Our pleasure," Jason replied.

Rachel shook her head slowly. "Not to be rude, but this is the craziest thing I've ever seen."

Jason couldn't help agreeing—although, amazingly, crazy things were starting to feel almost expected now.

The body set the head on the stump of the neck. Head and body instantly fused together without any mark to suggest they had ever been separated. Ferrin had a black eye and scrapes on his forehead and left cheek.

"Better?" Ferrin asked.

"Less weird," Rachel acknowledged gratefully.

Jason smiled. "I'm Jason. This is my sister, Rachel. Looks like you got beat up."

Ferrin flashed a lopsided smile. "The price I pay for being wizardborn."

"Was your father a wizard?" Rachel asked.

"Are you two as naive as you act?" Ferrin asked. "How can that be?"

"We're from far away," Jason reminded him.

"So far away that you haven't heard of displacers or the wizardborn races? Never mind, I don't mean to pry; you two just saved my skin. Rachel, when I say 'wizardborn,' I mean metaphorically. My race did not occur naturally. Displacers were created by wizards."

"I see," Rachel said.

"None of the wizardborn get much love from regular humans," Ferrin continued. "But displacers are especially despised—partly because we're hard to distinguish from regular humans, partly because our race is dying out, making us easy to pick on."

"Some bullies figured out you were a displacer?" Rachel asked.

"They were merciless. Once my head was in the sack, they kicked me up and down the road. A real group of princes, let me tell you. I suppose I should be grateful they wanted me to die a slow, torturous death, because now I may actually survive, thanks to your kindness."

"Did you know them?" Jason asked.

"Not personally. I saw them in an alehouse west of here. They must have followed me out of town."

"Where were you coming from?" Jason asked.

"Away farther to the west. I should have seen it coming. Too many of these small-town bumpkins prey on outsiders."

"We've noticed," Rachel said.

"Do you travel a lot?" Jason asked.

"It's all I do," Ferrin replied. "Displacers are wanderers. We're not like the drinlings or the Amar Kabal, with a homeland to call our own. We're unwanted, so we try to keep our identities secret and get by however we can."

"Do you know how we can get to Trensicourt?" Jason asked.

"You follow this road to the east, then take the northern fork when it splits. I happen to be going eastward myself. Unless you object to the company of a displacer, we could travel together. These are dangerous times."

"We'd enjoy some company," Jason said, looking at Rachel.

"We've run into some unpleasantness as well," she added.

"There can be safety in numbers," Ferrin said. "Fair warning: Traveling with a displacer can occasionally be troublesome. If others recognize my true nature, you could share in my unpopularity."

"To be honest," Jason said, "traveling with us might be risky as well." Rachel gave him a worried look, as if concerned he might say too much. "Servants of the emperor might be hunting us."

Ferrin clapped Jason on the shoulder. "I'm not surprised. Youthful siblings would not roam so far afield without reason. Maldor harasses everyone. He is not fond of travelers or visitors from distant lands. I am certain he has no great love for me, either. I will gladly risk traveling with you, if you will brave my company."

"It would be nice to have a guide," Rachel said.

"I agree," Jason said.

"Then it's settled!" Ferrin brushed some of the dirt from his sleeves and torso. "If I can't trust the pair who saved my life, who can I trust?"

They set off down the eastbound road.

"How do you make a living?" Jason asked.

"I do whatever I can find. Never one thing for too long. I've been a sailor, a horse trainer, a butler, a merchant, an actor, a farmhand, a hired sword—you name it."

"Sounds like an interesting life," Rachel said.

"Too interesting, sometimes," Ferrin replied with a grimace. "How about the two of you? What do you do?"

"We're students," Rachel said.

"We interrupted our studies to travel," Jason added.

"Ah," Ferrin said, nodding in approval. "The education of the open road. Reading about Trensicourt is no substitute for walking its streets."

"That's the idea," Jason said. "Do you know why traveling is so discouraged?"

"I can speculate," Ferrin said. "Maldor occupies this land, governing largely through officials selected from among the local populace. To discourage unified rebellion, he stifles interaction between communities. He prefers those he governs to remain divided and ignorant, especially in outlying regions far from his centers of power."

They proceeded in silence for a few minutes.

"You have provisions?" Ferrin asked.

"Enough for a few days," Rachel said.

"The bandits who jumped me cleaned me out," Ferrin said. "But I won't be a burden. They missed some money hidden in my shoe. There is a town a day's journey from here. We'll be fine."

"We had bad luck in the last town," Jason said.

"So did I," Ferrin chuckled. "We should be all right if we keep our heads down and stick together. As we draw nearer to Trensicourt, travelers become less conspicuous."

Ferrin kept scanning the side of the road, occasionally wandering some distance into a meadow or stand of trees to retrieve a stick. He discarded several before finding one he liked. "This may do," he said, examining it from different angles. "The item I most regret losing was my walking stick. It was perfect. I had it capped in silver. If not for the silver they probably would have left it." He used the sturdy, straight stick he had recovered like a staff for several paces. "Yes, this will suffice."

Before long Ferrin picked out a walking stick for Rachel. "Try it. It conserves energy. Let your arms do some of the work."

"Thanks," she said.

Soon thereafter he found one for Jason as well. As the day grew warm, Jason bundled up his cloak. Ferrin began whistling tunes Jason had never heard. The warbling whistle had a broad range, and Ferrin seemed to have good pitch. Rachel whistled

"Twinkle, Twinkle, Little Star." Ferrin liked it, learned it quickly, and soon began embellishing the melody. Then he started working on a harmony to whistle along with Rachel. The first few attempts were only marginally successful, but eventually he found one that worked rather well.

Jason spotted a couple of lizards longer than his foot. They darted away when he got near them. Ferrin warned him to stay away from a metallic blue beetle trundling lazily across the road. "You would be shocked how foul they smell if you get them angry. If you tread on one, you have to burn the shoe. It's that bad."

They chose a spot in a little stand of trees not far from the road to spend the night, and slept under the stars.

By noon the following day they were passing farms. For a drooma a man heading into town on a wagon gave them a ride. As they bumped along the road, Jason observed the countryside. Rippling oceans of wheat and barley turned farmhouses into islands. They passed a small, fragrant, fenced orchard, where bees hummed among the ripening fruit. Then three large windmills came into view, great white sails turning slowly in the gentle breeze.

The farms got progressively smaller. Before long they could see the town. It was much bigger than the little seaside village. The buildings were sturdy wooden structures, mostly unpainted, a few of them three stories high. The main street in town was broad enough for several wagons to move side by side, and it was interrupted by several wide cross streets.

"We'll climb down here," Ferrin said. The farmer reined in his team.

"Thanks for the ride," Jason said as he dropped to the road.

The silent farmer nodded, flicking his reins. The wagon lurched forward.

"I know a reliable place for food," Ferrin said.

Jason and Rachel followed Ferrin through the door of one of the largest buildings along the main street. Inside there were half as many people as tables, and a long marble-topped bar stood empty against the far wall. "This place gets busy in the evening," Ferrin said as they strolled up to the bar, taking seats on stools.

A heavy woman with frizzy brown hair came up, wiping the bar with a stained rag. "How can I help you?"

Ferrin leaned forward. "We want lunch, hearty portions with a bird involved."

She nodded. "To drink?"

"Cider for me."

She looked at Jason.

"Water."

"Do you have milk?" Rachel asked.

The corners of the barmaid's mouth twitched toward a smile. "Sure."

The woman walked off, then returned with drinks. Ferrin, Rachel, and Jason sipped and talked softly while they waited. The woman eventually brought out plates of roast duck, heavily seasoned and marinated in oily gravy, with vegetables and hot bread on the side.

"Good bird," Ferrin commented around a bite.

Jason nodded, blotting up some gravy with a piece of bread.

"Lots of bones," Rachel said, picking at the meat tentatively.

"How's the milk?" Jason asked.

"Good. Creamy. A little warm."

Ferrin finished first. "Pardon me, but I need to find the outhouse."

Jason stripped the last of the meat from the bones, then downed the last of his water. He sighed after emptying his glass.

"It's nice traveling with Ferrin," Jason said to Rachel.

"He's the most likeable person we've met since the Blind King."

Jason nodded. In spite of the detachable body parts, Ferrin seemed like the sort of person he might have become friends with under any circumstances.

A man came up beside Jason from behind. A sharp point pricked Jason's side. Another man walked up on the opposite side. "Don't move or make a sound," said the man with the knife.

Jason gave a start. It was the short, one-armed rescuer from the river. Except he now had both arms. Was that possible? Could this be his twin? Jason noticed that one of his eyes was brown and the other was blue, a detail he had missed when they first met.

The man on the other side was the lean man who had wielded the bow. He held a new bow, very fine-looking.

"He remembers us," said the lean man, as if the fact were endearing.

"Is there a problem?" Rachel asked the lean man. She had not yet noticed the knife.

"Clear out of here," the lean man threatened her.

"You might want to listen to them," Jason suggested.

Rachel backed away a couple of steps, one hand disappearing under her cloak. Jason hoped she wouldn't pull out the orantium. Hand grenades were not intended for close quarters.

"You played nasty with the wrong men," the shorter guy told Jason, relishing the moment. "We don't want a scene. Take a walk with us." He kept his cloak draped over the knife.

"Why should I?" Jason asked, not wanting to end up alone with these two.

"If you don't, I'll stick you right here and now. Then we'll stick your friend. You don't have to die today. Choice is yours."

Jason was pretty sure he recognized the voice. "Was it you two who broke into my room near the Tavern-Go-Round?"

The shorter man grinned. "You knew about that, did you? Don't know how you slipped by us. Good job there. Why don't you come along?"

"Are these friends of yours?" Ferrin asked politely from behind the trio.

The knifepoint poked persuasively into Jason's side. "Sure," he said without turning around. "What were your names again?"

"Tad," said the shorter one.

"Kale," said the lean one.

"Do you mind if I maim your friends?" Ferrin asked calmly.

Jason felt the point in his side waver.

"Why not?" Jason said.

Jason had his back to Ferrin, so from the corner of his eye he barely saw the walking stick swinging before it thumped Tad on the head, sending him sprawling. Kale dropped his bow and pushed back his robe to grab the hilt of a short sword. From his seat on the stool Jason kicked Kale in the hip as the man drew his weapon, knocking him sideways and inadvertently causing a stroke from Ferrin's walking stick to glance off Kale's shoulder rather than land on his skull.

The overzealous swing left Ferrin momentarily unprotected. Kale slashed fiercely, severing Ferrin's arm just above the elbow. Wielding the stick with his remaining arm, Ferrin deflected a thrust aimed at his chest. Rachel shoved Kale from behind, and as he stumbled forward, Ferrin clubbed him in the throat.

Kale crumpled to the floor, clutching his crushed larynx, legs jerking.

"What's going on here?" boomed a deep voice.

An overweight man wearing an embroidered bandoleer

entered the room, flanked by a pair of men with less fancy bandoleers, each holding a crossbow. Ferrin picked up his dismembered arm and reattached it.

Tad got up, eyes wide, hand over a bleeding gash near the crown of his head. "This *displacer* attacked me and my friend! We were just trying to enjoy a drink."

Kale continued to thrash on the ground, one hand on his throat, the other grasping helplessly, eyes rolling back.

"Not true," Jason blurted. "These men were trying to abduct me at knifepoint. My friend stepped in to help me."

"Lies!" shrieked Tad with surprising sincerity.

"The limb dropper struck first," said a bald man across the room. "I saw it plain enough, constable. He hit the little one over the head, then smashed his friend in the throat when he came to help."

"And the girl?" the constable asked.

"She entered the brawl," the bald man reported. "She helped the limb dropper take down the fellow on the floor."

The constable shook his head. "Sure as storm clouds bring rain, drifters bring trouble. You four will have to spend some time in the lockup, until we get this sorted out."

"Four!" Tad yelled. "I'm the victim! My best friend is dying!"

Kale's struggles were subsiding into random flinches and spasms.

"Then why aren't you trying to help him?" the constable asked. "You're protesting too loudly, friend. Harlin, did the little guy pull a knife on the young man?"

"He may have had a knife out when the limb dropper struck," the bald man said without much conviction. "Same knife you can see on the floor near his feet."

"Burn the limb dropper and call it even," a harsh female voice cried.

A few others muttered agreement.

The constable held up a hand. "I administer the emperor's justice. Under our laws even limb droppers get a trial. Patience. We'll make examples of these troublemakers, all in due time. Silas, how fares the man on the floor?"

A gray-haired man had crouched over Kale. "Not conscious. Still alive, for the moment."

Tad, Jason, Rachel, and Ferrin were led away.

The constable and his men took them to a low stone building, one of the only structures in town not made of wood. Three cells, with stone partitions between them, occupied the rear wall of a spacious room. The heavy bars of the cells were set close together. A bearded man sat in one cell, staring into a corner with his arms folded.

Jason's cloak was taken, and after a quick search his poniard was removed from a pocket. Ferrin, Tad, and Rachel were searched as well. Jason held his breath as a man checked Rachel's cloak, but he did not seem to notice the crystal sphere. Tad had left his knife behind in the tavern.

One of the men in bandoleers retrieved a key ring from a peg on the wall. Ferrin and Jason entered the center cell. Tad was placed in the cell to their right, with the bearded man. Rachel went to the cell on their left.

Once the prisoners were in their cells, the constable departed with three men. The remaining guard relaxed in a chair, leaning back, filing a piece of cream-colored wood.

Ferrin sat beside Jason in a rear corner of their cell. "I know the reputation of this constable," Ferrin said quietly. "He's a stern one. When Kale dies, and unfortunately he will die, the three of us will be sentenced to death."

"He mentioned a trial," Jason said.

"In this town Constable Wornser has final say in matters of sentencing. He'll be judge and jury. To acknowledge the law we'll receive a cursory hearing, and then we will be executed."

"Is there anything we can do?"

Ferrin smiled. "They evidently do not appreciate the abilities of a displacer. If they did, I would not be in a cell such as this."

Jason raised his eyebrows. "Can you split apart and slip through the bars?"

"Perhaps, though I would not risk it. Separating myself longitudinally is highly dangerous. If I place too much strain on my displacement field, I come apart permanently. Once the cross-dimensional connection is lost, my body would function just like yours. Namely, my innards would slop out all over the floor."

"Sounds appetizing. If you can't get through the bars, what can you do?"

"Wait until tonight when things quiet down. You'll see."

CHAPTER 12

JAILBREAK

When Jason awoke, a single oil lamp lit the room, casting parallel shadows of prison bars into the cell. Ferrin knelt beside him, shaking his shoulder.

"You have an astonishing capacity to sleep through commotion," Ferrin whispered.

Jason felt disoriented. Sleeping slouched in the corner had left his neck sore. He squinted at the displacer. "What's going on?"

"Not long after you went to sleep, the constable returned to report that Kale had died. People have been in and out all evening. Our hearing will be tomorrow. Fortunately, we won't be here."

"How?"

"You'll see. You knew those men who attacked you. Tell me about them."

Jason sighed. "I tried to save a bunch of musicians from intentionally going over a waterfall. I meant to help, but it turned into a mess. I knocked the shorter guy, Tad, into the water. He only had one arm back then. Kale fished him out. I knew they were angry, but I'm surprised they cared enough to track me down all this way."

"You say Tad had only one arm?"

"Yes. Unless this is his brother. Wait, maybe he's a displacer too!"

Ferrin furrowed his brow. "Probably not. More likely they were conscripted. Maldor has the power to restore limbs. A conscriptor must have used the replacement of his arm as leverage to gain his service."

Jason recalled how the Blind King had explained that Maldor had offered to restore his sight. "A conscriptor sent a boarhound after me as well."

Ferrin nodded. "They are masters of coercion. If conscriptors are sending assassins after you, the emperor must be more interested in you than I appreciated. On to more immediate concerns. Only one guard remains in the building."

Jason started to sit up, but Ferrin pushed him down. "No need to look. He has fallen asleep in a chair with his back to our cell. I suspect a second guard awaits outside the front door."

"How do we get out of the cell in the first place?"

"I do not wish to permanently harm the guards if possible. They acted against us with no malice. But we cannot allow ourselves to be unjustly executed. My first plan involves the two of us feigning sleep. You begin groaning louder and louder, as if in the grip of a relentless nightmare. I'll lie near the bars. When you hear me make my move, come lend a hand."

Taking off his shirt, revealing a sparsely hairy chest and moderately developed musculature, Ferrin plucked off his left arm at the shoulder and set it on the floor. He replaced his shirt, and then sprawled on the floor with his back to the bars, concealing the fact that he held his left arm in his right hand. He winked at Jason, who lay gawking at the disconnected appendage.

Jason closed his eyes. Rolling over, he uttered a mounting

series of moans culminating in a shout. Through the slits of his eyes Jason saw the guard stir in his chair. Closing his eyes, Jason let out a long, painful groan, tossing his head from side to side.

"That's enough," the guard growled.

Jason began panting, then commenced a fresh series of grunts and groans. He heard footsteps, and risked slitting his eyes fractionally. The guard stopped well out of reach of the bars.

"Hey, you, wake up and shut up!"

Jason turned his head away from the bars, then back. He groaned louder, growling at the end.

"Pipe down," called a voice from a neighboring cell.

The guard took a step closer. "Wake up!" he demanded.

Through his cracked eyelids Jason saw Ferrin leap to his feet and lean against the bars in a quick motion, holding out his severed arm to extend the length of his grasp. The hand of his detached arm caught the guard by the throat, and Ferrin hauled him brusquely against the bars.

Jason dove over to the bars, staying low and seizing the guard's ankles. Ferrin released his hold on the severed arm, which continued to squeeze the guard's throat. With his free arm Ferrin seized the man by the back of his head and pounded his forehead against the bars. Jason clung tightly to the struggling feet until the guard sagged.

After yanking the guard's legs and arms through the bars of the cell, Ferrin told Jason to keep hold of the guard's feet and to watch him closely. Welts began to discolor the guard's face. Ferrin took off his shirt again and seamlessly reattached his arm. Then he reached through the bars and made an underhand motion as if he were pitching a horseshoe.

As his arm swung forward, the hand detached from the wrist and sailed through the air, bumping against the wall near the peg where the keys hung. "Prongs!" Ferrin spat, using the word as profanity. The hand scuttled back to the cell on nimble fingers. Ferrin reattached it and tried again. This time the hand hit the keys but failed to catch hold of them. They jingled tauntingly as the hand slapped to the floor.

On the fifth try two fingers curled around the key ring, supporting the swinging hand precariously. The guard remained slumped, motionless, against the bars.

Moving dexterously, three fingers gripped the key ring while the thumb and index finger inched the ring off the peg. The keys jangled against the floor. Jason watched in fascination as the hand dragged the keys across the floor like a crippled spider. Ferrin's eyes were intent with concentration.

Ferrin reconnected the hand, picked up the keys, and pulled his shirt on over his head. Hastily reaching through the bars, he began trying keys. The gated section of the bars swung open. Ferrin scooped up the guard and hauled him into the cell. The man suddenly thrashed out of his grasp and twisted to lunge at Ferrin, who kneed the guard in the gut and shoved him to the floor. Ferrin pounced onto the man, hooking one arm around his neck in a choke hold while the other covered his mouth, muffling his protests. The man squirmed and lurched, desperate to break the hold, but Ferrin held firm as the guard's face reddened.

After the man lay limp, Ferrin maintained the stranglehold for a moment. "This one likes to play possum," he said. "Even when he's locked in the cell his shouts could bring trouble."

Ferrin rolled the guard onto his back and squatted beside him, staring. After a few seconds he swatted the man between his legs. The guard did not flinch. "He's out for now," Ferrin said, exiting the cell with Jason and shutting the door. He tossed the keys to Jason, who began stabbing keys into the lock of Rachel's cell.

"I wondered what all the groaning meant," Rachel said.

"Ferrin is a genius," Jason replied, inserting the correct key and opening her cell.

"Should I finish off your friend?" Ferrin asked, jerking his head at Tad, who stood glaring at them, hands fisted around the bars of his cell.

Jason frowned. "I can't see killing him while he's at such a disadvantage, all penned up."

Ferrin raised his eyebrows. "Chivalrous. You realize he will continue to hunt you once he gets free. His presence means he has taken a vow to see you dead. Were your situations reversed, he would end your life without a twinge of remorse."

Tad spat through the bars.

"No," Rachel said. "Don't kill him. Not like this."

Tad smirked.

"She's right," Jason said. "It's one thing to act in self-defense. This would be something else."

"It's your neck," Ferrin said. "You want out?" he asked the bearded man in the cell with Tad.

"No. I'm only in for another day. I caused a public disturbance. Matter of fact, would you mind giving me a knock on the head so the constable don't blame me for not raising an alarm?"

"Come to the bars," Ferrin said. He trotted over and punched between the bars, striking the man square in the eye. The man stumbled back and sat down hard, cupping a hand over the injury.

"Why doesn't Tad raise an alarm?" Jason asked.

"He can probably guess what I would do in self-defense," Ferrin said. "Give me the keys back." After unsuccessfully try-ing a couple keys, Ferrin unlocked a closet and retrieved their belongings. Jason wrapped his cloak around his shoulders. The closet contained no additional weapons. Ferrin crossed to a desk, reached underneath, and pulled out a loaded crossbow that had been cunningly suspended on hidden hooks. "I like to keep my eyes open when people don't think I'm watching," he said. "They might have other arms stashed someplace, but we have no time to search. The guard we subdued was unarmed. Let's see if we can get out the front door. Keep your knife handy."

Jason gently placed his thumb over the flower-shaped trigger, ready to eject the blade. Moving cautiously, Ferrin guessed the door key on the first try. He turned it and thrust the door open. A startled guard turned around. Ferrin leveled his crossbow at the man. "Make no sound. Come inside."

The guard, holding a crossbow at his side, hesitated. "Move now or die," Ferrin stated coolly.

The guard came inside. "Lay down your weapons. Knife, too." The guard put his crossbow on the table, along with a leather belt connected to a sheathed long knife.

Ferrin escorted him over to the cell where the other guard lay unconscious. Ferrin tossed the keys, and Jason unlocked the cell. Ferrin shoved the guard inside. "Kneel and hold still," Ferrin insisted.

The guard complied. Ferrin struck a measured blow to the back of his head with the heel of his hand. The man slumped to the floor.

"Is he out?" Rachel asked.

Ferrin nodded without checking him. Jason had a suspicion Ferrin had done this before.

Ferrin crossed to the table and buckled the belt with the long knife about his waist. He handed Rachel the other crossbow.

"Does it have a safety?" Rachel asked.

Ferrin glanced at the weapon. "To fire, slide this lever back, then use the trigger. Come."

The trio slipped out the front door into the night. "Walk carelessly," Ferrin advised. "No reason for us to look suspicious. We are merely escaped fugitives about to steal some horses to avoid a death sentence."

They strolled down a side street. Ferrin held his crossbow casually at his side. Jason clung to his poniard, keeping it under his cloak. Rachel hid her crossbow likewise.

At a signal from Ferrin, Jason and Rachel ducked into a small livery stable. A horse snorted and stamped. Ferrin put a finger to his lips. "You ride horses?"

"Only twice," Jason whispered, not mentioning that once was a pony ride at a circus as a child and the other walking single file along some trail in Arizona for a couple of hours on a guided excursion.

"I've ridden quite a bit," Rachel said.

Jason rolled his eyes. Of course she had!

Ferrin forced open a rickety closet door. Two of the horses started whinnying. Jason held his poniard ready as Ferrin saddled and bridled a big gray mount. Next Ferrin prepped a smaller white horse. He then bridled a roan with a long, thick mane, slightly shorter and broader than the first horse.

Ferrin led the gray horse out of its stall. He handed Jason the reins, nodded for Rachel to retrieve the white horse, and went to retrieve the roan. Jason patted the sleek neck, smoothing the fur.

"What do you think you're doing?" exclaimed a gruff voice. Jason turned to see a man entering the stable clutching a hoe like a weapon. He had messy hair and an open shirt that revealed a hairy chest.

Jason realized the man could not see Rachel and Ferrin, since they were currently in stalls. "I just love to pet horses," Jason said, his voice pathetically dreamy. "They're my most favorite ever. I can read their minds."

The stableman looked baffled. "These are private horses, son." An edge of stern accusation remained in his voice. He took a step closer.

Jason saw movement out of the corner of his eye. Ferrin stepped out of a stall holding his head in his hands. "Beware the boy," the head said. "He took my head. Yours will be next."

The startled man backed away, hoe raised protectively.

Ferrin's body set down his head, then seized a pitchfork and charged. The man threw down his hoe and ran. Ferrin's headless body flung the pitchfork sidearm so it spun end over end horizontally. The pitchfork tangled in the stableman's legs, and he fell heavily against the plank floor just shy of the door.

The body tackled the stableman as he began to rise. The gray horse tried to rear, nearly jerking Jason off his feet. He barely maintained his hold of the bridle.

"Toss me to my body," Ferrin's head demanded. "Make it a good throw."

Keeping one hand on the bridle, Jason crouched and scooped up the head. An underhand toss sent Ferrin's head spinning through the air to the outstretched hands of his body, which straddled the terrified stableman.

"That is much harder than it looks," Ferrin said while reattaching his head to his neck. "Catching your own head, I mean."

"I bet," Jason said.

The stableman lay motionless, breathing loudly through his nostrils, glazed eyes staring. "Leave me be," he pled.

Ferrin hauled him to his feet. "We mean you no harm, except to borrow a few horses. They will be returned. Just keep quiet and don't make trouble for yourself. Why don't you kneel right here?"

A practiced blow left the stableman unconscious on the floor.

"You need to teach me that one," Jason said.

"You all right, Rachel?" Ferrin called.

She led the white horse out of the stall. Pausing, she stared at the stableman on the floor. "Now we're real criminals."

"They made us criminals," Ferrin corrected, returning to the roan's stall. He led out the gelding, hoofs clomping on the planks. "Mount up," he said, bounding easily onto the roan's bare back.

Jason stuck his boot in a stirrup and hoisted himself up awkwardly. Rachel mounted the white mare smoothly.

Ferrin walked his horse over to Jason. "Don't stick your foot so far through the stirrup. If you fall you'll get dragged. And don't pull so tightly on the reins. They aren't there for your stability. Grip with your knees. Ready?"

"I guess."

Ferrin smiled. "You can read horses' minds. That was very nice. My kind of crazy."

"Thanks. The headlessness was a slick scare tactic."

"It kept our unfortunate friend off balance. Let's go."

Leaning down, Ferrin lifted a latch and shoved open the main stable doors. Rachel followed, and Jason trotted after them onto the street, bouncing up and down with the jerky gait. Then Ferrin touched his heels to the roan's sides, and the steed sped up to a canter. Rachel's mare started loping as well.

Without any urging, Jason's mount matched the pace of the other horses. For a horrible moment Jason thought he was going to get jounced out of the saddle to one side or the other. Each loping stride provided a fresh opportunity to lose his balance.

The town blurred by, dark buildings interrupted by an occasional lit window. Holding his reins loosely in one hand and clutching the pommel with the other, Jason tried to grip with his knees as Ferrin had instructed. Soon he discovered that if he let his body rock in synchronization with the horse's strides, the ride became less jarring.

They rode out of the town, Jason a few lengths behind Rachel and Ferrin. The town receded behind them, and Jason gradually grew more comfortable astride the running horse. He began to notice the cool night air washing over him, the bright stars glittering above through gaps in unseen clouds, the occasional twinkle of fireflies off to either side of the road. Somewhere in the night a pack of coyotes or wolves started howling. The howls rose in a cackling chant, intensifying until a heart-freezing shriek pierced the night. Jason's horse began to gallop, racing past Ferrin and Rachel, Jason tugging ineffectually at the reins. The howls ended abruptly. As he bounced along the dark road, Jason envisioned animals feeding on a kill.

He finally managed to yank his horse to a stop. Ferrin pulled up alongside him and dismounted. "We should walk for a while. These are hearty steeds, but we must conserve their strength." Rachel drew up and dismounted gracefully.

Jason clambered down. He rubbed his thighs. "Much more of this and I'll be bowlegged."

"You did fine," Ferrin laughed.

They led their horses along the lane.

"Will they chase us?" Rachel asked.

"Very likely. But not far beyond the outskirts of town. Now, your friend with the new arm, he is another story. I expect he will get released, so sleep with one eye open."

"Are we outlaws now?" Jason asked.

"Perhaps in that town. Not all towns have constables. And there is little communication between them. The only centralized power in the land belongs to Maldor."

"I'll wear a fake mustache and glasses if I ever go back through there," Jason said.

"Our manner of escape should help clear our names," Ferrin said. "Constable Wornser is no fool. We had plenty of opportunities to kill, if murder were our game. Still, if either of you ever comes back this way, go around the town."

They walked on in silence.

After a time they remounted the horses and trotted them. Jason marveled at how tireless the horses seemed.

As dawn began to color the sky, Ferrin led them off the road. They went over the shoulder of a hill and made camp in a hollow on the far side. Ferrin tethered the horses while Jason and Rachel laid out their blankets.

"I'll keep watch," Ferrin volunteered.

Jason fell asleep quickly but did not slumber long. He awoke with the sun barely above the horizon. He walked out of the shade of their hollow into the morning light, stretching the sore muscles in his legs.

"If you're up, I may catch a nap," Ferrin whispered.

Jason gave a nod. About fifty feet away stood a limbless stump of a tree, with a hole in its side the size of a dinner plate. Jason selected five rocks of similar size. He stood as if he were on a pitcher's mound, the first rock in his hand. He checked first base, went into a windup, and hurled the stone at the hole. Two of the five rocks went inside. Only one missed the tree entirely.

He wandered back over to the shade of the hollow. The horses nibbled at grass near where they were tethered. Rachel rested her head on her arms, her breathing slow and even. Ferrin lay on a patch of dirt, hands folded on his breast.

What a peculiar guy. He certainly knew how to handle himself in a fight. Whoever had jumped him and left him to die with his head in a sack must have really known what they were doing.

As Jason stood watching, the fingers and thumbs began

dropping off Ferrin's hands. They wormed off his body and squirmed toward Jason across the ground. Jason jumped back, his voice cracking. "Uh, Ferrin, you're coming apart."

Ferrin's mouth bent into a small grin, and he opened one eye. "Did I startle you?"

"You are weird."

Ferrin collected his fingers. "You have good aim with rocks."

"Do you know what baseball is?"

Ferrin shook his head.

"It's a game we have where I come from. One of the people in the game has to throw balls with a lot of accuracy. I used to do that."

"I enjoy sports. Tell me the rules of baseball."

Jason stared at the ground, wondering how to begin. He had never explained baseball to somebody with no knowledge of the game. "Well, there are two teams. While one takes their turn batting, the other team is on the field to defend against hits."

"What is batting?"

"I'm getting there. A pitcher throws a ball, and the batter tries to hit it into play, or over the rear wall, which is a home run, unless it goes foul."

Ferrin looked perplexed.

Jason rubbed his chin. "There are four bases arranged in a diamond shape, and the hitter is trying to advance around all the bases. When he gets to the fourth base, which is where he started, he's home and scores a run."

Ferrin began reattaching his fingers one at a time. "This is the most complicated game in all of history. I have no idea what you mean."

"Wait. I'm just laying groundwork. I have to define a lot of stuff before you'll be able to understand. I wish we could play a few innings. It's much easier to pick up when you can see the game being played."

"I don't care about baseball," Rachel moaned, her face buried in her arms. "I'm trying to sleep."

"You can tell me more once we get on the road," Ferrin told Jason. "Despite the long night, we should set off early today, just in case."

The horses acted restive returning to the road, so Ferrin let them canter along the lane for a good distance before slowing to a walk. This time, under the light of day, Jason enjoyed the ride. Despite feeling a little sore, he could see how people could develop a passion for horseback riding.

When the horses walked, Jason continued explaining baseball. Rachel added occasional clarifications. Ferrin began to grasp the concepts, and eventually the displacer could explain the difference between a ground-rule double and a double play. He even came to appreciate the necessity of the infield-fly rule.

Not long past noon they came to a small hamlet of low earthen buildings with thatched roofs. One of the houses had a corral fencing in a pair of horses. Ferrin dismounted in front of the door, handing his reins to Rachel.

A bald man with a hook nose answered the knock.

"Hello, friend," Ferrin said. "We borrowed these horses from a man in the town down the road. For a fee would you see that he gets them back?"

"The one without the saddle is Herrick's horse," said the man.

"The others were taken from the same stable. By necessity we borrowed them without permission. No doubt he will be most anxious to see them returned."

The bald man eyed Ferrin warily. "No doubt."

"Jason, pay the man eight drooma—three ones and a five."

Jason began fishing out his money bag. "Three for your trouble, sir, and five for Herrick. Please convey our apologies."

Jason climbed down from his horse and handed the bald man the money.

"Can I have your word the horses will be delivered as described?" Ferrin asked.

"I don't give my word to thieves," the man replied.

All friendliness vanished from Ferrin's countenance and expression. "And I don't deliver valuables via unsworn men. Swear or return the money."

The man looked uncomfortable. "I swear all will be as you say."

"Show no disrespect to thieves," Ferrin pressed, in an icy tone. "You know who claims to rule this land. Many of the best men living work outside the law. Along with the most dangerous."

The bald man looked thoroughly cowed. "I take your meaning. Forgive my words."

"I will forgive when you deliver on your pledge," Ferrin said, finally turning his back on the man.

The bald man accepted the reins from Rachel and Jason and began walking the horses toward the corral. Ferrin started down the road.

"You can be harsh," Jason said.

Ferrin smirked. "Among my many professions my favorite was acting." He slapped Jason on the back. "We are honest men again."

"And women," Rachel added.

"Precisely," Ferrin agreed.

Ferrin stopped at a seemingly random house, larger than most along the road. He knocked.

A disheveled woman answered. "We are weary travelers," Ferrin said. "Do you know where we might purchase some food here in town?"

"There is no inn. All I can offer is rabbit stew."

"Three bowls for two drooma?"

Her eyes widened. "Come in," she said, smiling hospitably.

Ferrin winked at Rachel and Jason. Leaning toward them, he spoke for their ears only. "With a few drooma in your pocket everyone is your friend."

CHAPTER 13

NICHOLAS

"The key to traveling without provisions," Ferrin explained on their third evening after leaving the road, "is learning to recognize a bubblefruit tree."

They stood in a dense grove surrounded by a sea of heather. "What do they look like?" Jason asked.

"Gray, mottled bark. Slender trunk. Rarely more than three or four times the height of a man. And broad, ferny foliage. Look for linear groupings of tiny leaflets."

"Right here," Rachel said, pointing to a nearby tree that fit the description.

"Do you see the bubblefruit?" Ferrin asked.

Jason walked over to the tree, squinting intently in the fading light. "No."

"That is why you must learn to recognize the tree. The fruit grows only on the highest limbs."

After Jason climbed the tree to procure a bunch, Jason and Rachel each ate a fruit, chasing them down with long sips of water. Jason recalled eating a bubblefruit hybrid at the Repository of Learning. The hybrid had tasted superior to the natural fruit. It seemed so long ago.

After abandoning the horses, Ferrin had suggested they forsake the main road to confuse any unfriendly pursuers. The diverging path wound through hilly country of heather and flowering weeds interspersed with mountainous bushes Ferrin called oklinders. The biggest oklinders rose over a hundred feet high and spread nearly twice as wide, the dense, spindly limbs abounding with dark, glossy leaves nearly all the way to the center.

Ferrin had explained that near the center of any oklinder hung moist white bulbs larger than watermelons, which were considered delicacies. Despite the delicious juice inside, few had the will to harvest them, because they were typically guarded by venomous thorns and colonies of aggressive wasps.

As they journeyed, Ferrin taught Jason and Rachel how to forage. They gathered nuts and berries, and used their crossbows to shoot bigger rabbits than Jason had ever seen. Each shot was carefully chosen, as they only had a single quarrel for each crossbow and could not afford to split one against a stone.

"Tomorrow we should see Trensicourt," Ferrin predicted, munching on a bubblefruit. "I will not be able to enter the city with you."

"Why not?" Rachel asked.

"Too many men in that city would prefer me dead. Years ago I was beheaded within those walls, part of a group execution. They failed to recognize I was a displacer. I feigned death for most of a day, trusting the word of a friend. The friend lost her life restoring my head to my body, and I only barely escaped. Trensicourt can be a delightful city, with enough money and the proper connections." He gave a wry smile. "But offend a nobleman over a woman, and the city turns on you."

"Then we'll part ways?" Jason asked.

"Nonsense. I'll not lightly abandon fine traveling companions such as yourselves. Besides, I still owe you for saving my carcass. Unless you intend to remain in Trensicourt. I was under the impression this was a temporary visit."

"It should be a short stay," Rachel affirmed.

"Then I will await you in the first town north of Trensicourt, at an inn called the Stumbling Stag."

"How long will you wait?" Jason asked.

"Until the sea dries into a desert," Ferrin said.

"Be serious," Rachel said.

"How about a fortnight?" Ferrin proposed.

"A what?" Jason asked.

"Two weeks," Rachel supplied.

"Should be long enough," Ferrin said. "If you do not join me, I will move on. Might I ask your business in Trensicourt? I am familiar with the city. Perhaps I could be of service."

Jason glanced at Rachel. They had not yet disclosed their true mission to the displacer.

"We're looking for a man named Nicholas," Jason said. "He once worked closely with Galloran. We can't share more particulars, because the information could endanger you."

Ferrin grinned. "I love intrigue. But by all means, if you feel it is necessary, keep your secret; I'll trust your judgment. Nicholas, you say. You can't mean old Nicholas Dangler, the weapons master?"

"We might," Rachel said. "Did he know Galloran?"

Ferrin frowned. "That is a name to mention with care, especially in Trensicourt. Yes, old Nicholas is a fallen nobleman. His family was heavily favored by Galloran. But once Galloran failed to return from his quests, the aristocracy turned on his favorite pets. If you want Nicholas Dangler, you'll need to inquire around the Fleabed, the poor district near Southgate."

"People in Trensicourt don't like Galloran?" Jason asked.

"The people?" Ferrin asked. "The people adore him. There was never a more popular prince, and his disappearance has lionized him, turned him into a myth. It's the current aristocracy who despises him. Never openly, mind you. They try to spread rumors to undermine his memory, and they have studiously ruined those who were once his staunchest supporters."

"Good to know," Rachel said.

"Take care in Trensicourt," Ferrin advised. "Its politics are cutthroat. With little warning the city can become most unpleasant."

Early the next morning Trensicourt came into view as the threesome topped a ridge. From the elevated position they gazed out over a lush valley of cultivated farmland crisscrossed with watercourses, hedgerows, and low fences of piled stones. Across the valley loomed a long, sheer plateau, crowned by the walls and towers of Trensicourt.

"Amazing," Jason breathed.

"It's a real city!" Rachel exclaimed.

The imposing city wall ran along the brink of the plateau, with square guard towers spaced at increments along the mighty granite rampart. A buttressed road doubled back and forth from the valley floor up to a yawning gate. Behind the wall rose the tops of buildings, some flat, some domed, some gabled, and overshadowing the entire scene soared the lofty towers of a proud castle. The rising sun cast a rosy glow over the landscape, glinting warmly off glass and gilded spires.

"I will draw no closer to Trensicourt than this," Ferrin announced.

"Thank you for guiding us," Rachel said. "We'll meet at the Stumbling Stag."

"If we don't get decapitated," Jason added.

Ferrin peered back the way they had come. "I've had a persistent feeling that we're being followed. I generally trust my intuition in these instances, but I've encountered no direct proof. Either our tracker is supremely talented, or my intuition has deserted me. In either case hurry to Trensicourt. The gates close at sundown. Don't dally, and watch your backs in the city."

"We'll be careful," Rachel promised.

Ferrin bent down and pulled off his shoe. From inside he removed two pellets, one gold, the other silver. "You've been paying my way and feeding me," Ferrin said. "I would have helped more, but the robbers took my copper and bronze. You may have need for gold and silver in Trensicourt. Either is worth enough to serve as a tempting bribe."

"We can't take this," Jason said.

"I insist," Ferrin said, waving a dismissive hand. "If you have no occasion to use it, bring it back to me. I'll feel better knowing you have it, and you will owe me nothing should you spend it."

"It's very kind of you," Rachel said.

"You can't imagine how seldom those who know I'm a displacer treat me like a person," Ferrin replied. "In case I wasn't clear, you may not want to mention our friendship inside the city. It could have negative consequences. I hope we meet again."

"So do I," Jason said.

"I'll create diverging trails, just in case we are being followed. You two should get underway. Crossing the valley will require much of the day. Safe journey."

"Safe journey," Rachel replied, giving Ferrin a hug.

Two or three hours of daylight remained when Rachel and Jason arrived at the foot of the road that climbed from the valley floor to the gates of Trensicourt atop the plateau. Neatly paved with red, square stones, the road rested on ingeniously constructed abutments braced against the face of the plateau. Jason had never witnessed a comparable feat of engineering. The precarious road was wide enough for large wagons to pass each other as they ascended or descended without bothering the foot traffic progressing along the railed walkways at either side.

By the time Jason reached the city gates atop the steep roadway, his calves burned. He felt relieved to find the great gates open wide, allowing traffic to move freely in and out. The guards at the gate, wearing feathered helmets and clutching tall halberds, paid him and Rachel no special attention as they entered.

Once through the gates they advanced up a cobblestone street overshadowed by tall, closely packed buildings. They came to a square with a fountain at the center. The majority of the water spouted from the upturned mouth of a hefty stone man struggling with armfuls of bulky fish. Lesser sprays of water issued from the mouths of the fish.

At the end of one long avenue rose a wide marble building with a golden dome surmounted by a slender spire. In the other direction loomed the castle, topped by pennants rippling in a breeze that Jason could not feel down in the square.

The crowd in the square milled about, a mixture of peddlers hawking their wares, shoppers dickering for better prices, farmers driving wagons or pulling handcarts, and an occasional fashionably appointed carriage slicing through the throng.

Jason noticed three scruffy boys dashing through the crowd, playing tag. They looked about ten years old. "Hey, come here," Jason said to a skinny one with big ears as he dashed by. The boy reluctantly answered the summons, and his two friends took off.

"What is it?" the boy asked uncomfortably.

"Do you know the way to the Fleabed?" Jason asked.

The boy glared, eyes darting between Jason and Rachel. "Got nothing better to do than mock strangers?"

"We're not teasing," Rachel said. "We're looking for Nicholas Dangler."

"The Dangler?" the boy chuckled. "Somebody dare you to knock at his door?"

"Something like that," Jason replied.

"Everyone knows where the Dangler lives," the boy said. "Leastways everyone who's ever set foot in the Fleabed. I'm not from the Fleabed myself, but I could find the Dangler's door easy enough."

"Two drooma?" Jason asked, taking the cue.

The boy brightened. "At your service." Jason handed over two pellets, and the boy stared at them as if he held diamonds. When the boy awakened from his temporary trance, the pellets disappeared into a pocket. "Follow me."

The nimble boy led Jason and Rachel away from the castle, toward the huge domed building. After traveling several blocks, they left the main avenue, soon veering to continue south beyond the enormous domed structure. They entered a maze of narrow, filthy streets and alleys. The buildings began to look like poorly stacked boxes. Furtive eyes peered through boarded windows, and lonely figures dressed in layers of worn clothing roamed the alleyways. Jason kept a wary eye on the people around them. Beneath his cloak one hand remained on his knife.

The boy led them around a battered lean-to in the mouth of an alley, where an old woman huddled behind a curtain of tattered rags. On one side of the alley a single solid building stood in contrast to the haphazardly overhanging levels on the opposite side. A gang of thin urchins scattered as Jason and Rachel followed the boy forward.

The boy stopped and pointed. "Up on the left is the Dangler's door. Whether you knock is up to you. Will you need help finding your way out of here?"

"I think we've got it," Jason said, unsure how long they might converse with Nicholas Dangler. He figured he could always hire another guide.

The boy looked up expectantly.

Jason fished out another drooma. "Thanks."

The boy stashed the pellet away and dashed off without another word. Rachel stepped nearer to Jason. "Is this safe?" she murmured.

"Has anything been safe?" Jason replied, his eyes following the boy as he ran away. "It makes me sad to think of all the kids growing up here."

"I can't think about that," Rachel said, her eyes misting up.

Jason sighed. "At least the Dangler's door leads to a sturdy building."

"There aren't many in the neighborhood," Rachel agreed. "I'm surprised this part of the city hasn't collapsed into the alleys."

"Let's knock." Jason approached the door and tapped it three times with his knuckles. The heaviness of the door dampened the sound. After waiting for several seconds, he knocked again, pounding this time.

"Maybe he's not home," Rachel said after a moment.

As Jason knocked a third time, locks disengaged, and the door whipped inward. A woman stood there, nearly his height, her shoulders broad, her dark hair tied back. She wore a sleeveless tunic, her bare arms plump with muscle. "What do you want?" the woman asked.

"We're looking for Nicholas Dangler," Jason said.

Her challenging eyes shifted from Jason to Rachel and back.

"Nicholas is ill; he can't abide visitors. If you want to commission work, I am running his enterprise. We could set up a consultation."

"We specifically need to speak with Nicholas," Rachel said.

"Then you should have visited years ago," the woman responded.

"Please," Jason persisted. "We're strangers to this city. We really need his help. Galloran sent us."

The woman sneered. "Your ridicule lacks invention." She slammed the sturdy door.

"Should you have brought up Galloran?" Rachel asked.

"Jugard said that Nicholas used to work for Galloran," Jason replied. "The problem is she thinks we're kidding." Slipping a hand into a pocket, he knocked again.

"Careful," Rachel said. "She looked like she could beat you up."

After a few bursts of knocking, Jason began to incessantly pound. When the door opened again, the woman held a sword. Behind her an older, smaller woman leveled a fancy crossbow at Jason.

"Walk away," the broad-shouldered woman suggested. "Do not force us to use violence."

Jason held up the ring Galloran had given him. "I am Jason, Lord of Caberton. The title came to me from Galloran. It seemed like you didn't believe me."

The smaller woman lowered her crossbow somewhat. The larger woman held out her free hand. "Let me examine the ring."

"It stays on my finger," Jason said, holding it up for her inspection. The last thing he needed was for the woman to take the ring and slam the door again.

The woman stepped forward and gazed at the ring. Jason twisted his hand so she could inspect different angles. Her interest shifted from the ring to Jason. He returned her stare. Despite her hard features she was not unattractive. The woman glanced up and down the alley. "Step inside."

Jason and Rachel passed through the doorway. The large woman shut the door, fastening multiple locks.

The shorter woman spoke. "I'm Kayla. This is my daughter, Minna."

"My sister, Rachel," Jason said, gesturing.

"I cannot guarantee an interview with Nicholas," Kayla said. "Do you mind waiting while I inquire?"

"Not a bit," Jason said.

The bare room had three strong doors besides the entrance—one to the left, one to the right, and one straight back. Kayla went through the door opposite the entrance.

"Forgive my abruptness," Minna said, the sword still in her hand. "Youngsters get dared to rap on our door, so when we answer, we normally find children running away. We make appointments for our business dealings. We have weathered numerous attempts to harm and disgrace Nicholas. These are uncertain times."

"I understand," Jason said. "We mean no harm."

"Any mention of Galloran will likely bring harm," Minna said uneasily.

Kayla returned. "Nicholas will see the two of you immediately." Jason and Rachel followed Kayla. As Minna moved to accompany them, Kayla held up a hand. "You will not be needed."

"We haven't searched them," Minna complained.

"Nicholas was explicit," Kayla said.

"That doesn't make him right," Minna groused. Kayla led Jason and Rachel down a short hallway. She motioned toward the door at the end of the hall. "Right through there."

Jason and Rachel passed Kayla and walked into a spacious

room crowded with workbenches, tables, tools, plans, and diverse contraptions in various stages of development. A graying man hanging in a leather harness glided toward them, suspended from an overhead track that snaked around the room. The man had no legs.

Tugging a strap, the man stopped sliding a pace from Jason, his body swinging in the harness. "Let's see the ring."

Jason offered him the ring. The man accepted it and removed a jeweler's loupe from a pouch in his harness. Staring through the lens, he studied the ring closely before handing it back. Apart from his lack of legs the man had a stout build. In fact, he looked vaguely familiar.

"Are you Nicholas?" Rachel asked.

"I am. And you claim to be called Jason and Rachel." He fixed Jason with a shrewd gaze. "How did you really obtain this ring?"

"Directly from Galloran," Jason said. "He personally named me Lord of Caberton."

"When?"

"About a week ago."

"Were you there?" Nicholas asked Rachel.

"Yes."

"And you expect me to believe you? Where did this happen?"

"I'm not sure we have the right to tell you," Jason said carefully.

Nicholas frowned. "What do you imposters want from me? If you came to kill me, there will be no more opportune moment to strike."

"We're not here to kill you," Rachel said.

"Good," Nicholas said, using his eyes to draw their attention to a strap he was holding. "One yank and I could pierce the two of you with a dozen arrows each."

Jason looked around the room, but could not see any bows ready to fire.

"They're concealed," Nicholas said. "I'm not bluffing. If you're not assassins, what are you?"

Jason decided to lay his cards on the table. "We're Beyonders. We were told you can help us find a word that might destroy Maldor."

Nicholas blanched. "How could you know about the Word? Who sent you?"

"Galloran," Rachel said. "More accurately Jugard, a man Galloran sent us to speak with."

Nicholas regarded them cautiously.

"You look a little like one of Galloran's men," Rachel said. "Brin the Gamester."

Nicholas glowered. "If you mean Brin of Rosbury, you had best be speaking the truth."

Jason now understood why Nicholas had appeared familiar. He did look like Brin.

"He never mentioned the name Rosbury," Rachel said. "He called himself Brin the Gamester."

"Brin was my youngest brother," Nicholas replied. "Did Galloran give you anything else?"

Jason showed the poniard to Nicholas, who examined the weapon, peering closely at the blossom that could eject the blade. "This appears authentic. It bears one of Galloran's seals, and it could certainly be the work of Brin."

Rachel pulled out her crystal sphere.

"Orantium?" Nicholas spluttered. "You could have shown me that first! It is almost better evidence than the ring. And you know about the Word . . . You say you are Beyonders?"

"We came to your world about two weeks ago," Jason said.

"Did Galloran bring you?" Nicholas inquired.

"No, but he knew the people who summoned us," Rachel said. "A woman, Erinda, and some musicians, the Giddy Nine."

"Already you pursue the Word?" Nicholas asked.

"The first place I went was the Repository of Learning," Jason said. "I learned the first syllable from *The Book of Salzared*."

"Have you discovered other syllables?" Nicholas asked.

"Two of the six," Rachel responded. "The first and the fourth. Can you help us?"

Nicholas sighed, glancing down at his harness. "Your words kindle memories of better days. Once I was Nicholas of Rosbury. Like my forefathers I served as chief engineer for the kingdom of Trensicourt. Now I am Nicholas Dangler, a maimed tinkerer hiding in the poorest district of a city my ancestors designed and constructed."

"Do you know any of the syllables?" Jason asked.

Nicholas closed his eyes, pain flashing across his features. "If Galloran lives, why has he neglected me? I am among the minority who have remained faithful! If Brin lives, how could he let us mourn him? We have lost so much!"

Jason felt torn—he would have expected Nicholas to react with joy at hearing that Brin and Galloran were alive. In Lyrian people's perspectives sometimes seemed stuck on the negative. So many of those he met seemed broken and hopeless.

"Galloran is blind," Rachel explained. "He was tormented by Maldor, and his mind suffered. He can't remember much about the Word, although he collected most of the syllables. Who knows what else he may have forgotten?"

"What of Brin?" Nicholas asked. "Is he well?"

"He seemed healthy," Rachel said. "He's helping watch over Galloran."

"You cannot tell me where they dwell?" Nicholas pressed.

"I don't think it's our secret to tell," Jason said. "Galloran has kept his identity a mystery. He goes by another name."

"I never envisioned him a free man in hiding," Nicholas murmured. "He was indomitable. I assumed Galloran was dead or in prison."

"He was in prison," Rachel said. "But not anymore."

"I do not know any of the actual syllables," Nicholas sighed. "But before I was ruined, Galloran confided some secrets to me about the Word. The third syllable resides here in Trensicourt, inscribed in the royal lorevault, above the entrance, fourth word from the left. Another lies on the island in the center of Whitelake. And I know that *The Book of Salzared* inside the Repository of Learning holds the first syllable."

"How do we get into the lorevault?" Jason asked.

Nicholas chuckled. "It's nearly impossible. Only two men are allowed inside the lorevault—the regent and the chancellor."

"Who are those guys?" Jason asked.

"Galloran was the last of the royal heirs to disappear," Nicholas said. "The regent, Dolan of Vernasett, rules in place of the king. For years the nobles have desired to formally crown Dolan, but the people still believe the royal line survives in hiding, and the nobles fear a revolt."

"Would the regent let us into the lorevault?" Rachel asked.

"Never," Nicholas spat. "Dolan would hunt you as ardently as Maldor if he knew of your quest. And the chancellor, a man called Copernum, is even more treacherous. Although officially Trensicourt remains a free kingdom, our regent, our chancellor, and virtually all of our nobility have quietly brokered deals with the emperor. They pay him tribute, and they obey his secret commands, which explains why Trensicourt remains untouched while battle rages in the east. Just you wait. After the great kingdom of Kadara falls, our aristocracy will hand Trensicourt over to Maldor without an ounce of blood spilled."

"Won't the people rebel?" Jason asked.

"Possibly," Nicholas conceded. "Which explains why Trensicourt is not already another of Maldor's fiefdoms. The nobles placate the populace by assuring them that our neutrality will shield us from conflict, that we have sufficient respect from the emperor to forever remain independent so long as we do not openly defy him."

"But you have your doubts," Rachel said.

"Maldor's ambition knows no limits," Nicholas assured her. "He plans wisely, fighting one battle at a time. He does not want Trensicourt involved as he conquers the remainder of the continent. Aside from the Seven Vales of the Amar Kabal, our kingdom boasts the best defenses in Lyrian. Taking Trensicourt by force would be an arduous task, even for the vast armies of the emperor. Should we elect to oppose him, we could raise a mighty host. Maldor wants to reserve Trensicourt for the end. Given his increasing hold on our ruling class, the mightiest kingdom of Lyrian may eventually prove the easiest to topple."

"All of this could change if we destroy Maldor with the Word," Jason said thoughtfully.

Nicholas fiddled with a buckle on his harness. "Galloran hoped to undermine our enemies with a single lethal stroke. I believe he shared secrets of the Word with me in the hope that I would follow in his footsteps if he failed. I tried. I knew that my first step would be to gain access to the lorevault. I challenged Copernum to a battle of wits, with the chancellorship in the balance. I lost. As punishment I was stripped of my title, Earl of Rosbury. Not long thereafter I was attacked, and I lost my legs, and with them any hope of adventuring."

"That's terrible!" Rachel exclaimed.

"All who remained loyal to Galloran were ousted from among the nobility," Nicholas recounted. "False accusations, ludicrous trials, and other political maneuvering concealed the injustice in the guise of legality. Many of the best men and women of Trensicourt were defamed, impoverished, or murdered, only to be replaced by the ambitious and unscrupulous. A handful of good people have managed to pretend enough loyalty to Dolan and Copernum to avoid destruction, at the cost of their honor."

"Have you sent others after the Word?" Rachel asked.

"My brother Roger embarked on the quest, opting to save the syllable inside the lorevault for last. He never returned. He must be dead or incarcerated. Brin followed Galloran on his early exploits and never returned. My sister, Hannah, could not endure the shame of our fall, and she married a lesser lordling who had risen to the position of count—a weak, scheming man. My two sons and one nephew perished while trying to incite a revolt against the present nobility. I live here with Kayla, the wife of my brother Roger, and her daughters Minna and Lisa. A few attendants have remained loyal to us from the early days."

"No offense," Rachel said, "but why have your enemies left you alive?"

"Not out of kindness," Nicholas laughed. "I know shameful secrets about many of our present nobility. I have taken measures to ensure they know that I know. They have been promised that upon my untimely demise those secrets will be made public. Aside from blackmail I keep up my defenses, and I stay out of the way in the Fleabed. I quietly provide architectural plans and various handy devices for members of the ruling class. They believe I have learned my place, which perhaps I have. Since I humbly remain the most talented engineer in the city, charging far less than my services merit, I have my uses."

"I'm so sorry," Jason said.

"It could be worse," Nicholas acknowledged. "Minna and Lisa are strapping girls, able to do much of the heavy work my designs require. I am successfully passing much of my knowledge to them. Kayla is a marvelous cook. I have no legs, but my harness suffices. I live in the Fleabed, but my residence is large and secure. My enemies rule over me, but they keep their distance. You may soon deserve my pity more than I deserve yours."

"I won't argue," Jason said.

Reaching up, Nicholas grabbed a couple of straps and pulled to shift his position in the harness. "Listen, son. Do you really think you have any chance for success? Getting the Word, I mean. Once Galloran failed, the rest of us should have quit. He was our best hope. Strong, smart, brave, inspiring, incorruptible; a peerless swordsman. How could others succeed where he had failed? Honestly, when I weigh all I lost, and how little was gained by that loss, if I could return to the days after Galloran fell, I would pretend to side with Dolan."

Jason frowned. The last thing he needed was fuel for his doubts. Looking into those grave, knowing eyes, it was hard not to waver.

"Galloran warned us that we have to see this through," Rachel said. "He warned us that Maldor knew we were after the Word, and would destroy us more swiftly if we departed from our task."

"He would know," Nicholas admitted. "And Galloran is right, to an extent. However, if you earn another syllable or two, you might garner an invitation to Harthenham. If you can survive until then, you can live out your days in luxury."

"Others have mentioned Harthenham," Jason said. "What is it?"

"The emperor's pleasure palace," Nicholas explained. "Only his staunchest enemies receive an invitation to the Eternal Feast. I have never been so honored. Those who accept live out their days in paradise, all cares forgotten. These days most who pretend to oppose Maldor are motivated by hope for an invitation. Few possess enough backbone to actually earn one."

"Was Galloran invited?" Rachel asked.

"Multiple times," Nicholas said. "Ever the idealist, he turned down the invitations. Want some practical guidance? If I were walking your path, my goal would not be to gain the Word. My intent would be to succeed enough to earn an invitation to Harthenham. After that your troubles could be over. Don't delude yourself. Maldor is a master manipulator. No matter how promising your prospects appear, he will not let you succeed. You can't imagine the resources at his disposal. Galloran failed years ago, and Maldor has only gained power since. If an invitation to the Eternal Feast ever arrives, take it. Deny it, and you will feel the full wrath of Maldor. Once the emperor truly wants you out of the way, your demise will soon follow."

"Thanks for the advice," Jason said, trying not to let it shake him. "Either way, for now we have to keep after the Word. What are our chances of breaking in to the lorevault?"

"Are you the greatest master thief Lyrian has ever seen?"

"No."

"Does some unknown magic from the Beyond allow you to walk through walls?"

"No."

"Then you have no chance," Nicholas said emphatically. "The lorevault was designed by my ancestors to be impervious. It has remained so for hundreds of years."

"Don't you know a weakness?" Rachel asked.

"On the contrary," Nicholas said. "I am simply more aware than anyone that the lorevault has no exploitable flaws."

"You challenged the chancellor to a battle of wits?" Jason asked.

"The office of chancellor is more vulnerable than the vault," Nicholas conceded. "But not by much. Since ancient times any nobleman of Trensicourt may challenge the chancellor to a battle of wits. The rule helps ensure that the cleverest nobleman will serve as chief advisor to the king."

"I'm Lord of Caberton," Jason said. "Would that qualify me?"

"Caberton lies in shambles," Nicholas chuckled. "But, yes, if your title were recognized as authentic, you would be qualified to challenge Copernum for the chancellorship. Be forewarned: He has been challenged thrice and never defeated. There is no end to his cunning."

"How does the contest work?" Rachel asked.

"The challenger poses three questions. After the chancellor answers each question, the challenger can attempt to supply a superior response. If any of the challenger's responses are judged superior, he becomes the new chancellor. If not, the challenger forfeits his title and property to the chancellor."

"So if you lose," Jason said, "you lose big."

"None know the consequences better than I do," Nicholas sighed. "Considering the risk, few have the boldness to issue a challenge for the chancellorship. The office is normally appointed by the king."

"This seems like our only way into the vault," Jason said. "At least in my case all I'd have to risk is a title nobody would want."

Nicholas grinned. "Nothing would delight me more than to see Copernum humbled. It will not be easy. First you must get Dolan to recognize your claim to Caberton. The ring is authentic, and it should serve as sufficient evidence, unless they bring forward false witnesses to label you a thief. The second trick will be actually defeating Copernum. Perhaps you know some unfathomable riddle from the Beyond?"

"I'll have to think about it," Jason said.

"I know some riddles," Rachel added.

"The question would have to be exquisite," Nicholas said. "Copernum has held his office so long for good reason. He is as keen as they come."

"Who judges the contest?" Rachel asked.

"Dolan," Nicholas said. "His word will be final. If there is room for doubt, he will side with Copernum. But if you clearly provide a superior answer, he will name you victor. Dolan knows that Copernum wields the real power in Trensicourt. I believe Dolan would gladly demote him if he could do so without blame."

"How do I establish my claim as Lord of Caberton?" Jason asked.

"You will need an audience with the regent." Nicholas sniffed and tugged absently at a strap. "You must not breathe a word about challenging for the chancellorship. Save that surprise for after your claim has been acknowledged. It would help if you found a sponsor." Nicholas bowed his head in thought.

"Could you sponsor him?" Rachel asked.

"My sponsorship would only harm his cause," Nicholas said. "In fact it should not be made public that the two of you came here for advice. If we were linked as conspirators, it would end badly for all of us. We must end this conversation soon, and you should not return."

"Does anyone know we're here?" Jason asked.

"Spies infest Trensicourt," Nicholas spat. "You must treat every person you meet as a potential traitor. Plenty of professional spies make a comfortable living in this town, not to mention the legions of casual busybodies eager to sell a secret as soon as they hear it."

"Do you think spies saw us come in here?" Rachel asked.

"Absolutely," Nicholas affirmed. "My alley is under constant observation. The watchers may not know your identities, but they know you are here. You will leave with crossbows. My models set the standard for all of Lyrian. The weapons may suffice as a legitimate reason for newcomers to Trensicourt to pay me a visit."

"Where should we go from here?" Jason asked.

"You want the legless ruin to lay out a strategy?" Nicholas chortled. His eyes grew thoughtful. "You are young, and you are strangers here. Perhaps I could help you avoid early missteps. My mistakes have taught me much. Be forewarned—politics in Trensicourt are ruthless. No amount of planning could insulate you against all the possible pitfalls."

"I get it," Jason said. "We're here. I have to try."

Nicholas wound a loose strap tightly around his hand. "Very well. How much money do you have?"

"This will cost?" Jason asked.

"You misunderstand," Nicholas said. "I mean to help you. The crossbows will be free, along with the advice."

"We have a gold pellet, a silver, and some change," Rachel said.

"Insufficient," Nicholas sniffed. "Money and connections mean everything in Trensicourt. One often leads to the other. Since you lack connections, you will need money. I will provide it."

"You're too kind," Jason said.

Nicholas snorted derisively. "I have much more money than I can use. So I will give you enough to make you dangerous to my enemies. Your risk will be tremendous; mine will be minimal. Not as generous as it may seem at first glance. Be on guard. Others will seek to use you likewise."

"Right," Jason said.

"You two should leave here separately," Nicholas advised. "You lack sufficient family resemblance for discerning eyes to accept you as relatives."

"But we really are—," Rachel began defensively.

"No need to explain," Nicholas interrupted. "I'm sure you have your reasons." He looked at Jason. "Keeping Rachel with you will needlessly endanger her and make your task to establish yourself more difficult. You will depart first. An agent of mine will hire a boy to guide you to the finest tailor and the best blacksmith in the city. Visiting other top-quality merchants will diminish the significance of your visit to me, and will allow you to outfit yourself properly. You are a good-looking boy. The right clothes will improve your credibility. Appear unattached—your bachelorhood could help soften hearts and perhaps open doors."

"What about me?" Rachel asked.

"I will hire a boy to escort you to a boarding house," Nicholas said. "Your story will be that you are awaiting your cousin, who is due to return from Rostenburg. Invent a name. He was away working as a mercenary."

"So I'll just sit and wait," Rachel said, offended.

"It will not take long for Jason to succeed or fail. You two would be wise to remain unconnected while in Trensicourt. Your enemies would gladly exploit your relationship as a weakness. If either of you is ever asked about the other, you met on the road on your way into town. When you discovered that you both meant to purchase items from me, you decided to journey together to my shop. That is all you know about each other."

"You say it won't take me long?" Jason asked.

"Your final stop after the shops will be the Upturned Goblet," Nicholas continued. "The proprietor is named Tedril. If he likes you, he could get you in front of the regent. The Upturned Goblet is the finest establishment in Trensicourt. The exorbitant prices allow only the rich and powerful to dine or sleep there. Unknown travelers rarely cross the threshold. Tedril will investigate you. If he believes you are legitimate, he will help you. If he smells a fraud, his bad opinion could ruin you."

"How do I smell right?" Jason asked.

"Tedril savors the smell of gold and silver," Nicholas chuckled. "Yet it will require more than riches to win his good opinion. Tell him you are descended from an old family who lost their holdings, and that you are looking to establish yourself as heir to Caberton. There are several such families, so don't get specific. Let him wonder. Show him the ring. Tell him Galloran gave it to you, but tell it with a wink. Tell him you're an old friend of Bartley of Wershon."

"Who?" Jason asked.

"A turncoat who neglected his family and sold his honor to preserve his place at court. A big, friendly fool, Bartley roars when sober and thunders when drunk. He rarely comes to town, but he spends like a sailor when he does. He has a soft spot for the downtrodden, so Tedril will believe the connection."

"Then what?" Jason asked.

"Rent a room. Let Tedril set the price, and don't bargain. I'll give you plenty. Then go gamble. Several nobles gamble at the Upturned Goblet. Be friendly. Lose lots of money. You will quickly find friends. Get one or two of your newfound friends to sponsor you at court. Hopefully, this will be enough to convince the regent to acknowledge your title."

"What about the competition?" Jason asked.

"Challenge the chancellor within a week after receiving your title," Nicholas said. "A novice attempting to navigate the politics of the upper class in Trensicourt will not survive for long."

"Do you know a question that might stump him?" Rachel asked.

"If I could stump him, I would not have lost my title. You must be able to prove the correctness of your answer. And it must not be some trivial trick, like asking how many fingers you are holding up behind your back. You'll need a question the other man could answer, and your superior response must be verifiable."

"Like a riddle," Jason said. "Or a fact. What if I asked him to name the first syllable of the Word that could destroy Maldor?"

Rocking in his harness, Nicholas let out a violent burst of laughter. "It would almost be worth it, to see the looks on their faces. None of them would know such a word existed. You would have no evidence. Nevertheless, in fear that the word might exist, the contest would end immediately, and you would disappear. Maldor would inevitably get involved. You, Rachel, me, Tedril—we'd all be slain. Along with many, if not all, of those who heard your words at court. While eliminating some of my old enemies, such an outburst would only hasten the downfall of Trensicourt."

"Then I probably shouldn't mention that I'm a Beyonder, either," Jason said.

"Not unless you fancy instantaneous imprisonment," Nicholas agreed. "You understand the parameters. My best efforts to topple Copernum failed, and the one time I advised another challenger, he failed as well. How you defeat Copernum is up to you."

"Can't I help him?" Rachel asked.

"If you have ideas, share them now," Nicholas said. "Jason should never contact me again, and you should avoid him as well until his business in Trensicourt is through."

"Remember any outstanding riddles?" Jason asked.

Rachel shook her head. "I don't know. The more you take away from me, the bigger I become."

"A hole," Nicholas said. "We have a similar riddle here."

Rachel scrunched her brow. "Twins stand at a fork in the road. One always tells the truth; the other always lies. One road leads to prosperity, the other to destruction. You can only ask one question to one of the twins. What question do you ask to find the right road?"

"I think I've heard this one," Jason said. "I can't remember the answer."

Nicholas stared down, lips moving without making a sound. Then he cleared his throat. "I ask either man which road his brother would tell me will lead to prosperity; then I take the opposite road."

"You know that one?" Rachel asked.

"No, I used reason," Nicholas said. "A riddle like this is not a bad idea, but Copernum is better at reasoning than I am. No matter what tactics you use, it will be difficult to flummox him."

"If I fail, all I lose is my title?" Jason asked.

Nicholas shrugged. "And your life, unless you hurry away from Trensicourt. For a newcomer who has defied Copernum, to remain in Trensicourt after failure would be fatal. He will want to make an example of you. Of course, after success your life will be almost equally endangered."

"And even if I beat him," Jason said, "Copernum only loses the office of chancellor."

"He'll maintain all other privileges and titles," Nicholas confirmed. "And after three months he will have the right to challenge you as you challenged him."

"I have more riddles," Rachel volunteered.

She rattled off several, and Nicholas answered all of them.

Jason could not have guessed the answer to most of them, and he began to lose faith that he could possibly succeed where Nicholas and others had failed.

When Rachel ran out of riddles, Jason cleared his throat. "Could I speak with Rachel in private for a moment?"

"By all means," Nicholas said. Tugging on a pair of straps, he glided away on his track to a far corner of the room.

Rachel leaned her head close to Jason. "What do you think?" she whispered.

"I think we'll never get another chance like this," Jason replied quietly. "With the money and advice from Nicholas I'll have a real chance of challenging Copernum."

"But can you beat him?"

"I'll never know unless I try. If I can get inside the lorevault, we'll have half the syllables. You gave me some good riddles. And I'll think hard between now and when I issue the challenge. Do you mind splitting up?"

"No. If all else fails, we'll meet up where Ferrin suggested, at the Stumbling Stag."

"Sounds like a plan."

CHAPTER 14

QUESTIONS AND ANSWERS

Not far down the broad avenue from the castle gates, the Upturned Goblet rose five stories tall, the massive stone structure receding from the street with each level to accommodate terraced balconies. Ornamental battlements and a trio of proud flagpoles crowned the building. A great paved hallway opened onto the street, enabling carriages to access a sheltered entrance.

With twilight fading, Jason entered and crossed a plush foyer to an ornate door on the far side. His new clothes felt too silky, but they fit him well. He tried to carry himself with confidence, as if certain he belonged here. A short man in a well-tailored outfit stood before a burly guard wearing a sword. "And who might you be, sir?" the short man inquired politely.

"I am Lord Jason of Caberton."

The man examined Jason suspiciously for a moment, eyes roving up and down. He seemed reluctantly satisfied.

The short man escorted Jason into an elegant common room, where richly dressed patrons dined on fine plates and drank from stemware. He led Jason to where a swarthy man with his hair slicked back stood conversing with an older couple seated before plates of half-eaten fish.

"Master Tedril, may I introduce Lord Jason of Caberton," the short man announced, interrupting the conversation.

"Lord Jason," greeted Tedril, making a much more obvious inspection of Jason's apparel than the short man had, "a pleasure to make your acquaintance." He nodded at the short man, who scurried away. Then Tedril turned to the dining couple. "If you will excuse me."

"By all means," the seated man said.

"This way." Tedril led Jason out of the common room and into a cozy office with a fruitwood desk and three wingback armchairs. Thick maroon carpeting covered the floor.

Tedril motioned for Jason to take a seat.

"I was unaware that anyone held the title of Caberton," Tedril said casually.

"I gained the title in the wilderness," Jason said, trying his best to sound sophisticated. The ring was on his finger, but to avoid seeming desperate or defensive, Jason made no motion to call attention to it.

"I see. How novel. A stranger to Trensicourt suddenly ranks among our nobility."

"My parents are not strangers to Trensicourt," Jason lied, his voice resolute.

Tedril held his eyes, weighing him. "The regent has recognized your claim?"

"Not yet."

"Perhaps I could be of service. How long do you intend to stay here?"

"A few days, at least," Jason said. "I would be happy to pay in advance."

"For a stranger without credit a two-hundred-drooma deposit would be appropriate."

Nicholas had schooled Jason in the currency. The gold pellets were worth a hundred drooma, the silver fifty. Two hundred drooma was a small fortune. Jason removed two gold pellets from his new money bag. The innkeeper accepted the payment, offering no sign that he was impressed.

"I've been traveling," Jason said. "It will be a relief to sleep in a bed."

"Have I met your parents?" Tedril asked.

"You would know their names. But we should not discuss them yet. They intend to join me here in time."

"I have fond memories of many exiles. You bear a resemblance to the former Baron of Leramy."

Jason shrugged. "I'm not supposed to comment."

Tedril smiled knowingly. "The public misunderstood the motives of the baron. Some called his actions treasonous. Others foresaw how he might be operating for the good of the kingdom. He simply acted too soon, before the monarchy had truly waned. How did you secure the title Lord of Caberton?"

"Galloran, of course," Jason said lightly. "He gave the title to my father in prison. My father kept it a secret. With his health failing, he recently passed the title to me. Unlike him I intend to claim my privileges."

"A fascinating story," Tedril said indulgently. "How did you come to hear of the Upturned Goblet?"

"The Viscount Bartley of Wershon recommends you."

Tedril brightened. "You are a friend of the viscount's?"

"I have met him."

"How fortunate," Tedril enthused. "Are you aware he is currently abiding with us?"

"I was not," Jason said, hoping his smile looked less brittle than it felt.

Tedril grinned as if certain this was all part of some prearranged strategy. "Come with me."

As Jason followed Tedril out of the room, he groaned inwardly. The innkeeper had been accepting his story. Why had he mentioned Bartley? The fake reference had been part of the plan, but with the conversation going well, it had probably become unnecessary. Jason tried to stay calm. His only hope was to try to bluff his way through this.

They walked across the dining room and down a wood-paneled hallway, then mounted carpeted stairs to a room with a small bar in the corner and a fire blazing inside a green marble fireplace. Several men stood around a long felt table casting dice. A big man whose wavy red hair fell to his shoulders slapped his thigh and let out a booming laugh. A few of the other men groaned.

"Viscount Wershon," Tedril said.

The red-haired man turned, smiling.

"You remember Lord Jason of Caberton."

"Caberton, you say?" Bartley repeated boisterously, staring blankly at Jason.

Jason felt like a fool. So far only Bartley was facing him—the other men remained occupied with the gaming table. His little gamble to establish credibility was about to destroy it. Holding Bartley's gaze, Jason winked.

"Yes, Jason, my friend, how have you been?"

Jason could breathe again. "Quite well."

Bartley strode over and put an arm around his shoulders. "Walk with me, my friend, so we can reminisce. Excuse us."

Jason did not look back at Tedril.

Bartley guided Jason to a neighboring room.

"So who in the blazes are you?" Bartley asked in a husky whisper. His breath reeked of spicy sausages.

"My family was exiled years ago. I'm here to help us regain some respect. I really am Lord of Caberton." Jason held up the ring.

Bartley squinted. "So it would seem."

"I'm hoping the regent will confirm me Lord of Rubble."

Bartley laughed explosively and slapped Jason on the back hard enough to knock him off balance. "Caberton is a start. You're dressed well. Your family had reserves?"

"I have money."

"You enjoy gaming?"

"I've never been a careful person."

"You play Bones?"

"I don't know the game."

Bartley paused. "But you have money?"

"Yes."

Bartley threw an arm around him. "This is a dream! A young, well-funded novice! I wish we were playing Knuckles! Tomorrow, perhaps. Come, join us." Bartley released the embrace but gripped Jason's elbow, pausing, his eyes suddenly sober. "But first you must tell me how you acquired the ring. It's authentic."

"My father spent time in prison with Galloran."

"No, really, the truth."

"My father bought it," Jason confided quietly.

"Bought it?" Bartley asked, his grip tightening.

"Right. I don't know all of the details. The merchant claimed it truly came from a prisoner who spent time with Galloran."

Bartley released his elbow. "Galloran," he whispered, looking haunted. "Did any knowledge come with the ring?"

"I have no reason to think Galloran survived," Jason said, since it seemed to be what Bartley needed to hear. "I plan to say my father was the prisoner who received the title and the ring. The real story could weaken my claim."

"You're too free with your information," Bartley said, recovering.

"My parents thought I could count on you," Jason said. "I decided to roll the dice."

Bartley harrumphed. "Right, the dice. Off we go." Bartley began walking, motioning for Jason to follow. "Bones can feel complicated at first. Two shooters. One shoots for the house, one for himself. Players can bet in several ways. Stay close to me; you'll catch on. You have bronze?"

"Gold and silver, mostly."

Bartley grinned. "I can make change for you."

Jason joined the men around the table. Bartley introduced him as Lord of Caberton. The house shooter wore a black vest with gold embroidery. He rolled a pair of ten-sided dice, one black and one white. The other man, a simpering gentleman wearing white gloves, threw a similar pair of dice, except one was blue and the other yellow.

Jason stuck to bets with decent odds. He won a bit, started betting more boldly, then lost a lot, falling more than a hundred drooma below even. After a risky bet paid off amid laughter and applause, he was back up two hundred and fifty.

The men laughed and shouted as money was won and lost. Sometime late in the evening Tedril reappeared. He seemed utterly won over. He gave Jason a key and told him a servant would see him to his room once he was ready. Jason could hardly hear the innkeeper over the commotion. Tedril promised to help acquaint him with the city and schedule an audience with the regent. A man in a fancy coat waved Tedril away, draping an arm about Jason's shoulders in mindless camaraderie.

Jason's winnings climbed to nearly three hundred before plummeting. He quit when he was fifty drooma above even, and left with Bartley.

"You fared well tonight," Bartley blustered. His face was flushed, almost matching his hair. "You won and lost more than some men ever see. As did I. But we both came out ahead of the house, and that is cause for celebration."

"Thanks for introducing me to the others."

"I'll vouch for you at court as well. The last twenty years have been hard on many families. Everyone deserves a second chance. Tell me, who are your parents?"

"They instructed me to confirm nothing to anyone, even you."

Bartley grunted. "Probably wise. You ever play Knuckles?"

"No."

Bartley grinned. "The finest card game ever devised! We'll see whether you can still afford my friendship after tomorrow. Ha! I'm jesting. We'll set reasonable limits. Good night, Lord Jason." He shambled off down a hall.

Jason pulled out his key and stopped a servant. "Could you show me to my room?"

"By all means, Lord Caberton."

At his door Jason tipped the man five drooma, and the servant regarded him in grateful awe. Once again Jason surmised that people in Lyrian must not tip very well.

The spacious room was nicely furnished. A set of doors opened onto a veranda with a wicker table and chairs. Jason crossed to a full-length mirror and examined himself. Days of travel had melted some fat from his frame, leaving his face leaner and more sharply defined. His new attire did look princely, although he imagined his friends from the baseball team would beat him up if they ever saw him dressed this way.

Sitting at his desk, Jason examined the contents of his knapsack. His money bag contained nine gold drooma and twelve silver, along with many new bronze pellets after gambling. More important than money, he had won acceptance at the Upturned Goblet. But how would he find a question to defeat a man such as Copernum?

Closing his eyes, Jason tried to imagine what might baffle the chancellor. Judging from the description Nicholas had given, it would be nearly impossible. Rachel knew lots of riddles, but Jason doubted that would be the best road. He needed trivial details, things a smart man might still miss. But what?

He knew some good trivia from biology class. He knew that the tip of the sternum was called the xiphoid process. He knew that flexing the foot upward was dorsiflexion, and downward was plantar flexion. He knew the cheekbone was called the zygomatic arch.

But who knew if anatomy had been classified the same way here in Lyrian? Who knew if anatomical details had been classified at all? And if they had, a learned man like Chancellor Copernum would probably know them.

He could think of some tough questions. Does a tree make a sound when it falls if nobody is around? How can you prove you exist? What is the meaning of life? The problem was, he not only had to stump Copernum—he had to provide a better answer.

Unsure how to force inspiration, Jason brooded miserably. Despite the late hour his frenzied mind did not feel sleepy.

Four days later Jason sat anxiously in the posh compartment of a sleek black carriage alongside the Viscount Bartley of Wershon, on his way to an audience with the regent. Velvet curtains screened the city from view. He wore an embroidered doublet, breeches that ballooned around his thighs, crimson stockings, and simple black shoes as soft as slippers. In his lap rested an overgrown beret with a crimson plume. He might have suspected the outfit was a joke had Bartley not worn similar attire.

A tailor had come to his room two days ago to measure him for the costume, then delivered the outfit the following morning. Despite the gaudy appearance, his clothes felt surprisingly comfortable.

Over the past few days Jason had lost nearly four hundred drooma gambling, most of it playing Knuckles, much of it to Bartley. He had spent another couple hundred on food and additional clothing.

Jason had used all of his free time to consider riddles and questions. Some of the riddles Jason remembered were silly jokes from his childhood. What's easy to catch but hard to throw? A cold. Why did the baby cross the road? It was stapled to the chicken. What do you get when you cross a cactus and a porcupine? Sore hands.

He felt most hopeful about some odd bits of trivia he had recalled, but still none of his ideas seemed like a reliable bet. He wished he had an Internet connection to his world!

The ride from the Upturned Goblet to the castle was brief. Before long the carriage clattered through the gates, and a footman helped them down.

"You will enter through the audience gate," Bartley said. "I will await you inside. See you soon."

Jason followed a liveried servant into the castle. They passed down a vaulted hallway. Ornate pilasters adorned the walls at regular intervals. Gold scrollwork embellished the ceiling. Enormous urns, intricately painted, dwarfed the rigid guards positioned along the immense corridor.

Jason and his liveried escort came to a heavy pair of bronze doors flanked by guards in ostentatious uniforms, complete with bandoleers, medals, epaulets, and ridiculously tall hats. The guards kept their gazes fixed down the hall, blinking infrequently, and never looked at Jason.

Another man waited outside the door. He wore a pointed hat and a long silk cape. A voice from behind the doors cried out, "Yosef, son of Pontiv." The doors swung outward. The pointy-hat guy entered, and the doors closed.

The servant stood silently beside Jason. The guards stared solemnly at the empty hall. Jason tried to calm himself. Obviously, the grandeur of the hall was meant to intimidate visitors. He tried not to stress. The best thing he could do if he wanted his claim recognized was to stay calm and look like he belonged.

"The purported Lord Jason of Caberton," echoed a voice from inside the chamber. The bronze doors swung outward. A long blue carpet edged in silver led across the polished stone floor toward the dais, where the regent sat upon a great ivory chair. Crowds of elegantly arrayed courtiers clustered in groups off to either side. A portly old fellow with plump, healthy features, the regent looked much more like a real king than Galloran. A bejeweled circlet rested on his head. Rings glittered on his fingers. His fine raiment was a rich purple trimmed in gold.

Jason advanced along the carpet to where it stopped at a raised, circular piece of marble directly before the throne. Jason stood upon the pedestal. Bartley had informed him it was called the Petitioner's Wheel. It gave an individual on the floor of the throne room the right to address the regent. Only those upon the dais shared the right to address Dolan directly. Currently two men stood upon the dais beside the regent, one dressed as a soldier, the other wearing long blue robes and an oversized tricornered hat, with a silver mantle wrapped about his narrow shoulders.

Standing upon the Petitioner's Wheel, Jason looked up silently at the regent. Bartley had cautioned him to wait for Dolan to speak first.

"Greetings, young man," Dolan said. "You claim the title of Caberton?"

"I do, sire." According to Bartley, "sire" and "Your Highness" were the forms of address etiquette demanded for the occasion. "Your Majesty" was reserved for the king.

"Hold forth your right hand."

Jason complied.

"Sound the tone."

A hollow metal tube, like a giant chime, hung from a chain off to one side of the throne. The man dressed like a soldier struck the long tube with a hammer, producing a deep, penetrating tone. Jason could feel his teeth vibrating. The ring on his finger began to glow, as did one of the regent's rings. Glancing around the room, Jason observed many other rings glowing, including a ring upon Bartley's hand.

The tone dwindled, and the light faded from the rings.

"Who bequeathed this title to you?" the regent asked.

"My father, who received the title from Galloran."

Courtiers leaned together, whispering soundlessly.

"While he lived," the regent said, "Galloran bestowed many titles. Though he was never king himself, with his enfeebled father, the honored King Dromidus, trapped in a cataleptic stupor, it became his right to manage the affairs of the kingdom. Yet I do not recall him bequeathing the title of Caberton, once that line failed."

"It happened twelve years ago. Galloran granted the title to my father in prison, who passed it to me."

The regent nodded. "Twelve years ago Galloran adventured abroad. Since he never returned, he could well have granted a title in the field without many knowing it. You do in fact wear the signet ring of Caberton, which Galloran had in his possession. Who was your father?"

"I do not wish to mention him," Jason said. "He was in prison, an enemy to the emperor, and I have chosen to distance myself from him."

"Even though he passed the title to you?" the man in the tri-cornered hat spoke up.

"He passed me the title to a heap of stones for three sacks of flour," Jason said, using a story Bartley had helped him prepare. "He was not man enough to make something of the opportunity. I will be. I intend to found a new line and to serve Trensicourt well."

"Will any man vouch for young Jason?" the regent asked.

Bartley raised a hand. Two others, both of whom Jason recognized from playing Bones and Knuckles, also raised their hands.

"Very well," the regent said. "Jason, do you solemnly swear fealty to the Crown of Trensicourt and to all agents of the Crown?"

"I do."

"In times of war and peace, through hours of need and years of prosperity, will you defend Trensicourt in word, thought, and deed for as long as you live?"

"I will."

"Your title is recognized, Lord Jason of Caberton. As of this moment you are free to stand in court when visiting Trensicourt. I fear your holdings are in considerable disrepair . . ."

At this point a titter ran through the assemblage.

". . . but the few artifacts in my treasury pertaining to Caberton shall be restored to you. And land is land. Make it blossom. Have you any other inquiry?"

Something small pelted Jason in the back of his head. Glancing over his shoulder, he saw a pretty young woman in an attractive dress trying to mouth something at him. It was Rachel, her short hair hidden under a fancy, flat-topped hat. Stunned to see her, he tried to read her lips. *Now*, she kept repeating silently, interspersed with a few other less decipherable words. Her imploring eyes glanced assertively at the dais.

"Has something else captured your attention?" the regent asked politely.

The crowd snickered.

Jason faced forward. "I beg your pardon, Your Highness. I have one other request. I would like to challenge Chancellor Copernum for the chancellorship."

The room exploded with reactions, a clamor of gasps and exclamations. The regent looked thunderstruck. Betraying no surprise, the thin man in the tricornered hat measured Jason with calculating eyes.

"Come to order," the soldier on the dais proclaimed. "We will have order, or I shall clear the chamber."

Jason felt dizzy. He hoped he had understood Rachel correctly. How had she gotten here?

The regent spoke as the courtiers quieted.

"Such is your right, as a lord of the realm. When do you propose to hold this contest?"

"As soon as possible," Jason said.

The regent turned to the brooding man in the tricornered hat. "What say you, Chancellor? Have you any objection to pursuing this challenge in summary fashion?"

Copernum narrowed his eyes. "I have no objection to annexing further holdings, however meager, to my own."

The regent nodded. "Very well. After a twenty-minute recess Lord Jason of Caberton shall compete with Chancellor Copernum for the chancellorship. You may step down, Lord Jason."

Jason stepped off the wheel. He watched Copernum, who had turned and was retreating through a door at one side of the dais. The slightly stooped man had a weak chin and a long, narrow nose, giving him an aerodynamic profile.

"Well," Bartley growled, slapping Jason on the back as he came up from behind. "Turns out I cannot read you as well as our card games have led me to suppose. You are full of surprises! Whether you win or not, you have earned a place in history for sheer audacity!" He shook his head. "Challenging for the chancellorship seconds after the regent recognizes your title—an unprecedented move."

"You have your questions ready?" asked another man. It was the fellow with the fancy coat from the Bones game. He had been one of the men who vouched for Jason along with Bartley.

"I think so," Jason said. "Unless you have any brilliant questions to share."

"No offense," Bartley grumbled, "but we are going to keep our distance. No man in Trensicourt can afford to make an enemy of Copernum."

"How long has it been since somebody challenged him?" Jason asked.

"Ten years," Bartley said. "That was when he stripped rank and title from the Earl of Geer."

"Give us a preview," the other man urged. "What do you mean to throw at him?"

"You'll see," Jason said, still not certain himself. "Do you have any advice? What are typical questions?"

Bartley shrugged. "Events from history. Strategies. Riddles. It depends. Copernum has betrayed no weakness. He knows history as if he lived it. He is a master strategist. And he solves riddles like he composed them. We should leave you to your thoughts."

Rachel approached as the other men walked away. "How are you?" she asked.

"Confused," Jason said. "What are you doing here?"

"Long story," she replied. "We have to watch what we say. There's no safe place to talk."

"Did you come up with any good questions?" he asked.

She moved closer and spoke more softly, her hand over her mouth. "Yes, actually. A great question. Which is why I went to see our dangling friend. He agreed that the question could help us. He had been doing some investigating through his own spies, and he discovered that Copernum already had his eye on the three of us, especially you. One of your gambling friends is one of the chancellor's top spies. He knows we're connected, and he might even know something about our quest."

"Great," Jason said. "What do we do?"

"You did it," Rachel said. "You needed to challenge him without waiting. It will be harder for him to destroy us if you beat him. And if you lose, we just do what we would have done anyhow. Escape Trensicourt immediately." She handed him an envelope.

"What's this?" Jason asked.

"Open it when the contest starts," she said. "It has some questions."

"Why wait?" Jason wondered, examining the envelope.

"Just in case," Rachel said. "According to our friend lots of people are watching you with spyglasses right now, reading your lips, observing your actions, trying to pick up clues."

"Gotcha. How'd you get in here?"

"Our dangling friend called in some favors," Rachel said. "We've been talking for too long. I have to go."

"You're not going to watch?"

"No. Trust me. It's better for both of us." She turned and vanished hurriedly into the crowd.

Nobody else drew near Jason, but he got plenty of elusive glances. He stood not far from the Petitioner's Wheel, tapping the envelope against his palm, wondering what questions it might contain. How had he gotten into this mess?

Over the next several minutes people poured into the throne room, claiming all of the available floor space except immediately around Jason. The galleries were mobbed, becoming a sea of expectant faces. The dais also became crowded. Jason figured he would be just as eager to witness an event like this if someone else had been willing to take the risk.

After what had to be much more than twenty minutes, the regent returned and took his seat. Copernum stood immediately beside Dolan, hands clasped behind his back, his expression proud and stern. As an attendant ushered Jason back onto the wheel, the room grew shockingly silent.

"You are certain you wish to pursue this challenge at this time?" the regent asked, staring at Jason, his demeanor graver than earlier.

"I am, sire."

"Very well. Chancellor Copernum has waived his right to postpone the contest. I shall judge the event. You, Lord Jason, shall pose three questions. If you can supply a better answer than Chancellor Copernum to any one of the questions, you will become the new chancellor. Chancellor Copernum would retain his titles and holdings, remaining the Marquess of Jansington, the Earl of Geer, and so forth. Copernum would become eligible to challenge you for the chancellorship after the space of three months.

"Should you lose, Lord Jason, the title of Caberton will pass to Chancellor Copernum, along with all holdings and privileges pertaining to the title. Are the conditions understood?"

"Yes, sire," Jason said, his mouth dry.

Copernum nodded.

The regent looked over at Copernum. "Have you anything to say before the contest ensues?"

"What education have you received?" Copernum asked Jason.

Jason looked around the room, unsure how to respond. "I'm almost in high school."

People in the room shifted and murmured. Copernum glared.

"Can you authenticate this claim?" Copernum asked. "I am one of only eight men living to have graduated from the High School at Elboreth, and I am well acquainted with each of them. I know of no prospective candidates."

"I never said the High School at Elboreth."

"That is the only recognized High School."

"I'll go to a different one, called Roosevelt High School. It's far away. I've traveled a lot."

"So it would seem. Your accent has a peculiar ring. English truly suits you." Copernum stared knowingly. Jason kept silent. "Enough banter. Good luck to you, lordling."

"And to you," Jason replied.

"Let the contest begin," the regent announced. "Chancellor Copernum has fifteen minutes to respond to each question. Should he wish to challenge the worthiness of a particular question, I will have the final word. A disqualified question still counts as one of the three. Copernum retains the right to pose clarifying questions, according to my discretion. I reserve final say as to who has supplied the superior answer to each question, should any controversy arise. Lord Jason, proceed with the first inquiry."

Jason swallowed. He wished he had a cup of water. He wondered if he should ask for one. No. Everybody was staring at him expectantly. Under the scrutiny of so many spectators he felt extraordinarily self-conscious as he tore open the envelope.

"I wrote these down to help me phrase them correctly," Jason said nervously, scanning the words as quickly as he could.

The assemblage chuckled in sympathy.

Question one is from our friend in Trensicourt. He said Copernum is ashamed of his father, so although he can answer this, it will provoke him and might put him off balance. Ask him the full name of his father.

"Chancellor Copernum, what is the full name of your father?"

Copernum's nostrils flared, his lip twitching toward a sneer.

"Is that the full question?" the regent asked.

"Yes, sire."

The regent signaled to a man, who overturned a large hourglass.

"Come now, lordling," Copernum condescended. "Tell me you are merely jesting, that you do not insult the renown of Roosevelt High School with inane questions such as this. Will the following question investigate my hat size? The answer is no mystery. Bridonus Keplin Dunscrip Garonicum the Ninth."

The regent looked to Jason.

"Wait, the loremaster?" Jason asked. "At the Repository of Learning?"

Copernum's gaze became predatory. For an instant hate flickered in his eyes. Then his expression relaxed. "Perhaps. His name is as I stated."

"Any rebuttal?" the regent asked.

"I have nothing to add," Jason stated.

"Copernum takes the first question," the regent declared.

The assemblage applauded.

"Apparently, you do not fully comprehend the situation into which you have ensnarled yourself," Copernum said. "Because of your youth, and your newness to Trensicourt, I extend the opportunity to withdraw. I am under no demands to extend such a courtesy, but you may do so if you wish. What say you?"

Jason stood frozen. After the message from Rachel he worried that if he stepped down, Copernum would arrest him or something. He had to see this through.

"That was my remedial question," Jason said.

The crowd laughed. Even the regent had to place his hand over his mouth before ordering the room to silence.

"Your second question," the regent prompted.

Jason glanced down at the note from Rachel.

Question two is the awesome one I came up with. Ask Copernum about the words above the inside of the lorevault. He should have no idea this is connected to the Word, and no reason to withhold an honest answer.

Grinning, Jason cleared his throat. "Inside the lorevault there is an inscription above the door. From left to right what is written there?"

"Is that the complete question?" the regent asked.

"Yes."

The regent waved a hand, and a second hourglass was overturned.

Chancellor Copernum fixed Jason with a grim stare. All condescension had departed. He seemed both suspicious and wary. The searching gaze continued for a long moment. Jason tried to keep his expression neutral.

"This is a peculiar inquiry, lordling," the chancellor finally said. "I will grant you that much. Are you suggesting you have been inside the lorevault?"

Sudden panic gripped Jason. If Copernum suspected Jason could not answer the question himself, he might refrain from responding, or give a false answer.

"My father disgraced us, but I come from an ancient family," Jason said simply.

Speculative murmurs rippled through the room. Scowling thoughtfully, Copernum turned to the regent. "Should I respond to this question in private?"

"I see no harm in responding here. Those words are not specifically secret."

"Very well," Copernum said. "The words are 'Elum Bek Nori Fex Fera Sut Copis Hostrum.'"

"How did you pronounce the fourth word?" Jason asked.

"Fex."

"And the seventh?"

"Copis," Copernum said impatiently.

Fex, Jason thought. *Fex. Fex. Fex.*

"Lord Jason?" the regent asked.

"I have nothing to add," Jason said, mind whirling.

<u> A </u> <u>   </u> <u>FEX</u> <u>EN</u> <u>   </u> <u>   </u>

"The second question also goes to Chancellor Copernum," the regent proclaimed.

Applause followed. Copernum smiled smugly.

"Enjoy your moment of notoriety, lordling," Copernum said. "Unless your third question is considerably less sophomoric than the first two, this will be the final time you stand inside this castle."

"Your final question, Lord Jason," the regent said.

Jason felt a compulsion to ask, *How much wood would a woodchuck chuck if a woodchuck could chuck wood?* He resisted and looked down at his paper.

Question three is your chance to use the best of what you prepared. Hopefully, question two made winning less urgent!

Jason sucked in his breath through his teeth. After reading the first two questions he had not expected to have to supply one of his own. His mind raced. Probably the best question he had come up with was an odd piece of trivia he had discussed one day with a kid named Steve Vaughn in his English class. The six letters in Steve's last name had inspired the conversation.

"What is the longest one-syllable word you can think of?" Jason asked Copernum.

"Is that the entire question?" the regent confirmed.

"It is."

A third hourglass was overturned.

"Point of clarification," Copernum said, brow creased. "Are you asking me to name the monosyllabic word containing the most letters?"

"I'll allow the inquiry," the regent said.

"I am," said Jason.

The chancellor stroked his chin, squinting up at the ceiling, as if lost in profound calculations. He folded and unfolded his arms. He rubbed his brow.

Jason crossed his toes for luck. It appeared the chancellor had never considered this question, which meant he had a chance. Ever since the conversation with Steve, Jason had noticed whenever he came across a long one-syllable word. The word he had in mind, if not the longest, was pretty close.

The chancellor stared darkly at the floor. Then he looked up, leering.

"I have your answer. How dare you pose such an absurd riddle? The longest monosyllabic word I can *think* of is *thoughts*. Eight letters."

All eyes shifted to Jason. He straightened. "Apparently, Chancellor, one-syllable words are not one of your *strengths*. Nine letters."

Copernum paled. He looked to the regent. "But . . . but he said the longest word *I* could think of. At the time the longest word *I* could think of was 'thoughts.' And the question functions like a riddle—one thinks thoughts."

Dolan shook his head. "You clarified that he was asking for the monosyllabic word with the most letters. There can be no debate. Lord Jason of Caberton has supplied the superior answer. Effective immediately he is the new chancellor."

The crowd roared. Jason smiled in shock, holding back tears of relief. Had he actually won? Was that possible?

The regent arose and retrieved the silver mantle from Copernum's shoulders and a ring from his right hand. The room only half quieted for his remarks. "Thank you, honored Copernum, Marquess of Jansington. Our kingdom will always be grateful for your years of venerable service. You are hereby honorably relieved of the office of chancellor." Copernum stood rigid with stunned disbelief. The throng applauded. There were a few catcalls.

"Ascend the royal dais, Lord Jason," the regent invited. Jason complied.

The regent spoke in a loud voice as he draped the mantle around Jason's shoulders and presented him with the ring. "Lord Jason of Caberton, you are hereby entrusted with the office of chancellor, making you guardian of the realm and chief advisor to the regent and acting sovereign, Dolan, Duke of Vernasett."

The crowd cheered enthusiastically.

Copernum stepped forward to clasp Jason's hand. "Congratulations, lordling," the former chancellor breathed, smiling kindly. "You will be dead by sunrise."

Before Jason could even react, the regent took Jason's hand and raised it as high as he could. "I call for a feast to welcome our brash new chancellor, to be held at the end of the coming week in my banquet hall." He turned to Jason, speaking for his ears only. "Well done, young man. You demonstrated great poise. We shall meet in private later this afternoon. I look forward to exchanging ideas with you."

Jason turned and looked for Copernum. The marquess had already departed.

CHAPTER 15

CHANCELLOR

That evening Jason sat alone on a black horsehair love seat, elbows on his knees, chin propped on his hands. He got up and went out to the blue-tiled balcony. Through the dimming twilight he surveyed the city of Trensicourt spread out beneath him, then let his gaze drift to the shadowed farmland below the plateau. Half-seen forms of bats or small birds wheeled and darted in the air below, flickering into view most clearly as they streaked past illuminated windows.

Copernum had vacated his quarters hours after losing the contest, taking his staff and his personal items but leaving most of the furniture. The apartments of the chancellor occupied the upper three floors of one of the castle's largest towers. The belongings Jason had left in the Upturned Goblet had already been transported to his new bedroom atop the tower.

Jason leaned against the stone balustrade, shivering in response to the chill breeze. Two levels below, in the rooms that now served as his offices, a page, a maid, a cook, a scribe, and two guards all awaited his orders. A bodyguard was stationed outside his bedroom door. None of them had served Copernum, but Jason had no idea how loyal they would prove. They all had been assigned to him by some administrator working under orders from the regent.

Jason studied the diverse buildings, the watch fires along the city wall, and the cultivated land beyond the wall atop the plateau. How could he be second in command of this sprawling kingdom? A few weeks ago his biggest worries had been getting decent grades and perfecting his curveball. He never would have imagined himself achieving anything like this.

Abandoning the view, Jason trudged to his bed, a sumptuous monstrosity that could easily sleep six. A pile of embers cast a warm red glow from the fireplace. He ran both hands through his hair. He would die tonight, if Copernum kept his promise. The threat could have been an idle exaggeration meant only to agitate him, but Copernum had sounded eerily certain.

Despite the soaring altitude of his accommodations, despite strong walls and solid doors, despite the multiple guards keeping watch, Jason had never felt more vulnerable. Up until last night Copernum had lived in these quarters and slept in this room. He could provide assassins with keys and a thorough description of how best to gain access.

To imitate a slumbering form, Jason arranged pillows under the fancy coverlet fashioned from soft rabbit pelts. The deep mattress was generously stuffed with down. No bed had ever beckoned more deliciously, but he crouched down and slithered underneath, bringing a pillow and a pair of blankets. The bed stood high enough that he had several inches of extra space above him as he lay on his back, one blanket beneath him, the other covering him. A fabric skirt shielded the space beneath the bed from view.

Jason lay staring up at the underside of the bed, his poniard clutched in one hand. He had never felt so alone. He missed Rachel. Could she be irritating at times? Sure. But she was also smart, and fun, and he knew he could trust her. Seeing her in the throne room had reminded him how much he had grown to rely on her. She had become a real friend. He wished she could have remained with him today.

Earlier that day, after the contest, the regent and his retinue had departed, leaving Jason to be tersely congratulated by Bartley, who notably kept his distance thereafter. The gambling acquaintance in the fancy coat had escorted Jason around the throne room, introducing him to a series of individuals who congratulated him with varying degrees of warmth. From most he got the impression that they did not wish to be seen acting too welcoming. He met counts and countesses, lords and ladies, scholars, poets, musicians, and artists. Names and titles all jumbled together.

Later, during a brief meeting with the regent, Jason had related the threat made by Copernum. Dolan had told him to be careful, and had explained that such threats were a burden of all men who held high offices. Jason had also conveyed the threat to Norval, his bodyguard, a solid man with a thick mustache, who had promised to remain vigilant at his door all night.

Jason had watched for an opportunity to slip away from the castle, but he had been surrounded by attendants all day, faking his way through meetings until he was delivered to his quarters in the evening. While dwelling in a tall tower held certain protections, it felt as inescapable as a prison.

Under the bed Jason bit his lip softly. He had hoped for communication from Nicholas or Rachel, but none had arrived. So now he had to survive the night. Alone. Hopefully, the dark hours would pass quietly. He promised himself he would find a way to escape his new job in the morning.

His thoughts turned to home. What were his parents doing right now? Had they figured out how to care for Shadow? He expected his dog missed him as much as anyone. What was Matt doing right now? Or Tim? Jason wondered if they had grown used to not having him around. He didn't feel like his whole self without them. He wished he could text them or call them up. What if he died tonight? How long would it take everyone to forget him?

The blankets began to feel very relaxing. It had been a long day, full of stress and confusion. He yawned, and shook his head to clear it. Soon he was slowly blinking; then he experimented with closing his eyes temporarily, just to rest them briefly. Sleep overtook him swiftly.

He awoke in the dark, certain he had heard a noise, feeling momentarily disoriented. His knife remained in his hand. He almost sat up before he remembered he was under the bed. Now that he was conscious and alert, Jason heard nothing. By the faintness of the glow against the material of the skirt he could tell that the embers had burned low. He waited, senses straining. All remained silent. Perhaps he had imagined the sound.

Breathing gently, he edged over until his face was beside the skirt at the foot of the bed. Feeling somewhat silly, he slid his knife from its sheath and with the tip of the blade raised the skirt just enough to peer out with one eye. By the feeble glow of the embers Jason saw the legs of a person stealthily advancing toward the bed. From the build it appeared to be a man. Jason's chest clenched in fear.

The furtive figure wore moccasins and made no sound as he moved. How had he gotten in? Jason considered calling for Norval. But this very well might be Norval! Or someone Norval had quietly admitted.

The intruder was about to pass out of view as he approached the side of the bed. Jason lowered the skirt and carefully scooted to the side the intruder was approaching, trying to breathe soundlessly. Again he raised the skirt with the blade. One of the intruder's feet was inches away. Jason thought of his uncle Kevin, who had hobbled around in casts and braces for months after snapping his Achilles tendon while playing tennis. Staring at the unprotected foot, Jason realized he could probably sever the Achilles tendon before the intruder knew what hit him. The moccasin did not rise above the ankle, and the pants were thin and close-fitting.

Jason heard the covers being thrown back, followed by a sharp intake of breath. The poor angle prevented him from putting all of his strength into the motion, but Jason slashed the back of the leg about an inch above the ankle. The blade of the poniard proved keen, slicing easily through the material of the pants and deeply into the flesh.

The figure sprang away using his good leg, then collapsed to the floor, clutching the injury, emitting an agonized growl.

"Help! Intruder!" Jason called, rolling out from under the bed on the side opposite the wounded assassin.

"Intruder!" Norval cried, relaying the alarm as he burst through the door, short sword in one hand, crossbow in the other.

Jason watched from his crouched position as a thrown knife buried itself in Norval's abdomen. The bodyguard staggered to one side, firing an aimless quarrel into the floor. Jason rose, his thumb on the trigger that would launch the poniard blade, just in time to see the dark figure scramble into the fireplace, scattering embers as he passed. Jason lunged to the large fireplace. Peering inside, he discovered that the flue extended both upward and downward. For a moment he could faintly hear the assassin fleeing down the flue somewhere below.

Jason backed out of the fireplace as four guards rushed into the room, weapons ready, a couple bearing torches.

"He's escaped through the fireplace, heading down!" Jason

shouted. "I slashed open the back of his ankle." Two of the guards left in pursuit. Two remained. One of the guards knelt beside Norval. The other held a torch and a sword. Jason approached the fallen bodyguard.

"The chancellor?" Norval coughed, voice tight, eyes squeezed shut, sweat shining on his face in the torchlight.

"Lord Jason is unharmed," the kneeling guard assured him. "Let me see the wound."

Norval clutched the haft of the knife in his gut with both hands. He shook his head. "End this," he grunted through clenched teeth.

The guard pried Norval's hands from the handle of the knife. The haft was black, the pommel shaped into the likeness of a grinning skull. "What the devil?" the guard murmured.

Thin tendrils of acrid smoke curled up from the wound. Norval began to convulse. His wide eyes rolled back, and perspiration drenched his reddening face. His lips twitched as if trying to speak.

"The knife was poisoned," Jason said.

"Bloodbane," the kneeling guard agreed. "A foul toxin, excruciating and without antidote."

The convulsions were increasing in violence. Norval held out a hand, the veins standing out so sharply on his sweat-glossed forearm they appeared on the verge of bursting through the skin. With a strangled cry he slumped into unconsciousness. His breathing continued in irregular gasps.

"This way, Lord Jason," said the guard with the torch, leading him out of the bedroom.

Jason looked back as he exited to the elegantly furnished antechamber. The other guard covered Norval with his cloak. The bodyguard's limbs continued to spasm in fluttering bursts.

Although Norval passed out of sight, Jason remained aware that the venomous knife had been intended for him. He could have been the one flailing on the ground, blood boiling in reaction to a vile poison, had he slept in his bed, or had Norval failed to respond so promptly to his cry for aid. Tears of gratitude to the dying bodyguard stung his eyes.

Several guards came into the antechamber. Most proceeded into the bedchamber. Others poked about the anteroom, as if they suspected the assassin might be hidden behind a wall hanging or in a drawer. A few gathered in hushed conversation.

Jason stood apart, deeply shaken, trying to process what had happened. Somebody had tried to assassinate him! It was one thing to know about a threat and quite another to see it carried out. If he had died, his loved ones would never have known what had happened to him. He would have forever been an unsolved missing-person case.

A broad guard with a fringe of graying hair around his bald scalp entered the antechamber and approached Jason. The other guards rose to attention, but he waved them back to their former activities. The older guard wore a pair of golden braids on his left shoulder that seemed to denote a high rank. "Lord Chancellor," the guard began, "I am Cedric, captain of the King's Guard. His Highness Duke Dolan requests that I escort you to his presence."

"Of course." Glad he had slept in his clothes, Jason followed Cedric out of his apartments and down several corridors. They entered a room where a pair of guards slid aside a plush sofa and rolled up an embroidered purple carpet to reveal a trapdoor in the floor. The guards raised the trapdoor, and Jason followed Cedric down a curving stairwell. A guard followed, bearing a lantern.

At the start of a narrow passageway beyond the stairs Dolan awaited, flanked by four guards, all wearing broadswords.

"Welcome, Chancellor Jason," Dolan said. "We lament word of the attempt on your life. Let us enter the lorevault to discuss these matters in greatest privacy."

"Lead on, Your Highness," Jason said.

They walked along a winding passageway until arriving at a round, iron door. The door had a grid of holes and seven pegs. The guards turned away from the door while the regent inserted the pegs. Jason moved to turn away, but Dolan insisted he watch. "You are the only person besides myself trusted with the combination," the regent said.

With the seventh peg came the tumbling of the locking mechanism. The regent removed the pegs, and two guards seized the great door. Heaving together, they swung it open.

Jason and the regent entered, bringing a lantern, and the guards closed the door behind them. The room was a spacious cube. The wall to the left of the door held books from floor to ceiling. The wall to the right supported stacks of rolled scrolls. The far shelves contained artifacts varying from fist-sized jewels to crystal vials to assorted weaponry. Above the far shelves were a few ventilation slats. A small table and two chairs occupied the center of the room.

Alone with the regent, Jason felt self-conscious. He resolved to try to sound as adult as possible. Glancing up, he noted the eight words emblazoned over the door. As Copernum had stated, the fourth from the left was "Fex." Jason felt relieved to have the matter confirmed. He officially had half of the Word.

A _____ _____ FEX EN_ _____ _____

"Your second question in the contest was unusual," Dolan said, apparently noticing Jason's interest in the inscription above the door. "How did you know about the inscription?"

"My father mentioned it once. I think he heard of it from Galloran."

"Were you simply trying to unnerve Copernum? He seemed perplexed by the inquiry."

"I only had one good question," Jason said. "My first two questions were to make him underestimate me."

Dolan considered Jason suspiciously. "I sense that you are full of secrets. Perhaps one day soon you will share them with me. Take a seat." In private Dolan seemed more direct and intense than the grandfatherly persona he portrayed on his throne.

They sat facing each other. Jason noticed that the table was a map. He saw the peninsula that projected westward into the ocean. Some distance inland Trensicourt was marked with a spot, as was Whitelake, a speck northward beside a small body of water.

"You like the map?"

Jason nodded. "Very much."

"Copernum insisted on it. After all, what use is a private chamber without a few secrets inside? Maldor would frown upon this map. He understands the advantage inherent in monopolizing such information."

Jason continued studying the map. The little fishing town at the oval inlet was called Flet. The town where he, Rachel, and Ferrin had been imprisoned must have been Carning. The place where Galloran lived as the Blind King was marked Fortaim, and the river to the north was the Telkron. The Repository of Learning was unmarked.

Many other names marked the map. Jason noticed Harthenham, a good distance north and east of Whitelake, beyond an empty green place marked the Sunken Lands.

"You did well surviving the attack," Dolan commended.

"Copernum told me I would not live to see the sunrise. I was trying to be careful. Norval, my bodyguard, will die in my place. How do we retaliate?"

"You believe Copernum masterminded the assault?"

"Considering his threat, I'm pretty sure."

Dolan sighed. "There could be many viable suspects. A newcomer to court earning the chancellorship at such a tender age could spawn any number of enemies. Harsh words spoken in a moment of embarrassment would not serve as sufficient evidence to accuse Copernum. The knife bore the black skull. Only the minions of Maldor use that ornament. The only material evidence we possess suggests an imperial assassin."

"Then Copernum must have planted it," Jason insisted. "Or maybe he called in a favor."

The regent frowned. "Copernum has strong ties to Felrook, but he is much too powerful to implicate without absolute proof. Did he orchestrate the crime? Probably. Using emblems of the emperor to attack you was his way of reminding everyone who backs him. The assassin somehow eluded our pursuit. All guards remain on alert, but considering the assassin has evaded us this long, I have little hope we will apprehend him."

"So I just wait until he tries again?" Jason could hardly believe the regent was so unruffled by the incident.

"Copernum might not strike again soon. He sent his message. He may now content himself with unseating you through a formal challenge."

"Instead of an informal murder."

"You have the idea."

Jason folded his hands on the table. "So there is nothing we can do to retaliate?"

Dolan cocked his head to one side. "There is little *I* can do. Surely you are not so naive to the art of statecraft as you pretend.

There is much *you* could do. But weigh your options carefully. Most men in this kingdom would endure anything to avoid an outright feud with Copernum."

Including you, Jason added silently. At first glance this ruler had looked much more authentic than Galloran. But on closer inspection he possessed neither the backbone nor the personal presence of the Blind King.

"If Maldor were behind the attack, would we do anything?"

Dolan made an indifferent gesture. "There is no definite evidence to implicate Maldor. As you suggested, the knife could have been a ruse."

"And if we had definite evidence?"

Dolan stirred in his seat. "Take care what you imply. I lost one of my finest bodyguards protecting you."

"Wouldn't you want revenge? Wouldn't you want justice?"

The regent ground his teeth. "Be reasonable. The semblance of freedom we maintain depends on keeping Maldor appeased. To a degree that includes keeping Copernum content. Should he openly align himself with the emperor against us, all could be lost. I like you, Jason. I admire the composure you showed facing Copernum. It was a daring stunt. Nevertheless you are an upstart about whom I know very little. In perilous times one must overlook greater injustices than a botched assassination in order to preserve peace. This kingdom cannot afford idealism. If you hope to endure, you must learn the art of compromise."

"I'm your main advisor," Jason said, flabbergasted. "An attack against me is an attack against you and your entire kingdom. What if I had been killed? Would my murderer simply have returned to his former position?"

"A wise man would know not to ask such questions."

Leaning his elbows on the table, Jason rubbed his eyes. How

could Dolan pretend cowardice was compromise? Did he believe his words? What hope was there for a kingdom whose leader was afraid to seek justice?

"Do not despair," Dolan said. "I called you to the lorevault because you have another option for survival. An attractive one, by the look of it."

Jason raised his head.

The regent withdrew an envelope from a pocket inside his robe. An elaborate seal held it closed.

"What's that?" Jason asked.

"It arrived for you tonight after the attempted assassination."

Dolan handed the envelope across the table. Jason opened it, removing a cream-colored card inscribed with silver lettering.

MY ESTEEMED LORD JASON,

YOUR PRESENCE IS HUMBLY REQUESTED AT THE ETERNAL FEAST AT YOUR SOONEST CONVENIENCE. A GLORIOUS BANQUET WILL BE HELD IN YOUR HONOR UPON THE DAY OF YOUR ARRIVAL. BE ASSURED THAT HARTHENHAM CASTLE PERMANENTLY STANDS UPON NEUTRAL TERRITORY AS FAR AS ALL POLITICAL MATTERS ARE CONCERNED. MANY DWELL HERE HAPPILY WHO, LIKE YOU, OPENLY OPPOSED OUR IMPERIAL LEADERSHIP IN TIMES PAST. ALLOW ME TO PERSONALLY ENCOURAGE YOU TO SEIZE THIS RARE OPPORTUNITY TO REST FROM YOUR STRUGGLES FOR A TIME AS MY HONORED GUEST. MAY MY HOME EVER BE YOUR HAVEN.

YOUR SINCERE ADMIRER,
Duke Conrad of Harthenham

The signature at the bottom carried a bit more flourish than the rest of the words. Jason reread the message.

Licking his lips, Dolan extended a hand. "May I see it?" Jason gave him the card. The regent studied the message, shaking his head. "I have never beheld an actual invitation to the Eternal Feast."

"I've heard of the Eternal Feast."

The regent shot him a sharp glance. "Who hasn't? It is merely paradise visiting the mortal world. A fortress against all concerns. A sanctuary of endless delights. Those invited are pardoned of all crimes, and they live out their days in careless luxury."

"Sounds like being a king."

"In many ways superior to kingship. A king has duties. Enemies. Fears." Dolan spoke like a man beholding a vision. "Those who dine at the Eternal Feast know hardship only as a memory."

"Have you gone there?" Jason asked.

"I would not be here if I had. None return."

"Foul play?"

"Quite the contrary. None who are invited ever choose to leave. Who would surrender paradise?"

"Have you been invited?"

"Alas, no," Dolan sighed. "The emperor needs me here."

"The invitation is from Maldor?"

"Indirectly. The emperor sponsors the feast. Conrad hosts it. You are most fortunate, Jason. You need not fear Copernum or any man ever again."

Jason held out a hand, and the regent returned the card. "So the feast is a prison."

Dolan chuckled. "In a sense, perhaps. A voluntary prison where none complain. Would that I could live out my days in similar incarceration."

Jason nodded. The ploy was obvious. The feast was a permanent bribe allowing Maldor to get rid of enemies. Still, the prospect of being out of danger was attractive. If he was stuck in some other reality, why not ditch his concerns and live a life of luxury? Nicholas had recommended that this should be his real goal. But if he caved and went to the feast, how would he ever get home? And what would happen to Rachel?

Glancing at the syllable over the door, Jason sighed. Maldor was evil. The men who worked for him were evil. The Eternal Feast might simply be another trap. How could anyone know how great it was if nobody ever returned? Besides, the fact that the invitation had been issued meant that Maldor was getting worried. He should be! Jason already had half of the Word that could destroy him.

Jason stared down at the map. He could not abandon the quest. He had another good lead, and Whitelake was not too far off. He could not abandon Rachel. He could not give up on getting home. He could not betray the trust Galloran had placed in him. Ferrin was waiting. Jason placed the card back into the envelope. He would hang on to the invitation. If he was ever cornered, perhaps he could save himself by accepting it.

"This is an amazing offer," Jason said. "Can I take a day to consider it? I need some time to think it over."

"Certainly. Jason, there is no shame in accepting this invitation. Should you abdicate, Copernum will be reinstated, and the kingdom will prosper. Be twice warned: Openly crossing Copernum, whether or not you feel certain he was behind the attempted assassination, will likely bring ruination. Let it go. In your position I would relinquish the chancellorship and join the feast. Any sane man would do likewise. You will be remembered as a daring lord and chancellor emeritus as you live out your days in blissful opulence."

Jason nodded. "I hear you. Is that all for now?"

The regent passed Jason a slip of parchment with seven pairs of symbols. "This is yours."

"The combination to the lorevault," Jason said.

"You are free to study here at will. The combination is not the same as it was yesterday. Should you resign, the combination will change again."

"I may need a coach," Jason said. "A way to travel."

"I take your meaning," the regent said, relief in his tone. "I can have a coach made ready within the hour, along with a tight-lipped driver. Should you elect to depart, no man would blame you."

Some would, Jason added silently. *Just not the sort you work with.* "Thank you, Your Highness."

Less than two hours later, with the sun rising, Jason stretched out in the compartment of a fine coach, the outside lacquered a shiny black and decorated with silver filigree, pulled by six powerful horses. He wore traveling clothes. On the cushioned seat beside him were provisions prepared by his cook, and some of the courtly attire he had worn as Lord Jason. His rings and mantle were stashed away, the rings in his cloak, the mantle rolled up with the rest of his gaudy apparel.

Jason moved the curtain to peer out as the coach descended the steep ramp down the plateau, then leaned back and closed his eyes. He could hardly believe he was leaving the stress and intrigues of Trensicourt behind. He hoped Rachel would have the sense to make her way to the Stumbling Stag. He didn't know how to contact her.

Once the coach leveled out, Jason became more comfortable and tried to doze. The jostling of the coach prevented him at first, but eventually fatigue won the contest.

When the coachman, a diminutive, knobby fellow, shook him

awake, they were stopped outside a tavern. Jason rubbed his eyes. The sign over the door showed a deer with forked antlers.

Jason instructed the coachman to wait for him, and climbed out of the compartment onto the packed dirt of the street. Ferrin leaned in the doorway. "Come inside, Lord Jason," the displacer said with a sweeping bow.

"Don't say my name so loudly," Jason muttered in a low voice as he drew near. "We don't want to stand out."

"Oh," Ferrin replied in an equally cautious tone. "Then you might want to rethink the elaborate carriage bearing the royal crest. Would you prefer I address you as chancellor?"

They went inside together.

"You know I became chancellor?"

"News of that sort travels on wings."

"Do you know Copernum tried to kill me?" Jason asked.

"No. You're ahead of that news. I wish I could pretend to be surprised. Now the same man has tried to kill each of us and failed. I guess that seals our friendship."

"Copernum ordered your execution?"

"Who else? I stole his cousin's fiancée, then killed his cousin in a duel. To clarify, the cousin insisted on the duel, and I fought fair. You hungry?"

Jason nodded. "What happened to the girl?"

"She found out I was a displacer." Ferrin flagged down a barmaid and ordered food.

Jason got out two gold pellets and two silver. "Here is your money back. With interest."

"Keep the excess," Ferrin said. "You weren't an investment."

"I can spare it," Jason said. "I grabbed a lot of money. Well, technically, an attendant grabbed it for me. Amazing the funds you can access as chancellor!"

Ferrin accepted the pellets. "I'll hold these until you need them."

"Any word from Rachel?"

"I was about to ask you the same question."

"We didn't stay together. I had no way to contact her. I hope she comes here."

"She'll come when she hears you fled." Ferrin tapped his knuckles against the tabletop. "Hopefully, she's already on her way. It would be hard to outpace a coach and six."

"You still want to join us?" Jason asked.

"Are you truly abandoning the chancellorship?"

"One assassination attempt was enough."

Ferrin raised his eyebrows and smiled. "The regent will be furious. Don't ever go back."

"I wouldn't enjoy working for Dolan. He seems like a coward."

Ferrin glanced hastily around. "Chancellor or not, lower your voice to express such things. We're still well inside the domain pertaining to Trensicourt. Some men would duel you over an insult to their ruler. Not that I'm disagreeing. Copernum ran that circus, and will again soon enough, I expect."

"So do you still want to come with us? I'm becoming a bigger target every day."

"Why do you think I was waiting here?"

"We're going to Whitelake," Jason said. "Do you know how to get there?"

"Whitelake? That's a little remote, isn't it? Not much of a town."

"We need to go to the actual lake, not just the town."

"Are we sightseeing? I've never gazed upon the actual Whitelake. It involves a climb. But if that's where you want to go, I'm willing."

"I have the coach," Jason said. "That should save us some time. I guess we just wait for Rachel?"

"Is the little driver the only man accompanying you?"

"Yes."

Ferrin stretched his arms. "In a coach like that, Whitelake is only a day or two away. The horses look amazing."

"The driver will take us far," Jason said. "I actually left with permission from Dolan."

"What? How?"

"I got invited to the Eternal Feast."

Ferrin blinked and shook his head. "Excuse me?"

"Dolan pushed me to accept. I basically told him I would, and he provided the coach."

"But you're declining the invitation?"

"No."

"Are you daft? Why not? Wait, why would you get the invitation in the first place? What have you been doing?"

Jason shrugged. "I guess because I became chancellor and survived the assassination attempt."

"That makes sense. Dolan has strong ties to Felrook, as does his former chancellor. They must have wanted you out of the picture in order to reinstate Copernum. But why not accept? Do you know how easy your life would be?"

"It might not be as great as everybody imagines," Jason said. "Nobody who goes there returns. The food might be good, but to me it sounds like a prison."

"Maybe," Ferrin mused. "Still, as prisons go, Harthenham would be my pick ten times out of ten. You're an interesting person, Jason. There is more to you than a glance would reveal. Who knows how long we'll be waiting for Rachel? Could be hours, might be days. You should instruct your driver to see to the horses and get himself some food."

"Good idea," Jason said.

"I'll wait here."

On his way out the door Jason noticed a pair of riders loping up the street. One was Rachel.

"Jason!" she called as they made eye contact.

Jason waved, relief flooding through him. As she approached, he realized how worried he'd been that she might have been hurt.

The riders pulled up near him, and Rachel dismounted. She wore new traveling clothes that actually fit her.

"Is this your destination?" the man asked, a rugged character with a crooked nose.

"Yes, thank you, Bruce."

"Very well. Safe journey."

Taking the reins of her horse, he rode away.

"Who was that guy?" Jason asked quietly.

"My escort," Rachel whispered back. "Nicholas took care of it. He's been much more helpful than he acted when we first met him."

"Once we left his shop, I thought we'd never hear from him again."

"Apparently Copernum linked him to us. And Copernum suspects we're Beyonders. Nicholas decided that the best way to strengthen his position was for us to succeed and escape. We met in person two more times, and he sent several notes. He was thrilled that you defeated Copernum and pleased that you survived the assassination."

"It was so freaky," Jason said. "You wouldn't believe it. I slept under my bed, and this guy came in and tried to stab me with a poisoned knife, but got my bodyguard instead."

"You're okay?" Rachel asked.

"I'm fine. I'm glad you got away safely. I was worried."

Rachel blushed slightly. "You got the syllable? I didn't wait around to hear."

"The third is 'fex.' I saw it inside the lorevault as well."

"Good question?"

"Great question."

"Is Ferrin here?"

"He's waiting inside."

Jason told the coachman that they would have a meal and then proceed to Whitelake, inviting the driver to get food and make whatever preparations he deemed necessary for the horses. Then Jason and Rachel entered the Stumbling Stag. They reached Ferrin's table at the same time as the barmaid.

"Perfect timing," Ferrin said. "Rachel can have my food." He ordered another meal.

"I won't take your food," Rachel said once the barmaid left.

"If you ignore the meal, it will get cold and stale. Eat," Ferrin insisted. "While you've been busy, I've been resting. So tell me, Rachel, have you married a prince and become the future queen of Kadara?"

"My time in Trensicourt wasn't quite as interesting as Jason's," she said. "But it was stressful enough that I'm relieved to get away."

"Leave city life to the masochists," Ferrin said, waving a dismissive hand. "It's the open road for us!"

CHAPTER 16

WHITELAKE

On their second afternoon after leaving the Stumbling Stag, Rachel stared out the coach window, trying to ignore the headache all the jerking and jouncing had created. They had reached rocky country with tall trees, steep hills, and rushing streams, and had not passed through a town all day.

She glanced over at Jason, who was trying ineffectively to nap. If *he* couldn't sleep, she knew it was a rough ride. What a funny guy. At first he hadn't struck her as the sharpest knife in the drawer, but she was starting to realize she could have gotten trapped in a parallel world with somebody much worse. She could hardly believe he had managed to become chancellor. Had he asked her the same question, she might have topped him. "Squirreled" had ten letters, although some people argued it wasn't a single syllable.

Her gaze shifted to Ferrin. The displacer had been their best find so far. He was the perfect guide—knowledgeable, skillful, and well traveled. Plus he was funny and not bad-looking. He acted so grateful for their friendship it made her furious at the rest of Lyrian for discriminating against his kind.

He noticed her looking at him. "The farther we get from

Trensicourt, the less we want this coach," he said, speaking loud enough to be heard over the clatter of their motion.

"We should start walking before my teeth rattle out of my head," Jason replied.

"I warned you we're heading into remote country," Ferrin reminded him. "The roads will only get worse, and the inhabitants less lawful. We've passed beyond the orderly kingdom of Trensicourt. This is a wild territory. Without an armed escort our coach will inevitably draw bandits. Out here a smart man wears a hard face and conceals his wealth."

"Sounds delightful," Rachel said.

"I'd prefer to avoid the town of Whitelake," Ferrin said. "It is no place for a pretty girl. The communities out in the wildlands are full of trappers, hunters, traders, and miners. Not to mention gamblers and outlaws. Many of them will take advantage of a stranger, given the opportunity."

"When do we ditch the coach?" Jason asked.

Pulling aside the curtains, Ferrin leaned out the window. "Before long we'll reach a trail that will lead us to the lake. It won't accommodate the coach, but the walk should require less than a day."

"How steep is the climb?" Jason asked.

"Nothing perilous," Ferrin assured him. "People stay away from Whitelake because it's cursed, not because of the ascent."

"Cursed?" Rachel asked.

"Supposedly the lake is bewitched," Ferrin said. "Even the hardy folk of the wildlands keep their distance, which should prevent us from meeting much interference."

"We need to get to the island in the middle of the lake," Jason said.

"The island?" Ferrin exclaimed. "Why? Are you on a tour of

the most dangerous and inaccessible places in all the land?"

"What makes you say that?" Rachel asked.

"Nothing floats on Whitelake. Not boats, not insects, not dust. Certainly not people. Everything sinks. Nobody knows how deep it is. Folks in town claim it goes down to the center of the world."

"But you've never actually seen the lake?" Jason checked.

"No," Ferrin responded. "You think people might be exaggerating?"

"Only one way to find out," Jason said.

Ferrin kept peering out the window. Half an hour later, pulling up the hood of his cloak, he called for the driver to halt. After they climbed down and collected their gear, Jason told the driver to return to Trensicourt.

"Are you certain, my lord?" the driver asked, eyes darting to Ferrin's hooded form. "Begging your pardon, this is far from the destination I anticipated, an uncivilized stretch of wilderness where you might come to harm."

Rachel had not heard the driver utter a complaint as Jason had issued prior instructions. Evidently, the man had reached his limit.

"I'm sure, Evan," Jason said. "I need to take a few detours before I go where Duke Dolan probably told you I was heading."

With practiced skill Evan produced a crossbow and pointed it at Ferrin. "If this man is trying to coerce you, I can take care of him, my lord."

"No, Evan, he's a friend," Jason assured the coachman. "Thanks for your concern, but I'm really here on purpose. You can tell the regent that I'm just taking care of some unfinished business."

Evan lowered the weapon. "Very well. Safe journey, my lord."

"You too, Evan," Jason said.

The driver flicked the reins, and the coach rumbled forward.

"How is he going to turn the coach around?" Rachel asked. The road looked much too narrow.

"He'll forge ahead until he finds a clearing," Ferrin said. "Come, we should get away from the road before nightfall."

The next morning, from a craggy hilltop, Ferrin pointed out the town of Whitelake, a rough-hewn settlement of log structures a few miles from the base of a squat, conical mountain. Golden-brown prairie land surrounded the town, beyond which forested hills and ridges continued into the distance.

"Where is the lake?" Jason asked.

"Atop the mount," Ferrin said.

"It looks like a squashed volcano," Jason said.

Ferrin rubbed his chin. "Volcanic activity might help explain tales of an unnatural lake."

They descended the hill and started across the open, grassy plain separating them from the mount. Rachel noticed that Ferrin kept checking behind them.

"Think we're being followed?" Rachel asked.

"Almost certainly," Ferrin said. "It's a single person, staying well back, I've half glimpsed him a few times. He might just be a hunter watching to ensure we leave his territory alone. Maybe he'll veer off now that we've left the forest."

"And if not?" Jason asked.

Ferrin shrugged. "Could be a scout for a team of bandits. Could be a tenacious spy from Trensicourt. Could be an agent of the emperor. Hard to guess."

"Let's hope he's a shy, lonely fisherman," Jason said.

"The mountain doesn't look too hard to climb," Rachel noted, looking ahead.

"True," Ferrin agreed. "The slope all around the mountain is strangely regular—fairly steep but never sheer. Anyone behind us will have a nice view of our ascent. But nobody will be able to sneak up on us."

They crossed the grassland without incident and started up the mountain. The slope was steep enough that hiking up it felt like climbing stairs. Rachel bent forward like Jason, using her hands as she advanced. Partway up they took a lunch break, having already gained an impressive view of the plains and forest behind them. As they finished, Ferrin announced that they seemed to have lost their tracker.

When they finally arrived at the top of the slope, Rachel's legs ached, and her back felt sore from crouching forward. Perspiration dampened her face. But her discomfort was forgotten at the sight of the odd lake.

The top of the broad mount looked like the round caldera of a volcano, filled almost to the rim with sludgy white fluid. A small island, little more than a rock pile, poked up near the center. The surface of Whitelake was unnaturally smooth. Heat radiated from the lake, making the air shimmer. A smell like overboiled eggs permeated the air.

"Come," Ferrin said, proceeding to the edge of the lake. Jason and Rachel joined him.

Ferrin held up a small, flat piece of wood, displaying it as a magician might before performing a trick. He handed it to Jason. "Light, isn't it?"

"Yes."

"Would normally float on water?"

"I guess so."

"Let's see what happens here." Ferrin handed the wood to Rachel.

She crouched, mindful of the heat radiating from the lake, and gently placed the piece of wood lengthwise on the creamy surface. The wooden fragment sank with hardly a ripple.

"What is the lake made of?" Jason asked.

"Not water," Ferrin replied.

"Looks like pancake batter," Rachel said. "Has anyone ever reached the island?"

"I have no idea," Ferrin said. "People say Whitelake is cursed. If nobody comes here, and nothing floats on the lake, I can't imagine anyone has been to that island. Nor can I imagine why you two would want to go there. I'd hate to watch you drown."

Jason glanced at Rachel. "Could we have gotten bad info?"

"Info?" Ferrin echoed. "Did somebody tell you to come here? Who? Why?"

Jason crouched, selected a flat rock, and winged it sidearm out onto the lake. It took a huge skip, then another, and several smaller bounces, until it had traveled a very impressive distance. When it lost momentum, the rock finally sank. "Did you see that?" he asked. "The rock skipped like ten times!"

"Yes," Ferrin answered in an intrigued tone.

Jason threw another with similar results. Rachel grabbed a stone, this one less flat, and threw it almost straight down at the water. It rebounded quite high, as if the surface were solid, then took a smaller hop and sank.

"Weird," Rachel murmured, taking a stone in her hand and kneeling beside the lake. Holding the stone firmly, she struck the white fluid sharply. The surface felt solid. She pounded it several more times. Nothing splashed. The surface barely rippled. She examined the stone, observing no fluid on it anywhere. Dropping the stone softly into the lake, it sank.

"The surface hardens against pressure," Jason observed. "Let's try a big rock." Together he and Rachel heaved a heavy stone against the surface of the lake. Sure enough, it rebounded once before losing momentum and sinking.

Rachel edged forward to the brink of the lake and stomped the surface with her foot. "Feels solid. Only yields a little, like a trampoline strung much too tight."

She dipped her foot in slowly. The syrupy lake folded around the bottom of her boot.

"No!" Ferrin exclaimed, springing forward.

Once part of her boot sank beneath the surface, an alarming suction pulled it farther. Jerking back sharply, she felt the fluid harden around the submerged portion of her boot, as if it were encased in cement. When she relaxed, the fluid sucked it deeper. Rachel yanked again, hoping her foot would come free of the boot, which was already half immersed, but it was laced too securely.

Ferrin and Jason reached her side, supporting her. "Pull steadily against the lake, but not too hard," Ferrin advised.

Rachel nodded. When she pulled too hard, the fluid solidified. Her only hope was to do this gradually. Braced by Ferrin and Jason, she resisted the suction just enough to prevent her boot from sinking deeper. Then, pulling only a little harder, she managed to slowly and evenly withdraw her boot from the liquid.

Once her boot was free, Rachel staggered away from the lake. She plopped down, panting. Her boot looked like it had been painted white almost to the ankle. While she watched, the fluid slid unnaturally off the boot and pooled in a little depression in the ground, leaving no indication her boot had ever been white.

"Thanks for the help," Rachel said. "If I had been alone, that would have been the end of me. I didn't expect so much suction!"

"The wood you placed earlier sank strangely," Ferrin said. "The lake seemed to draw it in."

"Can you imagine drowning in there?" Jason said. "You would be sinking, but as you struggled to swim, the lake would harden around you. Then when you relaxed it would suck you deeper. The perfect quicksand."

"It felt very warm, even through the boot," Rachel said.

Ferrin gave a nod. "Warm enough to burn bare skin, I expect. Do you still intend to try for the island?"

Rachel gazed out across the lake to the pile of rocks at the center. The image wavered with the rising heat. "How far away do you think it is?"

Ferrin squinted. "Hard to say. There is nothing near the island to lend perspective. The heat rising off the lake could also distort our perception. The island may be farther than it appears."

"Let me check if the lake will hold my weight," Jason said. "You know, just run out a short way and back."

"Allow me," Ferrin volunteered. "If a foot gets stuck, I can let it go."

"Right," Rachel said, "but how far will you get in the wilderness without a foot?"

"We won't sink unless we hold still," Jason insisted. "Watch."

He jogged out onto the lake, stamping his feet. The surface shivered slightly at the point of impact, but he did not sink. Jason turned and jogged back.

"Well done, chancellor," Ferrin said.

"That lake reeks," Jason complained. "Out on the surface you feel the heat more. Running to the island will be a nightmare."

"But running there is our only option," Rachel said.

"Unless we decide to hunt for entertainment elsewhere," Ferrin mumbled.

"We have to do this," Jason said with determination. "Well, I have to do it. No need for more than one of us to take the risk."

"No, it's my turn," Rachel said. "I'm a runner. I'll have a better chance. You jumped off the cliff, remember? Next cliff was mine."

"You two know something that you're not sharing," Ferrin probed. "You have an idea what might be out there."

"We can't tell you," Jason said. "Not knowing protects you. It has to do with why the emperor is after us, and why I had to become chancellor."

"It isn't fair that we keep you with us," Rachel said. "We're putting you in danger, Ferrin. If we explained, it would only make everything worse."

"Don't worry about me," Ferrin said. "I see more than I reveal, and I don't mean to pry. I just want the two of you to be sure whatever is out there is worth risking your lives."

"It is," Rachel said. "We have a lot riding on this. Jason, let me run to the island. I'm smaller, built for distance. I can make it."

Jason puffed up his cheeks and exhaled. He held up a finger. "If you slip, I'll never forgive you, or myself."

"I never trip," Rachel assured him. She studied the lake. She could easily maintain a brisk jog for three or four miles, but there would be unusual variables working against her. She had heavy boots, not running shoes. The heat from the lake might cause her to tire faster, and it might get hotter away from the shore. Plus, she would need to stamp down harder than she would with her regular stride, as insurance against her foot sinking through the surface. If that happened away from the shore, even just a little, she would be finished.

Despite the danger, she had to try. It was unfair to let Jason take all of the risks, especially when she legitimately had more chance for success than him.

"Wait a minute," Jason said, going through his satchel. "The loremaster gave me berries that boost your energy. This might be the perfect time for some extra endurance!"

Taking a bag from the satchel, he poured a small handful of shriveled berries into his palm. He lifted one darkly mottled berry to his nostrils and immediately gagged.

"They've gone bad," Ferrin said. "Eating them will do more harm than good."

"Perfect," Jason muttered, chucking the rotten berries into the lake.

"No worries," Rachel said, rubbing her legs anxiously. "I've got this. Just give me a few minutes to relax and stretch out."

She found a large, flat rock and spent a few minutes on her back, focusing on her breathing. Then she arose, rolled up her sleeves, and stripped off her unessential gear. She thought about running barefoot or in socks, but decided the extra weight of the boots would be justified by the protection they would give her feet against the heat of the lake.

She grabbed her ankle and pulled her leg back to stretch her quadriceps, holding the pose for fifteen seconds. Then the other leg. Keeping her legs straight, she leaned forward, touching the ground between her toes.

Rachel glanced at Jason. "Keep an eye on me. You don't want to sit around wasting your time if I fall."

"If you're going to fall, don't go," Jason said.

"I feel good," Rachel said, trying to convince herself as much as Jason. "I've got this." She walked closer to the edge of the lake.

"Step hard and quick," Jason urged. "It's going to be hot and stinky. If it becomes too much to handle, double back."

"Unless you're more than halfway there," Ferrin added.

"Okay," Rachel said. "Here I go."

Standing three paces from the edge of the lake, Rachel started trotting forward. She tried to ignore the reality that she was jogging onto the surface of a lake that minutes before had been sucking her under. It seemed suicidal.

Her first quick step onto Whitelake held her weight easily. After the first few strides she began to trust the surface and fell into a rhythm. The lake had enough give that it returned some of the energy she expended with her stomping strides. As long as she kept stepping firmly, she should be fine. Because she exerted extra force downward, she did not advance as quickly as when she normally jogged, but she found a good pace, and there was no hint of the liquid tugging at her boots.

She resisted the urge to look back, concentrating all of her energy on getting to the island and maintaining her shin-punishing stride. As she had feared, the farther she proceeded onto the lake, the higher the temperature became. In a short time the air she breathed went from uncomfortably warm to truly hot, and the stench intensified. The rapid increase in temperature alarmed her. How much hotter would it get? The white liquid did not bubble or boil or even stir. No steam arose. The only visual indicator of the heat was the rippling shimmer of objects far ahead, the trembling image of the island, wavering like a mirage.

Rachel's breathing grew deeper and more ragged much sooner than she had expected. She tilted slightly forward, trying to squeeze more forward motion from each stamping stride. Frustratingly, the island did not appear much closer. She wiped sweat from her brow with her bare forearm, which itself was damp with perspiration.

She fixated on the surface of the lake directly in front of her, ignoring the island. Her deep breathing coated her throat and lungs with the hot sulfuric smell that saturated the air. She could taste the odor. She tried to ignore the sensation, because it made her want to retch.

Soon her shirt was drenched with sweat. The temperature intensified to sweltering. It felt like jogging in a sauna. Scalding air tore at her lungs.

Rachel finally looked up. She was notably nearer to her destination, but not close enough. The temperature became hellish. Her exertion coupled with the heat radiating from the lake was overwhelming. Her head began to throb. A painful stitch burned in her side. The overtaxed muscles in her legs began to feel rubbery.

She broke stride and tried hopping in place. It required somewhat less exertion than jogging, and used different muscles. She struggled to choke down the bile in her throat, to ignore the suffocating heat searing her lungs. The island remained several hundred yards away.

The surface of the lake began to feel tacky. With each successive jump she felt increasing stickiness against the soles of her boots. Rachel realized she was getting lazy with her hopping. She was not thrusting her feet down briskly enough, nor lifting them quickly enough. If the sensation progressed beyond stickiness, a boot would get trapped, and she would die.

The thought impelled her forward. No use hopping when she could be making progress, especially once it proved to be less restful than she had hoped. Salty sweat stung her eyes. She wiped them clear. The nausea had diminished while she was hopping, but it returned as she jogged.

She took a bad step, almost stumbled, and for a moment the surface felt alarmingly wet. After recovering, she dashed forward faster than ever, eyes on the island. She was getting close.

The coppery taste of blood became more evident in her throat as her breathing became increasingly arduous. She was running inside an oven. Was the air shimmering more here, or was her vision blurring? She felt dizzy. The island was less than a hundred yards away. It looked bigger than it had from the shore. Not a rock pile. A boulder pile.

Anyone can run a hundred yards, she thought blearily. Each breath scorched her tortured lungs. The burning muscles in her legs verged on total exhaustion. She shed sweat with every stride. Her vision became edged in blackness.

The island was so close, but she didn't know if she could reach it. The human body had limits, even in emergencies. There were certain mechanical impossibilities. Any second now she would pass out, and that would be the end. In a way it would be a relief. Her legs felt clumsy and distant. She shuffled and stumbled instead of running. Against the soles of her boots the lake felt like freshly paved asphalt.

The island was only thirty yards away. *Anyone can go thirty yards.*

With a growling burst of exertion Rachel increased her pace to a full sprint. She had to reach the island before she fainted! Her legs refused to cooperate, and she fell.

Her left hand slapped the scalding surface. Then her right. She was going down, so she let herself roll forward, and with desperate effort used her momentum to regain her feet and continue running.

Vomit spewed from her lips as she reached the rocky shore of the island and pitched forward onto her hands and knees. As she held her head down, her stomach clenched again, and acidic foulness fauceted from her mouth.

She wiped the sickening taste from her parched lips. Her breathing felt ineffectual. Raising her head suddenly, trying to find fresh air above if it did not exist below, she experienced a peculiar rush as the blackness along her peripheral vision swelled inward, swallowing everything.

When Rachel regained consciousness, her cheek lay against a warm stone. She sat up gingerly. The sun did not seem to have moved, and her body was still slimed with sweat, so she did not believe she had been out long.

Looking back toward the shore through the trembling heat, Rachel could barely distinguish shapes that might have been Ferrin and Jason. The heat and atmosphere of the rocky island was almost as uncomfortable as the air directly over the lake.

She got up, massaging her elbow where an ugly bruise was forming. Why had she volunteered for this? Maybe she would stay on the island forever. She could not imagine crossing the lake again.

Rachel had never been closer to dying than when she had stumbled at the end of her run. How many near misses could she expect to survive? Her thoughts turned to her parents. They had built their lives around her. Her disappearance in the arroyo had to be driving them crazy. What would they do if she never made it home? No, she couldn't acknowledge the possibility. She had to make it home, for herself, and especially for her mom and dad.

The island truly seemed to be nothing more than a big heap of rocks, some big, some small. The highest point reached perhaps forty feet above the lake. The only evidence of life was tufts of purple-gray moss growing on some of the stones.

On wobbly legs Rachel began circling the island, looking for anything besides rocks upon rocks. The clue she needed might be scrawled on a stone. Or buried. Or not on the island at all. Maybe Nicholas had his facts wrong.

She was a quarter of the way around the island, picking her

way carefully so as not to turn an ankle, when she noticed a shadowy opening some distance up the slope from the shore. Could it be the mouth of a cave?

As she approached the opening, she saw that it extended back into the pile of rocks for some distance, sloping downward. The tunnel looked ripe for a cave-in, until she noticed that the chinks between the rocks of the walls and ceiling had been filled with mortar.

Rachel walked down into the shadowy tunnel. The farther she descended, the cooler the air became. The potent stench of the lake faded. She inhaled greedily, grateful for the reprieve from the intense heat.

The tunnel extended a surprising distance. Just as she was estimating she had to be at or beyond the center of the rocky island, the round tunnel opened into a domed chamber with a floor of solid rock and a pool of water at the center. The purplish moss she had seen outside grew plentifully. Several other shafts extended upward at various angles toward the surface. All were smaller than the tunnel by which Rachel had descended to the chamber, and most were inaccessible because they were too high on the domed ceiling. Daylight filtered into the chamber through the shafts.

Why was the chamber so cool when it was encompassed by the heat of the lake? And how had this place not been flooded by white goo years ago?

"It has been ages since I've had a visitor," a weak voice greeted.

Rachel jumped, eyes darting to find the speaker. She noticed the head of an old man on the ground near the edge of the pool, half hidden by a stone. The head smiled as she made eye contact.

Before knowing Ferrin, this sight might have been sufficient to make her pass out again. Even so, the severed head was disturbing.

"Are you a displacer?" Rachel asked.

"That I am."

The head had a long white beard and long white hair but was bald on top. The beard reached high onto the cheeks, hiding all of the face except the eyes, nose, and deeply creased forehead.

"Where is the rest of you?" she asked.

A movement glimpsed from the corner of her eye caused Rachel to turn. A wrinkled arm, severed just below the shoulder, wormed over the stone floor.

"That's all I have left," the head said.

Rachel turned back to the head. "How do you survive?"

The head cocked a bushy eyebrow. "I eat moss. It's specially engineered, full of nutrients, a strain devised anciently by some wizard. My arm brings it to me. My arm also brings me water from the pool, cupped in my palm."

"What happened to the rest of you?"

"You are full of questions."

Rachel opened her mouth to respond, but the head cut her off.

"I don't mind. It is pleasant to converse. You aren't a delusion, are you?"

"No, I'm really here."

"Why have you come?"

"I'm working with Galloran, hunting for the Word."

"Then Galloran lives!" the head exclaimed. "I expected if he still lived, Maldor would have fallen by now."

"Galloran failed," Rachel said.

"Tragic news. The odds have ever been against us. At least others continue to take up the cause. In answer to your previous question my body lies at the bottom of the sea. Would you care to hear the story?"

"Sure." Rachel squatted beside the head.

The head blinked and smiled. He seemed delighted to have

an audience. "Long ago I did the unthinkable. I spied on Maldor." He whispered the part about spying.

"For years I had served him faithfully, so I was a potent spy, deeply entrenched, and I helped frustrate him many times. I had come to trust a man called Dinsrel, from Meridon, who convinced me we had to depose Maldor and prevent an age of tyranny. I believed that Dinsrel could incite a revolution.

"I was cruising northward on a warship off the western coast when I discovered that Maldor knew of my treachery. I had been spying for almost a year, and I was embroiled in what was to be my most consequential betrayal.

"I knew I was in trouble when I awoke bound securely inside a canvas bag. It is hard to keep a displacer bound for long, but they had used generous portions of rope and cord both within the bag and without, so it must have been an hour before I made any real progress freeing myself.

"While I was making a hole to escape the bag, I heard a door open. Rough hands seized me and hauled me topside. They cut open the sack, and I beheld a dreadful scene. We were surrounded by the Black Armada. Maldor's entire fleet had assembled, including his flagship. The three warships belonging to Dinsrel had been captured. Maldor himself was present. He made me watch as Dinsrel and several other leaders were put in irons. The remainder of the rebels were executed. Maldor then publicly chastised me for my treachery, admonishing me and all who listened that any attempts to resist him would inevitably turn to his benefit.

"Somehow Maldor had learned I was unfaithful and used me to lure Dinsrel out of hiding. Dinsrel had hoped to capture the ship I was on, along with its precious cargo. Maldor had turned the attempted thievery into a masterful trap, beheading the nascent rebellion with a single blow.

"Once the executions were complete, the bodies were dumped overboard, staining the sea. I was transported to the flagship. The other ships departed.

"Maldor ordered my head severed, along with one arm. The rest of me was placed inside a heavy strongbox and thrown overboard. To this day I can feel the water around me, though I only notice it when I concentrate. I can touch the rusty insides of the strongbox. So long as my weary heart keeps beating on the bottom of the sea, I remain alive."

"How did you get away?" Rachel asked. Her ankles hurt from squatting, so she shifted to a kneeling position.

"I was held in a cell with a fellow called Drake, a seedman, one of Dinsrel's closest counselors, and Rex, Dinsrel's top assassin. Rex had smuggled a lockpick into the cell in his hair. During the night he sprang the lock to our cell. Rex killed the first guard silently, but the next one raised an alarm. There was no way to rescue the others. Drake and Rex fought their way topside with me in tow and leaped into the sea.

"Rex was slain by an arrow in the water. We were miles from shore, but Drake managed to swim the distance while keeping my head above water. My hand clung to the back of his neck the whole way. Had the ship been much farther out to sea, I would not be here today.

"When Drake made it to the beach, he was exhausted. Poor fellow collapsed right there on the sand. Before sunup I roused him by flicking his eyelid. He picked me up and headed inland.

"I spent a long time as a piece of luggage, passed from person to person. After a season I received word of another defection by a displacer: Maldor's chief scribe, Salzared. That was when I learned of the Word. A man who had learned the fifth syllable brought me here. Eventually he left. I have remained ever since, preserving a fragment of the Word, years upon years."

"Quite a story," Rachel said.

"Would you mind terribly lowering my lips to the water so I can take a drink? It is such a bother to shuttle water in my palm."

"Of course. Why don't you stay nearer to the water?" The head was about six feet away. It was a wonder the arm could bring any water to him. Rachel supposed he had a lot of practice.

"In case of a heavy rain. Twice I almost drowned, this place filled so quickly. I just barely managed to push my head away in time. It can be slow going with just an arm."

Rachel carried the hairy, wrinkled head to the edge of the pool and lowered it carefully, holding the long beard back as best as she could, until the lips touched the surface. The head drank greedily, finally stopping with a satisfied sigh. "I have not drunk so well since Galloran was here."

"Was he the last to visit you?"

"Correct. How did he fail? He was almost finished when he found his way here."

"I don't know all the details," Rachel said. "He was captured and brainwashed. He has forgotten most of what he learned. But he helped me and a friend begin our search for the Word."

"A shame. A good man, Galloran. You may return me to my resting place."

Rachel situated the head as it had been before.

"We have overlooked introductions," the head said. "I am Malar."

"I am Lady Rachel of Caberton."

The white eyebrows went up. "Caberton. A handsome estate."

Rachel shook her head. "Not anymore. Galloran gave my friend and me the title, but I have heard the estate has fallen into disrepair."

"A shame. In my day it was one of the finest. Times change when you are shut away in a cavern. This friend is male?"

"Yes?"

"And he let you brave the lake?"

"I insisted," Rachel said. "I'm a runner."

"You have spirit. He's a lucky man."

"We're not . . . We're just friends."

"I assume you desire knowledge of the Word."

"Yes, please."

"The fifth syllable is 'dra.' Have you visited the sea cave?"

"I have."

"What syllables do you lack?"

"The second and the sixth."

"You are doing well. The sixth is in the keeping of the Pythoness, in the heart of the Sunken Lands, north and east of here. The second lies very far to the southeast, in the Temple of Mianamon. I would not know where the second lay, were it not for Galloran. He is the only person I know to have ever found it."

Rachel sat down. She felt relieved to have a path again. Now she could put a name to the locations of the missing syllables! And they had two thirds of the Word! Maybe Ferrin would know about the Temple of Mianamon.

"You say you served Maldor, as did that other displacer, Salzared. Do many displacers serve him?"

The head chuckled. "Have you been in a cave yourself? They all do, by covenant. We are his spies."

Chills tingled up Rachel's back. "All of them? Are you sure?"

"To my knowledge only Salzared and I have ever betrayed him. Our race was created by Maldor's old master, Zokar. Things may have changed outside, but certainly not that much."

Rachel put a hand over her mouth. "We're traveling with a displacer."

Malar grimaced. "How did you not know any better? Are you a Beyonder?"

Rachel nodded.

Malar looked surprised at the nod, as if his question had been intended as a rhetorical expression. "Well, that explains it. Is it just you three traveling together?"

"It is."

"How did you fall into company with this *limb dropper?*" He spat the title as an expression of contempt.

"His head was dangling in a bag at a crossroads. His body was buried nearby. He said he had been robbed."

Malar looked downward, as if ashamed to be a displacer himself. "A predictable setup, playing off your ignorance. Has he been with you long?"

"A good while."

"He has been a faithful companion?"

"He feels like our only real friend."

"Then he is an observer," Malar said. "Confront him, and he should leave without violence, unless times have drastically changed."

"When should I confront him?"

"Immediately. Every move you have made with him in your company has been or will be reported to Maldor. Every strength you have, every weakness, every asset, every plan. And there will be other minions of Maldor nearby, ready to strike. After you break company with him, get away fast."

"This is a nightmare," Rachel said.

"Life gets no more difficult than when a person opposes Maldor. Believe me, I know."

"Do you mind if I take a drink?"

"Help yourself. You must be parched after the run across Whitelake."

Rachel bent over at the edge of the pool and began gulping down the water. It tasted strongly of minerals and was so cold it made her teeth ache. Despite the raging thirst the first sips awakened, she had to pull back several times because it was so frigid.

"How does the water stay so cold?"

"Magic."

Rachel stared.

"I'm not jesting. A stone that emits perpetual cold lies at the bottom. It prevents this room from becoming a furnace. Some old wizard designed this sanctuary."

"I have another question. Do you know how I can return to the Beyond?"

Malar scrunched his brow. "There I cannot help you. It is said that long ago there were more gateways to the Beyond than now exist. I myself know of none. There was a rumor in my day that Maldor guarded a secret involving such a portal. I learned no details, and the scant information I heard came from questionable sources."

Rachel sat down near the head. "I don't look forward to running back across the lake."

"I often wonder how many have died trying to cross it. In all my years here only four men have ever found me. I have dwelled here for decades. Although I was getting old when I came here, displacers age more slowly than other men and have hardier constitutions. Would you feed me some moss before you go?"

Rachel moved around the room, ripping up moss. When she squeezed it, a sticky fluid oozed out. She fed some to Malar.

"You should eat some," Malar said. "This stuff is full of energy. It will help in your dash over the lake."

Rachel smelled it. The moss had no scent, unless it was faintly like grass clippings. She tasted some. It was almost unbearably bland, and it triggered her gag reflex.

The head chuckled. "I wish I could say I have developed a taste for the stuff. All I can profess is a tolerance."

Rachel forced herself to eat more. She did not want to sink into the hot lake for lack of energy because she was a picky eater.

"Good girl," Malar encouraged.

Finally she ingested a good portion of the bland moss.

"Give yourself an hour or two," Malar recommended. "That is when your energy should peak. Have some more water. Don't drink any during the last thirty minutes before you run. Before you go, soak your shirt and hair. It will help you stay cool. And run to the shore to the east, right across from where you came in. It is closest, though not by much."

Rachel nodded. She drank more water from her cupped hand. Then she lay down and fell asleep.

She awoke with the head yelling. "Lady Rachel! Lady Rachel! Wake up!"

Rachel sat up with a start, squinting and rubbing her eyes. "What's wrong?"

"Nothing. It has been over two hours. You should probably get started."

Rachel stood and began her stretching routine. Afterward she submerged her head in the water, and came up sputtering and shivering. Then she soaked her clothes. Goose pimples stood out on her arms. "Hard to believe I will be hot in a couple of minutes."

"Believe it."

"I guess this is good-bye," Rachel said. "Do you want me to bring you with me? Get you out of here?"

"I must remain to protect my syllable," Malar said. "Powerful spells guard this chamber."

"Thank you for your help. Any parting advice?"

"Be firm with your displacer. We can be a slippery breed."

"See you later."

"I doubt it. May you prosper in your quest. Safe journey."

"Thanks, Malar. Safe . . . moss eating."

CHAPTER 17

JASHER

"Here she comes," Ferrin announced, rising to his feet and brushing dirt from his pants.

Jason looked up and saw a tiny figure scrambling down the rock pile toward the lake. Relief replaced anxiety. He had felt horrible when Rachel had tumbled at the end of her run, and then as he'd watched her motionless form on the rocky shore of the remote island. Finally she had arisen, disappearing into a cleft in the rocks. He and Ferrin had moved over to the side of the lake opposite the cleft Rachel had entered, but hours had dragged past without sight of her. Jason had begun to lose hope she would ever emerge.

When Rachel reached the lake, she started jogging across. The heat in the air distorted her miniature form.

"She's coming right at us," Jason said. "Should we go try to help her? Maybe carry her?"

"We might do more harm than good," Ferrin said. "One clumsy move and we all sink into the lake together. Hopefully, Rachel has recovered enough from her other run to make it back unaided."

Jason watched Rachel intently, determined to rush to her

aid if she started to falter. She kept a solid pace, and he gradually relaxed as she drew nearer to the shore. Her clothes and hair were drenched, her face was flushed, and she squinted with exertion, but her strides remained firm as she jogged off the lake and slumped to her knees, coughing violently.

"Are you all right?" Jason asked. "What can I do?"

"Just give me a second," she gasped, rising and walking with her hands laced behind her head.

"You are amazing," Ferrin said. "Did you find what you were looking for?"

"No," she replied, still panting. "We had bad information. I found nothing. Just an abandoned cave."

The displacer paused. "Why choose this moment to start lying to me?"

Rachel glared at him. "Because I just found out you've been lying to us."

An awkward silence followed. Ferrin scratched his nose. "What do you mean?"

"I mean you are spying on us for Maldor," she accused.

"What?" Jason exclaimed.

Rachel turned to Jason. "I learned on the island that Maldor uses displacers as his spies. They all work for him."

"Did I ever claim not to be a spy?" Ferrin said calmly.

"Are you blaming us?" Rachel ranted. "Were we supposed to ask? Where we come from, when you make new friends, it's implied they won't spy on you on behalf of your greatest enemy."

"The Beyond sounds wonderful," Ferrin said, his tone guarded.

"Wait, so it's true?" Jason asked in disbelief. He felt like he had been sucker punched.

"How much do you know about us?" Rachel asked.

Ferrin shrugged. "More than you've told me. I know you come

from the Beyond. I know you've consorted with Galloran. I know you're on a quest to find the Word that can destroy Maldor. And I'm sure you just acquired part of it on that island."

"You know about the Word?" Jason asked.

"Not many do," Ferrin replied, "even among Maldor's inner circle. Naturally, none of us know details."

"You've been a liar from the start," Rachel spat.

Ferrin shook his head. "Actually, I've mostly been genuine."

Rachel scowled. "You said you had been robbed when we found you at the crossroads."

"Yes. That was a lie. I told a few lies to gain your trust."

Jason balled his hands into fists. "You betrayed us." He wanted to punch Ferrin in the face. "No wonder everyone hates displacers. We were just too stupid to find out why."

Ferrin frowned and raised a finger. "I have aided and protected you. My presence has prevented numerous conscriptors and manglers from falling upon you. I have come along as an observer, not an enemy. I truly enjoy your company and think very highly of you."

Ferrin sounded hurt. Jason rolled his eyes. This was unbelievable. "So what now?"

"Come with me," Ferrin said. "I will take both of you to Maldor. You're good people. Maldor appreciates good people. If you pledge yourselves to him, he will likely grant you comfortable positions of considerable power. I will vouch for you. You could make worthwhile lives for yourselves."

"And if we won't come?" Rachel said, picking up her cloak and wrapping it around her shoulders.

Ferrin lifted his hands, palms outward. "I know you're reaching for your orantium, Rachel. I searched your things while you two slept. There will be no need for violence. Should you refuse my help, I will leave. I would never harm either of you. It is part of my role as an observer. I began my association with you knowing I was free to be your true friend. Maldor prefers it that way to help ensure more accurate intelligence. He is fascinated with the character of his enemies, and is always looking to turn the best of them into allies. At my discretion I can even help you, and I did, like when those men tried to attack you and we ended up in jail. I will never be asked to spill your blood, nor would I if ordered. I sincerely like and respect both of you. But once I am gone, you will lack my protection, and there are many enemies on your trail. Brave and resourceful as you are, you will not get far."

"Why don't you really help us?" Jason asked. "Abandon Maldor. With your help we might piece together the rest of the Word."

Ferrin laughed. "I would never change sides. I could pretend to switch sides, and keep spying, if you want. Life is far from ideal serving Maldor, but it's infinitely better than opposing him. I honestly am your friend and wish you no harm, but my first allegiance is to my duty."

Jason frowned. "This is insane."

"It is extremely sane," Ferrin assured him. "Displacers learned long ago what it meant to be on the losing side. The races Eldrin sired, the Amar Kabal and the drinlings, inherited homelands, while the races of Zokar became wandering fugitives, despised and hunted. Last time the displacers fought for the wrong wizard. This time we stand with the only wizard. Do not delude yourself. Maldor will prevail. His real struggle ended years ago. Now he's just mopping up."

"Not if we get the Word," Rachel said.

Ferrin laughed again. "You have no chance of finishing the Word! Maldor has monitored you this entire time. When I became your observer, I had details of everywhere you had been. When he wants to capture you, he will. If you send me away, his forces will probably swoop in immediately. You can't imagine the resources he could bring against you. Pray he does not send a lurker."

"We're not going to quit," Jason said.

"I never really expected you to resign," Ferrin sighed. "I just wish you would. Try not to resist when they come for you. They will kill you if you fight. Or you might kill yourselves, if you're not careful with that orantium."

"Thanks for the advice," Rachel said bitterly.

"Don't be so spiteful," Ferrin said. "You should be flattered. Maldor rarely dispatches an observer. He has not shown this much interest in an adversary for several years."

"We're deeply honored," Jason said dryly.

Ferrin folded his arms. "You're from the Beyond. Why do you care about stopping Maldor anyway?"

Jason shrugged. "It just sounded like fun."

"Be serious," Ferrin said.

Jason paused, reflecting. "I don't know. I came to Lyrian by accident. I found the stupid book by accident. Then I met Galloran, who explained about Maldor. Even after leaving him, I was still most interested in getting home."

"Why not make that your focus?" Ferrin encouraged. "I might be able to help you there. This isn't your world. This isn't your battle."

Jason frowned. "It's becoming my battle. This might not be my world, but it's a world. A whole world. Innocent people living in fear and having terrible things happen to them for no reason. Aster was killed, and Franny had her life ruined, just for being nice to me. Norval gave his life for me. The more I see of those who work for Maldor, and the more I see of the few people who try to go up against him, the more I realize this is truly good against evil. And good is losing. What if we can change that?"

"We have to try," Rachel agreed firmly.

"Maybe you're smart," Ferrin mused.

"Why?" Jason asked.

"Well, if you had submitted too easily, Maldor might have lost respect for you."

"That was a close one," Rachel said. "We really crave his respect."

"You think you're joking. His respect may keep you alive. It's your only hope."

Jason sighed. "We're running out of daylight."

"You won't get far," Ferrin predicted sadly. "Maldor's servants will fall upon you within a day. You'll resist, but it will be a fruitless exercise. Be smart enough to accept the inevitable. Nobody can blame you for that. Otherwise, no matter what you do, you'll shortly be killed or captured."

"None of your business anymore," Rachel said.

"I'll always take an interest," Ferrin asserted. "Where are you going?"

"Like we would tell you!" Jason huffed.

"Do you know where you're going?"

Jason shrugged.

"Let me warn you. To the northwest the mountains become impassable. North and east of here lie the Sunken Lands. You need serious provisions if you're headed that way. It's swampland. There's little drinkable water. South lies Trensicourt. Stay away from there. You'll find scattered towns to the west. The westward wilderness holds certain perils, but a person could lose pursuers there, and you will find plenty of bubblefruit if you keep both eyes open."

Ferrin opened a pouch, removing two silver pellets and two gold ones.

"I don't want your money," Jason said.

"Why not? I'm just returning a gift I didn't deserve. This may be my last chance to help you. I am headed far away."

Jason took the pellets.

"Take this crossbow too." Ferrin held it out to Rachel.

She shouldered the weapon.

"Sure you don't want to accept the invitation to the Eternal Feast?" Ferrin asked Jason. "I can probably exert some influence, get Rachel invited as well."

"I don't think so," Jason said.

"I recommend it," Ferrin urged. "I've been there. Harthenham isn't a ruse. The reward is real. This isn't your fight. Maldor might lose some respect for you if you quit, but at Harthenham that won't matter."

"We should get going," Rachel said.

Ferrin held her gaze before responding. "Look, final offer: Jason, accept the invitation to the feast. I'll take you there now, and I'll guarantee Rachel gets invited too. They'll call off the hunt. You won't have to face Maldor, or anyone. Meanwhile I'll try to find how you two can get back to the Beyond. I have reason to believe Maldor knows a way. He would never tell me, but I have a knack for digging up information. When I figure it out, I'll come get you and send you home."

Jason hesitated. He glanced at Rachel, who appeared thoughtful as well. The offer was tempting. A big part of what he had originally wanted was a way home. What if he could lounge in paradise until a way home was provided?

"You don't want manglers and conscriptors to drag you off to prison," Ferrin said. "That is going to happen before long if you walk away. I'm throwing you a lifeline. The scattered resisters who oppose Maldor won't be able to help you get home. Be smart. This is a better offer than I would make for anyone."

"I don't trust you," Rachel said.

"I'll follow through," Ferrin pledged, placing a hand over his heart. "I lied to earn your trust, but have I ever let you down? I've stood by you. Rachel, I know you want to see your parents. Don't skip your only chance to get home."

Rachel snapped. "Of course I want to see my parents!" Tears sprang to her eyes. "You can't imagine how close we are! You have no clue. But Jason is right. If we might be able to save this world, how can we walk away? Too many people around here have given up! Galloran said heroes sacrifice for causes; they do the things that others hide from. I may not be some great hero, but I won't hide from this. I could never live with myself."

"Me neither," Jason said, glad she was holding firm.

Ferrin shook his head. He picked up a rock and skipped it across Whitelake. He looked torn. When he spoke, he sounded sincere. "I might be able to understand this choice if you had any chance of succeeding. But you don't. I am telling you the truth. You will be dead or captured by tomorrow. The invitation to Harthenham will be revoked. It only remains valid if you come in voluntarily."

"No deal," Jason maintained.

Ferrin nodded. "Suit yourselves. I will convey a favorable report to Maldor. I'm striking off to the south. I won't be communicating with your pursuers. You should probably go into town for provisions, but be quick. Do not sleep there. Safe journey."

"You're a jerk," Jason said.

"Don't," Rachel murmured. "Things are bad enough."

"He's right," Ferrin said. "I deserve to lose your respect and your trust. I'm not happy with how this is ending. I'll always consider you my friends. Enough words; you need to move out. I won't be following. Forget about me. Hurry. I'd love it if you surprised me and got away." He turned and started walking.

Jason and Rachel watched the displacer make his way toward the south side of the lake for a moment; then they turned and headed east, toward the town. Scrambling down the eastern slope, they moved fast enough to make Jason nervous about falling.

"What did you learn on the island?" Jason asked as they descended.

"The fifth syllable," she replied. She told him the syllable and what she had learned from Malar about the location of the other two.

A ____ FEX EN DRA ____

"The Sunken Lands," Jason repeated. "According to Ferrin we'll need lots of fresh water."

"Thanks for being brave back there," Rachel said.

"You were pretty brave yourself. Sounds like you have great parents. It must be hard to walk away from a chance to see them."

She shrugged and looked away, her lower lip quivering. "Yeah. I miss them. And I'm sure they're worried about me. We do everything together. You have a close family too, right?"

"Sort of," Jason said. "My parents are good people. I'm sure they're worried about me. I have an older sister and brother. We all love each other, but they've always been closer with each other than with me. I've never totally fit in. The house got really quiet after my siblings left, unless I was butting heads with my folks. Honestly, I sometimes wonder if my parents meant to have me. My brother and sister both have these fat baby books full of photos and stuff. Mine is empty."

"I'm sure that doesn't mean anything," Rachel said. "Parents would be more into documenting their first kids."

Jason shrugged. "My dad is really into my brother, seeing him get into dental school. Mom has always been obsessed with my sister. The two of them love shopping together. My sister is the oldest. She married an endodontist. I'm the youngest by like ten years. When my siblings were home, at dinner I mainly listened. I think my parents try to be interested in me, but it always feels like they're straining. Dad doesn't even try with certain things, like baseball."

"I've always kind of wished I had siblings," Rachel said.

"Me too," Jason replied. "It isn't their fault. The age gap is too big. And our interests are really different. My brother is into school and debate. No sports. My sister is practically my aunt. I'm thankful for my parents. They take care of me. But we don't really know each other, not like you've described with your parents. I sort of do what I want. Even when they try to ground me, I just argue until I wear them out."

Rachel chuckled. "When my parents punish me, it sticks. But I don't get in trouble much."

"I'm going to get you home," Jason said seriously. "I promise. We'll escape whoever is chasing us, and we'll somehow finish this quest, and we'll go home, no matter what Ferrin thinks."

Rachel offered a small nod.

Jason could see the town of Whitelake in the distance, situated beyond the southeast base of the conical mount. The town would be dangerous. Despite his professions to the contrary, Ferrin might have guessed they would end up there, and he could have gotten word out. Enemies might be waiting. But in town they could buy horses, which might make all the difference as they tried to flee. He checked his knife.

"Keep that crossbow ready," Jason advised Rachel.

"I'll keep it under my cloak," she replied. "It'll be ready."

Whitelake was a dusty outpost full of burly men in rugged clothing. Many wore animal skins. Most had facial hair. The largest buildings were arranged along a central road, and scattered cabins, shacks, and lean-tos stood in haphazard clusters off the main street.

Jason avoided eye contact with other men, and they generally did the same. He found a store. An old man sat out front on a sawed-off log segment, whittling. Curled shavings lay scattered at his feet. Jason and Rachel entered the store. In one corner hung several water containers. He bought a pair of large, hairy water skins. They would be burdensome when full, so he decided he would wait to fill them until he had a horse.

He hung back to see what other men bought. Rachel waited at his side, keeping her head down. Many purchased a heavy flatbread they called gutplug. Dried meat was also purchased in considerable quantities. Jason purchased a good deal of the dense bread and some meat.

A crowd was forming in a corner, with a pair of brawny men at the center.

Jason hurried Rachel out of the store and walked up the street before they could get caught up in whatever trouble was brewing. Now they needed a pair of quality horses.

"Excuse me," said a voice from behind.

Jason turned. Before him stood a short man who once had only one arm.

Jason reached into his cloak and gripped the hilt of his poniard.

Tad held up a hand. "You are in no danger from me here. I've come to bargain with you."

Jason kept hold of the knife and placed his thumb over the hidden trigger.

"Save your breath," Jason said, taking a slow step away from the man. "We're not coming with you."

"I don't expect you to," Tad replied. "Apprehending you in town would cause a scene. We would rather handle this discreetly. I'm here to save everyone time. You are welcome to take my horse, if you wish to flee. We would prefer to apprehend you away from town. Naturally, if you want to save yourselves the trouble, you can accompany me now."

"Where's your horse?" Jason asked. "Does it have a wooden leg or something?"

"It's a good mount," Tad assured him. "It will carry both of you. Take it and go, if you please. Whatever you choose, you won't escape."

"What if I we take you hostage?" Jason asked.

"Getting ruthless? That man over there is the law in this town."

Jason glanced to his left and saw a big man leaning against a pole, examining his fingernails. He wore a heavy sword.

"I told him to keep an eye on me," Tad explained. "If you want to attack me unprovoked, have at it. But I'm really not worth the trouble. I'm the least of your problems now."

Jason glanced around, scanning the parade of faces moving up and down the street.

Tad chuckled. "The others aren't here with us. But they're watching. To lose them now, you would need wings."

"Does your horse have wings?" Rachel asked.

"Sorry."

"Let's see it," Jason said.

Tad shrugged. "Be my guest. It's the brown one tethered over there."

Jason peered at the horse. It stood beside a few others, and looked healthy. Jason narrowed his gaze at Tad. The short man stared back evenly, one eye brown, the other blue.

"So we can just leave?"

"Sure. You won't get far, but I was instructed to offer the option."

"What do you think?" Jason asked Rachel.

"I think we need two horses," she replied.

"They only gave me the one," Tad apologized. "You have money?"

"Plenty," Jason said.

Tad turned to the big lawman. "Know any horses for sale in town?" he called. "Good ones."

"I have an exceptional horse," the man replied. "Not for sale, though."

"Everything has a price," Tad replied.

"Okay, stranger," the lawman said, walking toward them. "What if I said two hundred drooma?"

Tad looked at Jason. "Can you cover that?"

Jason nodded. "What's he look like?"

"He is a she," the lawman said. "Intelligent and reliable. She's the black one near your friend's mount."

"Look okay?" Jason asked Rachel.

"Looks fine to me," she replied. "We need to hurry."

Jason fished out two gold pellets. "Can we take her now?"

"For two hundred?" the lawman snickered. "Be my guest."

"See you later," Jason said to Tad, turning and walking toward the horse.

"Count on it," Tad called after him.

Jason was relieved he had learned something about horsemanship. He managed to mount the brown horse and guide it down the street without much awkwardness. Rachel handled her mare like a pro. They rode out of town to the south, then curled around to head east. He scanned the surrounding prairie, searching for prying eyes marking his progress. His gaze repeatedly returned to the top of the conical mountain—anyone watching from that towering vantage point would have easily noted their little change of direction.

Rachel cantered beside him. "Think we have a chance?" she asked.

"I don't think they would give us horses if they thought we could escape," Jason replied. "I'm just not sure what else to do. Maybe they're counting on us making bad moves, or being lousy horsemen. Maybe we can surprise them. If we can make it to the forest, we'll be harder to spot. Keep that orantium ready."

The country around the town was covered in wild grass, and they made smooth progress for some time. Beyond the expansive sward, to the east and north, ranks of forested hills awaited.

Jason weighed their options. Perhaps they could dismount and let their horses loose. If they did it carefully, their pursuers might follow the hoofprints. He and Rachel could hide until after sunset, then sneak into the forest on foot. Of course, if their enemies were watching, or if they caught on to the ruse, the chase could end quickly. It was probably best to take their chances on horseback.

The sun was sinking. Jason kept a sharp lookout, but he viewed nothing across the surrounding terrain to arouse his suspicions, although the occasional scurry of a rabbit or squirrel made him start.

At a wide, shallow creek Jason and Rachel paused to let their horses drink and filled their furry new skins. They remounted and walked the horses across water-polished pebbles to the far side and up the shallow embankment.

Not far ahead arose the outliers of the forested hills. Sparse oak trees stood here and there about the sward, casting monstrous shadows as the sun plunged. Off to the left towered the bulk of an oklinder bush. Jason toyed briefly with the idea of concealing themselves in the huge mass of foliage, risking thorns and wasps rather than facing their pursuers. Of course, their enemies would probably track them there, then surround them and light the oklinder on fire.

At that moment from out of the massive bush sprang a gray horse bearing an armored rider. The bush was less than a mile away to the north, and the horse was dashing toward Jason at a terrific pace, churning up clods of earth from the ground.

"Jason!" Rachel cried.

"I see him." He kicked his horse, veering southward, and saw another, more distant horseman closing from that direction. In the west, the way they had just come, a third rider had materialized, made into a silhouette by the setting sun.

Where had they come from? He had been alert! Only the east appeared free of riders, so he urged his horse in that direction, yelling, "Yah!" like he imagined a cowboy would. He snapped the reins and nudged the steed's flanks with his heels.

Jason and Rachel sped eastward, their horses galloping wildly. Jason leaned forward, close to the brown neck, and rocked his hips in time with the horse's pounding gait.

As they raced along, the sun dipped below the western horizon, and shadows became muted in the softer light. Flecks of lather began to appear on the coat of Jason's horse.

Their pursuers herded them eastward. The riders had all drawn to within a hundred yards: one directly to their left, another to their right, and the third behind. When Jason tried to alter his course, they would draw in close, weapons flashing, forcing him to continue eastward or face confrontation.

Ahead gaped the mouth of a steep-walled ravine. He could feel his horse flagging. The other horses were bigger and more muscular than his mount, powerful animals that did not seem to tire. The men to either side wore similar armor. One clutched a battle-ax; the other held a spear.

Jason and Rachel rode into the mouth of the ravine. It was clearly a trap, but the walls were too steep for their horses to possibly climb. The horsemen at either side fell back to join the third trailing rider. Jason spurred his mount onward, noticing how the foam was thickening on the overtaxed steed.

Rounding a bend in the ravine, Jason learned where the horsemen were driving them. A fourth horseman stood in the middle of the ravine, flanked by three bizarre creatures. The horseman held a drawn bow in his hands.

"Rein in and dismount," the soldier commanded. He wore dark armor like the others.

Jason pulled on the reins, and his horse stopped, sides heaving. Rachel drew up beside him. They shared a worried glance. Jason heard the other horsemen trotting up behind them.

The horseman had his bow aimed at Jason. "I am Stanus, an imperial servant, and I demand your immediate and unconditional surrender."

Jason gazed at the creatures flanking Stanus. They stood upright like tall men, covered in rounded shell-like armor that curved up over their heads. Shiny black compound eyes stared out from the barbed masks protecting their faces. Hooks and spikes protruded from their armored bodies in all directions. Each creature had four arms bristling with cruel blades of varying length and shape. Various grinders and graters covered their torsos. Jason could tell the manglers were aptly named.

"Dismount!" the horseman repeated harshly.

Jason swung out of the saddle to the ground as the other horse-men pulled up behind, blocking their escape. Rachel dismounted as well.

"If you do not resist, we will not harm you," the soldier vowed. "You are trapped and outnumbered. Surrender your arms."

Jason glanced back at the men behind him. He assumed the horsemen were conscriptors. One of the three, the horseman who had come from directly behind, wore no armor and bore a long-sword. A patch covered one eye. The other horsemen wore hel-mets that screened their faces.

"Choose now," Stanus said. "Do not force us to lay hands on you."

Jason reached into his cloak, his hand closing over the haft of the poniard. There were too many adversaries both in front and behind.

"We have to surrender," he told Rachel. He wondered if it was too late to bargain using his invitation to Harthenham. It was worth a try.

"We're putting our weapons down," Rachel called, revealing her crossbow.

As she spoke, Jason heard a sound like breaking glass. A bril-liant flash originated behind a mangler, followed by a deafening explosion. The mangler blew apart, showering shards of blade and armor in all directions. A neighboring mangler also went down with the explosion, and Stanus was unseated from his horse as it reared and toppled over, a long fragment of a blade protruding from its side.

Jason fell flat after the explosion. His borrowed mount bolted back down the ravine, away from the blast. Had Rachel somehow thrown the orantium? How had it landed behind the mangler? Through the smoke Jason saw one of the manglers charging at him with alarming speed. Rachel thrust the crystal sphere into his hand. "You're the pitcher," she said urgently.

From his knees he flung the globe at the attacker. The crystal sphere shattered against the creature's spiked chest. For an instant the stone flared an intense white; then it exploded with a fiery roar.

As the hot blast wave washed over him, Jason pressed his face into the ground and clapped his hands over his ears. When he looked up, what remained of the mangler lay in a twisted ruin twenty feet farther away than before. A curved blade was planted in the earth inches from Jason's head.

Jason rose to his knees and turned to face the horsemen behind him, raising his poniard. Rachel aimed her crossbow. A long-haired man was bounding down the slope, a sword in one hand, a heavy doubled-up chain in the other. He headed toward the three riders, who appeared to have forgotten Jason as they faced this new threat.

Leaping the last twelve feet to the floor of the ravine, the newcomer swung the four-foot length of chain like a flail, taking the helmet off one of the riders and unhorsing him. The long-haired man rolled under the horse and regained his feet. The man with the eye patch was bearing down on him, brandishing his longsword. The long-haired man somersaulted toward the horse, just enough to one side to avoid being trampled, staying low enough to avoid the rider's reach. From the newcomer's kneeling position, a well-timed swing of his sword slashed the charging steed's foreleg, and the horse pitched forward, churning up chunks of soil. The rider took flight, landing violently.

Jason saw the conscriptor with the lance bring his horse around. He nudged Rachel, who aimed her crossbow carefully at the horseman and pulled the trigger. The quarrel did not fire. The safety was engaged.

The long-haired man did not require the help. As the rider reached him, he spun, using his sword to chop off the head of the lance, then the chain to slam the rider from his saddle. Pouncing, the newcomer stabbed the rider as he struggled to rise, the sharp blade finding a gap in the rings of his armor.

The rider who had lost his helmet was on his feet and approaching with an ax. Rachel, who had now released the safety, fired the crossbow. The quarrel missed by inches.

The long-haired man left his sword in the back of the fallen rider and held both ends of his doubled chain. With the chain he intercepted the downswing of the ax, turning the weapon aside. Lunging past his attacker, the long-haired man swung the chain in a vicious backhand that struck the rider's unprotected temple. The man collapsed and did not stir.

The enemy with the eye patch rose unsteadily, his clothes stained with dirt and grass, an ugly gash bleeding on his forehead. He stood ten paces away from the long-haired man, longsword grasped in both hands. "Jasher," he growled. "You chose the wrong day to interfere."

"I do not know your name," Jasher said, brushing some of his long hair out of his face, "though I am far too familiar with your kind." A good portion of his hair was caught up in a roll at the nape of his neck. To either side it hung more than halfway down his torso. He wore loose brown robes, and his feet were bound in animal hides with leather thongs. A leather baldric held a sheath across his back.

"I am Turbish."

"Are you ready to die, Turbish?" Jasher walked toward him, his chain held casually. He made no move to retrieve his sword.

"What makes you think you can best me?" Turbish snarled.

Jasher laughed lightheartedly.

The chain suddenly unfurled to its full length, snapping like a whip. Turbish's head jerked back, and one hand flew to cover his nose and mouth. When Turbish removed his hand, his nose lay broken sideways across his face. A second adroitly aimed lashing left Turbish cradling his remaining eye, his sword falling from his hands.

Jasher doubled the chain again, and a harsh blow to the jaw sent Turbish's head bouncing across the ground. The headless body lunged at Jasher, who sprang nimbly aside and tripped it.

Jasher retrieved Turbish's longsword, approached the displacer's head, and finished him. He promptly withdrew the sword and put the horse with the missing foreleg out of its misery. Leaving the longsword planted in the horse, he retrieved his own blade.

Weapons in hand, Jasher trotted past Jason and Rachel without a glance, over to where the manglers had exploded. He inspected the mangler bodies, thrusting his sword into one. The creature shrieked at a pitch almost too high to apprehend.

Jasher leaned over Stanus, who had been crushed when his horse fell. The injured horse was breathing, so Jasher dispatched it. "All dead," Jasher said, turning to Jason and Rachel. He spoke with a different accent than Jason had heard.

Jason gawked at their rescuer, still marveling at how thoroughly he had annihilated the enemy soldiers. "I'm Jason. This is Rachel."

"Jasher, exile of the Amar Kabal." He touched two fingers to his chest and briefly inclined his head.

Jason stood.

"That was an excellent throw with the orantium," Jasher said. "Galloran informed me you had one of his spheres." He spoke with the precise enunciation of a man using a second language he has mastered.

"You know Galloran?" Jason asked.

"He is a dear friend. He got word to me of your quest and bade me lend a hand. I almost reached the crossroads in time to prevent your meeting with the displacer. Once he was in your company, I chose to follow you, watching from afar. Now seemed the appropriate moment to intervene."

"I thought we were doomed," Rachel said.

"You were. Where are you going now?"

"Are you coming with us?" Jason asked hopefully.

"Of course, Lord Jason of Caberton. I will strive to keep you alive while you complete the Word."

"We're going to the Sunken Lands," Rachel said. "We need to find the Pythoness."

"A hard journey," Jasher said. "I have a horse, and fortunately two of your enemies' warhorses survived. We will ride part of the way."

Jasher retrieved the two warhorses. Both seemed unaffected by the wild skirmish. He handed Jason the reins to one. "I'll be right back."

Mounting the other, Jasher rode off down the ravine the way Jason and Rachel had come. Shortly he returned, leading the horses Jason and Rachel had ridden. "Transfer the gear you want to keep, and we'll let these poor beasts go."

Jason retrieved the furry water skin and some other articles. Rachel collected gear from her horse as well. Meanwhile Jasher heaped the bodies together and set them aflame.

"That should help blur the evidence of my handiwork. Nobody knows that I travel with you. We can use that to our advantage. Do you have what you want?"

"Yes," Jason said.

Jasher crossed to the horse Jason had ridden. He passed his hands over the coat of the beast, inspecting it closely. "Ah!"

"What?"

"Come see. You too, Rachel."

Jason moved closer to where Jasher stood inspecting the horse's shoulder. He had pulled back a small flap of fur to reveal a glazed human eye embedded in the horseflesh. Jason stared at the eye, disgusted and fascinated.

"Can you guess who this belongs to?" Jasher asked.

Jason shrugged. "It looks dead."

"Your displacer friend didn't teach you much. This eye belongs to the displacer I just killed—Turnip, or whoever he was."

"Ew," Rachel said. "How?"

"Displacers can graft parts of their bodies onto other living creatures," Jasher explained. "This talent more than any other makes them such potent spies. With his eye on the horse, he knew every move you made. Be wary of gifts from your adversaries."

Jasher swatted the horse gently and it trotted off.

"Unbelievable," Jason muttered. Now he understood why Tad had been so generous.

Jasher swung up onto one of the warhorses. "This ravine ends at an unscalable wall. We need to loop around to get my horse. Rachel can ride with me. Come."

Jasher helped Rachel mount behind him. Jason climbed onto the other horse, which proved a little tricky, since it was taller than the previous horses he had ridden. The powerful steed stamped restively.

"Ride with confidence," Jasher advised. "Your new mount is trained for battle. She can sense your uncertainty."

Jason followed Jasher out of the ravine. Jasher's hair trailed behind him like a banner as he cantered along. Once out of the ravine they curved around to the north and east. A small trail led up a slope to a third horse, which Jasher claimed. As he led them deeper into the forest, twilight deepened to darkness.

Eventually Jasher ordered a dismount and secured the horses. "Go to sleep quickly," he warned. "I will awaken you early."

Jason felt so fatigued from the day's activities that he needed no admonition.

CHAPTER 18

THE SUNKEN LANDS

The next evening Jason rested against a fallen log, his body sore from a long day riding. Jasher had led them on a winding route deep into the hills, often walking the horses up shallow streams or forging paths through heavy foliage.

Having been up since before dawn, Jason felt ready to sleep. The meal of gutplug and jerky settling in his stomach did not help his wakefulness. But Jasher had kept watch the previous night, and he had to be exhausted. "I'll take first watch," Jason offered.

"No need," Jasher said. "My kind never truly sleep. We recuperate from the day with a type of lucid dreaming. It's a trancelike state not far from full consciousness. No adversaries will surprise us while I rest."

These were more words than Jasher had spoken all day. Jason wanted to keep the conversation alive.

"Why do you keep your hair rolled up at the back of your neck?" he asked. He noticed Rachel paying attention.

"It is the way of my people, the Amar Kabal. It protects the amar."

"The amar?" Rachel repeated.

Jasher paused, regarding them with icy blue eyes. "'Amar'

means 'seed.' The Amar Kabal are the People of the Seed." He turned his head and lifted the roll of hair. At the base of his skull was a raised portion of flesh the size of a walnut.

Jason winced. It looked like a huge cyst. "What's it for?"

"The amar is the vehicle of our immortality. It dislodges at our death, granting new life when planted in the earth."

"You mean you grow?" Rachel asked in amazement. "Like a plant?"

"Buried in fertile soil, the man grows from the seed within a few months. Less fertile soil requires more time. If my seed dislodged in extremely arid terrain, I might never be reborn."

Jason leaned forward. "So you've died before?"

Jasher gave a small, grim smile. "Many times."

"And then you come back to life," Rachel murmured.

"Yes. The miracle of the amar preserves my memories until a new body germinates."

"You remember all of your lives," Jason said.

"Every moment until every seed has dislodged and become separated from my senses. Nine times I have perished in combat. Five times I have allowed my life to be taken, because my body was nearing the end of its usefulness and I wished to start anew. Once I drowned at sea. Once I fell to my death scaling a cliff. And my First Death."

"That must feel strange, becoming an infant with all of your former memories," Rachel realized.

Jasher laughed as if the idea were absurd. "No, we are reborn into the prime of adulthood, the age at which we first die. Our First Death is a ceremony held around age twenty."

"How long can your seed survive unplanted?" Jason wondered.

Jasher shrugged. "The amar can lie dormant for years. But eventually the seed would perish."

"So if Maldor wants to truly eliminate you," Jason said, "he would have to kill you and then destroy your seed."

Jasher's eyes flashed. "The destruction of an amar is the unpardonable sin. He who commits such an act incurs a death penalty, to be executed by the Amar Kabal, who from that moment onward will stand united as his enemy."

"I take it people don't usually destroy a seed," Rachel surmised.

"Not often." Jasher winced softly, as if the thought caused him pain. "On the brighter side, the hand that preserves and plants an amar may request virtually any service in return."

"You called yourself an exile," Jason remembered. "Are there others of your people wandering like you?"

Jasher shook his head. "Very few. I was cast out of the Seven Vales because I chose to oppose Maldor. My people enjoy independence from his tyranny. He respects their might and leaves them in peace, untouched by his corrosive influence, so long as they do not interfere with his efforts to dominate the other kingdoms. My rebelliousness endangered their peace, so they disavowed me."

"Then can Maldor kill your seed?" Rachel said.

"Not without incurring the full consequences of the unpardonable sin. There are no exceptions to our vengeance on that matter. If it could be proven that he was behind such an act, the Amar Kabal would rise against him, even though I am an exile."

"Why do you fight Maldor?" Jason asked.

Jasher looked into his eyes. "He committed the unpardonable sin."

Jason scrunched his eyebrows. "Then why don't your people oppose him with you?"

"To avoid a war Maldor pretended that the perpetrator of the crime, a displacer named Fronis, acted alone and against his orders. The Amar Kabal are not great in number, but there are mighty warriors among us, and our dead normally rise to fight again. Maldor has reason to fear us. He delivered Fronis to my people. The displacer, having been betrayed by his master, professed he was carrying out orders, but my people closed their ears and their minds and exacted their revenge on him alone. I confirmed through a trusted source that Maldor himself gave the order to extinguish the amar of my brother, Radolso. I testified to what I had learned, but since I myself did not witness the order, and since a war against Maldor could bring about the end of the Amar Kabal, my testimony was ignored. Therefore I seek my vengeance alone."

"So you're trying to kill Maldor?" Rachel asked.

"Yes. I bide my time, harassing him, slaying his servants, while I seek an opportunity to take his life. I must not fail, or else his sin will go unpunished."

"Are you seeking the Word?" Jason asked.

"I am not. Eldrin designed his races to have little aptitude for Edomic. There is a prophecy among us, spoken by Darian the Seer, that when the Amar Kabal seek to speak Edomic, it will mark the beginning of our downfall."

"But you want to help us," Jason confirmed.

"If you can obtain the Word and use it to destroy Maldor, my vengeance will be complete. I do not need his blood on my sword."

"You also helped Galloran?" Rachel asked.

"I was not present when he was taken. He had sent me on an errand. I would like to believe that had I been present, he would not have fallen. You have four of the six syllables?"

"Yes," Jason said. "How did you know?"

"An educated guess. I know where the fragments are located, all save the second. Long ago Galloran described to me the location of the Pythoness in the Sunken Lands. We will find her."

"The second syllable is in a place called the Temple of Mianamon," Rachel said.

Jasher grinned. "Then we know our destination after the Sunken Lands. I know of the Prophetess of Mianamon, but have never visited her temple. It lies deep in the southern jungles, beyond the limits of civilization. Let us hope the Pythoness can enlighten you. They say she has the true gift of prescience."

Jason scratched with his fingernail at a piece of meat in his teeth left over from dinner. It had wedged in there tightly.

"How did you two come to oppose Maldor?" Jasher inquired. "Galloran led me to understand you are Beyonders."

Jason and Rachel took turns explaining how they came to Lyrian, and how they crossed paths at Galloran's ruined castle.

"In the end," Jason summarized, "Galloran encouraged us to pursue the Word. He basically challenged us to be heroes. With Maldor already after me I'm not sure I had any other choice."

"Do not dishonor your involvement," Jasher chided. "For each of us destiny is a blend of potential, circumstances, and choices. You could flee and hide. You could bargain with Maldor. You have chosen a heroic path. Walk it without apology."

"I guess that makes sense," Jason admitted. "For what it's worth, I think I've finally really accepted the challenge."

"Me too," Rachel agreed.

"You have enjoyed much success," Jasher said. "Surely Maldor has offered you attractive alternatives by now."

"I got invited to Harthenham," Jason said.

"Ferrin hinted he might be able to help us get home," Rachel added.

"Yet here you are, toiling in the wilderness," Jasher emphasized. "The two of you picked the right road, even though it is the most difficult. This is the essence of heroism."

"You would know," Rachel said. "You walked away from your people to do what you felt was right."

"I have lived many lives," Jasher said. "I know myself. I could never have found peace while ignoring the crime against my brother."

"How far to the Sunken Lands?" Jason asked.

"This is rugged country," Jasher said, looking to the northeast. "The outskirts lie more than a week away. The contours of the land cause water to collect and stagnate there in a vast swamp, a festering breeding ground for foulness and slime. During a certain season the Sunken Lands become inaccessible due to rampant disease spread by impenetrable clouds of biting insects. This time of year we should survive if we take the proper precautions."

"So we'd better enjoy the ride in the woods while we can," Rachel said.

Jasher nodded. "The Sunken Lands will not be pleasant."

Traveling with Jasher proved simple. He gathered nuts and berries and supplemented their meals with fish and fowl. After two days of circuitous wandering to confuse pursuers, he began improvising easy routes across the gentlest available terrain, occasionally finding secluded paths to follow. Sometimes on high ground he climbed a tree to get his bearings or to check for enemies, but the days passed without hardship.

By their fifth day traveling together their path through the hilly wilderness trended down more than up. Early on the eighth day, from a hilltop, they glimpsed hazy, green lowlands to the north. Late on the ninth day, beside a rushing spring, Jasher informed them that they were filling their water skins for the last time before they left the Sunken Lands.

The next day Jasher left the horses on long tethers, and they proceeded on foot. He explained that the upcoming terrain was unsuitable for horses.

After leaving the horses, as predicted the ground became boggy and the air more humid. Jason's boots squelched in clinging muck so often he eventually ceased trying to avoid it. Persistent rafts of mud on his soles added weight to his strides and sometimes made it feel like he was wearing snowshoes.

As they progressed, Jason, Rachel, and Jasher all selected long walking sticks. Several times they were forced to double back because of quicksand or impassable mires.

Evening had fallen when Jasher paused beside a pool where a cluster of large violet flowers flourished. The striking petals looked venomously bright against the dull greens and browns of the surrounding foliage.

"I hoped to find some of these orchids before proceeding much farther," Jasher said. He plucked a closed bud from a stem and squeezed the tightly sealed petals. Blue gel oozed out. Jasher licked it. "The results are not entirely pleasant, but this nectar will keep most of the biting and stinging insects at a distance."

Jason ripped off a bud and ate the gel. It had almost no taste. Rachel tried some as well. Jasher plucked a few extra buds.

Not long after leaving that pool, Jasher found a section of higher ground covered in leafy ivy. They dined on gutplug and dried meat.

"We are at the threshold of the Sunken Lands," Jasher said as he bedded down. Jason and Rachel lay at either side of him on their backs, the ivy adding some cushion beneath their blankets. "Tomorrow you will see the actual swamp. The depths of the swamp cannot be negotiated without a watercraft. Fortunately, my people forage sporadically in the swamp to gather rare herbs and fungi. I believe I can guide us to a hidden skiff."

"What kind of animals live here?" Rachel asked. Her tone suggested she dreaded the answer, but couldn't resist asking.

"Our concern tonight will be serpents," Jasher said. "Should you feel a scaly visitor coiling against you in the night, keep still. Most snakes will not strike a person unless provoked. Be thankful the night is warm. On cold nights serpents are drawn to people for warmth. I once awoke with a black-ringed water prowler curled against my chest, inside my robes. Are you familiar with the species?"

"No," Rachel said, a quaver in her voice.

"The black-ringed water prowler is among the most poisonous of serpents. Its venom will claim the life of a strong man before he takes twenty breaths. The pain is instant and unbearable."

Jason leaned up on one elbow. "What did you do?"

"After I gingerly peered down my robes and observed the markings of the dread snake, I lay still and dreamless the remainder of the night, perspiring despite the chill air. I may live again after I die, but there is no guarantee my seed will be planted, and occasionally an amar is defective. Even under the best circumstances death can be highly inconvenient. In the morning the serpent stirred. It exited my robes past my neck, slithering against my cheek, as if daring me to flinch or cry out. Then it was gone."

"Are you trying to make me crazy?" Rachel asked. "Why would you tell a story like that on a night like this?"

"As a warning," Jasher said.

"More like psychological warfare," Rachel muttered.

"I hear the snakes like girls best," Jason teased. "Rachel can be our snake magnet."

"I'm walking back to Trensicourt," Rachel declared.

"You should sleep in the middle," Jasher offered. "It will offer some protection."

Rachel gratefully traded places with him.

Jason eyed the surrounding ivy. He rested his head on his arms. Every rustling sound in the night set his nerves on edge. It was a long while before sleep overtook him.

Jason wakened in the morning to an awful stench. He sat up, sniffing the rank air with sleepy disgust. A low fog hung over the marshland, fuming up from the surrounding pools.

Rachel remained asleep. Jasher lay with his eyes half open, crystal blue irises shifting eerily from side to side.

Jason put his nose near his wrist, and the unsavory stink was stronger. Sniffing at himself, he found that his entire body smelled putrid, his armpits unbearable, as if his natural body odor had been grotesquely magnified. Wasn't his own stench only supposed to bother other people?

Leaning over Rachel, Jason found she reeked even worse than he did. Leaning farther, he could smell Jasher as well.

Jasher fully opened his eyes. "The pungent odors of swamp travel," he said, sitting up and stretching.

"Ugh," Rachel griped, propping herself up, bleary-eyed. "What died?"

"We did," Jason said.

She sniffed her shoulder and made a revolted face. "That's us? What happened?"

"Think about it," Jasher said.

Jason shot Jasher a hard look. "The stuff from the flowers? You did this on purpose?"

Jasher grinned. "Trust me. To venture into the swamp without a means of repelling the insects is not merely inconvenient. It borders on suicide. Some of the pests are poisonous; others carry diseases. This time of year the stink should suffice to keep the insects away."

"And the bears," Jason said. "And the skunks. And the girls."

Jasher laughed, slapping his thigh. He reached up a hand, and Jason hoisted him to his feet. "Take this as a consolation. In the deep swamp there are insects as dangerous as any snake. Be glad you will not make their acquaintance. As for women, I suspect none of us will mind if the Pythoness keeps her distance."

"I wish I could avoid myself," Rachel mumbled.

The rising sun dispersed the mists. Rachel and Jason followed Jasher along a meandering route.

At length, with the sun high overhead, Jasher stopped and announced, "Here we are."

Jason had been focusing on the ground, watching for snakes. He had spotted nine so far. Two were pretty big.

Raising his gaze, he beheld the coast of a black lake, full of tall trees with spreading branches, huge arboreal umbrellas that blocked out most of the sunlight. Leafy vines hung in haphazard loops. Long beards of moss and glossy coats of slime added texture to the dark trunks. Out in the water, islands of filthy mulch and half-drowned logs showed that not all the swamp was submerged, though Jason had no trouble seeing why they would need a boat.

"You know where we are?" Jason asked.

"I think I know where our skiff should be," Jasher replied.

To reach the water's edge they weaved around a few reedy pools where cattails protruded like hot dogs on sticks. At one point the sludge became so deep it was almost over the top of Jason's boots, sucking and slurping with every step.

After reaching the brink of the gloomy swamp, they skirted the murky water for more than a hundred yards. Then Jasher began tearing decayed leaves and creepers off of a low mound by the waterside.

"Here we go," Jasher said, after stripping off enough vegetable matter to expose the wooden hull of the small vessel. "Help me uncover it."

Before long they removed the vegetation. Working together, they flipped the skiff right side up. An eight-foot snake uncurled from under the vessel and whipped away into the water, moving in a black blur.

"That was a dangerous one," Jasher said, staring at the ripples where the snake was lashing across the surface. "Did you notice the red dots behind the head?"

"I barely saw the snake," Jason said. "That thing was fast!"

"Mud viper. Big one. Be glad we were on land. They'll attack almost anything in the water. One bite causes paralysis. A few more bring death."

Jason shuddered.

"Snakes never really freaked me out before," Rachel said numbly.

"Don't worry," Jason said. "Your smell should keep them away."

"If your smell doesn't kill them first," she fired back.

Jasher inspected the skiff from bow to stern. "Looks watertight. Only one way to be sure."

They pushed it over the muddy bank into the water. "Get in," Jasher said.

Jason and Rachel stepped over the stern of the broad, shallow vessel.

"Move to the bow and sit down."

They complied, and Jasher sprang into the skiff, the force of his landing propelling the little craft away from the shore.

The skiff rode low with the three passengers, the gunwale scarcely six inches above the water. Jasher fitted the single long oar into the oarlock at the stern and began deftly sculling the vessel deeper into the swamp.

"Need any help?" Jason asked.

"No. I can do this all day. Better if you two stay in the bow. There is a species of predatory slime that drifts on the surface of the water. It will digest flesh down to the bone. Keep a sharp look-out so I can keep it from attaching to the skiff. It's yellow-green in color and floats listlessly until it senses prey."

Jason sat taller, scanning the water ahead. Off to one side he spotted a fat frog squatting on a floating log. Bigger than a rabbit, the frog bulged with warty bumps.

"Big frog," Jason said.

Jasher snorted.

"They get bigger?" Rachel asked.

"Big enough to prey on men, I am told," Jasher whispered. "I have never ventured deep enough into the swamp to behold one. Keep a sharp lookout. We should generally avoid speaking. Certain creatures have sharp ears. It would be better if we passed unnoticed."

Jason nodded. He kept watching the water. The only sounds were the gentle swishing of the scull and the mellow hum of insects. Jason glimpsed many more big frogs, both swimming and squatting. He saw a snake streak through the water, just as the mud viper had, and steal a big, hairy spider off of a tree trunk.

Insects abounded—dragonflies, mosquitos, gnats, water skimmers, and beetles in metallic greens and blues. As Jasher had promised, they kept their distance from the boat.

After some time Jason spotted an amoeboid shape floating in the water ahead, like a huge wad of snot. "I see some slime," he whispered.

Jasher navigated around it.

As night fell, the swamp blackened. Jasher found a soggy island, and he and Jason hauled the craft out of the water.

"The night is dreadful in the swamp," Jasher whispered. "Or so I have heard. I am told it is best to stay out of the water and to remain in your boat."

A deep, resonant croak, almost a bark, sounded somewhere not far behind Jason. He gasped and turned quickly but could see nothing through the murk. Jasher placed a steadying hand on his arm.

"Was that a frog?" Rachel murmured.

The croak was soon answered by another farther off. Before long the swamp was alive with a confused chorus of deep-throated croaking. Some of the croaks were like massive belches, others almost musical, others fierce and threatening.

Jasher moved between Rachel and Jason, whispering softly. "I had heard the night sounds of the swamp were unnerving. Never did I imagine it would be like this."

"I never imagined frogs freaking me out," Rachel whispered back.

"Swallow some insect repellant," Jasher suggested.

Jason and Rachel consumed the gel gratefully.

Soon it became as dark as the bowels of a cave. Jason found that closing or opening his eyes made no difference.

New sounds joined the frog chorus. High-pitched squeals began to warble in long, quavering notes. Low moans like the winding of giant horns drifted over the swamp from far away, as if some immense creature were mourning. A sudden clicking like castanets, sometimes alarmingly close, added a startling rhythm to the cacophony. The relative quiet of the day was utterly forgotten.

"Try to sleep," Jasher whispered loudly over the increasing din. "I will keep watch."

Jason had to curl up to lie in the skiff, and he had difficulty getting comfortable. His mind raced in the blackness, imagining cunning snakes stealing into the skiff, or methodical masses of slime oozing over the gunwale, mindlessly craving his warm flesh. The ghastly clamor of the swamp would not relent. Strange dreams invaded Jason's fitful slumber.

When Jason awakened, all was quiet again. And he could see, though the light was dim.

"Good morning," Jasher said in a hoarse, hushed tone. "Let's make haste today. I do not yearn for many nights like the past one."

"Is your throat okay?" Jason asked.

"A little sore," Jasher replied.

Rachel handed Jason a sandwich made of gutplug and dried meat. He wondered how long the other two had been awake. He found the sandwich difficult to chew, but his hunger made it delicious.

Jason stood up and could barely stretch because his back and neck felt so cramped. He noticed several dead snakes on the island beside the boat, heads crushed or severed.

"Were these here before?" Jason asked.

"I had a busy night," Jasher replied.

They got the skiff back into the water.

Jason knelt in the prow, scanning the turbid water for evidence of danger.

Jasher plied the oar expertly to maneuver them through mazes of muddy islands, tangled deadfalls, and slick masses of slime. Late in the afternoon they found a treeless lake. In the center was a long, muddy island, larger than any island they had yet seen in the swamp. At the far end of the island towered an enormous tree, both in height and girth: an arboreal skyscraper, dwarfing all the other trees within view. Its mighty limbs, themselves the size of the lesser trees, fanned out hundreds of feet above to overshadow the entire lake.

On the black mud of the near bank of the island squatted a frog the size of a horse, an obese creature disfigured by bulbous warts and crowned with sharp horns. It raised its heavy head, wet nostrils flaring, as the skiff moved out into the lake.

"We have arrived," Jasher whispered. "The Pythoness dwells within that monarch of the swamp." He gestured at the tree.

As they approached the island, the frog sat up high, revealing a fat, pale underbelly. The rest of its slimy hide was dark gray and green. The frog emitted a low humming sound. "Think you can work the scull?" Jasher asked. "I believe this frog means to challenge us."

Jason traded positions with Jasher, who moved to the bow, sword in hand. Under Jason's clumsy guidance the skiff veered right, then overcorrected to the left, and eventually made a zigzag path to the muddy bank.

Over his shoulder, Jason noticed that Rachel had pulled out her camera. She snapped a couple of pictures of Jasher approaching the frog.

As the craft ran aground, Jasher sprang forward into the muck. The heavy frog shifted, letting out a terrible roar, throaty and impossibly deep and loud. Jason flinched.

Jasher advanced slowly and evenly, walking sideways, sword held vertically in both hands. The gargantuan frog took a couple small hops forward, pausing five yards away from Jasher. Quick and sudden as a jack-in-the-box a long pink tongue lashed out and curled about Jasher's waist.

His sword flashed, severing over three feet of muscular tongue. The rest of the tongue retracted, blood spewing from the tip. The length of tongue around his waist clung there like a grotesque belt.

The frog roared with twice the previous intensity, its obscene body quivering, dark syrup gushing from its wide mouth. It squatted low, and its hide chameleoned to a darker hue that matched the surrounding muck. Its hind legs released, and the enormous frog leaped in a fantastic arc, its bulk soaring high over Jasher's head, beyond the reach of his slashing sword.

It crashed down near the skiff and slid across the slick mud to slam against the craft, bumping the vessel abruptly into the water, the sudden jerk toppling Jason over the side. Rachel screamed. Jason flailed his arms to keep his head above the surface of the tepid water. His cloak and clothes and boots weighed him down and made him flounder.

Something slick and muscular and somewhat elastic snaked around his arm and yanked him toward a gaping, razor-toothed mouth. Black liquid sprayed from the wounded tongue. As abruptly as it had seized Jason, the tongue released him, dropping him prone into the sludge on the shore with his legs still in the water.

Looking up, Jason saw Jasher carving wildly into the back of the frog with his sword. The great amphibian turned to confront the assault. A mighty sweep of Jasher's sword cleaved its horned head. Then he buried the blade to the hilt in the frog's throat, wrenching it free to open a gaping wound as the creature lurched spasmodically backward to lie in the mud, its powerful legs twitching.

"Rachel," Jason panted, rising.

The little boat drifted away from the shore, rotating slowly. Rachel grabbed the oar and began sculling it back toward the shore.

Jason and Jasher hauled the skiff well away from the water. Jason submerged himself at the edge of the water to rinse the majority of the grime from his sodden clothes.

"I've never seen a frog with teeth before," Rachel whispered.

"Nor I," Jasher replied softly. "Our adventure in the swamp is half done. Inside that tree you should find the Pythoness. You may want to consider entering one at a time. Galloran once cautioned that the tree plays tricks on the mind."

"My turn," Jason told Rachel.

"You're not coming?" Rachel asked Jasher.

"I will stand guard, protect the skiff. Without it we're doomed. You are the ones collecting syllables. Go swiftly."

"Is the Pythoness dangerous?" Jason asked.

"The question is how dangerous," Jasher replied. "I'm not certain. But she holds the syllable, and she should help you if you can convince her of your sincerity."

The long, narrow island widened around the tree. As Jason trudged closer to the towering tree, he observed several black mud vipers lying on the shore to his left. Rachel took his hand, her grip cutting off the circulation to his fingers. They watched the snakes carefully until they'd passed well beyond them.

At the base of the gargantuan tree Jason noticed clusters of spherical fungi, each with a small perforation in the top. Up close he marveled at the sheer girth of the trunk. He estimated it would take thirty men joining hands to encircle it. Maybe more.

They did not see an opening to the tree yet, so they began walking around to the far side. The damp ground was firmer here than anyplace else he had seen in the swamp.

Jason rubbed at his eyes. They felt itchy and drowsy all of a sudden. For a moment he paused. What was he doing? Oh, yes, looking for a way into the tree. He kept walking around and on the far side located a narrow gap tall enough for him to enter without crouching.

"You wait here," Jason whispered to Rachel. "I'll call if I need you."

"If snakes or frogs show up, I'm not waiting," she whispered back. "Be careful."

She backed away a few steps from the yawning gap.

Jason hesitated. Anything could await inside. He took his poniard from his sodden cloak. Why was his cloak so wet? He couldn't recall. He knew he needed to get inside the tree though. Why? For shelter? No. He needed more of the Word. He slapped his cheek and shook his head.

Cautiously he edged into the gap, continuing forward as the woody passage curved deeper into the colossal tree.

﹡﹡﹡﹡ CHAPTER 19 ﹡﹡﹡﹡

PYTHONESS

By the time Jason emerged from the long gap into the sizable hollow inside the tree, he felt utterly baffled. A lovely young girl in her teens sat staring at him in astonishment from a wooden rocking chair. A colorful throw rug lay on the ground, and two bookshelves loaded with literature stood against one wall. Light shone from a small crystal resting on a shelf.

Jason looked up. The hollow reached high, disappearing in shadow. Why was he inside a tree? And why was he holding a knife? Hurriedly he put it away.

"Who are you, visitor?" she asked, rising, her kind voice containing an undercurrent of apprehension.

"I . . . I'm . . . not sure."

She smiled. Her clothes were simple, but her fresh young beauty was entirely disarming. She was tall, with a slender build and a beautifully sculpted face. Her blond eyebrows arched delicately over striking eyes of the deepest green. Her skin was unblemished and fair. "You do not remember," she said.

Jason scowled, rubbing his forehead. He had a persistent suspicion that he was somebody. The answer felt barely out of reach.

He looked at his muddy boots, wondering if they held some clue. His clothes were wet. Something stank like rancid dung. Some investigative sniffing revealed it was himself. He tried to picture his own face but failed. "I really don't."

"No matter," the young woman said lightly. "I am Corinne."

"Sorry about my smell. I don't know why I reek like this."

"No need to apologize."

"Where am I?"

"Inside a tree," she said.

Jason gazed at the beauty of his hostess, trying to restrain his eyes from lingering impolitely. "Why am I here?"

"Judging by the knife you hid, you are probably seeking the Word. I recognize the emblem on the hilt."

Jason pulled out his knife and showed it to her. "Sorry about that. I'm not sure what I was thinking. What word are you talking about?"

"A word that can destroy an evil person. You probably can't remember."

Jason pinched his lower lip, squinting at the ground, trying to will memories to surface. What was his problem?

"You look distressed," she said.

Jason looked up. "It's frustrating. I'm almost positive that I'm somebody. But I can't remember a thing. Do I have amnesia? Should I know you?"

"We've never met." Corinne took his hand and led him to sit in a second rocking chair beside hers. "Are you hungry?" she asked.

Jason thought about this. "Yes."

She walked to a section of the wall covered with crumbly white cheese, broke off a handful, set it on a wooden plate, and handed the food to Jason. Then she went to a wooden spigot protruding from a different portion of the wall and turned it to fill a crude wooden cup. She brought the cup to Jason. It held dark brown syrup.

Jason found that the cheese had a powerful taste, sharp and persistent. The sap tasted semisweet and very rich.

"Thank you," Jason said.

"My pleasure," Corinne replied. "I rarely entertain company."

"But you're so pretty," he said, surprising himself with his candor. He fleetingly wondered if he had brain damage.

She averted her eyes. "Do you think so?"

"Definitely."

"Thank you." Some color came into her cheeks. "Let me fetch you a drink."

She dipped another wooden cup into a deep basin set against the wall and brought it back full of water. Jason drained it. He looked around. Clusters of spherical fungi clung to the walls of the tree, each with a tiny hole in the top. They grew thicker higher up, out of reach, ranging in size from golf balls to softballs. He also observed a big ironbound chest in one corner of the room.

"I need to conduct a test," Corinne told him. "It should help you remember why you came here. Would you mind if I slip this over your head?" She produced a handful of black, gauzy material.

"It won't hurt me?" Jason checked.

"No," she said. "It might help you remember."

"Sure, I guess."

She pulled the fine black mesh over his head. The material fit snugly and made him work harder to breathe. He could see almost nothing. His thoughts returned to his mysterious identity. And suddenly he remembered. "I'm Jason!" he exclaimed.

"Why have you come here?" a female voice asked from behind him. He felt a knife at his throat. "Don't move; just answer."

Jason felt bewildered. Why was he in a chair? What was over his head? His last memory was entering the tree. One instant he had been stepping through the entrance, the next he was sitting in a chair with his head covered and a knife at his throat. "I'm looking for information about the Word that can destroy Maldor." He hoped this was what the knife wielder wanted to hear.

"Who sent you?"

"Galloran," he replied.

"Why didn't Galloran come himself?" the voice asked.

"He's blind," Jason said. He heard a quick gasp. "He failed in his quest and passed the mission along to me."

"Fair enough," the voice said, tugging the mesh hood off his head.

Jason looked up, blinking, perplexed, at a beautiful young woman. Suddenly he recognized her. Of course, it was Corinne. "Why'd you take it off so quickly?" he asked.

"I'm satisfied that you deserve to be here," Corinne responded.

Jason thought about that. The hood had only covered his head for an instant. No words had been exchanged. He still had no recollection of who he was, or why he had come here. "Have you lived here long?" Jason asked.

"All of my life."

"You were born here?"

She shrugged. "My early childhood is blurred. I grew up here." She sat down in the other rocker.

"Is this a village of trees?" Jason wondered.

"No. This tree is encompassed by a deadly swamp. But we're safe in here."

"Why?"

"Do you see the puffballs growing on the walls?"

"Sure."

"They create an atmosphere that keeps all creatures away. Except people. The atmosphere here blocks the memory of any who enter, while unveiling another portion of the mind."

"So when I leave I'll recall who I am," Jason said, relieved and intrigued.

"And forget all that happened here. Were I to leave, I would lose my identity as you lost yours upon entering." She sounded sad.

"Are you a prisoner here?"

"In a sense. If I leave, I surrender most of my memories of my mother and her mission. I would hardly know myself. I must stay to preserve what I know of the Word. It is the only way to stop a very evil man."

"Do many people come seeking your information?" Jason asked.

"One man visited a few times when I was younger. Galloran. You know him, but you can't remember. His mark is on your knife."

"Where is your mother?"

"She died some time ago. It happened very suddenly."

Jason glanced around, not seeing any remains. He decided not to ask. "Tell me about this Word."

"I know only the sixth syllable, 'puse.' But I preserve another important piece of information. Galloran told Mother that the second syllable is the hardest to find. So, against the possibility that he would fail, he cheated to aid future seekers of the Word. The second syllable is tattooed just inside the shoulder blade of a man called Kimp. The letters are tiny, stacked one atop the other. Apparently, his body bears many tattoos."

Jason stared at Corinne. "All you know is one syllable of some word and information about another syllable?"

"It's a magic word," she said defensively. "You will remember its importance when you leave. Trust me. I am certain you came here seeking this information, though it clearly seems absurd to you at present."

Jason could see she was upset. This Word and her mission to preserve the sixth syllable obviously meant a lot to her. "I'm sure you're right. Wait, once I leave, I'll forget what you told me."

She nodded.

"Then maybe you should write it down."

"I'm not supposed to write any of this. Nor are you. It constitutes a heinous crime."

Jason furrowed his brow. "But you said Galloran wrote a syllable."

"And took a great risk. What he has done cannot be undone. If his action became known, all would be lost."

"I'm sorry, this just doesn't make any sense right now. What should I do?"

"Take a couple of puffballs with you. Their excretions will permit you to recollect our conversation. If all else fails, I'm sure you'll return shortly. We'll figure out a way to make this work. You're the first visitor I've welcomed on my own. My mother was called the Pythoness, but that will mean nothing to you at present."

"Okay," Jason said, struggling to grasp the situation. "If I get outside and can't figure out what to do, I'll be back."

Corinne plucked a pair of puffballs from a corner of the hollow. "Safe journey," she said, handing them to Jason. He liked it when their hands touched.

"Are you sure you don't want to come with me?" he asked hopefully.

Sudden tears shimmered on the surface of her green eyes. "I must remain."

Jason felt sorry for her. "Good-bye, Corinne."

On his way out through the gap he sensed his mind becoming muddled. He shook his head sharply. Surely he would not forget Corinne. He could overpower the mind-numbing effects of a bunch of mushrooms. He focused intently. Corinne. Puse. Second syllable tattooed on Kimp. Corinne. Puse. Second syllable tattooed on Kimp. He was almost through the gap. Corinne. Who was Corinne? Did he know her from school? Oh yes, he went to Kennedy! What a breakthrough! His name was Jason Walker!

He was outside the tree now. He was supposed to remember something, wasn't he? Yes, he had been swallowed by a hippo and was now in a swamp with an amazing swordsman named Jasher. Everything returned in a rush. Why did he have these puffball mushrooms in his hands? His last memory was sitting hooded in a chair while a woman asked questions.

"How did it go?" Rachel asked.

"I have no idea," Jason replied. "How long was I in there?"

"Pretty long," Rachel said. "Like half an hour."

He turned around, studying the gap in the tree. He could remember going inside. Then his memory skipped to sitting in a chair. The swamp was darker now. Had he fainted? Had he met the Pythoness? He had a foggy memory of a beautiful woman. He could not tell whether the beautiful face had been real or dreamed. Had the Pythoness cast a spell on him? His mind felt unclear.

"What's with the mushrooms?" Rachel asked.

"I don't know," Jason said. "Are they a clue?"

"You have two," Rachel noted. "Are we supposed to eat them?"

"I'm not sure," Jason replied, sniffing one of the mushrooms. He felt unsteady. Strange, he didn't recall actually exiting the tree, but now he stood outside, facing a strange girl. She was shorter than Corinne, and not bad-looking. What were these pretty girls doing in a swamp? "Who are you?"

"Are you kidding?" Rachel asked.

"I remember talking to Corinne inside the tree," Jason said, sniffing the mushrooms again. He squeezed one gently, and dusty spores the color of brown mustard smoked out of the hole in a little cloud. "These mushrooms let me remember her, but they block out everything else. Apparently we're searching for a word?"

"Yes," Rachel said eagerly.

"The sixth syllable is 'puse.' Does that make sense?"

"Absolutely. Anything else?"

He explained about the second syllable being tattooed on Kimp's back.

"Do you know where we can find this man?" Rachel asked.

"Corinne didn't explain," he said. "Should I ask her?"

"In a minute," Rachel said. "Tell me more about how these mushrooms work."

Jason explained the ability of the mushrooms to suppress memories and keep swamp animals away from the tree.

"Useful information," Rachel said. "Think Corinne would let us sleep in her tree tonight? It would be much safer than out in the swamp. This place is horrible at night."

"Can't hurt to ask," Jason said. "She seemed nice. Can you tell me what we're doing while I'm using the mushrooms? That way I'll be able to better explain our situation to Corinne."

Rachel rehearsed all sorts of information to Jason. He came from a state called Colorado in another world. He was on a quest with Rachel and Jasher. She related details about other syllables of the Word, warning him not to pronounce any of the syllables together. She went on and on. Nothing felt familiar, but the story was amazing.

"We should go talk to Jasher," Rachel suggested after concluding the recap.

"Okay," Jason replied, looking around. "Where is he?"

"On the other side of the tree. Watch out for snakes."

They hurried around the tree.

"Jasher, come quick," Rachel called in a hushed voice.

Jasher approached from the far side of the island, taking long strides, sword in hand. Behind him lay the corpses of three gigantic frogs in inky pools of blood.

Without repeating the sixth syllable, Rachel hastily explained what Jason had learned inside of the tree. She relayed their intention to remain inside the tree overnight.

"I know of the man you mentioned, Kimp," Jasher said. "You say the animals of the swamp will not approach the mushrooms?"

"That's what Corinne told me," Jason explained. "She would know."

"We should place some of those mushrooms in the skiff," Jasher said. "Hopefully they will protect it overnight and provide us with a safer journey out of the swamp."

"Great idea," Rachel agreed.

They gathered several of the puffballs from the outside of the tree and stashed them in the skiff. Then Jason set his mushrooms in the skiff as well. Away from the mushrooms he swooned, dropping to one knee. Since he'd forgotten Corinne again, Rachel and Jasher explained the plan to him. In the end Rachel leaned close and whispered the sixth syllable.

A _____ FEX EN_ DRA PUSE

With daylight waning, they gathered before the gap in the mighty trunk. Jason led the way in. Soon his only memories were his recent conversation with Jasher and Rachel and his discussion with Corinne.

Corinne rose as they entered. "Back so soon? You brought friends!"

"This is Jasher and Rachel," Jason explained. "I'm Lord Jason of Caberton. At least that's what they told me outside. We were wondering if we could stay the night in here, since it's getting dark out and the swamp is very dangerous at night."

Jasher stood staring back and forth between Corinne and Jason, blinking and rubbing his temples, eyes dazed. "You say my name is Jasher?" he asked Jason in a bewildered voice. "That doesn't feel right."

Rachel folded her arms, a line appearing between her eyebrows. "Rachel. Rachel. Doesn't ring a bell. What's the matter with me? What stinks?"

"We stink," Jason said.

"You are welcome to stay the night," Corinne said, after which she patiently explained to Jasher and Rachel why they could remember nothing. While she explained, she gathered cheese from the wall and two cups of sap. Jason declined more food but accepted a cup of water. Corinne knelt on the floor beside the two rockers and nibbled on some cheese.

"Since we have no memories, tell us about yourself," Jasher suggested. He seemed relaxed and happy.

Corinne looked shyly into her lap. "There is little to tell. I have lived in this tree for most of my life. The only people I have ever seen besides my mother are Galloran and the three of you. Since my mother died, I have lived here alone, protecting the syllable she believed was so important. I love to read. You don't have any books, do you? I have read all of mine so many times."

Jason and Jasher patted at their clothes and then shook their heads. Rachel checked her satchel. No books.

"What was your mother like?" Jason asked.

Corinne cocked her head slightly and stared blankly, as if gazing at her mother in her imagination. "She was always kind to me, and very patient. I grew taller than her before she passed away. In her youth she enjoyed much luxury, growing up in a noble house. She possessed a gift for perceiving future events, and some people despised her for it. They called her Pythoness because they believed she communed with unclean spirits. But her gift did not work that way.

"Mother was not old when she came here, entrusted with a portion of the Word that can unmake Maldor. Because of the puffballs the memories of her past came from her journal. Sometimes we would have discussions or do lessons outside the tree, but naturally, I can't remember any of that. She took the responsibility to guard the Word very seriously. She told me that before I was born, more people came here. But Galloran was her favorite. She cared for Galloran very much. She expected him to return for us someday, with news that Maldor had fallen. I've kept hoping for the same thing. Mother said she saw him leading me away through the swamp in a vision, and her visions were usually accurate. If he is now blind, that may never happen. The future is never certain."

"You poor girl," Rachel said.

Corinne gave a faint, sad smile. "The worst part was losing Mother. One day she fell to the floor, clutching her breast, gasping for breath. She reached for me and tried to speak, but I could not understand her. I never knew what she was trying to tell me. She was old when I was born. Quite old when she died. I did not know how to save her, so she perished in my arms."

Corinne spoke these final words as if in a trance. Now she stopped, regarding her visitors with her green-eyed stare.

"Would you like to get some sleep?" she asked.

"You read my mind," Rachel said. "I'm exhausted." She

stood up, slapping Jason on the shoulder. "We must have had a long day."

Corinne led Jason and Jasher to a thin mattress big enough for two. "Sleep here. Rachel, you can sleep on the rug using your blanket roll. I sleep just fine in the rocking chair."

Lying down on the soft mattress, Jason suspected he had not slept well lately. He fell asleep quickly.

A gentle hand was shaking Jason's shoulder. He opened his eyes to look up into a lovely face framed by long thick hair the color of honey.

"It's daybreak," Corinne whispered.

Jason elbowed Jasher, who sat up with a start. "Time to go," Jason said.

They arose from the mattress and ate some cheese. Rachel bundled up her blankets. Jasher wore a water skin, which Corinne insisted upon filling with fresh water.

"Would you like to join us?" Jasher asked as they prepared to leave.

"I must remain to protect the Word," Corinne replied. "If you succeed in stopping Maldor, perhaps you could send someone to notify me."

"We will," Rachel promised. "Thanks for your hospitality."

"Sorry we can't remember ourselves," Jason said. "I hope we would be more interesting with our personalities intact."

"I had a fine time with all of you," Corinne assured them. "You cannot imagine how lonely I get. Safe journey."

Jasher led the way out. By the time they had exited the tree, they were staring at one another in befuddlement.

"Did we go in?" Jasher asked.

"I think so," Jason said.

"This could be early morning or late evening," Rachel observed.

"The light is in the east," Jasher said. "I feel rested, and my throat feels better."

"So it's morning," Jason said.

"Do you remember anything?" Rachel asked.

Jasher squinted. "Not a thing. Do you feel dizzy?"

"A little woozy," Jason agreed. "Let's get back to the boat."

They walked around the tree and along the narrow length of the island toward the far tip where the boat lay. Jasher stopped short, raising a hand to halt the other two. A large, amorphous shape shifted ahead in the dimness.

They stood motionless, breathing softly, Jasher's hand on the hilt of his sword, Jason reaching for his knife. Up ahead something else moved. "Frogs," Jasher whispered. "A small army."

They held still, letting their eyes adjust. Soon Jason could make out at least a dozen gigantic frogs surrounding the skiff. Their skin blended with the mud. A few were bigger than any they had yet encountered: huge muddy boulders, almost elephantine in size. "They know we need the boat," Jasher murmured in disbelief.

"At least they didn't think to sink it," Rachel whispered.

"Don't give them any ideas," Jason worried.

"The puffballs probably saved the skiff," Jasher guessed. "Although the frogs surround it, none are too close. Looks like the frogs I slew yesterday are gone."

"Cannibals," Jason muttered. "What now?"

Jasher motioned for them to lean in closer. "All else failing, we retreat to the tree. I have one more orantium globe. A good blast should destroy a frog or two and might disperse the others. There is no chance we will overpower them by the might of our blades alone."

"Especially since mine is hardly big enough to lance their warts," Jason said.

"I'll want a little more light before we move," Jasher said.

They stood in silence. The frogs made no noise and no aggressive movements. Occasionally one or two would shift position. The nearest stared at them unblinkingly. The light increased. Jasher got out his orantium globe.

"Wait," Rachel whispered. "Why don't we try throwing mushrooms? If the puffballs kept them out of the boat, they might drive them away."

Jasher grinned. "At least one of us is thinking. Back to the tree. No sudden movements."

Slowly and quietly they returned to the tree and collected several puffballs each, taking care not to squeeze them. Once within throwing distance of the congregation of immense frogs, they began lobbing puffballs into their midst. The mushrooms soared in high trajectories before landing in faint bursts of yellow-brown dust.

As the first three landed, the frogs sprang for the water, colliding with one another in their panicked haste. Only six puffballs were thrown before Jason and his companions stopped to watch the last of the monstrous amphibians scrambling and splashing into the murky water.

Still bearing several puffballs each, Jason, Rachel, and Jasher raced to the skiff. Near the small craft Jason felt hazy. He remembered Corinne, and he realized that the puffballs had masked his memories again. Jasher and Rachel appeared confused.

"Move the mushrooms to the front of the boat," Jason advised. "It doesn't really matter whether Rachel and I have our memories. Jasher, try covering your nose and mouth."

They moved the mushrooms. Jasher took a sash from his robes and wound it around the bottom half of his face.

"I'm back," Jasher said. "I take it the mushrooms were flummoxing us."

"We'll keep them at the front of the boat," Jason said.

The three of them shoved the skiff into the water. After Rachel and Jason climbed to the front, Jasher launched them.

"Keep watch," Jasher said, his voice muffled by his sash. "I intend to make use of these mushrooms. We're going to sacrifice stealth for speed. I want out of this swamp before nightfall."

"We'll keep watch," Rachel assured him.

"Anything specific we're looking for?" Jason asked.

Jasher told them about the slime. "I forget that you two don't have your memories."

"Not many, at least," Jason replied. "Which reminds me: Corinne asked us to let her know if we succeed and destroy Maldor, but without the mushrooms we might not remember."

Jasher held up a finger. "If you overthrow the emperor, I promise to personally inform all of the custodians of the Word."

"We're not going to overthrow anyone if we don't get moving," Rachel said, staring around uneasily.

Jasher began sculling aggressively, the long oar sloshing loudly in the water, throwing big ripples across the otherwise calm surface. Jason sat attentively in the bow, occasionally giving a puffball a gentle squeeze, hoping to keep creepy animals away.

The day was hot and humid. Jason enjoyed the strange and exotic sights of the swamp. He wondered whether he had appreciated the scenery as much on the way in. He doubted it. After all, this time the sights were among his first memories. The animals he glimpsed stayed a good distance from the skiff. Only the floating masses of slime seemed indifferent to the cargo of puffballs.

* * *

The light was dimming when they finally saw the muddy bank marking the end of the swamp and the beginning of the marshlands. Jason noticed an unusual, fat frog sitting on a log.

"Look," he told Jasher, pointing. "That one has a third eye."

Jasher instantly fell flat. "Get down. A human eye?"

Jason and Rachel huddled low in the vessel. "Maybe. It's on the chest."

"Blast!" Jasher jerked a small knife from his boot. In one motion he rose to his knees and flung the little weapon.

Jason peeked over the gunwale and saw the knife pierce the frog just above the foreign eye, sending the amphibian backward off the log. Grimacing, Jasher speedily guided the skiff to the bank. "Somewhere, a displacer has learned where we are and that I travel with you. Someone must have stumbled across our trail. There must be quite a manhunt underway. We should move swiftly."

He and Jason dragged the boat out of the water and overturned it. In the waning light they hurriedly concealed the vessel. Jason noticed that Jasher's hands were raw and covered with dried blood and the flattened remains of burst blisters.

Night fell as they marched away from the edge of the swamp. Unseen clouds blotted out many of the stars. Well after dark they found a fairly dry spot to bed down. Rachel had kept many of the puffballs from the boat, and she arranged them around their little campsite. The presence of the mushrooms let Jason rest easier.

The next morning, before any evidence of sunrise had colored the sky, Jasher awakened Jason and Rachel. They set off immediately, munching on the last of the gutplug while they walked.

"We must clarify our next move," Jasher said.

"Okay," Jason agreed. "Who is this guy Kimp?"

Jasher smiled. "That was the best news we took from the

swamp. Finding the Temple of Mianamon would have been a daunting journey. Now locating the second syllable will be simpler, though perhaps equally perilous."

"At least it's still perilous," Jason said with mock relief.

Rachel elbowed him. "This is serious."

"Kimp serves Maldor," Jasher said. "Not long before Galloran was taken, he captured Kimp. That must be when he placed the tattoo. You must understand, Kimp collects tattoos. Most all the surface of his body is marked in green and black ink. Assuming the mark left by Galloran remains, all you must do is read it off his shoulder blade."

"Do you know where this guy is?" Rachel asked.

"That is the best part. I do. I spend a lot of my time monitoring Maldor and his chief henchmen, searching for opportunities to strike. Kimp currently dwells in Harthenham Castle, where the Eternal Feast is held."

"I have an invitation to the Eternal Feast," Jason reminded everyone.

"It has been on my mind," Jasher said.

"Will they still accept it?" Jason wondered.

"Have you formally rejected the invitation?" Jasher asked.

"No."

"This is your first invitation?"

"Yes."

"There was no expiration listed?"

"No."

"Then it remains in force."

"Did it go in the water with you?" Rachel wondered.

"No," Jason said. "I had it in my bag in the skiff. It should be fine."

"Where is the castle?" Rachel asked as they pushed through a stand of thick reeds.

"Several days east of here," Jasher said. "Assuming our horses remain where we left them. On foot the journey could take weeks. We'll have to approach our mounts carefully. If our pursuers found them, it would be an ideal location for an ambush."

"What can you tell me about the Eternal Feast?" Jason asked.

"Maldor invites his most dangerous adversaries to the Eternal Feast at Harthenham Castle. Duke Conrad presides over the festivities. None who have answered the invitation have ever returned."

"Is it a trick?" Jason asked. "Are they killed?"

"Supposedly not. At first guests typically send correspondence explaining that they intend to prolong their stay. Inevitably word comes that they have chosen to remain indefinitely."

"Must be good food," Jason said.

"I'm sure they don't make leaving easy," Jasher said. "Getting in should require little effort. Getting away will be the challenge."

"Have you been invited?" Rachel asked Jasher.

"Three times."

"But you never went."

"I never considered accepting. Nor did Galloran. But now Jason must. Traveling to Mianamon would take months, and it would lead us into the most dangerous and unexplored terrain on the continent."

"Could you and Rachel come with me?" Jason asked.

"I would if I could," Jasher said. "My opportunity to accept has passed. The third invitation issued an ultimatum. It was dated, and I let the date lapse. I am the only man I know of against whom Maldor has issued a standing death warrant. He no longer cares to beguile me. I am to be killed at any opportunity. If I joined you, I would be slain on sight."

"What about your seed?" Rachel asked.

"If he could destroy my amar in secret, Maldor would not

hesitate. Otherwise I suppose it would be locked away where it could never be planted."

Jason rubbed his chin. "So we need to separate," he said reluctantly.

"What about me?" Rachel asked. "Why can't I get invited?"

"That could happen," Jasher said. "It would take time. Jason's high-profile maneuvers in Trensicourt brought the invitation more swiftly than usual."

"I know five syllables of the Word," Rachel said.

"Maldor can't imagine you know more than four," Jasher replied. "The clue in the lorevault is something Galloran did on the sly, since the fourth syllable required a voyage to a distant island. The syllables you get in secret, like the one at Harthenham, give you a huge advantage. If Maldor thinks you only have four syllables, he may feel sufficient confidence to enter your presence, giving you the chance we've been waiting for."

"It all depends on getting this last syllable from Kimp," Jason said.

"We need to act quickly," Jasher said. "This opportunity could dissolve."

"I get it," Rachel said. "There isn't time to build my reputation enough to get me invited."

"Hopefully, our separation will be brief," Jasher said. "Rachel will remain with me. We'll await you, Jason, outside of the castle. We'll be there to help, horses ready, when you make your escape. You must keep foremost in your mind the understanding that you are not there for the feast. Forgo all pleasures and diversions. Accept as little hospitality from your hosts as you can. Beware gifts from Maldor. He gives gifts to people much as fishermen offer worms to trout."

* * *

Five days later, from the cover of a wooded hillside, Jasher, Jason, and Rachel watched a rider clad in scarlet galloping in the distance, his bright cloak flapping like a flag. With Jasher as their guide they had recovered their horses and made their way across the wilderness without incident.

"The Scarlet Riders are Maldor's couriers," Jasher explained. "This is one of their regular routes. They carry no arms, and therefore we in the resistance do not harm them."

"I just flag him down?" Jason asked.

Jasher nodded. "It would be the quickest way to redeem your invitation and access Harthenham Castle. Rachel and I will never stray far from you. But if they ask about me or Rachel, we parted ways three days ago. I'll keep us hidden."

Jason nodded. It was now or never. He nudged his mount with his heels and flicked the reins. The responsive steed charged down the hillside. Within moments Jason rode out of the trees and waved his arms at the distant rider. The rider reined in his horse and watched as Jason approached. At length the rider spurred his mount toward Jason.

A few minutes later the rider pulled up beside him. The chestnut horse was the biggest Jason had ever seen, making his own large steed appear average.

"Speak," the rider demanded in a powerful voice, using far more volume than seemed necessary.

"My name is Jason."

His eyes widened. "Lord Jason of Caberton?"

"Good guess. I have an invitation to the Eternal Feast, and I want to accept it."

Jason held up the invitation. The rider was speechless.

"It got a little wrinkled and dirty," Jason apologized. "I'm tired of trying to be a hero. It's pointless to resist the emperor. Can you help me out?"

The young man in the scarlet cape looked nervous. He surveyed the area in all directions.

"This isn't a trick," Jason said. "How do I declare my acceptance of this generous invitation?"

The scarlet rider relaxed a little. "This preempts the message I'm carrying," he said. "I will see you safely to Bresington. An official escort will take you from there to Harthenham."

"Lead on," Jason said, forcing himself not to glance back toward where his friends were hiding.

~*~*~*~ CHAPTER 20 *~*~*~

THE ETERNAL FEAST

A carriage advanced along a well-kept dirt road, passing grassy fields divided by whitewashed wooden fences. From the window Jason stared across the pastoral expanse at his first view of Harthenham Castle.

Tall and graceful, white walls gleaming, the castle seemed plucked from a fairy tale. Beautiful towers abounded, topped by steep conical roofs aflutter with banners. Elegant flying buttresses linked several of the towers to surrounding walls. Dramatic statues of majestic figures glistened on the parapets like angelic gargoyles. Elaborate gold and silver traceries embellished the stonework. Bright flags and standards decorated the great outer wall, which shimmered with opalescent sparkles.

Count Dershan, who sat in the carriage alongside Jason, gestured at the castle. "Many tons of fine crystal were crushed into the mortar to give the walls of Harthenham their ethereal glitter," he recited reverently. He leaned toward Jason as he spoke, stroking the bushy mustache that flowed into his shaggy sideburns.

"It's spectacular," Jason agreed, glancing at the man who shared his compartment. Count Dershan had met him back in

Bresington about an hour ago with the carriage and a change of clothes. After almost two days following the scarlet rider Jason was again bedecked in courtly finery and seated comfortably in a plush compartment.

"The highest figure on the castle, the warrior Elwyn, is constructed of pure gold, and his sword is composed of burnished platinum."

Jason could see the warrior, one hand clinging to the loftiest spire, the other holding his sword aloft. Jason imagined the spire snapping, sending the proud golden warrior on a breakneck plunge into some hidden courtyard. He wished it would happen just so he could see the look on Dershan's face. The count obviously took great personal pride in the opulence of Harthenham.

"Sadly, we cannot observe the grounds from here," Dershan continued. "The topiary is exquisite. The garden unparalleled. From the proper perspective the reflecting pool creates a perfect illusion of the castle inverted, complete with clouds and sky."

"I can hardly wait," Jason said, hoping to seem like the model newcomer. "I hear the food is pretty good."

Count Dershan chuckled at the understatement. "Over two hundred specialists devote their lives to collecting and preparing delicacies from all over the continent. No king has ever dined as we do."

Before long the carriage rattled over the drawbridge and came to a stop beside a portico in an immaculate yard. Several servants stood at attention, wearing powdered wigs and fine livery. None bore weapons, and Jason noticed no guards.

Under the portico awaited a dignified man of about forty years with excellent posture. He wore an impeccable white uniform, complete with a profusion of medals on his chest and gold-fringed epaulets on his shoulders. A rapier was belted to his trim waist. His black hair was clipped short and slicked back, emphasizing his widow's peak. A meticulously trimmed goatee bristled at the end of his chin. His bronze skin contrasted with the light uniform.

A footman opened the carriage door and set a stool on the ground. Jason followed Count Dershan out of the coach, accepting a hand down from the sallow-faced attendant.

Dershan guided Jason directly to the uniformed gentleman. "Duke Conrad of Harthenham, allow me to introduce our esteemed guest, Lord Jason of Caberton."

Duke Conrad inclined his head and torso stiffly. Jason mirrored the slight bow. "A pleasure to make your acquaintance," Conrad said, his words clipped and precise. He extended a gloved hand, and Jason shook it, the firmness of the grip catching him by surprise. Duke Conrad stood a few inches shorter than Jason and stared up at him with keen, dark eyes. His face had a narrowness that accentuated his hollow cheeks and aquiline nose. Jason noticed that Conrad had twisted his gloved hand slightly so that Jason was shaking with his palm upward. A friend had once told Jason that whichever hand was on top won the handshake. Jason opened his hand, ending the subtle contest.

"I was glad to receive your invitation," Jason said.

"And I am overjoyed to welcome you into my home," Conrad said with little enthusiasm, his perceptive eyes weighing Jason. "Please feel at liberty to explore the castle and the grounds. Consider all of it yours."

Jason felt a sudden temptation to ask if he could have one of the duke's medals. Or maybe just unpin one and put it on. But the goal was not to make this man an enemy. The goal was to appear docile. "I appreciate your hospitality," he said.

"Come," Conrad instructed, whirling briskly and leading

Jason through an elaborate set of double doors. "Your feast of welcome is in the final stages of preparation."

Jason followed Duke Conrad down a grand hall to a marble fountain. Emerald liquid splashed from the spout to the basin, giving off a fruity scent. A massive gold and crystal chandelier hung from the vaulted ceiling, hundreds of candles flickering. A row of evenly spaced servants stood unmoving against the wall.

"Would you rather dine immediately or retire to your rooms for a time?" Conrad inquired.

"What would you prefer?"

"An answer."

Jason felt chagrin. Conrad had abrupt arrogance down to an art. "Then I would like to see my rooms first, and eat soon afterward. Will that work?"

"You are the guest of honor," Conrad said dryly. "We are overjoyed to accommodate your schedule. Derrik."

A pale servant detached himself from the wall. "Yes, milord."

"See that the feast is set to commence in thirty minutes."

The man bowed low and hurried away.

"Cassandra. Conduct Lord Jason to his apartments."

A woman against the wall lowered her eyes and curtseyed. Jason could not help noticing that several of the female servants were very pretty.

"This way, milord," Cassandra said courteously.

Jason followed her down halls and up stairs, past magnificent hangings and sculptures, until they reached a set of white doors accented with golden scrollwork that resembled leafy vines. The doorknob was worked into the likeness of a rose.

Cassandra opened the doors and escorted Jason inside.

Jason paused in the doorway, gawking.

He had never seen a more elegant room.

Blues dominated the color scheme, complemented by whites and silvers. Artful arrangements of brilliant flowers blazed from ornate vases, making the room smell like a blossoming field after a gentle rain. Masterful paintings and sculptures were spaced tastefully around the spacious salon. Unobtrusive murals of pastoral scenes decorated the high ceiling. Jewels studded the luxurious furniture. Jason could envision any article in the room behind glass in a museum.

In a neighboring chamber he found an enormous bed. His parents owned a king-size. This was emperor-size, piled with infinitely soft pillows. The deep mattress felt ready to embrace him. The silky sheets were cool and smooth. The fur comforters folded at the foot of the bed surpassed the plush covers at Trensicourt.

"Are the accommodations satisfactory?" Cassandra asked hesitantly, as if half expecting him to launch into a disgusted tirade.

"It's perfect. Thank you."

"I'll let you know when the feast is ready to begin," she said, gliding from the room.

Upon further exploration Jason discovered another room with a beautiful bathtub carved out of polished azure stone. His balcony overlooked glorious gardens and manicured hedgerows. Fountains of colored water geysered high into the air. Peacocks strutted about the lawn, some fanning out their spectacular plumage. There were peacocks with feathers of lustrous blue and violet, and others with plumage shimmering in vibrant shades of lime green and yellow, or fiery hues of red and orange. One exotic plot was devoted to a topiary teeming with elaborate hedge sculptures. Some were shaped geometrically, some like fanciful animals; others appeared to be people. One was clipped into a striking likeness of Duke Conrad standing rigid in his uniform.

Jason sat down on the balcony tiles, chin in his hands, considering the allure of Harthenham Castle. Who wouldn't crave to be a permanent guest here? It would be like living at a luxury resort, the sort of life most people could never attain no matter how hard they worked.

But he knew it was a prison in disguise. A beautiful distraction designed to sidetrack enemies of the emperor. He wondered if the servants were secretly the guards. Certainly they were spies. He wondered if Cassandra carried hidden weapons or poison.

He would need to remain vigilant. He had to find Kimp and make a hasty exit. Despite the size of his bed, he would have to avoid getting too comfortable.

Jason rose and wandered his rooms, examining the artwork. He was thumbing through one of the books in his modest personal library when Cassandra entered.

"The feast is ready, milord," she said with a curtsey. She escorted him to the dining hall, passing him off to a stiff young servant who directed him to the foot of a very long table that dominated the room. The dining hall was an elongated rectangle with a high roof. Painted carvings hung on the walls. Many guests were already seated. Others were filing in. At the far end of the table sat Duke Conrad. To his immediate left Count Dershan sat grooming his mustache, and to his right a bulky bald man leaned forward in his seat, a feathered hoop dangling from one earlobe, his bare scalp crawling with tattoos. Judging from the tattoos, the bald man was probably Kimp. Jason wondered how often he took off his shirt.

Duke Conrad met eyes with Jason and gave a slight nod. The smug contempt in his gaze implied that Jason now belonged to him.

As Jason scanned the rest of the people at the table, a familiar face surprised him. About halfway down on the left Jason spotted Tark. He looked the same as he had in the revolving tavern, except he was dressed like a prince. Their eyes locked, and Tark waved feebly, clearly embarrassed.

Duke Conrad arose from his high-backed chair, and the remaining guests scurried to their seats, assisted by servants. Many of the other guests were overweight, several grotesquely so. Jason was comfortably the youngest guest in attendance. Duke Conrad cleared his throat, and the room became silent.

"We are gathered here to welcome our newest comrade, Lord Jason of Caberton, who joins us in seeking refuge from a hostile world." Conrad raised a crystal goblet. "To new friends."

"Hear, hear; to new friends," the crowd babbled, hefting goblets and drinking to the statement. Jason filled a spare goblet with water and drank.

"Let the feast commence," Duke Conrad exclaimed, gesturing like a showman.

The guests cheered. Doors swung open, and an army of servants stormed the table bearing heavily laden trays. Jason could scarcely believe the bountiful variety of edibles that was soon spread before him.

Steaming slabs of prime rib, legs of lamb, cuts of ham, heaps of fowl, fillets of fish, rows of sausage, morsels on skewers, and platters of tender shellfish all vied for his attention. Bowls of fruit, some peeled and slathered in cream, some whole, sat opposite plates piled with vegetables both familiar and foreign.

Jason watched the guests attack the food without restraint. Soon flabby chins dribbled with grease wherever he looked. Chubby fingers were occasionally dipped into silver bowls of scented water and wiped clean on linen napkins only to instantly become messy again as they shuttled more food to eager mouths. Each person at the table had a full complement of silverware, but few paid heed to spoons or forks. Jason noticed that Duke Conrad, Count Dershan, and the tattooed man all ate in moderation with utensils, abstaining from the frenzy displayed by the other guests.

Jason selected a thick cut of steak and found it was the most succulent, perfectly seasoned meat he had ever tasted. It was pink through the center, with a hint of red, and melted juicily in his mouth. As he sampled other delicacies, he began to understand the exuberance displayed by the other guests. He ate decadent shellfish marinated in buttery sauces, chilled fruit that exploded with sweet flavor, and poultry smothered in melted cheese.

Everything was superb.

The variety of delicious tastes was overwhelming.

Only the obscene gluttony of the other guests distracted from the perfection of the meal. Jason noticed that Tark ate little. He did not look over at Jason again. As more courses arrived, Jason tried to pace himself, savoring the food instead of wallowing in it, trying soups, breads, and tangy cheeses.

As the meal proceeded, a group of servants appeared, bearing white, bulbous fruit the size of watermelons. "Oklinder" was repeated around the table in excited whispers.

Servants ceremoniously punctured the glossy white sacks, catching the spilling fluid in silver decanters. A servant carried the first decanter to Jason and filled his goblet. The fluid was clear. He took a probative sip, then gulped down the contents. The natural juice was sweet enough to please the palate, but not so sugary as to make it unrefreshing. The delightful taste was unlike anything he had ever sampled. Since the servant was hovering, he held out his goblet for a refill.

Fresh platters of food continued to appear. The eagerness of the guests began to abate. Jason picked at salty stuffed mushrooms. His stomach felt full of lead.

"And now for dessert," Duke Conrad cried at last, dabbing his lips with a napkin.

"Dessert, dessert," echoed many in the company.

Jason wiped his mouth with a napkin. How could he eat anything else?

"I wonder," the Duke began slyly, directing his gaze toward Jason, "if our new friend has ever sampled the liver of a wizatch."

Jason found the entire party staring at him. "I haven't had the pleasure," Jason said, trying to sound formal, "unless I know it by another name." Interested murmurs followed the declaration.

Liveried servants busied themselves clearing away the remains of the feast. Tark got up and left the table, shoulders slumped.

Duke Conrad coughed into his fist. "The wizatch is a rodent unlike any other. The finicky creature feeds exclusively upon the nectar of the cheeseblossom—it would starve before taking nourishment from another source. Cheeseblossom nectar is, of course, poisonous to all other known organisms.

"Inside the wizatch, cheeseblossom nectar undergoes a transformation wherein the poison is neutralized and the taste is refined. The liver becomes saturated with purified nectar. Consumed fresh, the liver of a wizatch is the most delectable delicacy of my acquaintance. As you are one of the uninitiated, I insist you inaugurate our dessert by sampling the first batch."

"Hear, hear," resounded voices up and down the table.

Jason could not conceive of a more disgusting after-dinner treat than rodent livers, but he succumbed to the general pressure with a grin and a nod. "I'll try anything once."

Servants placed a silver bowl before each guest seated at the table. Jason's contained five beige livers, each smaller than his thumb. Beside Duke Conrad an officious servant held up a shaggy rodent with three tails. "This fortunate wizatch will be spared," the servant announced.

"Until tomorrow!" shouted a flat-featured man with black hair down to his shoulders. The diners laughed at the remark.

Jason held his fork tentatively. He glanced down the long table. A double row of expectant visages offered encouragement.

"No time to lose," prompted a blubbery woman wearing a necklace of enormous pearls.

Jason peered into the bowl. The livers looked raw and squishy. He lifted one with his fork and put it in his mouth. As he bit down, his eyes widened. The liver had ruptured, and the warm creamy interior tasted delicious, somewhat like sweetened vanilla with a hint of cheese and banana.

"What is your recommendation?" Duke Conrad inquired, as if the reply were inevitable.

"You were right—these are delicious."

"Then let us proceed," Conrad replied, taking a bite.

All along the table people began eating the tiny uncooked livers. Jason greedily finished his without hesitation. With each his enjoyment grew. He could tell he would crave them in the future.

"Now that our palates have been cleansed, bring forth the rest of the dessert," Conrad commanded with a jovial wave of his hand. Cakes, pies, tarts, éclairs, cinnamon rolls, fruit breads, sugared nuts, puddings, and sherbet appeared in towering quantities. The guests welcomed the onslaught of sweets.

Jason already felt ready to burst, but he tasted a few of the desserts, finding them as delicious as the entrees would have led him to suspect. He could see how living at Harthenham would easily lead to obesity. Across the busy table Duke Conrad saluted Jason with an upraised goblet.

~✦✦✦✦ CHAPTER 21 ✦✦✦✦~

DUEL

Jason spent the next couple of days becoming familiar with the castle. He roamed the grounds, discovering an aviary, a menagerie, an archery range, a kennel full of big boarhounds and mastiffs, two swimming pools, and a large area of closely mown grass for playing a game that seemed a hybrid between soccer and croquet. Inside the castle he found game rooms featuring billiards, darts, duckpin bowling, strategic board games, gambling, and an enclosure where animals were pitted against one another in mortal combat. He came across an area for fencing, a music room full of instruments, and an intimate, elegant theater.

Importantly, on the first day exploring, Jason also found a bathhouse. Inside, men waded and bathed in scented pools of varying depth and temperature. He went by several times after discovering it but had not yet seen Kimp.

Although subsequent meals did not display varieties as extravagant as Jason's feast of welcoming, they retained sufficient quality to delight the most discriminating critic. Beverages and snacks could be obtained all day and night from various locations.

On the evening of his second day exploring, Jason located a

strange room deep belowground where castle guests, lounging on divans and futons, munched on small, individual pies. Pungent incense permeated the air, and in one corner musicians tapped at marimbas and plucked peculiar stringed instruments. Several of the reclining diners were people Jason had seen at his welcoming feast. Others were emaciated wretches, with waxy skin and greasy hair.

The flat-featured guest with long black hair who had joked about the wizatch relaxed on a nearby divan. He used his fork to motion Jason over.

As Jason approached, the man swallowed a bite of his pie. "Have you ever experienced lumba berry pie?" he asked quietly, dabbing his lips with a fabric napkin.

"No," Jason replied.

The man offered his fork. Jason declined. "I can get my own." He could see two attendants carrying trays of pies around the room.

"My name is Drake."

"Jason."

Drake took another bite. "One mustn't overindulge in lumba berries," he confided, eyes rolling with pleasure. "Their more common name is hunger berries. No other food tastes more divine, or leaves the diner more satisfied. But a person who regularly consumes the berries rarely lasts long."

"Why?"

"Lumba berries do not truly nourish. In fact they rob your body of nutrients. When consumed in significant quantities, they destroy your appetite for any other food. Soon only lumba berries will satisfy, and you blissfully devour them until you starve to death."

Jason glanced around the room, paying more attention to the diners who looked unhealthily skinny. "Do you limit yourself?"

"Sometimes. It can be hard to resist such a pleasurable poison. Lumba berry pies have killed me three times."

Jason scowled. "What brought you back?"

Drake grinned, showing a gold tooth. "I am something of an oddity. I have the dubious distinction of being the only member of the Amar Kabal to accept an invitation to Harthenham."

An attendant approached a neighboring patron, an obese man wearing a silk robe. Using pinchers the attendant held out a pie. The man considered for a moment, then held up a hand, stood, and walked away.

"You're a seed person," Jason said.

Drake nodded. "You strike me as an oddity yourself. I kept an eye on you at the feast. Proud. Vigilant. Pensive. Not characteristics of a young man who has turned his back on the world and surrendered."

"Maybe."

"You're clearly here with an agenda. Others have started out that way. If I noticed, Conrad noticed. He doesn't miss much."

Jason didn't like how much Drake was guessing. "What brought you here?"

Drake stretched. "Boredom. Weariness. My people lead an austere existence, treasuring simplicity and avoiding addictive indulgences. After enduring many lifetimes I no longer found joy in living. I tried devotion to various causes; I tried love; I tried conformity; I tried creative endeavors; I tried solitude. I contemplated destroying my amar by fire. Then I received an invitation to the feast. I had never fully explored reckless self-indulgence. So I came here to conduct a final experiment."

"Any conclusions?"

Drake smirked. He took a small bite of pie. "My people are right. Indulgence is emptiness. I have probed the limits with food and frivolity. There is no real fulfillment in meaningless rushes of pleasure. You try to conceal the emptiness with more extravagance, only to find the thrills becoming less satisfying and more fleeting. Most pleasures are best as a seasoning, not the main course." He held up the pie. "However you try to disguise it, you end up feeding without being nourished."

"So why stay?"

Drake studied Jason. "Empty or not, the lifestyle is addictive. It breeds fear of real life. By abstaining for a season, I can restore some of the thrill to certain delights. Outside these walls I am an embarrassment to my people, an enemy to an emperor, and much less able to bury my shame in excess."

One of the nearby cadaverous pie-eaters began to cough violently. Thin muscles stood out on her neck. Nobody in the room paid her any mind.

"Should somebody help her?" Jason asked.

Drake regarded the coughing fit. "She is in the final stages of starvation. Nobody can help her now. All she can do is keep ingesting hunger berries to distract her from her condition."

Drake took another bite.

"What a waste," Jason murmured.

"Eating lumba pie is a dangerous game," Drake acknowledged. "Sampled in small quantities on occasion, the pie can be a harmless and delightsome diversion. But the more one eats, the more one craves the berries, and the deeper they seem to satisfy."

"I get it," Jason said. "I think I'll skip the pie. How many lives have you spent at Harthenham?"

Drake took another bite, holding the food in his mouth, his eyes closed, savoring it before finally swallowing. "Six. Some were quite brief. None were long. But this is the last."

Jason raised his eyebrows. "You're going to destroy your seed?"

Drake shook his head slowly, setting the remains of his pie aside. "That choice has been taken from me. After my last rebirth my amar did not form properly. Occasionally this defect occurs among my people. Perhaps the reckless living caught up with me." He rubbed the back of his neck. "Most of my seed already fell off. There is no question. This will be the last of my many lives."

"I'm sorry."

His eyelids drooped. "If anything I should feel sorry for you and your kind. You only live once. Most of the guests here are drowning in gluttony having hardly lived. Shed no tears for me. I have experienced plenty. I brought this doom on myself, poisoning my system through pleasurable excess. I do not ascribe my condition to chance."

Jason watched as Drake settled back on the divan. "Don't you want to make something of your last life?"

"Let's not dwell on me. Look to yourself. What are you doing here? Spying? Fishing for information? Planning to redeem some forgotten hero? A word of caution. If you do not mean to stay, you need to leave now, and you need to leave quietly. Whatever your intentions might be, this place will get a hold of you."

"I won't be here long."

Drake smirked. "Nearly every person here but me has told themselves the same thing. Be careful what you eat. Lumba berries are not the only perilous delicacies here. Many of the foods and seasonings are deliberately addictive, including wizatch livers."

Jason nodded. "I know another seed person."

"Who would that be?"

"His name is Jasher."

For the first time Drake looked truly interested. "I know him mostly by reputation. I traveled with his brother for a time."

"His brother is dead."

"Radolso?"

"Yeah, that was his name."

"In the ground, you mean?"

"His seed was destroyed."

Drake leaned forward, distressed. "How?"

"I don't know details. But Maldor did it."

"Are the Amar Kabal seeking vengeance?"

"There was no hard evidence. Maldor claimed the killer was acting alone, and he delivered some displacer to them. A source who Jasher trusts knew the killer was acting under orders, but his people wouldn't believe him. Your people have a treaty with Maldor. Jasher chose exile, and he's out for revenge on his own."

Drake leaned back and closed his eyes. His voice became mellow again. "The things one misses when one wallows in ecstasy. Are you working with Jasher now?"

"I better not say."

"Understood, understood. Pleased to meet you. I need to sleep."

"Have a good nap."

Drake smiled faintly.

Jason suddenly recalled a detail Rachel had related about her visit to the middle of Whitelake. "Wait a minute. Drake. Did you know a displacer named Malar?"

Drake raised his eyebrows, but his eyes remained closed. "Sure, sure, the traitor, I knew him." His voice was dreamy and distant. "Found him, did you? Clever lad. A regular Dinsrel. I need to rest." His head sagged, and his breathing became regular.

Jason left the room feeling disgusted.

The next morning, after a light breakfast followed by a delicious massage, Jason headed for the bathhouse, determined to stay there until Kimp showed up. He had confirmed by talking to other guests that the large man seated near Duke Conrad at the welcoming feast had indeed been Kimp. Jason carried some fruit in a basket in preparation for his stakeout.

On his way to the facility he noticed Tark sitting on a stone bench beside a row of blossoming rosebushes. It was the first time Jason had seen Tark since the musician had walked out of the welcoming feast.

"Hello, Tark," Jason said, coming alongside the bench.

Tark glanced at him with bloodshot eyes. He grunted a greeting.

"Mind if I sit here?" Jason asked.

The short, stocky man shrugged indifferently, then bowed his head, placing his face in his meaty hands.

"When did you get invited here?" Jason asked.

Tark looked up. "I suppose I need to face this," he grumbled in his raspy voice. "I arrived just over a week ago. The temptation overcame me. I figured that since I had caused enough harm to Maldor to get invited to Harthenham, I would quit fighting and spend the rest of my miserable life surrounded by other deserters. Better to die a gluttonous failure than a hungry one. I almost believed the lies I told myself. Then you showed up. I know a sign when I see one. Once again I have betrayed my friends. Just like before, I started off right and then quit when the opportunity arose."

He returned his face to his hands and shook with ragged sobs.

Jason waited politely.

Finally Tark lifted his tear-streaked face. "You must have been up to some mischief to get in here." He wiped his leaking nostrils with the back of his hairy-knuckled hand.

"I do what I can."

"Tell me."

"I became chancellor of Trensicourt. I also helped kill a bunch of conscriptors, manglers, and a displacer."

"I never got a displacer," Tark said in admiration, sniffling. "Good work."

"How did you end up here?"

Tark brightened a bit. "It all started the day I left you. I felt really good, full of resolve, ready for my penance. As it happened, on my way up the road out of town I was stopped by a conscriptor. He had questions about a fellow who fit your description, and a girl who sounded like Rachel. I acted very compliant, and then I put my knife through his back. His mangler friend came at me, blades whirling, and I was sure I had arrived at the brink of my waterfall, if you take my meaning. But I flung the knife, and it found a weak spot, slaying the monstrosity. I could hardly believe it.

"I retrieved my knife and raced off into the woods, leaving behind the corpses and the horse. From that day onward I have waged a private war against the minions of Maldor. I sank a barge, burned down some warehouses, even undermined a bridge. In a pass east of here I buried a whole column of conscriptors and manglers in a landslide. I'd wager that stunt was what finally earned me an invitation to the feast."

Jason nodded. "Do you plan to remain here?"

Tark stared at his feet. "I had intended to stay. Not a soul has ever left. They die wallowing in vices, all of them men and women who once bravely defied Maldor. Some expire choking on lumba pie. Others are so fat they can't leave their beds. I stumbled across Bokar the Invincible my third day here—you know, the great hero from Kadara? Legendary swordsman. A placard beside the door proclaimed his identity. He was lying on his back on an enormous bed like a beached sea elephant, his face drowning in blubber. Attendants were cramming meat pies down his greedy throat. I asked if he was really Bokar the Invincible. He said he was, his mouth full of food. I asked why he gave up. He said he hadn't. He said he was planning to leave in a couple of weeks. I almost laughed. The only way he was going anywhere was in a really big wagon pulled by a whole cavalry of horses. Strong ones.

"I decided some undignified end like that would be fitting for a coward like me. But now my mind is mending. I could be convinced to leave. What about you?"

Jason lowered his voice. "Wait a day or two, and we can leave together."

Tark grinned. "My will is reviving. Fate has made you the guardian of my self-respect. Once again I will abandon self-pity. I will join you, Lord Jason." He pulled out the same heavy saw-toothed knife he had wielded in the Tavern-Go-Round, holding it so the sun glinted on the polished blade. He scrunched his heavy eyebrows. "If you mean to leave so soon, why accept the invitation in the first place?"

"It's a secret. But I had a legitimate reason."

Tears pooled in Tark's eyes. "You came to show me the way." He spoke with amazed realization. He slid off the bench, dropping to his knees. "I knew it. Tell the truth, are you a mortal being or some heavenly apparition?"

Jason stifled a smile. "I'm a friend. I'll warn you when I plan to leave. Try to stay out of trouble."

Tark blushed, swiping a hand over his nose again. "As you say, Lord Jason. I'll scout the perimeter. I've noticed they tend to keep the drawbridge shut. We're never permitted beyond the castle wall. They may resist our attempt to depart."

"We have to find a way," Jason said.

"Aye, we'll set a new precedent. Perhaps others will follow."

"We'll see," Jason said, rising. "I need to visit the bathhouse."

"On your way." Tark shooed him. "We'll talk later."

Jason's fingers and toes had shriveled into pink prunes by the time Kimp appeared. Jason had been in and out of the water all day, watching the servants use heated rocks to adjust the temperatures of the various pools. Count Dershan had come and gone, as had other men Jason recognized from his explorations of the castle.

Jason was relaxing in a cool, shallow pool when Kimp entered. The man was built like a power lifter, his bulging physique graffitied in green and black ink. Only his face was unmarked.

Kimp waded into the hottest pool, an almost comical expression of relaxation transforming his gruff face. Transferring to the hot pool, Jason sloshed over to Kimp, the water just above his waist.

"We haven't met," Jason said, extending a hand. "I'm Lord Jason of Caberton."

"Kimp," the hulking man grunted, giving Jason's hand a limp shake. "This is where I come to unwind."

It was an unmistakable invitation to leave him alone, but Jason pretended to miss it. "I haven't seen you around since the feast."

"I stay busy here. I'm the duke's majordomo. And I tend the dogs. You don't ever want to upset the duke, friend."

"I don't plan to."

Kimp sniffed and twisted, arms raised. Jason heard joints popping.

"I like your tattoos," Jason said.

Kimp cocked an eyebrow. "Do you, now?"

"They're really intriguing. Astounding artwork. Where were they done?"

"All over." His demeanor became much friendlier. "My back has the best one." Kimp turned around.

Jason could not believe his good fortune.

Just inside the left shoulder blade, beside the mast of an elaborate ship spanning the majority of Kimp's broad back, inscribed so tiny that Jason had to lean in close, were three letters arranged vertically and spaced unevenly. The second syllable was "rim."

A RIM FEX EN DRA PUSE

"The detail is amazing," Jason said, trying to bottle his excitement. He had the Word!

"You ever see a jollier picture? My own idea. An artist in Ithilum rendered it. Name of Sgribbs. Only fellow to see for quality work. Took seventeen hours."

The sailors on the ship were all women. They climbed the rigging, hauled lines, hefted frothy mugs, and tussled with one another. On the bow stood a disproportionately large woman wearing a captain's hat and an eye patch, her hands on her rounded hips.

"That is the most intricate tattoo I've ever seen," Jason said respectfully. "You're a walking gallery."

Kimp turned back around, grinning. "You want one?" he asked, giving Jason a friendly slap on the chest with the back of his hand.

"A tattoo? Well, I'll have to think it over."

Kimp frowned. "Nothing complicated. Start simple. How about a shark on your chest? I do great sharks." He lifted a leg with sharks all over the front of the thigh to prove it. They were pretty good sharks. One was devouring a terrified woman.

"You do tattoos yourself?"

"I'm an expert. I have all of the equipment. If you don't like sharks, I can do wolves. How about it?"

"I'll get back to you."

"Is it the pain?" Kimp asked. "The process only stings a little, not bad at all. Then you have the rest of your life to enjoy it. Nothing could look more lordly."

"I'll get back to you."

"Once in a lifetime opportunity."

"So is drowning in quicksand. I expect I'll agree; just let me think it over. Decisions always take me a little time. I'll get back to you."

"You do that."

That night at dinner Jason and Tark sat together at the long table. Duke Conrad, Count Dershan, and Kimp were also present, along with many of the guests who had attended Jason's arrival feast. Drake sat across the table from Jason, not paying him much attention.

Servants wheeled out a tremendous cooked bird on a cart. The enormous fowl was called a ponchut; it was big enough to rival an ostrich, with soft, pink meat. Servants moved the cart around the table, portioning out slices of the bird along with a creamy sauce.

"You want to leave now?" Jason murmured to Tark.

Tark glanced over. "Whenever you decide."

"I've looked around; the wall is high, and there are no doors. The drawbridge never seems to open."

"I've reached a similar conclusion."

"Might be hard to scale the wall."

"Seems designed that way."

Jason ate some of his meat. The sauce made it delicious.

"I think we need to declare our intent to leave," Jason said. "We should do it publicly, so there will be pressure from the other guests to let us go."

"Might be worth a try," Tark said, fidgeting with his napkin.

Jason ate more meat. He took a sip of fruit juice. Then he stood up.

"I have an announcement to make," Jason declared.

Everybody froze, including a servant in the middle of handing a plate to a plump woman. Only Duke Conrad made announcements at dinner.

"I want to publicly thank Duke Conrad for his hospitality," Jason continued. The other diners visibly relaxed. Several tapped their stemware with their forks in approval.

"I have thoroughly enjoyed my stay here," Jason said, nodding graciously at Conrad, "but the time has come for me to depart."

Silence.

Drake covered his mouth with a napkin, stifling a laugh.

Conrad's features hardened. Muscles pulsed in his lean jaw. Count Dershan forced a laugh. "A fine jest, Lord Jason," Dershan approved hopefully.

"No. I am leaving this evening. I don't mean to offend anyone."

Duke Conrad arose, tossing his napkin aside, and walked down the table to Jason. The two stood facing each other. "No man has ever refused my hospitality," Conrad said softly, his tone lethal, his eyes demanding submission.

"Neither have I," Jason replied. "I accepted it. I thank you for it. And now I'm leaving."

Duke Conrad frowned. "My invitation offered indefinite participation in the Eternal Feast," Conrad said. "All who come here recognize this. To accept less insults my honor."

"I mean no insult," Jason said. "I was under the impression I was welcome to stay but free to leave when I wanted."

"All men are free to do as they will," Conrad said, his voice dangerously reasonable. "But you have not even remained here a week. Such an affront is insupportable. Are you resolved to pursue this course of action?"

"I am."

"Then you force my hand. I, Duke Conrad, challenge you, Lord Jason of Caberton, to a duel!"

"No, milord," exclaimed Kimp, rising from his chair. "Let me handle this miscreant."

Duke Conrad motioned for Kimp to be seated. "Lord Jason is a member of the aristocracy. Disputes among nobles are best settled by nobles." Some of the guests nodded sagely at this statement. "I repeat myself—I challenge you to a duel, tomorrow at dawn."

"I refuse," Jason said. "Can I go now?"

Several of the stunned guests stifled laughs. Drake tried to pretend he was coughing. "I am your superior in rank," Duke Conrad insisted, voice quavering with indignation. "You have no right to refuse."

"I do anyway."

"Let me rephrase. I will not allow you to refuse, no matter how great your cowardice."

"In that case I accept."

"Rapiers at dawn," Conrad declared.

Jason thought about movies he had seen where people challenged each other to duels. "Wait. You made the challenge. Don't I get to choose the weapons?"

"Perhaps, if we were of comparable rank, but it is unthinkable that I should condescend to permit an upstart lordling the selection of arms. Consider yourself fortunate I do not simply let Kimp dispose of you."

The injustice of the situation made Jason's ears burn. He had an audience. He needed to state his case convincingly.

"I am not only Lord Jason of Caberton," Jason explained, partially restraining his anger. "I am the chancellor of Trensicourt, second in command after the regent."

The guests murmured. For an instant Conrad's rigid expression faltered. "Untrue. You abandoned your office, and Copernum was reinstated."

"I abandoned nothing!" Jason reached into his pocket and pulled out the chancellor's signet ring. "I left secretly on a private errand. Anyone who claimed my title in my absence will answer to me when I return. Should I go get my mantle?"

Duke Conrad was clearly taken aback by Jason's vehemence.

"Furthermore," Jason pressed, taking advantage of the shifting momentum, "I am a guest in your house. You invited me, which implies some equality between us, even if I had no title. Or do you consider your guests inferiors?"

Around the table eyes glared. Conrad searched for support. Count Dershan shrugged.

Conrad cleared his throat. "The weapon with which I dispatch you is of little consequence," he said. "Choose."

To his mild astonishment Jason had won the argument, leaving him unsure what weapon to select. He knew what he didn't want. Conrad would hack him into lunch meat with swords or axes or any traditional armaments. What if they wrestled? Jason was bigger. Conrad probably knew moves that would take away the size advantage. Everyone was awaiting a response.

"Billiard balls," Jason said.

"Billiard balls?"

"Is there an echo in here?"

"I am unfamiliar with the tradition."

"Among my people it's a common practice," Jason invented.

"The combatants stand at opposite ends of a billiard table full of balls, then throw the balls at each other until one is dead."

"How novel," Conrad sniffed. "Very well. An absurd death for an absurd lordling."

"Hold on. If I win, will I walk out of here untouched by your henchmen, free to leave with my insult to your honor settled?"

"This castle represents neutral ground," Duke Conrad said. "Besides, no man may be compelled into a mortal duel twice in the same day."

"How comforting. Tomorrow at dawn then?"

"At dawn in the billiard room. Count Dershan will serve as my second. Who will serve as yours?"

"I will," Tark blurted, standing up. "And I will depart with Lord Jason when the conflict is resolved."

Duke Conrad nodded briskly, eyes narrow. Those around the table sat openmouthed. Jason and Tark walked away together.

At the door, aware that all eyes were still on him, Jason paused to address a servant. "See that my meal is sent to my room."

"Yes, milord," the man replied.

"I prefer 'Your Mightiness.'"

"Yes, Your Mightiness."

"See to it, then."

"Why billiard balls?" Tark asked. They stood in the topiary.

Jason shrugged. "Conrad would cut me to ribbons if I fought him with a sword. I can throw balls hard. Hopefully harder and better than he can." He picked up a stone and chucked it at the hedge shaped like Conrad. It missed.

Tark pretended not to notice.

"Think you could swipe some billiard balls?" Jason asked.

"No problem."

"Would you wake me up early? I want to have time to prepare."

The sky was gray when Tark awakened Jason.

Before a big game, Jason often had trouble sleeping. Last night had been his worst such experience. No matter how he tried to calm himself, Jason had felt too wired to sleep. He had paced. He had done push-ups. He had tossed and turned in the huge bed. He doubted he had slept more than an hour when Tark woke him.

Eyes burning, mouth nasty, Jason got up and did several stretching exercises. Then he began pitching billiard balls at folded fur comforters propped against the wall until his arm felt limber. An errant throw shattered an ornate jade vase and sent flowers flying.

Not long afterward a knock came at the door. It was Count Dershan, clad in a dapper uniform.

Jason and Tark followed him downstairs. They brought their belongings so they could leave when the duel was over. They proceeded directly to the billiard room. A crowd of guests and servants stood outside the doors. The crowd parted to let the participants pass.

Jason noticed several people giving him encouraging looks. Was he really about to fight someone to the death? He had no choice! Conrad had forced the issue. The Word was worthless if he remained trapped in Harthenham his whole life. Maldor would never be stopped, and he would never get home.

Once they entered the room, Dershan closed the doors, shutting out the onlookers. Inside, Duke Conrad awaited, medals glinting on his uniform. The onyx billiard table had sixty balls spaced equally across its maroon felt surface.

"We have our witnesses," Conrad said. In response to a gesture

Dershan and Tark took their places against a far wall. "You are more familiar with this form of combat than I am. How do we begin?"

Jason flexed his fingers. He had been thinking about the reality that he might die. Conrad was an athletic man. Luck would play a large role in this showdown. Jason tried to remind himself that he could throw fastballs at over eighty miles per hour. Without training, nobody could throw that fast. This was not a hopeless contest like fencing. Despite the danger, he had a real chance of winning. "We stand at opposite ends of the table, no balls in our hands, and your man drops a handkerchief. When the handkerchief lands, we take up balls and throw them at will."

Conrad nodded as if this met his expectations. "Shall we, then?" he asked, as if they were about to begin a game of checkers.

One thing Jason had to give Duke Conrad—he showed absolutely no fear. His nonchalance was unnerving.

Conrad and Jason took their places. Conrad stared coldly. Jason knew Conrad would kill him given the chance. But Jason hoped to end the contest without anybody dying. If he could hurt Conrad enough to get the upper hand, hopefully the duke would yield.

Jason felt sweaty. He rubbed his palms against his trousers. This was a different kind of nervous anticipation than he had ever experienced. No points would be tallied today. If he threw well he would live. If not, he would die. A strange tension hummed in his mind and body. His senses were in overdrive. The uneasiness he had sometimes felt before a ball game seemed ridiculous by contrast.

Dershan held a handkerchief aloft and let it fall. Jason hastily grabbed a ball in each hand. As a pitcher he had hit a batter once or twice, but now he would be trying to inflict serious injuries. Plus the batter would be throwing back.

As Jason released his first ball, Conrad's first ball breezed past his ear. Conrad twisted in an attempt to avoid Jason's first throw, but the ball struck him solidly, high in the back. Jason shifted the second ball to his right hand. It missed Conrad when he ducked. Jason lunged sideways in an attempt to dodge Conrad's next throw, which glanced off his side, stinging but not stunning him. Jason hurriedly grasped for more balls.

In order to hamper Conrad's ability to throw, Jason had hoped to bombard his arms, but in the heat of the moment it was difficult to aim with any precision. In unison they threw their next balls. Conrad's went wild, missing by a few feet. Jason's tagged the duke squarely on the collarbone. Jason threw another and barely missed the duke's elbow. Conrad's next throw was made awkward by his injury, but the ball hit Jason on the forearm, hurting plenty.

Jason snatched two more balls. Conrad fumbled as he reached for more. Jason remembered a trick he had used during water balloon fights. With his left hand he lobbed a yellow ball underhand fairly hard. It glanced off the high ceiling on its way toward Conrad, whose eyes followed it while he grasped for balls. Before the first ball fell, Jason whipped the second ball sidearm as hard as he could. It caromed off Conrad's head, and the duke flopped to the floor.

Jason gasped. He had been aiming for the duke's throwing arm, but Conrad had ducked right into the path of the throw. The ball had connected with so much force that Jason paused for a moment, grimacing in empathy. Tark noisily cleared his throat, and Jason hastily grabbed two more balls, holding them ready.

Except for his chest rising and falling, Conrad lay motionless.

Breathing hard, his arm and side stinging, Jason remained poised to throw. The duke stayed on the floor. Was he really unconscious? Could the duel be over?

Jason glanced at Dershan. "Is that good enough?"

Count Dershan looked pale. "Duke Conrad asked for no quarter. It is your right to ensure his demise."

Jason wondered if Count Dershan coveted Conrad's job. "I think I'll take my chances. I was forced into this duel. I don't want to kill Duke Conrad. What happens to him now is no longer any of my business."

"As you wish," Dershan acquiesced.

"Let's get out of here," Jason said shakily, sickened by the brutality but relieved to be standing and relatively uninjured.

"Right," Tark grunted. "I've had my fill of Harthenham."

"Farewell," Dershan said. "I'll have the drawbridge opened. You comprehend that your asylum ends once you pass without the castle walls."

"It doesn't surprise me," Jason said.

He and Tark exited the billiard room. The crowd stared silently. Someone coughed.

"Any who want to join us are welcome," Jason said. "You may not get another chance like this. Fair warning: Once outside the castle walls, we will probably be attacked."

Everyone in the crowd found something to look at besides Jason. Except for a tall, heavyset man, his reddish-brown hair thinning on top. A longsword was strapped over his shoulder. "I'll come." Considering his size, his voice was pitched higher than Jason would have expected.

Jason had never particularly noticed the man. "We leave immediately."

The big man hoisted a pack. "I am Tristan, son of Jarom. Once I held a noble title, though I forfeited it long ago."

"Lord Jason of Caberton," Jason said. "And Tark."

"Of the Giddy Nine," Tark explained.

Jason nodded. "Let's go."

CHAPTER 22

ESCAPE

Jason, Tark, and Tristan hurried to the front door, trailed by the crowd of bystanders. A pair of male servants flanked the door, standing at attention. The servants made no move to impede their departure. Once outside, Tristan drew his sword, and Tark produced his heavy knife. Jason unintentionally still clutched a billiard ball.

"Hold," called a voice behind them. They turned. Drake came striding down the hall, wearing a long, plain coat and tall boots. His hair was tied up in a ponytail, and a sword was fastened around his waist. "I need to come with you."

Jason smiled. "Please, join us." His eyes swept the onlookers. "Anyone else? Last call." A short, slim man with a narrow face met his gaze. Frowning slightly, he shook his head. Nobody else would look him in the eyes.

The four men trotted out under the portico, across the courtyard, and through the front gate over the lowered drawbridge. They abandoned the lane leading away from the castle and struck off at a loping pace across a field of alfalfa. The morning was cool. Low clouds hung in the sky. Dew from the alfalfa stalks dampened their trousers.

"What made you join us?" Jason asked Tristan.

"I was never proud of my decision to come here," Tristan panted. "Seeing men with the courage to defy Duke Conrad and forgo the protection of the castle inspired me. I resolved yesterday that if you won your duel, I would go with you."

"Glad to have you," Jason said, a little worried that Tristan was getting out of breath so soon.

"You realize we are about to die," Drake said.

"Probably," Tristan agreed. "But this is a better way to go."

Jason kept silent.

From behind, dogs began baying in an exuberant chorus. The four men looked back and saw nearly twenty eager mastiffs and boarhounds tearing after them, followed by a horseman.

"They don't waste much time," Jason muttered bitterly.

The four men broke into a sprint. Tristan discarded his pack. On the far side of the alfalfa field they vaulted a low wooden fence. Tark caught his foot on a post and went down hard, scrambling back up with the adrenalized vigor of a man about to become dog chow. The next field was a wide expanse of knee-high grass. Jason glanced back. The pack of fierce canines was already halfway across the alfalfa field. The man on horseback was now visible as Kimp, cantering along easily behind the dogs, a flanged mace in one hand.

Already Tristan was breathing in ragged gasps, his face red and sweat-glossed. His pace was beginning to flag. Jason slowed his pace to stay with him. Tristan angrily motioned him forward. "Go on," he wheezed.

Drake had the lead. Tark raced with remarkable speed for such a compact man. Jason could barely keep up with them. He concentrated on his feet beating against the grassy ground, trying to lengthen his stride and make his legs pump faster. The yowling of the pursuing dogs was rising in intensity.

Jason already felt a stitch forming in his side, like a screw twisting inward. He rubbed at it. Tark was a couple of steps ahead, his short legs churning desperately.

Glancing back, Jason saw that Tristan had turned to face the approaching dogs, longsword clutched in two hands. The dogs were almost upon him.

Jason witnessed Tristan's last stand in a strobe of backward glances.

Tristan slashing a leaping mastiff.

Tristan down on one knee, hacking at a boarhound, whines now mingling with the vigorous baying.

Tristan fighting to his feet, fists swinging wildly.

Tristan on the ground with dogs swarmed around him, gutting a mastiff with a dagger as a boarhound found his throat.

Jason stumbled and went sprawling on the dewy grass.

Tark skidded to a halt and yanked him up.

A dozen dogs still pursued them. Jason had dropped the billiard ball in the fall. The only weapon he now bore was his poniard. Tark had his knife. Several paces ahead Drake held his sword.

Out of a grove of trees on one side of the field came Jasher on a splendid black charger, riding straight toward Jason and Tark. He was leading a gray horse.

"Prongs!" shouted Tark, swerving to the left.

"No! He's a friend!"

Jasher raised a crossbow. He fired a quarrel. It was a long shot to the dogs. Jason glanced back. A boarhound pitched forward, a shaft protruding from its chest.

Jasher discarded the crossbow and produced another one. A mastiff fell. The crossbow went into the grass, replaced by another. Another mastiff went down with a yelp.

Jasher was almost upon Jason and Tark as he produced a fourth crossbow. "Take the horse," he ordered, releasing the reins.

The freed horse thundered straight at Jason. How was he supposed to stop a speeding horse? He dove out of the way, reaching back halfheartedly for the loose reins. He missed the reins, and the horse raced past, gradually slowing.

Jasher leveled his crossbow and shot another boarhound.

"Turn and fight!" Drake called. He flung a short sword end over end. The blade stuck in the ground at Jason's feet, and he seized it.

Jason and Tark whirled to face the remaining dogs. With a fifth crossbow Jasher reduced the dogs to seven as he bolted past them to intercept Kimp.

Drake trotted away from Tark and Jason, creating some space. Brandishing his sword, he shouted at the onrushing canines. Four of the dogs veered after him.

Three dogs—two boarhounds and a mastiff—charged at Jason and Tark. Jason sidestepped the leap of the mastiff, slashing its head as it soared past. A bounding boarhound rammed Tark into a backward somersault, taking his heavy knife through the chest in the process. The second boarhound came at Jason low, sweeping his legs out from under him with its rushing bulk.

The boarhound tore at the leg of Jason's pants, teeth penetrating to the flesh. Suddenly the mastiff he had slashed was upon him as well, going for his throat. Jason gave it his forearm instead. He had dropped the short sword. With his free hand he desperately pushed against the writhing bulk of the ferocious canine.

The boarhound was no longer savaging Jason's leg. Then Tark tackled the mastiff. Arm pistoning frantically, Tark stabbed the dog repeatedly, until it went limp.

Sitting up, Jason observed that the boarhound at his feet had also been dispatched by Tark. Off to one side, untouched, Drake stood calmly with a bloody sword in hand, surrounded by four dead dogs. Turning his head, Jason saw Jasher and Kimp closing on each other. Jasher held his doubled chain. Kimp brandished his flanged mace. Both horses galloped wildly.

As they reached each other, Kimp sprang from the saddle, straight at Jasher. Jasher swung his chain, but it was too late— Kimp collided with him, and both men flew off the back of Jasher's horse to roll in the grass.

Both men arose immediately. Kimp used his free hand to intercept Jasher's chain on its way to his tattooed head, while simultaneously swinging his club with a quick, one-handed backhand that struck Jasher in the chest.

The hasty blow from the mace was not particularly forceful, but it was accompanied by the sound of breaking glass. There came a brief glare of intense light, and then Jasher blew apart in a roaring explosion that hurled Kimp backward in fiery ruin.

Jason gaped in disbelief. Some distance away a flock of birds took flight. Smoke mushroomed up from the blast. Kimp lay motionless, his clothes aflame. Just like that both men were destroyed.

"Jasher was a seed person," Jason gasped, sprinting toward the fallen warriors.

Tark followed.

"His seed pops out when he dies," Jason told Tark. "If we find his amar, we can save him."

"Be quick," Drake warned, scanning the surrounding area as he hurried to join them. "Others will come after us. We're losing our chance to flee."

Jason found Jasher's scorched head and neck still attached to part of his torso, lying face up, long hair matted in charred tangles.

Jason turned the remnant of his former protector facedown and checked beneath the roll of hair at the nape of his neck. He found an empty socket.

"The seed got out," Jason said, on the verge of tears. "Search the grass!"

The three of them fanned out, combing carefully through the knee-high grass.

"Maybe it was destroyed," Tark said.

"No," Jason said, refusing to consider the possibility. "He saved us. We're going to find it."

"The amar is normally quite durable," Drake muttered, studying the ground.

The circle of their search continued to widen. Jason periodically looked back toward the castle for evidence of additional pursuit.

Tark returned to where Jasher's head lay, and squatted, searching meticulously. A moment later he held up the gray, walnut-sized seed. "We missed it. The seed was half buried. It must have detached while he was lying there, before you flipped him over."

Jason sighed with relief. "We have to plant it in a safe, fertile spot."

"Far from here," Drake said.

Tark nodded, slipping the seed into a pouch on his belt.

One of the horses, the black one Jasher had ridden, remained close by. Kimp's steed had started grazing over a hundred yards away. The gray horse Jasher had led had run off a good distance across the field. It began grazing as well.

"I'll bring the gray horse back," Tark said, mounting Jasher's horse.

"I'll get Kimp's mount," Drake called over his shoulder, already running toward the stallion.

Jason looked around. Where was Rachel? Jasher must have insisted she hang back.

The gray horse shied away from Tark when he got close, but Tark rode it down and caught hold of the reins.

Blood trickled down Jason's arm to his hand as he watched Drake mount Kimp's horse. Jason hesitantly inspected his wound. His sleeve was tattered above ugly tears and punctures in his skin. Maybe he could cut a strip of material from his cloak and fashion a bandage.

Tark was waving an arm, pointing in Jason's direction. Jason turned around. No less than twenty horsemen were emerging from the trees behind him at full gallop. These were not reinforcements from the castle. They came from off to one side.

Drake sat astride his horse, sword in hand, frowning. Behind Drake, across the field, Jason saw Rachel emerge from the edge of the woods on horseback. Tark was returning for Jason, the gray horse in tow. Neither Tark nor Drake could possibly make it in time. Jason waved them away. "Go, go, go!" he shouted. "Drake, save Rachel! Tark, tell her 'rim'! Tell her 'rim'! Go!"

Saluting with his sword and spurring his mount, Drake rode away from the soldiers. His horse jumped a fence and galloped madly up a gentle slope toward where Rachel waited.

Tark reined in his horse, hesitating.

"Get out of here!" Jason yelled. "'Rim'!"

Tark released the gray horse and took off, veering away from Drake.

Jason turned to face the riders. With no recourse he raised his hands in surrender. Most drew up around him. Four went after Tark. Five others chased Drake and Rachel.

Several lightly armored men dismounted, seizing Jason roughly. These were not conscriptors—or if they were, they wore less impressive armor than the ones who had previously tried to capture him. Their helmets had no face guards. They searched him and relieved him of his poniard.

"Lord Jason of Caberton, I presume?" asked a man still seated on horseback, apparently the commander.

"Yes." Jason felt defiant. He was captured, his friends were on the run, and he had little to lose. "How'd you know?"

"We were warned early this morning of your possible defection. A recent signal confirmed your decision. Is this the seedman Jasher?" The commander indicated the charred remains.

"It's his identical twin."

"We know he traveled with you until recently. Where is his amar?"

"I ate it."

"This is a foolish time for flippancy."

"I panicked. It tasted horrible. Do you have any mouthwash?"

"Search the vicinity," the commander ordered his men. "And check the young lord thoroughly."

They methodically searched Jason and his clothes. Crouching soldiers scoured the surrounding area with painstaking care. "The amar is not here, sir," a soldier finally reported.

"Search again," the commander directed. "There can be no error. And bind the prisoner's wounds."

A stinging salve was applied to Jason's torn arm and leg, after which they were wound with linen bandages. Nobody found a seed.

"One of the other men has it, then," the commander concluded. "They should be apprehended by now."

"Your men won't be back," Jason said. "Do you know the kind of people who live at Harthenham? I'm not talking about the fat ones. I'm talking about the sort who kill guys like you as a hobby."

"Enough nonsense."

Several minutes later a lone rider returned, his horse lathered.

"The man who went north rides Kimp's stallion, Mandibar. The girl had an excellent mount as well. The horses were too fast. The others remain in pursuit, but unless they make a mistake, our only chance lies in anticipating a destination and heading them off."

The commander scratched his cheek. "Where was he going?" he asked Jason.

"How should I know? He was running away."

"Tell me about your friends."

"I hardly knew them. The one who ran off with the girl is named Christopher Columbus. Tall guy. Really skinny. Green hair. Fangs. Six fingers on his left hand. About a hundred years old. Lots of wrinkles."

"I trust you are enjoying yourself," the commander sneered. "You are currently protected by orders to inflict no unnecessary harm. Otherwise I would teach you to guard your tongue. Your impudence will not go unpunished for long." He turned to his men. "Edmund—go to Harthenham and ascertain who we are pursuing. Bradford—take two men to Orin and find the pair who fled north. Cecil, take two men and track the man Eric pursued to the west. The rest of us are off to Felrook."

❊❊❊ CHAPTER 23 ❊❊❊

THE WORD

A -rim-fex-en-dra-puse. *Arimfexendrapuse.* The stupidest word Jason could have imagined. Utter nonsense. Supposedly it would unmake Maldor. He repeated the odd syllables in his mind, varying the inflection. If it failed, he could always try "supercalifragilisticexpialidocious."

For the past several days Jason had ridden east, under the watchful eye of Ian, the commander who had captured him. Six other heavily armed guards rode along as escorts. Ian had promised that before sunset today Jason would behold Felrook.

Throughout the journey Ian had remained tight-lipped about what specifically would happen to Jason. The commander gave ample hints that it would be unpleasant but offered no particulars. Jason hoped they would bring him before Maldor. Since the emperor should not suspect Jason had the entire Word, getting captured could turn into the perfect opportunity to finish his quest.

If he succeeded in destroying the emperor, Jason knew he might face immediate execution. But he was already facing torture or death in the dungeons of Felrook. How great would it be to take down the emperor instead! He thought about the joy it would bring to Rachel, Galloran, Jasher, Tark, Nicholas, and all of the others who had helped him. He had already beaten the odds by surviving as long as he had. Maybe he would find a way to survive after defeating Maldor.

Still, he couldn't keep a variety of fears from haunting him. What if they planned to brainwash the syllables out of his memory before bringing him before Maldor, to minimize the risk? Galloran was evidence that such precautions were within their power. What if they opted to never even bring him before Maldor? Or what if they gagged him?

With the sun approaching the horizon, Jason and his captors came through a narrow pass. A large valley spread out before them to the north, with Felrook in the distance. Jason did not know what exactly he had expected, but the reality surpassed anything he had anticipated.

A monstrous stronghold of iron and stone, the huge castle surmounted a tall island of rock in the center of a sprawling lake. The sheer cliffs of the island rose to great heights above the water, augmented by the monumental outer wall of the fortress. Four lesser rock formations surrounded the central island. Atop these satellite islands perched smaller fortresses, the two largest connected to the central stronghold by stone bridges, the other two by suspended walkways.

Further fortifying the intimidating complex, the ferry granting access to Felrook was encompassed by a formidable wall of its own. Three hills loomed near the lake, each crowned with a mighty keep, from which reserve forces could sally to harass assailing armies. Without atomic bombs or high explosives Jason could not conceive how Felrook could ever fall.

"Has Felrook ever been taken?" Jason asked Ian.

Ian snorted. "Felrook has never been attacked."

Jason could believe it.

"Are we going to make it there tonight?" Jason asked.

"You have one last night to contemplate your fate," Ian replied. "We'll camp not far from here, then deliver you late tomorrow morning. I hope you're ready to answer for your crimes. You cannot imagine the horrors that await."

"Will I go to the dungeon?" Jason asked.

"You will answer for your behavior," Ian promised cryptically.

Jason said nothing more as they rode forward and set up camp. After eating, all but two guards bedded down. Hands bound in front of him, Jason rested on his side. He had already tried to run off one night, earning a lump on the back of his head and a black eye. Jason knew it was futile to attempt another escape. All of his hopes were now focused on earning an opportunity to stand before the emperor.

Despite the long day riding, Jason found sleep elusive. He could not ignore that this was probably the final night of his life. His parents would never see him again, nor would his brother and sister. He would never see Matt or Tim. He would never play with Shadow. None of them would ever know what really happened.

When he finally slept, frustrating visions troubled him. He dreamed of his teeth falling out, of arriving for exams unprepared, and of searching for his parents in a chaotic crowd.

Until Drake shook him awake. "You're the heaviest sleeper of the bunch," the seedman chuckled.

Jason sat up, disoriented, hands unbound. The fire had burned low. He could see the figures of the soldiers sleeping around him.

"Keep your voice down," Jason whispered urgently.

Drake grinned. "They can't hear us anymore."

"You mean . . ."

"The only tricky part was the sentries," Drake said. "And they weren't much of a challenge."

Jason could hardly believe his ears. He looked around. "Who came with you?"

"I delivered Rachel to Tark and sent them northward," Drake said. "I've been stalking your little caravan for days. I figured we might as well let them bring you most of the way."

"You know about the Word?" Jason asked.

"Rachel filled me in," Drake said. "Tark gave her the last syllable. The second, correct?"

"Yes."

Drake rubbed the back of his neck. "I can hardly believe somebody finally pieced it all together. Rachel wanted to come. She tried to insist. But I reminded her that if you failed, she would become our last hope. Besides, I knew that alone I could successfully slip past our enemies and track you. Another person would have made the outcome less certain."

"If I fail," Jason said, "Rachel should share the syllables with someone else."

"I'll keep that in mind," Drake said. "But you won't fail, not if you have the syllables right."

"You know how to get me in front of Maldor?" Jason asked.

"I do," Drake replied. "Might be a one-way trip, and you'll have to go alone, but I know how. Are you willing?"

The question made Jason pause. Drake had rescued him. They could run away. "Will there ever be a better opportunity?" Jason asked.

"To get in front of Maldor?" Drake verified. "The emperor no longer leaves Felrook. The only sure way to gain an audience with him is to ring the gong near the gate to the ferry. By imperial decree anyone can ring it and talk to the emperor. In practice nobody ever touches it. Guards protect it, and everyone under-stands that while ringing the gong guarantees an audience with Maldor, it provides no assurances regarding the consequences of that audience."

"So what do we do?" Jason asked.

"We leave now," Drake said. "We get to the ferry before sun-rise. I'll create an opportunity, and you'll ring the gong."

Jason realized that unless he wanted to spend the rest of his life running from agents of the emperor, he had to finish this. Drake seemed committed and able. Here was a real chance to succeed where so many others had failed. If the gong would grant an audience with Maldor, he could fulfill his mission and maybe move on with his life.

"Let's go," Jason said.

Outside the wall protecting the ferry was a town considerably big-ger than it had looked from afar. Drake and Jason rode into town before sunrise, both wearing clothing and armor taken from the fallen soldiers. Drake carried a bow and a quiver of twelve arrows. Jason had recovered his poniard, along with a regular sword and a crossbow. They passed numerous stables, several warehouses, vari-ous inns, diverse shops, and multiple garrisons.

After tying up their horses, Drake led Jason down a series of alleyways. From the shadowy shelter of an alley Drake indicated a roofed platform accessible by stairs on three sides. Sheltered by the roof, hardly visible despite the burning cressets nearby, the round shape of a large gong dangled from a crossbeam. Beside it hung a mallet on a chain. Jason counted four guards.

"I'll climb onto the roof of that building across the street," Drake said. "You'll make your way to that shed over there." He pointed.

"I see it," Jason said.

"I'll make my presence known by loosing arrows. Once I get started, you run for the gong and ring it loudly. I'll ensure you get there."

"What will you do afterward?" Jason asked.

"Try to get away," Drake said. "My chances are poor. But as long as you ring that gong, and then say the Word when the time comes, it will be well worth the sacrifice. I've been waiting for this, Jason. I'm not sure I knew I was waiting, but I was. We should move before it gets any lighter. Ready?"

"Okay."

Drake strolled across the street. Following his example, Jason wandered casually down the road to the shed. From the shed he would be able to approach the platform from the side while Drake shot arrows at the front.

Once he reached the shed, Jason kept out of view from the gong guards while watching the roof. Just as he was wondering why Drake was taking so long, he heard a strangled cry, and a guard toppled down the platform steps.

Jason broke from cover and rushed toward the platform. Guards were shouting and motioning at the roof, then dropping with arrows in them. Another pair of guards issued from a small building on the far side of the platform.

As Jason reached the base of the steps leading up to the gong, only one guard remained on the platform. He had taken cover behind a thick post holding up the roof. When he saw Jason charging up the steps, he emerged from his position, sword in hand, and an arrow instantly pierced his side.

Lunging up the steps two at a time, Jason reached the mallet, grabbed the handle, and smashed the head into the gong like he was swinging a baseball bat. The long, shimmering crash hurt his ears, but he wailed the gong again, and again, figuring the more times he hit it, the less room there would be for argument.

"Enough!" called a guard, one of the two who had emerged from the guardhouse, and the only one without an arrow in him. He stood at the foot of the steps in front of the platform.

"I wanted to make sure," Jason explained, wondering if Drake might still shoot the final guard.

"You'll get your audience," the guard assured him. He turned toward the roof where Drake hid. "He'll get his audience," he yelled. Then he looked up at Jason. "You may not like what happens afterward, but you'll come before the emperor. Can I get your name?"

"Lord Jason of Caberton."

The guard huffed. "Should have known. Word has gotten out about you. I thought you were captured after fleeing Harthenham?"

"So did my captors," Jason said mysteriously.

"You're just a lad," the man realized, coming up the steps, hands raised. "Well, it was a bold run. I hope you can handle facing the end of it."

"Me too," Jason said honestly.

"I'll have to relieve you of your weapons," the guard said.

"How do I know I'll get to see the emperor?" Jason asked.

"At this hour all of Felrook heard that gong," the guard said. "They all know the rules."

Jason handed over his sword.

Perhaps an hour later, with the sun poised to rise, Jason and the gong guard boarded a ferry. It could have held a hundred men, but they were the only passengers. They crossed the lake to a quay projecting from a small landing area at the base of the central island. The fortress loomed above them, seeming to stretch upward forever. A switchback path had been carved into the face of the precipice. As Jason marched up the path behind the gong guard, several other guards fell into step behind them.

Jason imagined at least some of the guards might have bragged if they had apprehended Drake. He hoped their silence meant the seedman had managed to slip away.

As he climbed the path, the Word burned in Jason's mind. What if one of the syllables was wrong? Did pronunciation matter? He wished he could practice saying the Word aloud, but supposedly, once he uttered it, the Word would vanish from his memory. He would have to wait.

After the long ascent they passed through the two tremendous gates of the thick outer wall, walking under several massive raised portcullises, only to discover an inner wall nearly as high as the first. Nothing in the fortress was beautiful—everything existed to repulse and intimidate attackers. Riddled with loopholes and trapdoors, the battlements projected over the walls, making them virtually impossible to scale. Heavily armed guards patrolled everywhere, some accompanied by manglers. Catapults and trebuchets stood ready to help repel invaders. The main building was a blocky structure, warded by a series of parapets that receded from the courtyard in a progression of crenellated terraces.

Across the courtyard and into the stronghold they strode, down bare, solid hallways and up broad stairways, until they stood outside a massive pair of black iron doors, each embossed with a grinning skull.

A tall man, dressed like a conscriptor, instructed Jason's other escorts to depart. After they moved away, the conscriptor thoroughly searched Jason, finding no new weapons since the others had already all been confiscated. Then he pulled twice on a chain dangling from a hole in the wall. The doors swung open. "Lord Jason of Caberton," the tall conscriptor proclaimed.

Clenching his jaw, the Key Word repeating in his mind, Jason entered the vast audience hall. Huge pillars supported the roof, their bases carved like human feet, their tops shaped like hands splayed against the ceiling. Torches blazed in sconces on the walls. Flames leaped up from kettle-shaped braziers standing about the room on cabriole legs. A long black carpet led to an obsidian dais, where a man clad in a sable cloak sat upon a dark throne bristling with spikes. Off to the sides courtiers milled about, all eyes on Jason.

Starting at the base of the dais, on either side of the black carpet, ran long tables draped in black silk. At the tables sat many men and a few women. Most had empty eye sockets and only one ear. Many were missing limbs. Those who could see regarded Jason solemnly.

The tall conscriptor ushered Jason to a position ten yards from the dais, between the black tables, then backed away. The man on the throne had white hair and hard gray eyes. He was clean-shaven, with handsomely chiseled features and a cleft in his chin. A steel pendant featuring a huge black gem hung over his chest.

He sat with an elbow propped on an armrest, a single finger resting against the side of his head. He wore a bemused expression. "Greetings, Lord Jason." He spoke in a melodious baritone.

Jason felt like everyone expected him to kneel and beg. "Are you Maldor?"

Maldor chuckled. As if this granted permission, low laughter rippled through the room. "I am. Why have you sought audience with me?"

"I want to have a word with you," Jason said. "Just one." Maldor leaned slightly forward, eyes sharpening with alarm and disbelief.

Jason wondered what would happen after he said the Word. He was deep inside the fortress. Escape would be highly unlikely.

"Arimfexendrapuse!" Jason shouted.

Jason could feel the energy of the word as he spoke it. For an instant he almost sensed the meaning. The utterance left a buzzing aftertaste in his mouth.

Maldor gazed at him questioningly. Around the room courtiers murmured.

With a jolt of panic Jason realized he must have mispronounced the word. But when he tried to say it again, he could not remember how it started. Or how it ended. Or what came in the middle.

He strained his mind. He remembered *The Book of Salzared*. He remembered Jugard and the crab. He remembered the lorevault, and Whitelake, and the Sunken Lands, and Kimp. But the syllables were gone.

Calm had returned to Maldor. He folded his hands in his lap. "Anything else?"

"That was all," Jason replied uncomfortably. What else could he say?

"How unfortunate that the one word you wished to share with me was gibberish," Maldor said, bewildered. "You are dismissed."

Jason's mouth opened and closed soundlessly.

"Groddic," Maldor said. "Take this confused youngster to a holding chamber until I select a punishment."

The tall conscriptor bowed deeply, seized Jason by the arm, and guided him from the room out a side door. Jason glanced back over his shoulder at Maldor, who returned the gaze with puzzlement.

Groddic led Jason along a hall, then down a cramped, winding staircase to a corridor lined with iron doors. The three soldiers manning the small antechamber at the front of the corridor came to attention and saluted.

"I need a holding cell for this one," the tall conscriptor said.

One of the soldiers produced a key ring and opened a door on the left side of the hall. Groddic manhandled Jason into the room, which was bare except for an iron chair bolted to the floor.

"Secure him," Groddic said.

Jason saw no use in resisting. What could he expect to do, run wild through the fortress, find a way out, swim the lake, and escape into the wilderness? Still, he pushed off one of the soldiers and lunged for the door. A large hand caught him by the back of the neck and flung him brusquely to the floor. From a supine position Jason looked up at Groddic, who had so easily thwarted his escape. The tall man glowered.

"Sit in the chair."

Two of the soldiers had swords drawn. Jason went and sat in the hard chair. One soldier approached and began fastening him in. There were manacles on the armrests for his wrists, manacles on the legs for his ankles, and an iron collar affixed to the high back of the chair that clamped around his neck. The soldiers secured straps around his chest, thighs, and upper arms.

Groddic and the soldiers departed without a backward glance. A feeble ribbon of light glimmered into the room from under the door.

Jason had no way to measure time.

The confining straps and manacles allowed him virtually no room to even squirm. The iron collar was so snug he could feel every pulse of blood through his carotid artery. The darkness and confinement made him begin to feel claustrophobic. He closed his eyes and tried to breathe slowly, tried to pretend he was strapped to the chair by choice and could release himself at will.

He could not believe the Word had failed. He had gone through so much to obtain it! It would be one thing if absolutely nothing had happened. But the Word had felt powerful as he'd spoken it, and it had erased itself from his memory, which meant the syllables had probably been correct, and he had pronounced it just fine.

Maldor had not burst into flames. He had not melted into a bubbling jelly of biomaterial. He had not vanished with a thunderclap, empty clothes falling to the floor. The ground had not rumbled, the castle had not tumbled to ruins, and the courtiers had not fled the room in terror.

Instead Jason had been the focus of an awkward moment for less than a minute and then unceremoniously escorted from the room. Now he sat chained to a chair.

What if the Word worked slowly? What if the effects took time to manifest? Hours, days, weeks? It didn't seem likely. Magical or not, the Word had been a dud.

Jason sighed. He kept trying to ignore the restraints.

He tried counting heartbeats but gave up when he reached a thousand.

He imagined happier times. He pictured his dad drilling a tooth. He envisioned his mom walking Shadow. He imagined Matt turning in an English assignment. He visualized Tim cracking jokes at lunch, getting the whole table laughing.

Then he pictured Rachel. She was on the run with Tark someplace. He found that he missed her more than anyone, perhaps because he knew the others were safe. What would become of her? Somebody needed to warn her that the Word was a dud.

Hours passed. His mouth became dry. His stomach gurgled. He pictured himself dining during his arrival banquet at Harthenham.

How long would they keep him here? Besides being hungry and thirsty, he was developing an itch beside his nose. He attempted to reach it with his tongue but could not come close. Eventually he quit trying.

Much later—it was impossible to determine exactly how long—the door opened, bringing blinding light. Jason squinted while his eyes adjusted.

A pair of men carried a table into the cell. A third brought a cushioned chair. The two men spread a clean white cloth over the table and placed a bottle in a silver bucket of ice beside a glass. The other man set a lantern on the corner of the table.

"At least this place has room service," Jason said, his voice cracking. His mouth was dry. He had not spoken for hours.

The men did not acknowledge his comment or his presence. They exited the room and closed the door.

Not long after they had departed, the door opened again.

Maldor entered unaccompanied.

The door closed behind him.

"Greetings, Jason," he said, sitting in the chair at the table.

Jason swallowed. The pulse in his neck quickened.

"You are in a difficult situation," Maldor said, pulling the bottle from the bucket and wiping off the beads of moisture with a linen napkin.

"I have an itch by my nose. It's beginning to fade though."

Maldor set the napkin aside. "Oklinder, with a hint of lumba berries." He uncorked the bottle. "Let us speak plainly, man to man."

"Sounds good."

"Congratulations." Maldor poured pink liquid into the glass and raised it toward Jason. "You have uttered the dreaded Key Word in my presence. You surprised me. I would not have chosen to let you speak the Word in public. I did not realize you had all of the syllables. Those who heard it will not remember it, but still, I dislike being surprised. Although you were not rewarded with the desired effect, you had the Word right."

Jason stared blankly. "I did? Then what happened?"

Maldor gave a small smile. "You tell me."

Jason frowned. "The Word was a hoax?"

"Perceptive."

"A big diversion," Jason realized.

"What value does the Word have as a diversion?" Maldor coaxed, taking a sip.

Jason's heart sank. "It would keep your enemies busy, chasing after false hope."

Maldor inclined his head in agreement. "You have the idea. Only myself and Salzared know the truth. And now you."

"Salzared was in on it?" Jason felt dizzy. The faceless hero who had stolen the Word was a fraud!

"The displacer Salzared lives a life of pampered luxury inside this stronghold. It is his skin that binds the book scribbled in his blood, his eye on the cover."

"What about the people guarding the syllables?"

Maldor waved a dismissive hand. "Everyone else who knows of the Word believes it is real. Those who guard the syllables believe they reside in magical refuges beyond my reach. They are very well protected, but were the Word an authentic way to destroy me, I would have found a way to eliminate at least one of them long ago."

Jason studied Maldor. "How did the Word vanish from my mind after I said it?"

"You said a true key word," Maldor explained. "It was the word that could obliterate a past enemy of mine, a fellow student of Zokar named Orruck. That was why the Word and its syllables could withstand scrutiny even from the wise. The word you spoke and forgot is indeed capable of undoing a wizard. But not me."

"Did you use it to destroy Orruck?"

"I held the Word in reserve but never had occasion to use it, until I employed it as decoy to divert the efforts of some of my staunchest adversaries. Amazing what even intelligent men will accept as truth when they desperately want to believe it."

Jason scowled in silence. Could it really be true? So much effort all for nothing? So many people placing their hopes on a falsehood? He felt shattered to his core. With Maldor as an enemy no wonder so many had given up hope.

"Why are you telling me this?" Jason asked. "Is this just another trick?"

"I'll be interested to learn how you obtained all of the syllables," Maldor said. "By my count you had four: the original syllable from the Repository of Learning, the syllable guarded by Jugard in the cave, the syllable held by Malar on Whitelake, and the syllable protected by the Pythoness in the Sunken Lands. You never visited the Temple of Mianamon, nor did you set sail to the Isle of Weir. I suspect the hand of Galloran in this, but how he concealed these syllables from me is perplexing. Perhaps he was not as thoroughly broken as my tormentors assured me."

"Maybe I'm psychic," Jason said.

"That could be tested," Maldor said. "I'll learn the truth from you. Not now, I expect, but soon enough."

"Why are you telling me so much?" Jason asked.

Maldor swirled the fluid in his glass. "In private I only engage in candid conversations. I want you to comprehend your situation. Anything I tell you can be erased from your mind should that become necessary. Or I can simply have you executed."

"You seem very powerful," Jason said. "Why all the subtlety? Why the games?"

Maldor took a slow sip of oklinder juice. "I could crush the populace of every province I control, even if they rose united against me. But I enjoy experiments in governance, finding methods for holding power more securely, employing strategies to debase my opponents. No empire is ever too secure. I want mine to endure for millennia."

Jason licked his dry lips. "I still don't get why you're talking to me."

Maldor drank the remainder of the fluid in his glass. "Another purpose served by the hunt for the false Key Word is to identify my most capable adversaries. I take a keen interest in my opponents. Long ago I promised myself that any man who succeeded in obtaining the Word would receive the opportunity to join my elite circle."

"You want me to join you?"

"You have demonstrated your worthiness in many ways. You thwarted several attempts to capture and kill you. You overcame a variety of obstacles to gain the syllables. You eluded the titan crab. No others have done that. You bested Copernum in a battle of wits. Again, an exclusive accomplishment. Your friend crossed Whitelake, and you visited the Pythoness. Unbeknownst to me or my agents you obtained two syllables secretly. You found allies when necessary. Ferrin spoke highly of you. You are not eager to shed blood but will do so when cornered. You overcame Duke Conrad in a duel. You had enough self-possession to forgo the pleasures of Harthenham. You have proven yourself intelligent, brave, tenacious, resourceful. In short you are the type of man I prefer at my side rather than resisting me."

"Do you try to turn all your enemies to your side?"

"All of the most valiant ones."

"Then Galloran refused."

Maldor shrugged. "To Galloran, his stubborn ideologies

were more important than wielding real power. Had he joined me, he could have regained his kingdom and accomplished most of his goals. Instead he chooses to grow old in a rotting keep. Incidentally, he was my only other adversary to obtain the entire Word. Truth be known, he said it to me in this very dungeon. Of course it had no effect except to erase the syllables from his mind. I convinced him that he uttered the Word to a decoy, to explain why it failed to destroy me. He had been recently blinded, so he had no reason to doubt me."

Jason furrowed his brow, his heart aching for Galloran. "Why toy so much with your enemies? Why not just kill them?"

"You keep asking *why*. Curiosity can be admirable, but yours is so lazy. Can't you deduce the obvious answers? No, too late, I will divulge further unearned knowledge. 'Toying with my enemies,' as you phrase it, is simply another experiment in statecraft. Murder begets murder. I want the world to fear me, without inflaming that fear into rebellion. I slay many inconsequential enemies. But slaying powerful enemies creates martyrs, rallying their followers, allowing fear to become emboldened into anger. So I do not kill my most effective enemies. Great men who oppose Maldor know they will be ruined. Not killed, but utterly broken. They end their lives addicted to the pleasures of Harthenham, or, after long imprisonment and extensive conditioning, they are released into the world as feeble shadows of their former selves, burdened with physical and mental handicaps. Walking testaments to the futility of resisting my authority. Rather than spark rebellion, they are pitied and forgotten."

"Unless they switch to your side," Jason pointed out.

"Correct. And nothing is more demoralizing to my opposition than when their leaders join me." Maldor poured a little more juice into his glass. "My opponents have no heroes. Their best men and women either sell out or fail catastrophically."

"Ruthless."

"Only if you are foolish enough to oppose me. My power has never been seriously threatened, nor will it be." He sipped some juice. "Often the most dangerous enemies are former allies. My potential enemies, within my ranks and without, are kept separated and monitored. In conquered provinces I establish competent leaders of limited vision who will never aspire to the absolute power I wield. Their highest aspirations are to find favor in my sight. Something you have already accomplished." Maldor set down his glass.

Jason scowled thoughtfully. "If I joined you, how could you ever consider me a trustworthy servant? How would you know my loyalty was real?"

Maldor pursed his lips and placed his palms together. "Admirable. You have cut to the center of the issue. Your probable disloyalty is my chief concern in welcoming you into my inner circle of colleagues. The principal solution entails you receiving an eye and an ear from a displacer to replace your own, thereby rendering you incapable of secrecy. The temptation toward disloyalty would thus be removed."

"Now I get why Galloran refused your offer to restore his sight."

Maldor shrugged. "I could have forced a grafting upon him, but since it appealed to his sense of dignity to live out his life as an anonymous blind pauper settling petty disputes in a ruined castle, I was willing to accommodate that desire."

Maldor took up his glass and drained it. Jason shifted in his seat as much as the restraints permitted. "Those people at the tables by your throne are all displacers?" Jason asked.

"Better. A conjecture rather than a *why*. They are all displacers. They sacrificed body parts to serve as my intelligence network. I keep the most important ones close to me so I can receive significant tidings instantly. You are a Beyonder. Tell me why you came to this world."

The request jarred Jason.

"Honestly, it was an accident. I worked in a zoo, where I fell into the hippopotamus tank, got swallowed, and came out of a tree beside a river."

Maldor rose from his seat and walked over to Jason, looking down at him.

"A peculiar quirk of fate. Why did you elect to oppose me?"

Jason got the impression Maldor was very interested in this response.

"I read the book because I was curious. I knew it was forbidden, but I was hoping it might contain information about how to get home. Anyway, I read it, then met up with Galloran, who explained that my best chance to stay alive was to pursue the Word like the book said."

"I believe you," Maldor said. "Your tale fits the evidence, and I have a knack for spotting lies. Because your involvement against me was the result of unfortunate luck, I may show you mercy. But first tell me how you came to possess the second syllable. I know you never went near the Temple of Mianamon."

Jason considered the request. Kimp was dead, so he was no longer protecting a valuable secret. Unless Maldor would exact revenge on Galloran for placing the tattoo. That was a huge breach of his rules and would probably get the Blind King in trouble.

"I can't tell you. But honestly, nobody could ever discover the second syllable the way I got it."

Maldor considered him for a long time. "Again I believe you. And I can interpret much from your answer. Galloran must have disregarded my rules. I will learn more of this later." He began pacing back and forth before the chair.

"What now?"

Maldor stopped pacing and grinned. "Only men in your unfortunate situation are permitted to sit while I stand."

Jason stared in silence.

"I have a fondness for Beyonders," Maldor said. "I formally invite you to serve me. There is much I can offer. I will exalt you above the petty squabbles that trouble my lesser servants. You have proven you deserve to live beyond such nonsense. Using the secrets that extend my health and youth, I can prolong your mortal life to many times its normal duration. We will work together directly, until I find the best way to employ your talents. You will have to work hard, but will also enjoy many rewards. And you will retain a measure of freedom. You will be released immediately, and I will forgive all of your friends for any crimes involving you."

Jason contemplated the trust Galloran had placed in him. He thought of Jasher sacrificing his life and Drake risking his final life at the gong. He pictured Tark and Rachel riding desperately to escape Maldor's soldiers. He saw Tristan being ravaged by a pack of dogs. He remembered Norval infected by a poisoned knife. He imagined Aster the hobo being mutilated by manglers. He considered the arrogant, spiteful evil of men like Copernum and Conrad, along with the spinelessness of Dolan. He remembered the deceit Ferrin had employed. And now the man who rewarded evil people and punished good ones wanted Jason to serve him.

"What will happen when I refuse to serve you?" Jason asked.

"You will be turned over to my tormentors, to begin your reconditioning. Believe me, you cannot imagine the exquisite suffering they elicit. They have terrible methods involving magic and toxins along with a wide array of more traditional discomforts. You will languish for years under mind-rending tortures that will eventually decimate your very identity."

"My identity would be more decimated if I joined you."

"Well spoken, however unwise the sentiment. You are determined not to serve me, even at the cost of unspeakable torture?"

Easy to act brave now, Jason thought, before the consequences of this decision came to fruition. Would this private moment of valor be worth long years of unguessable torment? But how could he pledge himself to Maldor? How could he let displacers graft eyes and ears to him, to ensure he would live out his days doing evil?

He recalled Galloran stating that being a hero meant doing what was right regardless of the consequences. The thought sent a thrill through him. Galloran had been in this same situation and had made the right choice. Jason felt less alone. Maldor had claimed that his opponents had no heroes among them. But Galloran was proof to the contrary. And Jason would be evidence as well.

Jason took a deep breath. "I will not serve you," he said. "Your servants are frauds and murderers. You say your opponents have no heroes, but I disagree. The only heroes I have met here have been your enemies. Besides, you've already proven yourself an expert liar. How can I know whether anything you have told me now is any truer than your fake key word? How can I expect any good to come from making a deal with you? We have a saying where I'm from. Fool me once, shame on you; fool me twice, shame on me."

"We have one here as well. A lie twice believed is self-deceived."

"It rhymes. That'll help me remember."

"Where in the Beyond are you from? You sound American. California, maybe?"

"Colorado. Do you know how to reach the Beyond?"

"I do."

"Why not just send me home?"

"I do not reward my enemies unless they serve me." Maldor smiled and produced a small vial with a crystal stopper. "You have my admiration for resisting my offer. My esteem will bring you no mercy—quite the contrary—but you have it, as did Galloran. All who oppose me must be broken. I trust your convictions will be good company once your conditioning ensues. Adieu."

Maldor unstopped the vial and held it under Jason's nostrils. Jason held his breath, refusing to inhale. Even so, the fumes rising from the tiny hole were making him woozy. When he finally inhaled, unconsciousness overcame him abruptly.

CHAPTER 24

PRISONER

Jason awoke on a cold stone floor in a bare cell, wearing only a flimsy cloth. The single door was so thick that when he pounded with his fist, it sounded like he was hitting a wall. High above the door the light of a lantern shone through a barred window. One wall had a mysterious round hole the size of a baseball, at about the height of his waist. The only other things in the room were a small loaf of dark bread, a reeking hole in the floor near a corner, and a shallow depression near another corner where water had pooled.

Jason shivered and rubbed his bare shoulders. He picked up the bread. It felt petrified. He gnawed through the tough crust to the softer inner portion. He began tearing pieces off and cramming them into his mouth. Any bite that included crust took a long time to chew.

The bread was bland with an unpleasant aftertaste, but Jason kept eating until it was gone. He went over and squatted by the puddle. Leaning down, he sniffed the fluid. He touched his tongue to the surface. It tasted relatively clean. After a tentative sip, he began gulping it down.

He sat back and wiped his mouth. There remained enough water in the depression to last a few days, even if some evaporated.

Jason crossed the room to examine the hole in the wall. No light came from it. He could see that it curved away upward. He could not quite fit his hand inside.

He wondered if it allowed his jailers to hear what he was doing.

He put his mouth up to it. "Yeah, I'd like a cheeseburger and fries with a large Coke, easy on the ice."

No response came.

Could it be a drain? What if it connected to a toilet in a higher cell? Jason backed away.

He paced out the dimensions of his cell. It was a rectangle, seven paces wide, nine paces long. The ceiling was high, maybe fifteen feet. The barred window was well out of reach.

After his brief exploration Jason scavenged for crumbs that had fallen from the bread, collecting them in his palm. Then he sat with his back to the wall, nibbling on them. He wondered when he would get fed again. He wondered if they would bring him water, or if he'd have to just rely on the puddle. He wondered when the torture would begin. Maybe they would just let him sit and stew for a few days. Or weeks. Or years. Or decades.

Jason had been awake perhaps three hours when the snake squirmed out of the hole. It was at least five feet long and had a sleek azure body with dark violet markings.

As the serpent entered the cell, Jason scrambled to his feet. He had been sitting against the wall opposite the hole. The snake curled on the floor beneath the hole.

Jason moved as close as he dared. The head of the snake bulged on the sides, suggesting venomous pouches. A slender ribbon of a tongue flicked out of the mouth, testing the air. Jason backed away, glancing down at his bare feet and legs.

He scanned the cell with new intensity. There was no loose article he could use as a weapon, not even a pebble. Though not perfectly smooth, the stone walls were unclimbable, devoid of any handholds.

The snake uncurled and slithered lazily toward Jason. He backed away. Suddenly it advanced toward him with alarming speed. He had to run in a wide circle to keep away from it, splashing through the puddle.

Jason stood watching the serpent, his body tense, as if he were about to steal a base. The snake raised its head, its flat black eyes expressionless, and probed the air with its tongue.

Without warning the snake streaked toward him again. It seemed to be trying to shepherd him toward the corners of the room, but Jason kept dodging around it before he became trapped.

Moving strategically, he got the puddle between himself and the snake, but the snake went right through it.

Eventually the snake stopped again.

This was a pretty devilish torture. He could evade the snake for a long while, but without intervention the aggressive serpent would eventually strike him. He couldn't stay awake forever.

"My only hope is to kill you," Jason told the snake. It had curled up, tucking its head away in its coils.

"Are you peeking at me?" Jason asked, squatting.

The snake did not move.

"You really came after me. I had no idea any snakes were so aggressive. Did they train you to hunt people?"

The snake offered no response.

Jason scratched above his ear. How could he kill a poisonous snake when he had lots of exposed skin and no weapons? He wished he had retained the bread. That crust might have been hard enough to do some damage. Of course, his jailers had probably confirmed that he had eaten it before placing the snake in with him.

What about the tiny cloth he was wearing? Wrapping it around his hand might offer a little extra protection. Then again it was nice to have a little extra protection right where it was.

Jason supposed that if he could grab the snake just below the head, he could crush it against the walls or ground. Or if he got it by the tail and kept swinging it really fast, he might be able to bash it to death against the floor.

Now seemed like a good time to try. The snake had not stirred since it coiled up.

Jason could not see the head, but the tail was in plain view. He would have to grab it and start twirling violently. Even then the serpent might be strong enough to turn and strike him, no matter how vigorously he whirled it.

Holding his breath, Jason crept closer, one hand stretched forward. He was only a couple of feet away. Suddenly the snake struck, the head moving in a blur. Jason jerked his hand back and leaped away, letting out an involuntary shout.

The snake had moved too early. It had missed.

The serpent reared up, and for the first time a hood unfolded. It was some kind of cobra.

The snake stayed coiled, but the hooded head rose higher, swaying gently.

Jason backed to the far side of the cell.

Head high, hood spread, it came at him. The hood made it scarier. As before, Jason ran around and around until the snake stopped pursuing. It finally curled up again.

Jason stood panting, staring at the sinuous loops of blue and violet coils. There was no way he could grab the snake faster than it could strike. He considered going over to the snake and letting it bite him. It was bound to happen eventually. Unless this was some sort of test. Maybe if he lasted long enough, his jailers would come take the serpent away.

Incalculable hours passed. Periodically the snake would charge him, but never with the prolonged vigor of the earlier attacks.

Jason dreaded the drowsiness he felt overcoming him. He slapped himself. He splashed water in his face. He spit water at the snake, which hissed loudly in response, for the first time baring a pair of slim, curved fangs.

"Nice teeth," Jason said. "Hollow, right? Like a pair of syringes for injecting venom. Oh, I know a thing or two about snakes, pal. Just because you're going to kill me, don't pretend I'm not onto you."

As time passed, Jason caught himself nodding toward sleep standing up. His head would sag and then jerk up, his eyes blinking. Finally he awoke as he was toppling over, but he managed to catch himself. The snake attacked, and it was all he could do to hop clear of the striking serpent.

The near miss helped refresh his senses.

But the clarity did not last. Before long he became sleepy again. All he wanted was to steal a brief nap. The snake was still. Maybe he could sneak a few winks.

No! He slapped himself on the cheek, then began beating his bare chest and legs. As soon as he stopped, his eyes were drooping.

He had felt like this once on a road trip with his family. They had decided to push through late, and at almost four in the morning Jason was riding up front with his dad as they drove along a featureless stretch of highway outside of Mesquite, Nevada. His mom and brother were asleep. His job was to stay awake and watch his dad. He had caught himself nodding and had kept pinching himself to stay conscious. He repeatedly warned himself that if he fell asleep they would all be killed, and that seemed like sufficient motivation to avoid snoozing.

But deep down he had realized he was only the safety net. Every time he'd looked over, his dad had seemed alert. Jason had leaned his head against the window. The next thing he knew he woke up with the car tearing along the shoulder, churning up a huge fan of dust. His dad had overcorrected, screeching across the highway almost to the opposite shoulder. They easily could have died. His dad had taken the blame, but Jason had felt horribly guilty.

Here he was again. Except here he wasn't just the safety net, and there was no end in sight.

"Help!" Jason cried. "Just so you know, I can't stay awake much longer! Just so you all know!"

He heard no response.

With a shuddering sigh Jason sat down opposite the snake, back to the wall. After a moment the snake streaked toward him. Jason scrambled to his feet. The snake gave a long chase. Finally it quit.

Jason sat again. Maybe he could teach the snake that even when he was sitting, it would never catch him. Maybe then he would have a chance it would leave him alone when he inevitably succumbed to his drowsiness.

The second time he sat, the snake remained coiled up. Jason stared, tense, ready to hop to his feet. After a long while the snake attacked. He leaped to his feet and sprang away. The snake gave almost no chase.

Jason sat against a wall again. He could feel himself slipping. He closed his eyes momentarily.

And awoke when the snake struck his arm. He shrieked, rolling over. As he staggered to his feet, the snake struck him on the calf.

Disoriented, Jason examined the two spots of blood above his wrist. He had quietly planned that once the snake struck him, he would fearlessly throttle it for some measure of revenge. Now he didn't care. The persistent snake struck him again on the leg, but it felt distant. He swooned, extending his hands to catch himself as he collapsed to the rocky floor. Was that the door opening? *Too late, guys!* Consciousness retreated.

Consciousness returned. Jason was secured to a table in a dazzlingly bright room. An old man with a narrow, creased face stood over him.

"I'm dead," Jason mumbled.

"No, far from it," the stranger replied calmly.

Jason struggled feebly, testing the snug restraints. "I feel faint," Jason said.

"I'm sure you do. Is the light too bright?"

"Yes." Jason blinked several times. "I feel like I'm floating. Did I just start floating? How can I float when I'm strapped down?"

"You aren't floating. How is the light now?"

"Better. Still bright."

"I can't shield the candle any more or it will become impossible for me to see. Your eyes are currently extra sensitive. Squint if you must."

"You sure I'm not floating?"

"Yes."

"Are we in a hot-air balloon?"

"No. Do you remember where you are?"

"In the dungeons of Felrook."

"And how do you feel about that?"

Jason squinted thoughtfully. "Not too bad right now. I guess I should feel more upset. I didn't want to be here. And that was a mean trick with the snake."

"But you're trapped here, so why worry?"

"Good point," Jason agreed dreamily. "Very good point. That should be my motto."

"Just relax. The venom will help. I need to ask you some questions."

"What's the matter with me? I feel . . . really good but kind of nauseated at the same time."

"You were struck by a rare serpent whose venom induces an altered state of consciousness. The potency is enhanced when the subject is exhausted."

"Yes," Jason exclaimed. "I remember being asleep and hearing it coming—its scales against the stone, but I just couldn't wake up. Then it bit me. I was too tired."

"The powers of your memory have been magnified. I need you to answer some questions."

"Who are you?"

"Call me Damak."

"I read from a book by a guy named Damak once."

"Did you really?"

"Yes. *Subtleties of Manipulation.* 'Manipulation is a quiet tool of majestic power. Artfully manufacturing desires in others to suit one's own needs can be accomplished on an individual basis, or on a worldwide scope. Clearly, a study of manipulation requires a profound understanding of the selfish motivators that drive men to action. Different motivators function depending on the nature of the minds one seeks to dominate. Manifold motivators are available, including fear, the desire for wealth or respect or power, lust, duty, obedience, love, even altruism. Endless combinations may be employed to reduce the staunchest will to a malleable plaything. Learning to discover the appropriate mix of motivators for—'"

"Did you read the entire book?" Damak interrupted.

"No. I could tell you more. I remember every word."

"So do I, more or less. I wrote it. You are feeling lucid?"

"Yes. I feel very lucid. Good word for it. I can remember so many things. I can remember the colors of the animals that hung from the mobile over my cradle. I had forgotten all about them. They were puffy. A yellow and blue checkered elephant. A red and white checkered lion. A green and—"

"Well done," Damak said. "Very interesting. That is enough about the animals for now. Do you remember Galloran?"

"How could I forget?"

"Did he reveal any plans to you?"

Jason pressed his lips together, concentrating. "No real plans. He just talked to me up in his tower. He helped me make plans."

"Did he manifest any desire to oppose Maldor?"

"He said his only remaining purpose of any consequence was advising those who dare to challenge the emperor."

"How did he help you?" Damak inquired.

"He gave me a poniard and dubbed me Lord of Caberton. By the way, fun fact, a poniard is a knife. He introduced me to Rachel, and gave her a crystal sphere with orantium inside. He gave me directions to the cave where Jugard dwells, but could not recall how Jugard would help me. He told me to use his name among those who oppose Maldor because it would open doors. And he told me that heroism means doing the right thing regardless of the consequences."

"Did he tell you about a syllable he wrote down?"

"No, I learned about that elsewhere. He didn't remember."

"Where was the syllable written?"

"Tattooed beside Kimp's shoulder blade. I got it at Harthenham. It was 'rim.'"

"Don't tell me specifics about the Word," Damak said hastily.

"It doesn't matter. The whole thing is a hoax."

Damak clapped his hand over Jason's mouth. "Say no more regarding the Word." He looked away fiercely. "Did you hear anything about the Word?"

"Certainly not," a nervous voice responded. Jason could not see the speaker, but he could hear the scratch of a quill on parchment.

"Then you transcribed nothing of the sort," Damak verified.

"Certainly not."

Damak removed his hand. Jason stared with wide eyes. "Do not be alarmed," Damak soothed. "I would simply rather not hear details about the Word. Another syllable was written down. Where?"

"Inside the lorevault at Trensicourt. Strange, I remember that syllable too."

"Interesting. Tell me about Ferrin. Is he loyal to Maldor?"

Jason scrunched his brow. "He said he has no great love for Maldor, and he helped me quite a lot before Rachel found him out, but that was all part of tricking us. He explained that as an observer he could help us at his discretion. I believe he is loyal to Maldor. In the end he betrayed us and refused to relent."

"Very well. Tell me about the girl, Rachel. She is a Beyonder as well?"

"Yep. From Washington. She's incredible. I mean, she can be a little pushy, and sometimes acts like a know-it-all, but she really is smart, and she isn't all talk. You should have seen her at Whitelake! Have you ever met her?"

"No."

"She's really cute. I've never liked any girl as much as her. I'm really worried about her. I wish I could go to her and help her. Funny, I can't think things without saying them. It's like my mouth is tied to my brain. Bad for privacy. Good for you, though!"

"Did you know her in the Beyond?" Damak asked.

"Nope. I met her here."

"Did either of you come here on purpose?"

"Nope. By accident."

"How much of the Word does she have?" Damak asked.

"All of it. 'Arimfexendrapuse.'"

His expression horrified, Damak belatedly clamped his hand over Jason's mouth. He looked over to the unseen scribe. "You heard nothing?"

"Less than nothing. Must have been the wind."

"Do not say any of the Word," Damak urged, taking his hand away.

"Sorry. It just popped out. I couldn't remember it before, no matter how hard I tried. Funny, I still remember it, even after saying it again. I guess the snake venom works really well."

"Let's change the subject," Damak suggested. "You escaped Harthenham with a member of the Amar Kabal. Tell me his name."

"Drake. He liked dangerous pies."

"Why did he join you?"

"Who would eat pies that could take over your life? Why risk it?"

"Focus. Why did he join you?"

"Say no to death pies. Another good motto. I'm getting a headache."

"Why did he join you?" Damak repeated.

"Tough to say. Maybe because his amar went bad. I think he wanted to die with some honor. You should have seen the dogs he chopped up." Jason gave a soft whistle. "Poor doggies."

"And the runt who made off with Jasher's seed was called Tark, the surviving member of the Giddy Nine."

"Correct. Your eyes are very close together." Jason grinned sleepily.

"Stay focused."

"How do you stay focused? You're practically a cyclops."

"Stay with me. We need to discuss your fears. Of what are you most afraid?"

"Getting killed by a puppet. Like a marionette or a ventriloquist's dummy."

Someone in the room snickered. Damak looked in the direction of the snickering. "You getting this down?"

"Yes, sir," came the controlled response.

"What else frightens you most?" Damak asked.

"Enclosed spaces. You know, claustrophobia? Not every type of enclosed space. Some are worse than others. I heard a story about some prisoners of war who were squeezed into these confining boxes for a long time. I would hate that." Jason shuddered.

"What else? List some."

"Having body parts crushed or maimed. Finding out nobody has souls. My friends or family getting killed. Suffocating. Getting brain damage. Heights, if I'm not secure. Getting gangrene. Getting radiation poisoning. Titan crabs. Having my eyes poked out. Getting rabies. Having a toothache and no dentist, then trying to yank the tooth out, and having half my jaw break off. Getting cancer. Puking. Having my belly button come untied. The devil. Being tortured. Manglers. Leprechauns. Forgetting a class I signed up for and then remembering on the day of the final. Drinking rotten milk.

Earaches. Catching on fire. Getting lost. Dying. Finding out—"

Jason stopped speaking and began to lurch against the immobilizing straps. It felt like somebody had lit a string of firecrackers inside his head. His eyes rolled back, and he jerked and trembled while Damak steadied him.

"What else do you fear?"

Jason opened his mouth to speak, but only a tiny gasp came out. The spasms increased.

"The venom is wearing off," Damak said to someone.

He uncorked a vial and waved it under Jason's nose. The seizures subsided, and Jason sank into a dreamless sleep.

Jason awoke in what looked like the same cell where the snake had bitten him. His muscles felt sore, as though he had spent the previous day strenuously lifting weights for the first time in months.

He sat up and looked around. A new small loaf of dark bread sat close by.

He picked at the scabs from the snakebites on his arm and legs. He could remember an old man asking him questions. The man had written the book about manipulation Jason had read in the Repository of Learning. What was his name? He could not recall. Yes he could: Damak.

He remembered learning that the venom of the snake was a mind-altering substance. The conversation with the old man seemed like a vaguely pleasant dream. Had he been floating? Maybe it hadn't really happened. Maybe it had all been in his head. He hoped so. He had spilled his guts about Galloran and a lot of his fears, but the specifics remained vague. He had remembered the Word, but he recalled none of it now.

Jason crawled over to the puddle for a drink. Then he retrieved the bread. Even as hungry as he was, Jason crammed almost half the loaf into the hole in the wall to plug it up before devouring the rest.

He felt tired after eating the bread, dimly realizing as he slumped to the floor that it must have been drugged.

When Jason regained consciousness, he could barely move. Everything was black and smelled like metal. He was inside an iron container tailored to the contours of his body. He was lying on his back. He could wiggle his fingers and squirm a bit, but that was the extent of his capacity to move.

He closed his eyes and tried to resist his rising panic. He hated tight spaces. He had told them that in his dream. It must not have been a dream. He began breathing faster. He tried to thrash against the container but could hardly twitch. Was this a sarcophagus? A coffin? Had he been buried alive? No, he could breathe. There were slits near his nostrils.

He was hyperventilating and getting sweaty. He cried out, and his voice sounded close and muffled.

Jason kept his eyes closed and concentrated on breathing more slowly and deeply. Nobody was going to free him, so he had to get used to this. He tried to go back to sleep but was unable.

The silence was oppressive. He began singing songs. Songs from the radio. Television theme songs. He hummed themes from movies.

He wiggled his body as much as he could. It was tough being encased in such a tight space. The only sounds came from his voice. The only smells were musty iron and his own sweat. The perfect darkness left nothing to look at.

After a long time he heard a door open. He heard footsteps; then a hatch over his face opened. The torchlight was blinding until his eyes adjusted.

A pliable hollow tube brushed against his lips. He could see a hand holding the tube. "Drink," a male voice said.

Jason sucked on the tube and eventually began swallowing water. He paused, then drank more. He had not realized how thirsty he was. The water tasted flat, but he could not get enough of it.

The tube was removed. Dirty fingers began feeding him cold wads of stringy meat. It was not good. It was too salty and may have been raw, but Jason ate greedily. The fingers gave him stale bread, followed by another sip from the tube. Then the hatch closed, returning him to darkness.

"Hey," Jason complained. "I have to pee."

"Then do it."

"I'll drown."

"It'll drain."

"Wait, I have some questions—"

He heard the door close.

Time became Jason's nemesis. He was trapped with virtually no sensory input. He tried to keep himself company. He recited quotes he remembered from movies. He prayed aloud. He sang. He flexed his muscles and wiggled. He slept as much as he could.

Sometimes he thought about the people he had left behind—his parents, his brother, his sister, his baseball team, Matt and Tim. He wondered if his face was on milk cartons. He wondered if he had been on the news. By now there might even be a headstone in some cemetery with his name on it. Wherever they imagined he was, he doubted any of them would guess he was locked within a sarcophagus in the dungeon of an evil wizard.

He thought back over his adventures, marveling how Maldor could have instituted and maintained such an elaborate fabrication.

He wished he could get a message to Galloran that the Word was a fraud. He wondered if Tark and Rachel had completely escaped, and if they had planted Jasher's seed. He wondered what Drake was doing.

Nobody visited except to bring him food and water. After the few words on the first visit the man who fed him would not speak.

Jason did not know how many times a day he received food. He was losing all concept of time. He thought he was fed twice a day. But it might have been five times a day. Or once a week.

The sixth time the cell door opened since he had been imprisoned in the iron container, Jason was dosing. He awoke at the noise. "I have to . . . um . . . do more than pee," Jason groaned.

There came no answer.

"Don't tell me it will drain."

There was a sound like a body falling to the ground.

"Hello?" Jason called.

The hatch opened. Jason squinted because of the light. As his eyes adjusted, he saw a familiar face peering down at him. Ferrin.

"You look full of goma worms," the displacer said.

"Full of what?"

"No time to explain."

CHAPTER 25

DEEP PORTAL

F errin? What are you doing here?"

"I came to recite original poetry. You're the perfect audience."

Jason coughed out a laugh. "You're here to torture me?"

"I bet you love it here. You can just sleep all day." The displacer winked, then glanced to one side. "Listen, we need to make haste. I have received a new assignment from Maldor. Since I'm leaving, I thought I might bring you along."

"But how—"

"Pay attention. I've done some snooping. I had to take some risks and use up some favors, but I now know of a way to return you to the Beyond. The portal is in a cave not far from Felrook. I am not supposed to know about it, but I figured it out. If you swear you will return directly to the Beyond, I'll sneak you out of here."

"But I learned some very—"

"No, no, no. There is no room for negotiation. I have committed some minor deviations against Maldor in the past. All right, some major ones. But never anything comparable to smuggling a prisoner out of Felrook. I need your word on this. If I smuggle you out, will you go directly back to the Beyond? Yes or no."

"Is this some kind of trick?" Jason asked. "I don't get why you're doing this."

"Before you found out what I was, we became friends. I regret how our association ended. I'm doing this to show how sincerely I value you. No trick. You're stuck. I'll get you out and send you home. It couldn't be more straightforward. Yes or no."

"Yes."

"Good."

Jason heard latches snapping. Ferrin heaved open the heavy lid of the sarcophagus, then helped Jason out.

Jason was relieved to find he was not too wobbly. He twisted and stretched and rubbed his limbs.

Ferrin knelt beside a fallen conscriptor and began stripping his gear.

"What's going on?"

"Remove his boots."

Jason went to work. The conscriptor breathed gently. "I take it I'll be wearing his clothes."

"Good guess. I think he's about your size."

Soon the conscriptor was undressed.

"Get clothed," Ferrin said. "Hurry." He picked up the naked conscriptor, dumped him into the container, and closed the lid.

"You knock him out?" Jason asked, pulling on a pair of trousers.

"Drugged him." He held up a small crystal vial like the one Maldor had waved under his nose. "A potent solution. I needed to be sure he would stay out for a while."

"Thanks for doing this."

"I tried to tell you that I remain your friend. Convinced?"

"More than I was an hour ago. How did you know where to find me?"

"I'm a spy. Gathering information is my specialty. It helps that

I rank fairly high around here. Felrook is a gigantic bureaucracy. Hurry."

Ferrin helped Jason arrange his sword, armor, and helmet in proper conscriptor fashion.

"Stay close to me. Be confident. Your face is inscrutable behind that face guard. Say nothing, even if questioned. If I'm asked who you are, I will say, 'He is not here.' That will imply that you accompany me anonymously on a highly secretive mission. Which works well, because Felrook is plagued by such secrecy."

"Sounds good."

"The only thing that could possibly stop us would be if we encountered Maldor. But that will not happen." Ferrin wore a chocolate brown robe. He pulled the cowl over his head. "We must move quickly. When Rumus awakens, he will rant and threaten until somebody investigates his claims. By then we need to be far away. You carry the torch."

Jason picked up the torch. Ferrin used a long key to open the door.

A pudgy man was waiting outside. He had matted black hair and a nose like a potato. He was eating stringy meat from a clay bowl when the door opened, but instantly stopped, wiping a greasy hand on his tunic. He nodded submissively at Ferrin.

"What are you doing out here?" Ferrin demanded.

"Waiting to feed the prisoner, master." Jason recognized the voice and the dirty fingers.

"It appeared you were feeding yourself."

The man stared at the ground in shamed silence.

"Finish it, for all I care," Ferrin said. "I assume considerable nutrition is required to sustain your girth. We administered a toxin to the prisoner to elicit information. He will not awaken for some time."

"Very good, master." His eyes remained downcast.

Ferrin led Jason down a hall. Guards opened an iron door, and Ferrin signed a register. Nobody paid particular attention to Jason.

They mounted a long spiral staircase, passing other iron doors. At the top Ferrin signed another register; then the guards opened a heavy door.

Without a word Ferrin strode past them, Jason at his heels. He led Jason through a network of passages, then out a heavily guarded door into a courtyard. The soldiers saluted Ferrin. He paid them no heed.

It was night outside, and overcast. In one portion of the sky a hidden moon made the clouds glow. Covered lamps and cressets shone in the courtyard and on the walls. The paving stones of the courtyard were glossy with moisture, but no rain was currently falling. Jason breathed deeply of the fresh, humid air. He had never felt so happy to be outside.

Jason followed Ferrin across the yard toward an enormous gate. A man wearing a long chain-mail hauberk approached them. "Who goes there?"

Ferrin lowered his cowl.

"Ferrin, you're dressed to travel," he said. He had a scar that ran through his upper lip.

"Sorry night for it."

"Who's your friend?"

"He is not here."

"Come off it. Who is he?" The man squinted at Jason, as if trying to penetrate the visor of the helmet.

Ferrin glanced around, never looking directly at Jason. "I see no one."

"Have it your way. Travel well."

Ferrin led Jason to the great gate and spoke briefly with a

guard, who let them out through a narrow postern door. It began to sprinkle as they made their way down the slick switchback. By the time they reached the landing at the bottom and boarded a small ferry, the rainfall had become drenching.

Ferrin in his hooded robe stood silent beside Jason in his borrowed armor, the only passengers on the ferry, watching the raindrops disturb the lake by the light of a lantern as the craft advanced toward the shore. Jason shivered. The dampness magnified the chill.

The craft landed, and the two passengers disembarked. They walked along a quay to a low building with a slanted roof. Jason waited under the eaves while Ferrin went inside. A young man exited the building and jogged off into the rainy night.

When the young man returned leading a pair of horses, Ferrin came outside.

"Ready to ride?" Ferrin asked. Something in his intonation warned Jason to try to seem like an experienced horseman.

Jason put a foot in a stirrup and swung onto the saddle. His days riding with Jasher had left him feeling much more comfortable on horseback. Ferrin led the way.

As they approached, the gate in the wall protecting the ferry opened. Ferrin and Jason trotted out, Jason squeezing his mount with his knees, trying not to be jounced too much by the jerky gait. The gate closed behind them.

Jason glanced over at the gong. Four big guards flanked it, two under the roof on the platform, two on the steps with hoods up against the deluge.

Ferrin increased the pace, and Jason followed. Once they left the ferry town behind, the night became almost impenetrably black. Only the muted glow of an unseen moon provided luminance.

"Stay close," Ferrin called back. "I know this country well. Even with the weather we'll reach our destination in a couple of hours."

Eventually the rain relented. They followed a narrow lane beneath the cover of trees. Water dripping from overhanging leaves made the rain seem to continue for some time.

A group of men stepped out into the path, barring the way, one of them lighting the scene by unhooding a lantern. Ferrin reined in his horse.

"Who goes there?" inquired the lantern bearer.

"Ferrin the displacer and an unnamed conscriptor, on urgent duty." He held up a token.

The soldiers cleared out of the path.

At length Ferrin left the lane. The horses squelched across a sodden field as the rain began to fall again in large drops. They pressed through damp undergrowth to pass over the shoulder of a ridge, then followed a rain-swollen stream in the dale beyond.

Ferrin drew up his horse and dismounted near a group of mossy boulders beside a low bluff. Jason did likewise. They tethered the horses, and Ferrin grabbed a bundle from the back of his saddle, leading the way between the largest boulder and the steepest portion of the bluff to the hidden mouth of a cave.

Ferrin paused just inside the opening to ignite a small oil lamp. Holding the lamp aloft, he led Jason deeper into the cave. They climbed upward for a time and then had to wriggle into a horizontal cleft on their bellies and slither forward for about thirty feet. After that the way widened again, descending until they came to a roomy grotto where long stalactites hung over a placid pool of water.

"Come look," Ferrin said, approaching the brink of the pool.

Jason came up to the edge. The water was remarkably clear.

By the light of the lamp he could see a long way down, but the bottom was not in sight. "Deep," he said.

Ferrin nodded. "This is a gateway. You need to hold a heavy stone so you sink fast. Once you reach a certain depth you will pass through into the Beyond. The portal only works in one direction. You won't be coming back."

Jason dipped a finger into the water, sending concentric ripples across the glassy surface. "It's frigid."

"Sorry, but this is the only way I know to send you home. And you have to go home. Maldor will not rest until you're recaptured."

"Will they link you to me?"

"Probably. I went into the dungeon using one of my false identities, but I expect to be discovered. When they find me out, I must be able to claim I rescued you to mercifully dispatch you and spare you the agony of the tormentors. I will claim to have dumped your corpse in the sludge pits. When I make that assertion, I need to be certain the lie will never be detected."

Jason glanced at the deep water. "That isn't what you're doing, is it? Tricking me into killing myself?"

"No," Ferrin said gravely. "I know it requires trust, because you will have to sink to a depth beyond the point of no return. But this truly is a portal to the Beyond. One of the last reliable passages from our world to yours. A closely guarded secret. If Maldor knew I was aware of it, I would probably be killed. Jump in holding a heavy stone. You will not return to the surface. But neither will you die."

Jason clenched his fists. "I learned something very important from Maldor."

"What?" Ferrin asked, clearly eager to uncover a new secret.

"The Word is a hoax."

Ferrin stared. "What do you mean?"

"He invented the Key Word as a decoy for his enemies. The Word we learned was real, but it had power to kill a different wizard, not Maldor."

Ferrin closed his eyes and tilted his head back. He rubbed his forehead. When he spoke, he seemed to be thinking aloud. "That makes perfect sense, but the possibility never entered my mind. The very existence of the Word is a zealously protected secret. Few who serve Maldor have even heard rumor of it. I always thought Maldor was flirting with disaster by not vigorously attempting to remove those who guard the syllables—at least one of them. I assumed they must be protected by some unnamed magic. Now it makes sense."

Ferrin opened his eyes. "How did you uncover such a secret?" There was urgency in his manner.

"I got the whole Word. It didn't work, and Maldor later explained it was a hoax, when he tried to convince me to join him."

"You got the entire Word?" Ferrin exclaimed in flustered admiration. "Well done! I heard you called out something strange when you were brought before the emperor. I assumed it was a guess using whatever syllables you had accumulated. So you had the complete Word, and it failed; then you rejected an opportunity to join Maldor, even though the only alternative was endless torture?"

Jason nodded.

Ferrin plopped down on a rock. "That is integrity," he muttered to himself. He looked up at Jason. "I've gotten myself into much more serious trouble than I anticipated."

"Why?"

"You have information that could spoil one of Maldor's most

elaborate and secretive intrigues. I mistook you for a prisoner who had failed to obtain the Word. This alters everything. If Maldor suspects I know what you just told me, I'm finished." Ferrin rubbed his throat. "Not only that, when he learns I instrumented your escape, knowing what you know, I'm finished."

"So join me. Switch sides. We can escape together, take this information to Galloran. We have to stop everyone from focusing their attention on this wild goose chase."

"No, no, no." Ferrin wagged a finger. "Abide by your promise. You go home. My latest mission will take me far away for a time. I will keep an ear to the ground. I may not be implicated. If I am, I'll have to drop off the map."

"They'll piece it together."

Ferrin arched an eyebrow. "I can't argue. I was spotted leaving with an unnamed conscriptor near the time of your escape. The identity I used when signing the register is one I have employed before. I kept my face hidden in the dungeon, but that won't be enough, not with how hard Maldor will be looking."

"Did the conscriptor know you?" Jason asked. "The one you placed in the sarcophagus?"

"He did not. That was the main reason I used him. He thought he was coming to observe while I extracted information from you. I kept my face obscured and gave him the same name I signed to the register. Still, he knows enough that when they put together the pieces, I'll be implicated."

"You wouldn't have rescued me if you knew the whole story," Jason said.

Ferrin sighed. "Probably not. I neglected to fully investigate those details. I simply couldn't imagine you had completed the Word. Still, all the more reason I need to be able to claim I killed you, so Maldor can believe your secret perished with you. I will behave as though you told me nothing. I have kept secrets from Maldor before. Nothing this crucial, but I might be able to do it. Don't worry about me. One way or another I'll take care of myself. All you need do now is return home. Isn't that what you want most?"

Jason bit his lip. He imagined how relieved his friends and family would be to see him. He considered some of the conveniences of modern life he had once taken for granted—grocery stores, refrigerators, hot showers, air conditioning, toilets. "It was. But this information is so vital. Everyone chasing the Word is wasting their time. And I'd be abandoning Rachel. Maldor is a bad man, who rewards bad people. Would you honestly regret it if someone defeated him?"

"No, assuming someone worse didn't take his place. But he will not fall. The Word was his only weakness, and it isn't real. This is not open to debate. If Maldor finds I've set you free, we'll both be dead sooner than you can imagine. You must leave this world. I'm protecting both of us. We should hurry and find a suitable rock."

Jason hesitated. "Okay."

They began searching around the perimeter of the pool, looking for a good stone to serve as a weight. Jason tried to pick up a large round one, but it was too heavy. When he turned and looked at Ferrin, he saw the displacer lifting a rock at the edge of the water, his back toward him.

"How's that one?" Jason asked.

"Not bad. I brought you a change of—"

Jason shoved Ferrin in the back, sending him into the water, and then sprinted toward the mouth of the cave. He fell flat and began scooting through the low cleft, heedless of scratching and bumping himself. As he came out the far side, Ferrin was entering the crack, dripping wet, bearing the lamp. "Wait!" he called. "You stop and I'll stop!"

Jason hesitated, looking back through the low gap at the soaked displacer thirty feet away.

"What are you doing?" Ferrin asked calmly.

"I have friends who need the information I know. I can't just abandon Rachel. She'll think I failed, and try to use the Word. She'll end up in the dungeon."

"You swore you would return to the Beyond if I freed you."

"Let me see, have you ever lied to me? I think now we're even."

"I'll catch you before you reach the horses."

"No you won't."

"If I fail, you will get picked up by a patrol. Or get apprehended once you are found missing and the manhunt begins. You'll end up back in the dungeon."

"I might. You might too."

Ferrin shook his head in frustration. "At this point Maldor might even send a torivor after you. Have you heard of them? More commonly called lurkers?"

"I've heard the name."

"You don't want to meet one. Trust me. Just go home. This may be your only chance. Don't pass it up. Saving you probably cost me my life. Don't you want to go home?"

"Believe me, I really do. But not as much as I want to help my friends. Too many good people have wasted their lives chasing a lie. Now I know a way home. I can use it later."

"You'll be dead by sunrise."

"I've heard that one before."

Ferrin sighed. "Fine, you win. If you're adamant about staying here, let me come with you. I can guide us to safety."

"Sorry, Ferrin, I can't trust you. A lie twice believed is self-deceived. You'd never believe who taught me that one. If you really want to help me, catch up with me later, at a time when I can trust your sincerity. I would love to have you on our side."

"I will catch you," Ferrin promised, voice grave.

"Don't chase me," Jason said, picking up a stone. "Do you have any idea how much damage I could do to you while you squirm through there? Ask Duke Conrad."

Ferrin paused, frowning. Then he blew out the lamp. Jason could see nothing. He heard Ferrin scrambling, and blindly winged the stone sidearm into the crevice. He turned and hurried toward the mouth of the cave, hands outstretched. Several times he stumbled. Three times he fell hard, only to jump back up and blunder onward.

He could hear Ferrin fumbling along behind him, gaining ground.

Jason burst from the mouth of the cave in a wild sprint. Rain fell in a torrent. He could scarcely see. Splashing through puddles and slipping in mud, he wound through the boulders toward where the horses stood tethered.

A body slammed into him from behind, tackling him with a muddy splash. Jason tried to squirm free. His helmet was jerked off, and as he tried to rise, a sharp blow to the back of his skull knocked him forward, robbing him of consciousness.

Rachel waited beneath a rocky outcrop, wondering whether Tark would return. Lightning blazed across the sky, and for a flickering instant fir trees strobed into view. Thunder boomed loud and close.

She smoothed her hand along the neck of her horse. It was not the same horse she had ridden while escaping Harthenham, nor was it the mount she had used after that. She had traveled on foot, in wagon, by boat, and on several different horses as she and

Tark led their pursuers on an epic chase. Time and again, when it seemed they had finally gotten away, a new patrol would start after them.

Shivering, Rachel pulled her cloak tighter. She wondered whether Jason was alive. She wondered if he had used the Word yet. Could Maldor already be destroyed? How would they know if he had been?

Lightning flashed again, temporarily throwing harsh highlights over the landscape. Where was Tark? Could they have taken him? No, he would be back. He always came back.

The rain started pattering hard again. Rachel waited patiently. Eventually she detected the sound of an approaching horse. Or could it be horses? She grew tense as a pair of horses loped into view. Tark sat on one. The other held a taller figure.

"Rachel?" Tark called.

"I'm here," she answered. "Who's with you?"

"Drake found us," Tark replied.

The two men joined Rachel beneath the outcrop. Lightning glared. Sure enough the other rider was Drake.

"How did you find us?" Rachel asked.

"I rode hard," Drake said. "It was no challenge to follow the patrols on your trail. You create quite an uproar wherever you go."

"What about Jason?" Rachel asked.

"When I left him, he was entering Felrook for an audience with Maldor. I have kept my ears open but have heard no news since. Perhaps he was not granted an audience. If Maldor had perished, we would have heard."

Rachel bowed her head. She had hoped that if she and Tark could hang on until Jason destroyed Maldor, everything might change. What now? Could the emperor have killed Jason? No, she would not accept the possibility. They had locked up Galloran—

they would lock up Jason as well. He might not be comfortable, but he was probably alive. And if he was imprisoned, eventually they would find a way to rescue him. She had to believe that.

"Drake figured out why we can't shake our pursuers," Tark said.

"A lurker is aiding your enemies," Drake said. "Maldor rarely sends out a torivor. Escape is unlikely, but I will try to help you."

"What's a torivor?" Rachel asked.

"I would rather not say," Drake replied. "They can sense your thoughts. The less you know about them, the better."

Rachel bit her lip. "What do we do?" she asked.

"The quick answer?" Drake said. "What you've been doing. Perpetual motion. If you stop, you will be taken. The time may come for us to split up. For the present we need to ride."

"They're not far behind," Tark said.

Trying to ignore her weariness, Rachel followed Tark and Drake out into the rain. Lightning flashed. Thunder roared. Her horse weaved among half-glimpsed trees, heading down a slope. She had almost forgotten what life was like not on the run. She wondered if she would ever feel safe again.

When Jason awoke, he barely opened his eyes. He was back beside the pool in the cave, lying on his side near the edge of the water. His head throbbed.

"Welcome back," Ferrin said.

"I was trying to play possum," Jason complained.

"Your breathing changed. Sorry about thumping you on the head."

"You better be. It's pretty sore. Do you have any idea how many times I've been drugged or knocked unconscious lately? I bet I've lost a million brain cells."

"I had no alternative. You must return to the Beyond. I was

BEYONDERS: A WORLD WITHOUT HEROES

only waiting for you to awaken so you could hold your breath on the way down."

Sitting up, Jason saw that a sack was bound to his leg by an elaborate series of knots and lashings. He was dressed in a plain shirt and twill trousers. "Quite a knot."

"There is no chance you will unloose it before you sink to the Beyond."

"You took away all of my conscriptor stuff."

"Better that you enter the Beyond looking nondescript."

"This outfit will make me look like a hobo."

Ferrin shrugged. "Best I could do."

"If you're Rachel's friend, tell her the Word is a fraud."

"I wish I could. I'd be killing both her and myself. Take a deep breath. Farewell." Ferrin shoved the sack of stones into the water and gave Jason a push as he struggled to rise. Jason caught hold of the displacer's hand, and both of them plunged into the pool, sinking rapidly.

The water was shockingly cold. Ferrin was above him, being towed deeper underwater headfirst. The displacer thrashed, but Jason had a secure grip. Ferrin jerked and yanked but could not break Jason's two-handed grasp. Ferrin pulled Jason close and tried to push off with his legs, but Jason kept twisting so the displacer could get no leverage. Meanwhile the bag of rocks pulled the pair swiftly downward. Ferrin went limp. Jason squeezed his hand relentlessly. Looking up, Jason could see lamplight dancing on the surface of the water high above.

Ferrin gave a final jerk, and then all Jason had in his grasp was the hand. Above him, silhouetted against the lighted surface, he saw Ferrin stroking upward.

Jason maintained a tight grip on the hand. It tried to squirm free, to no avail.

Jason continued to sink. His lungs began to clench for want of oxygen. The water was frigid. How could water this cold not be frozen?

Before long he was in absolute darkness. The surface was no longer visible. Maybe, after all he had suffered, he was simply going to drown.

But suddenly something was different. Without changing direction it felt as though he was now rising rather than sinking. Was it an illusion spawned by disorientation? His speed was increasing. The water seemed to be getting warmer and thicker. The bag of rocks no longer pulled him. His lungs burned, but Jason resisted the urge to inhale.

Abruptly he slammed into a yielding surface with great force. He smelled soil and sensed sunlight, although his eyes were closed.

Opening his eyes, Jason found himself lying on his back in a cornfield, soaking wet and covered in dirt. He could not clearly discern whether he had fallen there or risen up through the ground, though it seemed like the latter. Great clods of soil had been dislodged by his arrival, and several tall stalks of corn had been uprooted and scattered.

He sat up, shaken but uninjured, except for his throbbing head.

All he could see in any direction was corn.

He stood, looking around. Endless rows of corn shifted in a gentle breeze beneath the midday sun. Where was he?

"This better be a cornfield on Earth," he muttered, trying to brush mud from his clothing, succeeding only in smearing it around.

He still had Ferrin's hand. He set it down and examined himself. His only clothes were the shirt and the pants. They were crude, and the mud made them look much worse. He had no shoes. He hoped he would not have to walk far.

The hand began to crawl across the ground. Jason picked it up and gave it a slap. The fingers opened and closed rapidly as if to express outrage.

"You're my only souvenir," Jason told the hand. "I hope you realize I have to get back there somehow."

Jason shoved the hand into one of the two deep pockets in the front of his trousers. Whenever it moved, Jason slapped it firmly.

It took Jason ten minutes to unbind himself from the sack of stones. He checked inside the bag, to be sure he wasn't leaving anything interesting behind. It only contained rocks. He took out the rocks and placed the hand in the bag.

Jason struck off in a straight line. He figured if he went straight long enough, he would find civilization. Somebody had planted and was tending this corn. Eventually he would reach a road.

Before long he came to a farmyard. It had a nicely painted house and a barn. A couple of trucks and four-wheelers were parked in the big driveway. A tire swing hung from a branch. Some toy cars had been left near the swing. Ferrin had been right. This was Earth.

For so long all he had wanted was to get home. But now all he could think about was getting back to Lyrian. He couldn't leave Rachel stranded there! He couldn't deprive his friends of the knowledge he now possessed!

He went to the front door of the house, opened the screen, and knocked. A middle-aged woman in a sleeveless shirt answered the door. "Can I help you?"

He suddenly felt unsure what to say. All he knew for certain was that he couldn't tell the truth. "Hi. My name is Jason Walker. May I please use your telephone?"

ACKNOWLEDGMENTS

I am thrilled to have the first book in the Beyonders series written and into the hands of readers. This series has been in development for more than ten years, and I'm looking forward to sharing the two upcoming installments. This first book has been through many drafts over several years. When I first attempted to write it, I did not yet have the ability to tell the story effectively. I believe that it has finally become what I was initially aiming for. Hope I'm right. Anyhow, many people have encouraged me and helped me along the way.

First off, my wife, Mary, helped me create time to write the first draft of this story back before I was getting paid to write, so the biggest thanks goes to her. Without her support, this series specifically, and my writing career in general, may never have happened.

Huge thanks also go to my editor at Simon & Schuster, Liesa Abrams. She helped me find some key characters and moments to add, and provided smart feedback on issues large and small. She deserves credit for helping me get this book finished and polished. Smart lady.

Simon Lipskar, my awesome agent, got this project organized, and has provided important feedback on the story as well. The whole team at Simon & Schuster deserves lots of credit, including Mara Anastas, Fiona Simpson, Bess Braswell, Bethany Buck, Anna McKean, Paul Crichton, Lucille Rettino, and Lauren Forte. Sammy Yuen Jr. and Lisa Vega deserve big high-fives for designing a cool cover.

Many other readers contributed to the story. Some read early versions years ago—others read more recent updates. These readers include Mary Mull, Bryson Mull, Cherie Mull, Summer Mull, Pamela Mull, Gary Mull, Jason and Natalie Conforto, Dean Hale, Randy Davis, Jake and Dion Gulbransen, Chris Schoebinger, Tony Benjamin, Lisa Mangum, Liz Saban, Nancy Fleming, Sean Fleming, Mike Walton, Ryan Hamilton, and any others I may have missed. Tucker Davis provided a meticulous read and extensive notes. Very extensive. I practically have post-traumatic stress syndrome.

Thanks also to my amazing family, especially my kids: Sadie, Chase, Rose, and the new one who isn't named yet, maybe Calvin Emmett, we'll see. Also Tiff, Ty, Cy, Marge, the cousins, the nephews, the nieces, the aunts, the uncles, and the in-laws. Especially the mother-in-law, who recently provided a very memorable moment while hiking in the canyon near my home, when she laid down on a high trail and puked off a cliff. True story.

And thank you, reader, for trying this book. I hope you liked it. If you did, don't miss the next two! Also if you liked it, please spread the word. People telling other people means everything for books. Visit me online at BrandonMull.com or on Twitter.

SO . . . WHAT NEXT?

Welcome to the end of the first book in the Beyonders series. I'll be writing two more books in order to finish the story I started with this one. The second book, *Seeds of Rebellion*, will be out in spring 2012, then the third will follow in spring 2013. I have the rest of the story all figured out—the next two books will build on this first one in cool and exciting ways.

In the meanwhile, I do have some other books already published. If you haven't tried my Fablehaven series, those books are fun as well. It's about a brother and sister who discover that their grandparents are the caretakers of a secret wildlife park for magical creatures. The whole series is already finished, so there are five books waiting to be read. I've written one other novel so far, called *The Candy Shop War*, and a picture book called *Pingo*.

Thank you, reader, for trying *A World Without Heroes*. To stay updated, feel free to visit BrandonMull.com and to follow me on Twitter.

READING GUIDE QUESTIONS

1. How does Jason cross from our world to Lyrian? How does Rachel cross over? How have characters in other stories crossed from our reality to a fantasy world? Invent a way you have never heard of for a character to cross into a fantasy world.

2. Rachel is homeschooled and shares a close bond with her parents. How do you think that affects her personality? Share examples.

3. Jason is confused about his future and isn't very close with his parents. How do you think that affects his personality? Share examples.

4. Do you think Jason and Rachel would have become friends had they met in our world? Why or why not?

5. According to Galloran, Maldor would rather not kill his greatest rivals. Instead he tests them. He wants to control them or break them. How might turning the heroes of Lyrian into sellouts or broken failures cause more harm in the long run than just killing them?

6. Many people in Lyrian have stopped believing in heroes. Do we have heroes in our world? Who are some of your heroes?

7. Heroes in America can range from performers and athletes to political leaders and teachers, from soldiers and rescue workers to family members. Have any of your heroes ever disappointed you? How can a hero try to repair the damage caused by their mistakes?

8. Who do you think has the potential to be the greatest hero, Jason or Rachel? Why?

9. Many of the heroes of Lyrian are no longer resisting Maldor. Why is the Blind King no longer fighting very much? Why did Nicholas Dangler stop? Why did the seedman Drake stop? What are the differences between their reasons for stopping?

10. Of all the heroes we met in this book, who do you think will have the hardest time rejoining the fight against Maldor? Why?

11. What character from Lyrian would you most want on your side if you were part of this story? Explain.

12. What character from the story would be the most fun to hang out with? Explain.

13. If you could visit one place in Lyrian, which would you choose? Why?

14. Galloran says that being a hero means doing what is right, no matter the consequences. Is that an easy way to live? Why or why not? How can people find the strength to live that way?

15. Jason spent much of the story trying to get home. By the end he was forced to return home against his will. Why didn't he want to go? How would you feel in his position?

Dear Readers,

Many of the characters who only play small parts in this first book end up joining the fight and filling larger roles throughout the rest of the trilogy. One such character is Drake, the seedman at Harthenham. Since his character will play an important role in the upcoming story, I thought it might be fun to let you guys see his point of view the night before Jason dueled Duke Conrad at Harthenham. You already know what choice Drake must have made that night, but this extra scene lets us see him struggling with the decision.

DRAKE'S DECISION

The fire had burned low within the wide marble fireplace, but still Drake could not relax and slip into a restful trance. In fact he could not even sit down. He paced back and forth like a newly caged predator, not seeing the thick bearskin underfoot, nor the rich furnishings positioned about the room, nor the ornate hangings texturing the walls. Despite the late hour, rest was not presently a consideration. He could not even convince himself to remove his boots.

He had a weakness for good people who did the right thing against terrible odds. It invariably got to him. He wanted to laugh at the fools, to warn them that it was pointless, like trying to smash a boulder with your bare fist. You simply hurt yourself and accomplished nothing. He yearned to scoff at those still resisting Maldor, but whenever he witnessed a truly noble attempt, the laughs still turned to sobs.

Earlier tonight Jason had openly defied Duke Conrad and Maldor together by announcing that he was going to leave Harthenham. Lots of people talked about leaving. It was a frequent topic of idle conversation. Nearly everyone had mused about it at one time or another. Nobody ever took action. Yet Jason had, with boldness and considerable flair.

The boy was too young. Too idealistic. Humans didn't stand a chance. They only had a single lifetime to figure out how to live. Drake felt his dozens had not been enough. The courage he had witnessed in Jason had resulted more from lack of experience than anything. An inability to anticipate consequences. An inability to judge with a seasoned eye. A reckless regard for his own existence.

That had to be the truth of it. Because if it was the truth, it would justify where Drake now stood, the decisions he had made. But it didn't feel true. Not at all.

What had felt true was the thrill that went through him as Jason stood up to Conrad in front of the others. The boy had left Conrad no recourse. The public insult meant the duel had to happen. But the boy had not been witless. Had he allowed the contest to be decided with swords, his fate would be sealed. But billiard balls? Such a bizarre choice of arms left at least some doubt regarding the outcome. Perhaps the boy had practiced with billiard balls. Perhaps he might even have an advantage.

Drake rubbed the back of his neck. Who was the fool? Jason, for his ludicrous defiance? Or himself, for letting the boy's actions infect his mind? Tomorrow the boy would live or die. Either outcome would change nothing. If the boy survived, he would be immediately apprehended outside the castle walls. Maldor would continue to rule. If the boy perished, he would certainly not be the first.

Life would continue unruffled at Harthenham either way. If Conrad lived, all would remain the same. If Conrad died, there were plenty of others to take his place. The duel meant nothing.

So why couldn't he settle down?

Drake rubbed his temples. He had always tried to be true to himself. Honest with himself. He hadn't cared that it was unacceptable for a seedman to go to Harthenham. What did he care about the opinions of his brethren? It was unacceptable to him that as a people the Amar Kabal had opted not to challenge Maldor. Sometimes unacceptable things happened.

The luxury of Harthenham was seductive. Ultimately unfulfilling, but so easy. He had expected to wrap himself in opulence like a burial shroud. Collectively, the Amar Kabal valued simplicity. He had gone the other way. Over the past years he had probably enjoyed more physical comfort than any of them had ever known. And his seed had withered, as he had known it might. So his long existence would finally end. On his terms.

He stood in the middle of the room—in his opinion the finest room in all of Harthenham—his eyes drinking in the extravagance around him. Who else lived like this? Not kings. They had concerns. The wealthiest merchants? Even more hassles and uncertainty than kings. Only those at Harthenham ate like this, dressed like this, relaxed like this, with nothing required, nothing expected.

Nothing except closing their eyes to the evil that was overrunning Lyrian.

What if he went to Lord Jason right now? Encouraged him. Advised him. The boy must feel alone and overwhelmed. No, by now the boy would be sleeping, and he needed his rest. Drake crossed his arms. He could wait until after the duel. And say what? If Jason lived, he and Tark were still doomed. Drake glowered into the fireplace. If he lent his aid, might he help them survive their departure? Probably not. They lacked mounts. It would be three against many, with nowhere to run.

He needed some fresh air. Needed to talk to somebody.

Drake stalked out of his room.

Harthenham never truly slept. It dozed. Without responsi-bility, some people became nocturnal. Some lacked any regular sleep pattern whatsoever. Most of the humans here generally stuck to the tradition of sleeping at night, but not out of neces-sity. There were no crops to plant, no battles to fight, no chores to accomplish. They could sleep their lives away if they desired.

Bokar might be up. And if not, the blob could awaken. The sluggard could catch up on his sleep whenever he wanted.

Drake went directly to his room. A placard beside the door gleamed in the lamplight: BOKAR THE INVINCIBLE. Beyond the door lay a man who had nearly grown to match the size of his reputation.

Drake pounded and then opened the door without waiting. The room was dark.

"Who goes there?" called a voice—not alarmed, just curi-ous. The voice did not sound groggy.

"It's Drake. Did I wake you?"

"No." He raised his voice. "Denton! Light a lamp."

"I can get one—" Drake began.

"Nonsense. What are servants for? Denton!"

"Coming, Your Greatness," answered a timid voice. A door opened, letting light into the room. Bokar had a fine room. Not quite so fine as Drake's; the emperor had never been so delighted as when he'd finally corrupted a seedman. But Bokar had been a prize as well—an extraordinary swordsman, a fear-less leader, large and strong and able.

A little man emerged from the door, blinking sleep from his eyes. He set the lamp he bore on a bedside table. "Anything else, Your Greatness?"

"Quicker with the light next time," Bokar griped.

"I keep a lighted lamp beside my—"

"I don't need the particulars," Bokar snapped. "Just be quicker. Whatever it takes. Stop dreaming, if necessary."

"I'll do my best," the little man apologized.

"Off with you," Bokar said, waving a fleshy hand.

"Yes, Your Greatness."

Not much of Bokar was visible. Just his bloated face and the top of the flabby rolls that descended from his chin. Embroidered quilts covered the doughy mountain of his body. The bed was vast. Only an immense bed could accommodate him. He lay propped up on an array of pillows and cushions, wheezing air in and out of his burdened lungs.

"You're too good to your servants," Drake commented dryly.

Bokar watched the door close, then turned an eye to Drake. "All that man has to do is light my lamps and give me food. And he has others who share the duty. You know many men with an easier life?"

"Around here?"

"No, no, out there, in the real world. Denton has accomplished nothing, and yet he dwells under the same roof as me. The man should bless every insult I throw his way, and cherish every instruction. Small price to pay. Very small."

Drake smirked. "He never made an impression on the world to rival Bokar the Invincible. Why not have him address you as 'Your Invincibleness'?"

Bokar scowled. "Why do people act like I should be ashamed of my title? I earned that title. Paid for it in blood. Not much of it *my* blood, but the price was paid. There are plenty of piles of bones around Lyrian that once belonged to warriors who tested my title. There they lie, and here I persist."

"I'm not sure you could stand any more easily than they could."

Bokar chuckled, blubber jiggling. "I'm still invincible. Not all the food in Harthenham could do me in."

"It has certainly enjoyed a fair opportunity."

Bokar laughed and coughed. "Why did you come here? To trade insults? Why is the seedless seedman prowling Harthenham at this hour? Are there no more lumba berries to be had?"

"Maybe I needed to remind myself why I like it here so much."

Bokar smiled broadly. "Is this about the young upstart? The lordling? I heard all about it. The castle is abuzz. A duel, they say. With billiard balls, no less. I've tried all evening but failed to devise a more ridiculous way to die."

"It was a cunning move," Drake replied. "He chose a weapon with which Conrad has no expertise."

"Because it isn't a weapon! But yes, ludicrous or not, it was wiser than naming swords. You are impressed by the boy?"

Drake shrugged. "Impressed might be taking it too far. I was moved by his courage. It tainted my mood."

Bokar guffawed. "Again! Don't tell me you're having another crisis of conscience! Drake, how many times do you have to die here before you accept the choice you made?"

"Just once more, actually."

Bokar rolled his eyes. "Walk away from here and they'll cut your throat before you take ten steps. Maybe they'll bury you beside the little lord. For good or ill, you made the bargain. Enjoy the spoils!"

"You make a compelling point," Drake mused. "This is my final life. Would I rather be buried beside you or Lord Jason?"

Bokar's expression changed a bit. "Are you serious? Or are you just baiting me? I guarantee that your corpse will be much older if it rests beside me."

"But will it rest as comfortably?"

"So long as they don't bury me on top of you."

Drake tried his best to smile.

"Don't show me the feeble grin of a shy youth!" Bokar admonished. "Laugh like a man! Maybe when I go I'll have them burn me. It will light up the countryside."

"It will be the greatest test fire has faced."

"Or they could dump me in the sea. That would be a sight! Imagine the splash!"

"The sharks will feast for weeks."

Bokar glared at Drake. "You're saying the right words, but your heart isn't in it. What's the matter? Don't tell me this deluded lordling actually got to you?"

"Nobody gets to me," Drake said. "But his example started me thinking." He gestured at his surroundings. "I might be changing my mind about all of this."

"I'd think you were jesting if I hadn't heard it all before! Don't be daft! You're too late, Drake. Go have some lumba tarts and slip into a trance. You'll be good as new by morning."

Drake frowned. "I'm not sure I will be. I've changed my mind in the past. About other things, I mean. I've uprooted myself and shifted from one form of living to another."

"You made this choice a long time ago. Well before I came here. You knew it was permanent."

"I had my reasons," Drake said. "Mostly it was my way of surrendering. Partly I wanted to experience the opulent lifestyle. Partly I wanted to bring shame upon my people. They deserve it."

"So what has suddenly changed?"

Drake shrugged. "I tired long ago of this lifestyle. My people were right about decadence. It is comfortable but empty. This is my last life, Bokar. I might not want to die here. This boy, Jason, gives me a reason. An excuse. Another new resident, a man called Tark, means to leave with Jason if he wins the duel. If Conrad falls, perhaps I should join them."

"The three of you will die together."

"Probably. I've dodged death before."

"Tell yourself whatever you like. Why come to me? Sounds as though your mind is made up."

"It helps to talk about it. It helps to hear your thoughts." Drake paused, gazing into the eyes of a once-great man. "Honestly, Bokar, if you could be back in your physical prime, would you consider leaving here?"

"We should not speak of such things in soberness."

"Humor me. I want to know your mind on the matter."

Bokar sighed. "I joke all the time about leaving here. Many of us do. I know it won't happen. What would I do without servants to rub ointments onto my bedsores? I enjoy the ridiculous bravado of the idea. I enjoy pretending I'm not finished. It stings to consider the notion seriously. If I could be back in prime condition, I might toy with the idea. And I might get away with it, no matter how many tried to stop me. In my prime I was someone to be reckoned with. But that is all academic. I'll never be in my prime again. My heart should have failed long ago."

"Strong heart," Drake murmured. "If you worked at it, changed your habits, you might manage to walk again."

Bokar snorted. "Who needs to walk when you have Denton? Don't make any plans to bury me yet. Obese or not, I'll still outlive you."

"Yesterday I might have disagreed. Today I would say that is highly possible."

"You really might walk away from all of this tomorrow?"

"If Jason wins, I really might."

Bokar nodded and scowled. "You seem to mean it. If you want my word on the matter, you should probably do it."

"You're joking," Drake said. "Why?"

His face became more serious than Drake had ever seen it. "Because the thought of you leaving makes me intensely jealous. That's the truth."

Drake narrowed his eyes. "Is this a ploy? Giving me approval so I'll reject the idea?"

Bokar snorted a chuckle. "The choice is yours, not mine."

"I'll keep thinking on it."

"I tried to leave heavy matters behind long ago. Can I get some sleep now?"

"Sure." Drake rubbed the back of his neck. "The boy might lose the duel."

"The boy will probably lose the duel, no matter how absurd the weaponry. This palace is full of heroes, and not many of them could take Conrad."

"Perhaps I'll see you tomorrow."

"You know where to find me."

"Want me to extinguish the lamp?"

Bokar shooed him away. "You trying to disappoint Denton? The man lives to assist me with these trifles."

Drake walked to the door. "Give Denton my regards."

"I'll give him no such thing. The man already has too high an opinion of himself. Drake, if they go, you had best join them. Otherwise I expect I'll get no sleep for months."

"You that anxious to be rid of me?"

"We all die. In here, out there, sooner, later—it all makes little difference."

"It might to me," Drake muttered, and exited.

KEEP READING FOR AN EARLY LOOK AT HOW
JASON'S AND RACHEL'S ADVENTURE CONTINUES IN

SEEDS OF REBELLION

A cold wind swept across the narrow ridge. On either side of him, a sheer drop fell away into darkness. Unsure of how he had gotten there, Jason sensed that something was deeply wrong. He had to hurry. Crouching low enough to almost touch the rocky ground with his fingertips, he moved forward, choosing his steps with care, trying to remain in the center of the jagged spine, despite the buffeting gusts.

From one side came a monstrous roar, like an approaching landslide. A mighty blast of wind lifted Jason off his feet and hurled him to the edge of the ridge. He landed roughly, with his legs dangling over the void, desperately hugging the rugged ground as a flood of wind rushed over him.

As the gust relented, Jason pulled himself forward, swung his legs up, and got to his feet. His torso and the underside of his arms ached and burned with bruises and scrapes. Returning to the center of the knifelike ridge, he staggered forward, currents of air rising and falling, swirling and whistling.

The fierce wind lashed at him with increasing violence. To keep his balance, he leaned into the gale which suddenly switched directions, and his own effort helped the new gust shove him toward the dizzying brink. He fell to the unforgiving ground time after time, trying to grip with his entire body to avoid being flung to his doom.

He wanted to lie still and wait until the raging windstorm abated, but he had to press on. What was he doing here again? Was something after him? Was the storm going to worsen? He did not understand the logic of his need, but an innate sense urged him to hurry.

He got to his feet and shuffled onward, unpredictable currents thrusting him in different directions. Ahead, through the dimness, he saw where the ridge ended. At the extremity of the rocky spine awaited a table with one empty chair and an occupied seat.

Shouldering his way against a persistent gust, Jason stumbled to the empty chair and sat down. The other person at the table was Rachel! The wind did not seem to touch her, although it continued to half blind and half deafen Jason.

"Why have you returned?" Rachel asked. He could hear her soft words despite the howling gale. "You should have stayed home. You don't belong here."

"I couldn't just leave you behind!" Jason yelled. "What are you doing here?"

"You should not have come," she whispered, her expression neutral. "You have condemned the both of us."

Jason could hear the sound of the wind rising, louder than ever. He knew it was about to hit them like an avalanche. He stood and shoved the table aside. "We have to go!" He took her hand, shocked by how icy cold her skin felt.

Rachel rose. She stood significantly taller than him. Her hand gripped his firmly, so cold that it burned. Her eyes were black—no whites, no irises. "Stay away from me." She released his hand, and at the same moment, the wind hit, like a tsunami.

Jason tumbled helplessly off the ridge and into the stormy void, arms pinwheeling, legs thrashing. Powerful updrafts slowed his fall, then heaved him sideways and upward. A succession of unpredictable gusts thrust him in various directions, as if he weighed nothing. Had he dropped into a tornado? With wind screaming around him, Jason fell and flew, flipping and twisting, his orientation so disrupted that he lost all instinct for up and down.

Each time he opened his mouth to cry out, wind rushed into his lungs, drowning his protests. Questions surfaced through his panic. How high was the ridge? When would he hit the ground? How hard would he hit it?

The wild fall continued until Jason finally managed a shout. At that instant, his eyelids flew open, and he found himself on his back, beside a path, beneath a sunlit sky. A dark, featureless figure towered over him.

The events of the previous evening returned all at once. Using his heels and elbows, Jason scooted away from the shadowy form without taking his eyes off it. The figure did not move.

After putting a few yards between himself and the dark entity, Jason paused. Fear lingered from the nightmare. His heart raced. Everything had felt much too real. Jason checked his arms, expecting to see scrapes and bruises from the stony ridge. There were none.

He detested that the shadowy figure had been standing over him as he slept. He wondered if the creature had gotten even closer. He wondered if it might have touched him. The thought made him shudder.

The events of the dream left a foul aftertaste. Jason found his hands trembling. There had been other nightmares before the stormy ridge. He could almost remember them. What had they been about? The details dissolved under scrutiny.

Taking a steadying breath, Jason arose. The featureless figure held still, its surface perfect blackness, even under the sunlight, like a void in the shape of a man. Jason had hoped dawn would have driven the apparition away, like a vampire or something. But the inky creature appeared indifferent to the brightness.

Wiping sleep from his eyes, Jason hesitantly approached the creature. "What do you want?"

The tenebrous being offered no indication of understanding.

"Why are you following me?"

Nothing.

"¿Hablas español?"

Nothing.

Jason circled the creature, scrutinizing its smooth shape. They stood about the same height, roughly six feet. The face had no contours to suggest ears or eyes or a mouth. The hands had fingers, but no fingernails or other details. The feet lacked individual toes. The being was like a man reduced to his simplest geometric form.

No matter how Jason positioned himself, the flawless surface of the figure reflected nothing. It was a black that should have been impossible under the light of day. What material could absorb light so completely? Did it have any more substance than a shadow? Maybe that was how it moved so silently.

"I'm not going to harm you," Jason soothed.

He extended a hesitant finger toward the being's shoulder. Would it feel spongy? Hard? Would his finger pass through the surface? The instant before his fingertip would have made contact, the figure moved in a blur, seizing Jason by the wrist and shoulder and flinging him through the air. Jason sailed off the path, turning a three-quarter somersault and landing on a bush.

Stunned, Jason lay quiet for a moment. Would the creature pounce? Follow up the attack? He rolled over, rose to his knees, and saw the figure standing on the road, fifteen yards away, as if nothing had happened. His wrist ached from where it had gripped him. The dark hand had been ice cold.

Jason waded through undergrowth back to the path. "I get it," he said, brushing leaves from his shirt. "Hands off, right? You don't need to tell me twice."

As usual he received no acknowledgment. Jason felt angry. He wanted to strike the calm figure, if for no other reason than to earn a reaction, but he had a suspicion that if he attacked, the shadowy entity would knot him into a pretzel.

"Did you give me those bad dreams?" Jason asked, rubbing his wrist. "Was that you impersonating my friend? You both have really cold hands."

As usual, the being gave no reply.

"Are you a lurker? A torivor? A creepy puppet? Can you speak? Can you understand me?"

No response.

"Nod if you can understand me. You just chucked me into the bushes. You must have a brain. Wiggle a finger if you understand. Tap your foot."

Nothing.

Jason sighed, exasperated. "Well, looks like I can't talk to you and I can't beat you up, and the sun doesn't bother you. I guess you're going to tail me for as long as you want. Don't expect me to smile about it."

Jason took out a protein bar and finished the water in his canteen. He then set off to the north, determined to distance himself from the giants. The dark figure followed less than ten paces behind.

The groomed path dwindled to an indistinct trail, but continued northward. Jason filled his canteen when he crossed a brook, and ate trail mix. He wondered if his parents were freaking out back home. This time witnesses had seen him get swallowed by a hippo. Everyone would think he was dead. He hoped they wouldn't blame the animal.

Where was Rachel right now? Safe? On the run? Captured?

He wished he could know that he wasn't too late to help her. What about Tark? If the shadow creature was chasing Jason, hopefully that meant Tark had escaped with his vital message. As he munched on raisins and nuts, Jason wished he had packed a wider variety of food. Maybe next time.

Not long after the path began to run parallel to a little brook, Jason finally spotted a bubblefruit tree. He hungrily devoured some fruit, grateful for something fresh and juicy. Ferrin had once claimed that a watchful wanderer could survive in the wilderness on bubblefruit alone.

Standing near the trunk of the tree, Jason wondered if the shadow creature ever ate. How could it survive otherwise? He watched it. How could something capable of movement remain so perfectly stationary? It didn't seem to breathe. Maybe it absorbed air through its icy skin. Maybe it absorbed food. Maybe it was magical and didn't need air or food. Jason decided to try to get some answers.

Holding up a bubblefruit, he approached the dark figure. "Do you eat? I haven't seen you eat. These are pretty good. Want to try one?"

The figure did not stir.

Jason pantomimed taking a bite of the fruit. "I know I'm supposed to be terrified of you, but I started to wonder whether you might be hungry. Here's some food. I'd hate to have you pass out and then stop following me."

Jason held out the transparent fruit. When the dark being made no move to accept it, he tossed it underhand. The graceful creature stepped sideways, caught the clear fruit in one hand, and quick as a blink flung it back at Jason. There was no time to react. The bubblefruit splatted squarely against Jason's forehead, spraying his face with juice and sending him reeling onto his side. He remained on the ground for a moment, stunned, his head smarting from the impact and his eyes stinging from the juice.

Clenching his fists, Jason calmed himself. If he attempted to retaliate, he knew the creature would dismantle him. In fact, that could be precisely what the creature desired.

"I don't get you," Jason growled, getting up and using his shirt to wipe juice from his face. "If you want to beat the snot out of me, why don't you just do it? I can tell you could."

As expected, the being offered no response.

"Seems like you only react if I invade your space. Don't worry, I won't try to give you anything ever again. I'll leave you alone. I wish you'd return the favor."

The trail flanked the brook for the rest of the day. By the evening the brook joined a larger stream. Near the intersection, Jason found another bubblefruit tree. He offered nothing to his eerie escort.

By sundown, Jason could smell the sea. He felt exhausted after the long day, and curled up near the creek. After getting comfortable, he raised his head to look at the dark figure.

"You keep away from me while I sleep. Don't even think about hijacking my dreams. I'm going to be ready this time, just in case. Fair warning."

Jason rested his head on his jacket and tried to prepare his mind to dream about happy things. He pictured Rachel excited to see him instead of possessed and warning him that he should have stayed away from Lyrian. He told himself that coming here was the right decision, that he would make a difference, that he wouldn't die alone in the woods. And he promised himself that if he had another bad dream, he would recognize it and take over.

Jason stood on Zuma Beach in Southern California. He had been here once before, a few years ago while visiting his brother for a long weekend. But today the beach was deserted, including the light blue lifeguard stations spaced evenly along the sandy expanse. Low gray clouds muted the sun and made the sea look grayer than he remembered it.

A helicopter came up the coast, flying directly toward him. It hovered loudly above, and a male voice called to him through a loudspeaker. "Sir, you do not belong here. The evacuation has been in force for hours. Your life is in danger."

A rope ladder unfurled from an open door, and the helicopter came closer to the ground. Jason ran forward, the sand hampering his strides. The ladder dangled almost within reach. He squinted as the wind from the rotors blew particles into his eyes. Suddenly the helicopter rose, along with the flimsy ladder. Charging hard, Jason jumped, but barely missed the last rung.

"We're sorry," the voice informed him. "We're too late. We have to climb now or none of us will make it out."

Jason gazed out to sea and saw the horizon curl upward, steadily rising as a mountain of water like he had never imagined approached the shore. Awed by the sight, everything inside of Jason seemed to drop, and despair filled the emptiness.

Turning, Jason recognized that there was no escape. At best he might make it to the parking lot. Looking back at the sea, the leaden water continued to ascend. This wave would break over not just the beach, but the coastal mountains as well. He doubted whether the swiftly rising helicopter could escape it.

Still, he ran away from the oncoming tsunami, panting as he plodded across the sand. Could he possibly ride it out? Hold his breath and hope he might somehow make it to the surface before drowning? No, not through miles of water. This would be like having the whole ocean fall on him.

When Jason reached the parking lot, he turned to look back.

The great wave was almost to the shore, curling up so high that the top disappeared into the overcast sky. The water before it had receded dramatically, turning the coastline into a sloping desert of moist sand.

"Not the best way to go," said a gravelly voice at his side.

Glancing over, Jason found Tark beside him, wearing a Hawaiian shirt and sandals. Otherwise he looked exactly as Jason would have expected.

"How'd you get here?" Jason asked, panic giving way to curiosity.

Tark shrugged, staring up at the looming wall of water. "Serves us right, you know. This is what happens when you bite off more than you can chew."

"We can run," Jason said. "We can try."

Tark grasped his arm, his hand so cold, it burned. "Better to accept the inevitable."

Jason tugged and pulled, but couldn't break his grip. For the first time Jason recognized that Tark's eyes were entirely black.

"Wait a minute," Jason said, the realization hitting him hard. "This is a dream. You're not really Tark. I'm not really here."

Tark grinned darkly. "Tell that to the wave."

Looking up, Jason saw the wave curling over him—over the entire coast—the wave to end all waves, falling forward, stretching so far beyond Jason and the little parking lot that he could hardly imagine a place beyond its reach.

The sound was like being at ground zero during an atomic blast, so loud that Jason knew he would never hear again. Then he was tumbling helplessly through turbulent water that surged with unfathomable power. He immediately lost all sense of direction and found it impossible to keep the salt water from painfully invading his nose and mouth.

Jason woke up screaming, eyes squeezed shut, drenched in sweat, his body curled into a defensive ball. He opened his eyes and found himself staring at a faceless black head, inches beyond his nose, and screamed again, recoiling as best he could. The dark figure that had crouched beside him stood upright, took a step back, and held still.

Jason rolled away from it, deeply shaken, grateful that predawn light had begun to illuminate the forest. "I knew it was a dream," he panted, trying to let go of the terror that had owned him. He was on dry ground. He could breathe. "It was horrible and realistic, but I called it. I knew it was you. I couldn't stop it, but I knew what was up."

The shadowy figure remained still. Jason found it infuriating to think that this voiceless, motionless creature was getting inside his head and manipulating his dreams. He despised the thought of it following him sedately all day, only to attack him mentally, when he was at his most vulnerable.

Seething, Jason lurched to his feet. The creature did not twitch, but Jason reminded himself how quickly it could move when attacked. If he tried anything physical, he would only get hurt.

Jason stalked over to the figure and stood close, glaring at its blank face. "You're a coward!" he yelled. "Stay out of my dreams! If you're going to kill me, let's get it over with. I'm serious. What's your point? Why are you here? To make nightmares? Or is that just extra credit?"

The figure withstood the tirade without flinching.

"Are you trying to make me doubt my friends? To make me sorry I came back to Lyrian? Are you trying to provoke me into attacking you? Are you a spy? All of the above?"

The figure gave no acknowledgment of Jason's presence.

Disgusted, Jason turned away. Why was he wasting his breath? It was like complaining to a mannequin.

Torn by worry and frustration, Jason kicked a small rock into the bushes. "I'm not sure what you're trying to do," he murmured bitterly, "but I think it's working."

*   *   *

They tethered the horses, and Rachel followed Drake deeper into the grove. He kept a hand on his sword. The trees were not very tall, but they had thick trunks with deeply grooved bark. Heavy, twisting limbs tangled overhead. She imagined that after nightfall the place would look haunted.

The undergrowth remained sparse enough to proceed without a trail. At length, Drake waved Rachel to a halt. He pointed up ahead, and she saw a long string of colorful beads looped around the knob of a fat tree. Three feathered hoops hung at the bottom of the strand.

"What is it?" Rachel whispered.

"Charm woman!" Drake called, raising his voice enough to make Rachel flinch. "We have met before! Please console us in our hour of need!"

They waited. Drake held a finger to his lips to discourage Rachel from speaking.

"You may pass" came a reply, well after Rachel had stopped expecting one. The sonorous female voice sounded younger than Rachel had anticipated.

Drake led Rachel past the strand of painted beads. As they advanced, she noticed various trinkets—some fashioned out of metal, some of bone or ivory, others of stone—dangling from other trees and shrubs.

They reached a small clearing. In the center awaited a large tent composed of stitched animal hides in mottled shades of gray and brown. The head of a wolf, still attached to the pelt, lolled over the entrance. Small carvings and graven figures surrounded the tent in a loose circle.

A woman appeared, taller than Rachel, but hunched, with ratty silver hair and a face that looked too young and smooth to match her spotted, wrinkled hands. She wore crude brown garments belted at the waist, and a colorful shawl. In one gnarled hand she held a staff topped by dangling trinkets that clinked when in motion.

"Drake," she greeted, her voice melodious. "I believed we would meet again."

"I would not have bet on it," he answered. "Until recently I expected to rot and die in Harthenham."

"You have brought a visitor," the charm woman said. "What is your name, sweetling?"

"Rachel."

Her attention returned to Drake. "What is your need?"

"We're being chased by a lurker."

The woman squinted. "Yes, I have sensed one nearby. It has been years since Maldor deployed a torivor."

"Can you help us?" Drake asked.

"You have brought a terrible threat my way. But that harm is already done. We shall see if I can help you. Remove your footwear."

Drake took off his supple boots and Rachel squatted to untie hers. The woman slipped strings of dark beads accented with teeth over each of their heads, mumbling quiet phrases.

The charm woman stepped back and invited them into the tent. Barefoot, Rachel ducked through the doorway. Three large bearskins lay on the ground. Elaborate mobiles hung from the ceiling, displaying a variety of gently spinning ornaments and crystals. Simple dolls made of wood and yarn sat opposite the entry in a staggered row. Incense burned inside hollow statues, aromatic smoke filtering through tiny holes, the heady scent mingling with the earthy smells of ashes and old leather.

The charm woman crouched on a low stool and gestured for Drake and Rachel to sit on the bearskins. The thick fur felt soft.

"How long has this torivor been after you?" the woman asked, her eyes on Drake.

"Five weeks," Drake said.

"Has it guided soldiers to you?"

"Yes, until I led Rachel far into the wilderness."

"The torivor has remained with you?"

"I continue to see it. Not clearly or often, but consistently."

The woman rubbed a coin with a hole in the center that hung from a cord around her neck. "When was the last time you saw it?"

"Last night," Drake replied.

"Has it visited your dreams?"

"No."

The charm woman turned to Rachel. "How about your dreams?"

"How would I know?"

"You would know." Her attention shifted back to Drake. "Is it more interested in you or the girl?"

"Almost certainly the girl."

"Why?"

Drake glanced uncomfortably at Rachel. "I'm not sure we should confess why, charm woman. It could place you in greater danger."

The woman laughed, quick and loud. "I could not be in greater danger. The emperor has hunted me for years. You have brought a torivor to my threshold. Speak candidly. The more I know, the better I can help."

"The girl is a Beyonder," Drake said. "She knows all of the syllables of a word that can unmake Maldor."

The woman regarded Rachel with new interest. "I know of this word. You have all of it?"

"Yes," Rachel said. "So did my friend Jason, another Beyonder. He has been captured by Maldor, but it doesn't seem like he's had a chance to use the Word."

"He could be dead," the charm woman said.

Tears clouded Rachel's vision. "He could be."

"Though I expect that he lives," Drake inserted. "He rang the gong and was admitted to Felrook. Maldor has never been quick to dispose of a significant enemy once captured."

"You were close to this other Beyonder?" the charm woman asked Rachel tenderly.

"We became close," she said, trying to bridle her emotions. She had cried enough over Jason. There was no need to make a scene in front of a stranger. "I didn't know him in the Beyond. I met him here."

"By what power did you cross over from the Beyond?" the woman asked. "Most of the ways have long been closed."

Rachel explained how she had followed a butterfly through a natural stone arch and how she had entered Lyrian near the cabin of a spellweaver named Erinda, on the same day the solitary woman had died. Rachel also mentioned how the Blind King suspected that Erinda had summoned her.

"Intriguing," the woman said. "Erinda was a former apprentice of mine. I have long wondered what became of her. She always displayed a profound interest in the Beyond. You have acquired an Edomic key word. Have you any experience speaking Edomic?"

Rachel blinked. "A little."

"The girl can call fire," Drake specified.

"Indeed?" The woman licked her lips, her gaze becoming more intent. "Who taught you this secret?"

Rachel glanced at Drake.

"I did," he said.

"What business does a member of the Amar Kabal have speaking Edomic?" the woman challenged.

"I'm an exile," Drake replied. "I've dabbled in many pursuits uncommon among my people."

"You know the prophecy," the woman pressed. "When the People of the Seed grow familiar with Edomic, their downfall will have commenced."

Drake flashed his crooked grin. "I'm no longer among my people. I prefer to conclude that I don't count. Besides, anyone can see that our downfall has begun. We might as well go down fighting."

"Perhaps," the charm woman mused, stroking her chin, the liver-spotted hand incongruent against the more youthful skin of her face. "Prophecies aside, the wizardborn normally show little aptitude for Edomic."

"I'm no spellweaver," Drake huffed. "It doesn't come easily. I know a few practical tricks."

"How long did it take her to learn?"

"She saw me call heat to light a campfire one evening. She asked how I did it, and I told her. She lit a candle that same night."

"The same night?" The charm woman gasped. "How long did it take you to light your first candle, Drake?"

"Years of practice. She clearly has an unusual aptitude."

The woman fixed Rachel with a suspicious stare. "Where did you study Edomic before?"

"Nowhere," Rachel replied. "Never. I know the syllables to the word that can kill Maldor. Otherwise, the first Edomic words I heard came from Drake."

"This was how long ago?"

"A couple of weeks."

"You can light a candle whenever you choose?"

"Pretty much."

"Show me." The charm woman arose, collected a long reddish candle, handed it to Rachel, and returned to her stool.

"Now?"

"At your pleasure."

Rachel felt a mild surge of stage fright. She hadn't done this trick under such scrutiny. The woman had made it sound like lighting a candle with Edomic should have been difficult to learn. The skeptical attitude magnified Rachel's nervousness. She took a breath. She had done this hundreds of times. She spoke the words, focused on the wick, and a flame flickered into being.

"Remarkable," the charm woman said. "Blow it out." She gestured at Drake. "Take the candle to the other side of the room."

Rachel handed him the candle, and he carried it to the opposite side of the tent.

"Light it," the charm woman ordered.

"I've never tried this from so far away," Rachel explained.

"Same idea," the woman said. "Will heat to the wick."

Rachel said the words, concentrating on the wick. She could feel an inexplicable resistance, like the first time she had tried to use Edomic to light a candle. Her attention began to waver, as if some distractive force were willing her eyes away from her target, but she redoubled her effort, pushing mentally, and whispered the words again. Across the room, a new flame was born.

"That was harder," Rachel said, wiping perspiration from her forehead.

The charm woman considered Rachel curiously. "Yet you made it look relatively effortless." The woman looked at Drake. "What are the chances of Rachel remaining with me as an apprentice?"

"You would have to ask her," he replied with a slight frown.

"Well?" the woman asked.

Rachel felt flustered and flattered. Did this mean she showed serious promise with Edomic? It would be amazing to learn more, but the timing seemed off. "I don't think I can. We need to figure out how to rescue Jason, and I need to get in front of Maldor, so I can use the Word. Plus, I need to find a way home."

"I can offer you as safe a sanctuary as you are likely to find in Lyrian," the woman replied. "Study with me for a year, and you will become much more formidable. You learned to call fire with abnormal ease. For most, those words you uttered would convey meaning only. Heat would hear but not respond. If you can continue as you commenced, you could exceed the abilities of any practitioner remaining in Lyrian."

Rachel looked to Drake.

"This is a high compliment," the seedman admitted. "The charm woman would not make this invitation lightly. Nor offer such encouragement."

Rachel pressed her lips together. "Wait a minute. Is this why you really brought me here? To see if she thought I could become a wizard?"

Drake shrugged innocently. "I was interested in her opinion regarding your aptitude. And we needed to lose the lurker. Both needs aligned."

"Only one person in Lyrian could help you become a true wizard," the charm woman said, "but Maldor does not take apprentices. He crushes any who aspire to learn Edomic. Our best lore on the subject has been lost. Only scant fragments of what we once knew are preserved by stragglers like myself. Still, there is much I could teach you."

"What do you think?" Rachel asked Drake.

"You are in a difficult situation," the seedman replied. "Maldor wants to apprehend you more than any rebel in recent memory. The torivor proves that. You hope to return to the Beyond, but we have no idea how. You wish to rescue Jason, but we currently lack any realistic chance of accomplishing that as well. Alternatively, if you could arm yourself with greater power . . . who knows what options the future might hold?"

Rachel bowed her head. To agree to study with the charm woman would mean admitting some uncomfortable things. It meant that Jason would be in Felrook for a long time. It meant that she would remain in Lyrian for a long time. In fact, an apprenticeship like they were discussing might be the first step toward admitting she would remain in Lyrian for the rest of her life.

But wasn't that just accepting the reality of her situation? Jason had been captured. He might be dead. Nobody knew of a way back to the Beyond. The emperor was out of reach. Whether or not Rachel studied Edomic, she was in serious trouble. Her options were limited. If this woman could provide a safe haven while empowering her to have a better chance of surviving on her own, shouldn't she seize the opportunity?

Besides, wasn't she curious to learn what else she might be able to do using Edomic? If lighting a candle brought an exultant thrill, how would it feel when she mastered more ambitious abilities? Didn't she crave the rush that came when a few words supported by her will set the forces of nature in motion?

Rachel wrung her hands. Did she want to study Edomic? Absolutely. Maybe too much. Maybe so much that all the other reasons she had in mind were really just excuses.

BE SURE TO CATCH

FABLEHAVEN

Available from Aladdin

FROM ALADDIN · PUBLISHED BY SIMON & SCHUSTER